Thunder from Above Book 1

~ HARSH INNOCENCE ~

By
Tracy Van Gorp

PublishAmerica
Baltimore

© 2010 by Tracy Van Gorp.
All rights reserved. No part of this book may be reproduced, stored in a retrieval system or transmitted in any form or by any means without the prior written permission of the publishers, except by a reviewer who may quote brief passages in a review to be printed in a newspaper, magazine or journal.

First printing

All characters in this book are fictitious, and any resemblance to real persons, living or dead, is coincidental.

PublishAmerica has allowed this work to remain exactly as the author intended, verbatim, without editorial input.

Hardcover 978-1-4512-9606-8
Softcover 978-1-4489-4376-0
PUBLISHED BY PUBLISHAMERICA, LLLP
www.publishamerica.com
Baltimore

Printed in the United States of America

Kathy,
I hope you enjoy.

T. Van Camp

This is for gramma, Edith Pahl

And in memory of grampa, Gilf Pahl

I couldn't ask for two better grandparents

CHARACTER LIST

Skiringssal (in Vestfold):
Lord Valr Vakrson – Jarl (Chief) of Skiringssal
Lord Rafn Vakrson – "The Raven" – Warlord
Lady Kata Vakradottir – Sister to Valr, Rafn and Orn
Lord Orn Vakrson – youngest brother
Dagstyrr – Rafn's 2nd in command and best friend
Lady Geira – Valr's wife
Father Duncun – Christian Monk living in Skiringssal
Esja – Head Servant Woman
Agata – Maid to Seera
Leikr – Warrior
Hachet – Warrior
Ranka – Orn's betrothed
Fox – Ranka's brother

Dun'O'Tir (Fortress by the Sea; in Pictland):
Eorl Airic – Ruler of Dun'O'Tir and representative of King David in Pictland
Lord Peder – Heir to Dun'O'Tir and the King's soldier
Lady Seera – younger sister of Peder and Christian woman
Jakob – Seera's squire
Iver – Peder's lieutenant and best friend
Father Albert – Priest

Ribe (in Jutland):
Lord Drenger – Jarl
Hwal – "The One-Eyed Giant" – 2nd to Drenger

Lady Gillaug – Drenger's wife
Yrsa – Hwal's slave girl
Abiorn – warrior
Klintr – warrior
Lene – warrior

Trondelag:
Kobbi – Jarl
Lady Auga – Kobbi's wife and Dagstyrr's sister

Meadow in Mountains:
Systa – The Seer
Joka – Warrior woman and Systa's sister

PROLOGUE

Thunder cracked and static rippled through the air in the dwelling. Invisible fingers reached above the bed and sparked as they traced the skin of a sleeping young face.

A boy of twelve struggled in the furs that covered the pallet he slept on. An instant jolt caused him to jump, but not wake. Rumbling waves of a powerful storm washed over him, reaching for his soul. Dark clouds of premonition wrapped around him, pulling him tight in an embrace. Hands that could not be seen reached inside him...searching...testing...

Satisfied, the storm pulled back to wait.

A scream split the night and Rafn bolted from his bed to stand sweating on the cold wooden floor. His gaze swept the dwelling, searching for the danger.

He stared in alarm at the shadows dancing across the dark room. He smelled smoke and sniffed the air for the source. It was not the smoke that escaped the banked fire in the hearth, but one of burning pitch and straw.

"Attack!" He thought with a sudden certainty.

He focused sharply on his eight year old brother sleeping next to him. Orn's eyes opened slowly to focus on Rafn standing beside the bed. He blinked and wrinkled his nose in concern.

Rafn laid a finger against Orn's mouth before the boy could speak. Rafn stepped silently on bare feet across the floor to the chest that held his tunics. He grabbed one from the top and pulled it over his head. Not taking the time to reach for either trousers or boots, he tossed a tunic towards Orn.

Their older brother, Valr and their father, Vakr joined them in the central room. Both were dressed and armed with spear and sword. Rafn met the sharp gaze of his father and knew that his instincts spoke true. Another terrified scream—closer now!

Rafn's mother and ten year old sister appeared behind him. Kata clung to their mother with eyes as wide as a doe. Valr thrust Rafn's practice spear in his hand. The weapon was not as good as the sword Valr had already earned, being three years older. It was not even as sharp as a warrior's spear, but he gripped it tight and drew Orn closer to him.

Kata jumped in panic at the shuffle of feet outside the dwelling.

Rafn watched his father's expression grow hard. A trap lay beyond the door were they to use it.

Vakr, lord and Jarl of Skiringssal called to his family. "Come." He led them not to the wooden door that offered freedom and death both, but to the back wall. With an axe he began to hack at the wooden boards. Something landed in the straw above them. Rafn yelled in horror. "They have ignited the roof."

Valr rushed to their father's side and helped him yank the board free. His father threw it behind him and beckoned his wife and daughter towards the hole.

"You first," he said. For a moment Vakr held the gaze of the woman he loved. A noise drew their attention as a man tore open the front door as if he'd guessed their intent.

In only seconds the entire roof was consumed. Rafn's panic grew as he crowded closer to his older brother.

Vakr caught Valr's arm. "Get them to safety." Valr nodded, but Rafn was not so calm.

"Father, no." Rafn couldn't move as fear warred with reason. Only Orn's insistent yanking on his hand made Rafn turn away from his father to see that the opening was about to be overtaken by flames.

Rafn pushed Orn ahead of him, searing his arm as the flames closed behind him. He coughed on the heavy smoke as he heard his father's blade meet the warrior's. The clang of metal against metal seemed oddly loud.

His father was swallowed by an inferno as they ran through the rows of houses. The village men fought half dressed against fully armored Viking warriors, who bore the mark of those from Smaland. The small village that his father had founded had become a burning nightmare.

Valr directed them away from the flames of their home. A splintering noise made them stop and stare back in horror. The wooden beams of their dwelling had collapsed. All sides were consumed by flames, and their father was in the center of it.

A desperate rage seized Rafn. Putting all his strength behind his spear, he threw it at the nearest enemy. It failed to find its victim and sailed by a bear of a man, twice his size. The bear warrior had a wild mass of black hair and beard thick with ash. He turned and caught sight of the noble family's escape and sneered. He lifted his sword, dripping with the blood of those who lay dead around him.

Valr watched in horror as Rafn bent down and picked up the sword of a fallen warrior. "Rafn, no!"

It came alive in Rafn's hand like a living serpent. Its power shot up his arm and through his body, until it reflected in his eyes. Valr sucked in a breath at seeing it.

From Rafn's side Orn looked up wide eyed and mouth gaping. Rafn shoved Orn in Valr's direction. "Take him from here."

Valr drew not only Orn back with him, but Kata and their mother.

Rafn glanced away from his mother's tears. He would not die. Power awakened in him as thunder rumbled through the darkening clouds. Rain did not come, but the thunder moved closer, as if the boy himself called it.

The bear-warrior laughed at Rafn, whose scrawny arms could not possibly possess enough strength to wield a sword that was far too big for him. He raised his sword to humor the boy's bravery. He met the boy's eyes as something sparked and made them shine brighter than the fire that blazed around them. He hesitated.

Rafn stood as still as stone as the thunder boomed directly over their heads. A streak of lightning shot straight down and scorched the ground behind him.

The warrior watched the bolt hit the boy, and yet the boy still lived. The thunder sounded closer. His eyes widened as Thor's hammer trembled across the sky. The bear-warrior shivered with the sudden knowledge that the mighty god Thor was claiming this boy for his own. Rafn's shoulder stung from a spark that burned through his tunic. The lightning bolt had been so close his hair sizzled with its energy, but he felt no fear to have been touched by a god. Confidence washed through and he knew no man could stop him.

Rafn yelled out his rage, as he lifted the sword which no longer felt heavy in his hand. Caught in a dance not of his making, he spun around on his feet, giving momentum to the swing of the weapon.

The long-sword sliced through the air, singing a song that only Rafn could hear. The bear-warrior lifted his sword in time to stop the blade from reaching his chest. He staggered back.

People pressed in closer to watch Rafn pit himself against the warrior. A hush traveled through the crowd as they saw he was winning.

The bear-warrior knew it too. He knew that he would sup in the halls of Valhalla that night as he caught a glimpse of the Viking warrior that this boy would grow to be and regretted that he would not be there to see it.

Rafn didn't know why the bear-warrior smiled as his blade found flesh, but the killing rage still touched him, and his eyes widened with madness as the man fell to his knees. Not stopping in his action he swung around in the final steps of his dance and brought the blade across the man's neck.

Blood from the wound sprayed Rafn, who tilted his head and yelled to the sky above him. An echoing call of thunder answered him, causing the remaining warriors from Smaland to stop and stare at the boy in wonder, as if they were seeing a prophecy come to life. Rafn stood covered in blood, dripping red from head to foot and from the tip of his stolen blade; the curse of Thor alive in his eyes.

Another warrior pushed forward. He was smaller than the first. A nasty scar was all that was left of his right ear. He glared in contempt at the boy, even as he brought up his sword. A shield was held against him, where Rafn had none, but the boy showed no fear and more than one person gasped.

The god led Rafn as he fought with the strength of a man. His arm was quick, his reflexes even quicker as the warrior tried to find his vulnerability. The other Smal warriors stopped to watch, but they became nothing more than a blur at the edge of his vision.

Rafn's eyes narrowed. His concentration was on the man he faced and nowhere else. So focused was he, he pushed aside the scream of a woman and the cry of a small boy. He could not acknowledge what would bring him pain later, for to do so would bring his own death.

He felt the thunder roll across the sky, closer and closer, until he felt its vibration sweep over him, through him, and become a part of him. The thunder was now inside, even as the lightning lit the sky to reflect in the eyes of the warrior who was but a few steps in front of him.

The Smal warrior feared too late the boy that could kill a man. Rafn's thrust came down hard, and somehow managed to break the shield that the warrior clutched. Now useless, he tossed it aside, and began to fight desperately, foolishly and Rafn's blade found his heart. He died with a look of shock frozen in his eyes as he glimpsed in his final breath that the boy did indeed belong to Thor.

Taking this as an omen, the attacking men retreated to their longships and pushed back out to sea. Their superstitions were enough to drive them from Skiringssal's shore. Those warriors still left in Skiringssal let them go, for they too were gaping in shock at the boy they knew, who'd been chosen before their eyes by one of the most powerful gods of the Aesir.

Rafn turned as Valr came up behind him and saw that Orn was alright. Relief was instant. Orn clung to their brother's hand in terror, but he was uninjured. Kata held Valr's other hand and he noted the tears running down her face. A tremor ran through him.

"Where is mother?" Rafn asked. He felt sick by her absence. The memory of her scream rushed back at him and he felt it sink in, now that the danger to his life had past.

Valr's face tightened. "She has fallen."

Rafn clenched his teeth in anger. If there had been anyone left to fight, he would have gladly battled another. The thunder was still in him, and he felt it brewing into a dark storm. He was ready to give himself to it.

"Rafn," Orn said. He let go of Valr's hand and took an uncertain step towards his brother.

Rafn met Orn's eyes and saw the plea in them. He latched onto that need and tried to ignore the thunder. Orn held his gaze and Rafn saw in them a place of calm in a storm of chaos. He held onto it until he'd centered himself again. He let the anger slip from him and managed a smile to reassure his little brother.

The rain came then; strong, thick and refreshing. It washed the blood from Rafn. It cleansed the smoky air and squelched the flames. He looked to the ruin of their family's dwelling and felt as if he were locked in a dream.

The four of them, three brothers and one sister, held on to each other. They vowed that Skiringssal would be rebuilt. That it would be bigger and more fortified than it had been that day.

The sky rumbled one last time as Rafn understood that he would meet his future as a great and fierce warrior that others would come to fear.

CHAPTER 1

Lady Seera rode in the center of a small party of mounted travelers. She stretched her back and squinted at the sun as it dipped low on the horizon. She knew they needed to stop soon for the night, but she wanted to push on a little longer. Seera pulled her woolen green cloak tighter around her as the wind quickened to a sharp chill.

Jakob, her squire turned to watch Seera, his cheeks coloring from more than the cold. "You are relieved we are heading home?"

"Extremely so." Seera managed a smile for her childhood friend. Jakob steadied his gray stallion as its foot stepped into a pit in the road. The horse was quick to regain its coordination. The animal was of fine stock, given to him by the Earl of Dun'O'Tir, the Fortress by the Sea.

"I thought you enjoyed the King's court?" he asked.

"Normally I do." She pushed an escaped lock of her light brown hair behind her ear and tossed the rest of her braid back over her shoulder. "The Queen is enjoyable company."

"Why, then, did you insist on leaving a day early?"

"Because if I had to endure one more conversation with that dour Lord Kent from King Alfred's court in Wessex, I would have gone mad." Seera frowned. An unbidden image of the insufferable man came to her mind. She shook her head to dispel the unpleasant image.

"The other ladies find him quite charming," Jakob said.

"Then they are welcome to him." The scathing look she shot him made him laugh.

"He is from a reputable family." The squire lost his smile and became serious. "It would not be such a bad match."

Her temper flared at his words. "How could you say that? You, who are my companion and friend, how could you wish that I marry a man I loathe?"

"I don't wish such a thing." He held her gaze and she saw something in them that she was perhaps not supposed to. It was gone before she could make sense of it. "Your brother will insist on a marriage soon, my lady." He turned to watch the road they traveled. Behind and in front rode the guards. Her maid kept close.

Seera's mood shifted towards more pleasant thoughts and she found her laughter returning. "Maybe if we find him a wife, his mind would be elsewhere."

"Lord Peder does not seem inclined to choose a bride."

"He is elder," she said. "He should be concerned about siring an heir, and let me find my own husband."

"You know that's not how it works, my lady."

"I am all too aware that as my brother, it will be Peder's choice, but I don't have to like it. He would choose such as Lord Kent."

Jakob turned his attention to the trees. Seera was quick to notice that something was wrong. A sudden apprehension ran through her. Fear blossomed as dark shapes materialized within the shadows.

They came from the night, shattering the tranquility in a moment of brutal rage. There were a dozen of them, dressed for battle in metal breast plates and helmets. In an instant they surrounded the group which was escorting The Lady of Dun'O'Tir home. Seera's horse balked at the abruptness of their appearance. She made an attempt to grab the reins in an effort to calm the gray, but the horse rose on hind legs and Seera failed to hang on. The ground met her with a hard impact as her horse tore off into the night.

Startled, Seera was forced to watch as Jakob was plucked from his horse and a long broad sword was pushed into his side. He looked at her, his mouth set in a silent scream. The raider pulled the sword back out and Jakob teetered on his feet before collapsing.

Seera screamed as large, rough hands grabbed her and lifted her with little effort from the ground. Seera fought, but he only tightened his grip and laughed; a sound that sent a chill through her.

The man turned her to face him and glared at her out of his one remaining eye. The other was a nasty puckered scar that made her cringe. He had shaved his hair so short that only a stubble of hair remained. He was the largest and scariest man Seera had ever seen. Fear spread its wings through her despite her will to remain in control.

"You're a pretty one." The man's gaze roamed over her, his teeth yellow through his menacing smile.

"Let me go." She demanded with as much conviction as she could muster. As an answer she got a hard hand across her face. The sting of it was a shock, for she'd lived a life of being protected and cosseted, in a castle where servants saw to her needs and a father and brother who watched her every move. How she'd hated their over-protectiveness.

How she wished for it now.

"Stop, Hwal." Seera watched another man come forward. He was shorter than the one who held her, but just as fierce. Hwal turned to the other and nodded, giving Seera an insight into who held the power.

The one-eyed giant was not the leader, she thought. Seera caught a glimpse of contempt flash in Hwal's squinted brown eye, before he hid it from the man he answered to.

"You want her, my lord?" Seera felt Hwal's anger tremble through his arm.

Seera was forced to look at the new unattractive man. She noted his eyes were too small and his mouth was twisted into a permanent scowl. The gray that peppered his hair told her his age, though she did not doubt that he had the strength to equal any of the younger men.

From over the leader's shoulder Seera saw one of her guards lose his battle against the Viking he fought. His sword clattered to the ground giving the enemy a clear opening. As the sword was stabbed through his gut, blood rose to his mouth and Seera's eyes widened in horror as he choked on the red froth.

Hwal gripped her possessively for a moment before he passed her off to his lord and Seera found herself looking into the leering black eyes of the leader of these Viking men. He sneered, making the lines on his face more pronounced.

His lust filled stare caused her gut to tighten. No man had ever dared to look at her in such a way. She was a Lady. Had any man ever looked at her thus, they would have had to deal with her brother. It was a death wish knowing Peder's reputation as a soldier. Seera realized with growing fear that this man did not know the Lord of Dun'O'Tir, or fear his wrath.

"You will not speak without permission." His order was harsh and she was not about to disagree with him. "I am Drenger, you now belong to me."

A tremor vibrated through Seera at the mention of the Jute lord's name. He was known among the Norse as being a nasty and merciless leader. He was the Jarl; the leader of Ribe in Jutland. She had not thought he ever came to Pictland, which was ruled by David, a Norse King who had chosen the path of Christianity, and denied the pagan gods that ruled the Vikings of his native home.

From the corner of her eye she saw all four of her guards bleeding on the ground unmoving. Seera grit her teeth against the sob that threatened to escape. She could not show this man weakness.

Drenger grabbed her chin and forced her to look back at him. He smiled at her reaction. She tried to keep the fear from her eyes, but thoughts of her father and brother…of the safety of home, the beauty of which she knew she would never see again…brought tears.

"Tie her." Drenger snap his order before walking away and leaving her to Hwal.

Hwal grabbed a length of rope from one of the guard's horses, and Seera took this opportunity to run. Without stopping to think of the wisdom of her decision she plunged into the trees to her left.

The earth was spongy from a recent rain, and the leaves wet with moisture. The branches snagged on her clothing as she ran, ripping the precious material of her dress and the smock underneath. She lost the cloak she'd been wearing to a low lying branch.

She did not stop. Could not stop! Death's breath was tingling on her neck, its greedy fingers almost touching her.

She stumbled on a hidden stump. The ground met her as she put up her hands to stop herself. Something sharp sliced her palm, the warmth of her blood a contrast to the chill on the air.

It was only a moment's mistake, but it was enough for the large man to catch her. He yanked her arm as he forced her to stand and stare up into his contorted face.

He raised his free hand to hit her. Seera saw the struggle as he forced his hand to remain poised. He wanted to strike to her. This she saw in his one eye. Fury spread across his face as he found his control. Having been claimed by his lord, he could not discipline her without permission.

Growling his frustration he dragged her back to camp, regardless of the branches that shredded her dress. Hwal bound her hands and feet to a tree and left her. Seera met her maid's eyes as she lay sprawled only feet away. They were sharp with pain. A red stain spread across her dress and soaked into the ground.

She kept her gaze locked with the girl's until the maid's eyes dulled and the pain ebbed away. Seera stared at the girl's lifeless form as if it were not real. Her maid had not been beautiful, but surely her youth would have been valued. As she continued to study her maid's young face she thought perhaps the girl was the lucky one. For who knew what lay ahead for Seera?

Her body stiffened in fear, as the giant appeared beside her to cut the rope. His foul breath made her cringe as he leaned in close a dagger. She fell away from the tree.

Drenger shouted an order for his men to head to the shore and their double-prowed long-ship that was waiting. Hwal's fingers dug into Seera's sides as she was lifted and thrown over his shoulder. She was forced to stare at his back as he carried her. She was brought on board and tossed in the front of the ship. He left her tied with the ropes biting deep.

Thoughts clogged her mind as she watched through stinging eyes the strange and brutal savages who'd taken her from her land. None looked her way as if they knew to do so would bring swift death from the man who'd claimed her.

She prayed continuously, but never aloud, for she feared what they would do to her if they heard her speak, and to a God that was not theirs. They sailed across the North Sea, east and south across open water. Seera had never been this far from land.

Her father had taken her out in boats before, but always along the coast. He'd never taken her out so far that land was no longer visible. The swell of the waves on occasion blew harshly and she clung in fear to the side. The men were unaffected by any weather. Whether the wind blew or rain fell, they continued on as if they had been born of the sea. When there was not enough wind for the sail, they rowed using the many large oars that lined each side. Seera could not help but notice the strength of each man's arms, and feared more readily what lay ahead.

She was left where Hwal had dumped her for two days without anyone approaching her before Hwal came and undid the ropes from her swollen wrists and ankles. He grabbed the long braid of her hair and dragged her head back. With his other hand he poured water into her mouth. She choked as she tried to swallow. He growled when half the water ran down her chin.

Hwal walked off and snapped an order to one of the men, but his words failed to reach her. Moments later the same man brought her some dry bread and moldy cheese which he managed to shove at her without actually looking at her. He moved swiftly back to his position at one of the oars and resumed rowing.

Drenger remained in the center of the ship. He never so much as glanced at her the entire journey across the sea. Seera had managed to numb herself of all feeling, except that of the shivering cold that consumed her, until land came into sight. She had no idea what lay ahead for her, but she knew her noble blood would not help her.

They came to the port of Ribe, and the long-ship pulled up to the dock. Few people came down to meet the ship, an ominous quiet claiming the village. Almost as if they were afraid to speak lest they anger their Jarl.

Hwal grabbed Seera and threw her over his shoulder once again. He carried her through the gathered crowd, which was not difficult for there were not many, and into the compound enclosed behind fortified walls. His stride was long and far too soon they came to a dwelling that was larger than the other homes. He kicked the door open and threw her on the bed.

He stared at her with such searing hate she felt scorched by the intensity of his single eye. Just under the surface another emotion lay. Seera shivered at the undeniable lust as he ran his tongue over yellowed teeth. For an instant she was sure he would reach for her, but he turned sharply and left without a word.

Seera sat up and looked around the dwelling. She needed to escape. She couldn't stay in this place and be expected to do…what? Serve the man who'd taken her from her home? Though she lived in the new land of Pictland with her father, she had heard the stories of his birth place in Hordaland. The Viking warriors from that district were among the most renowned. Only those from the town of Skiringssal, in Vestfold were considered fiercer, and said to always be in conflict with the Jutland warriors.

Seera sat on the fur that covered the bed and concentrated hard on not giving into her fear before it paralyzed her. She had to get out now! She rose from the bed and looked to the window. The door would be guarded, but would the window?

Before Seera could act, a woman came in. Her hair had the beginnings of white streaks. As she cautiously approached Seera the woman was forced to look up. A stern expression claimed her face as if it was rare to see a smile upon it.

"I am Gillaug," the woman announced rather than introduced. "I will be in charge of you."

"In charge?"

The woman was not pleased by the interruption. "You will speak only when asked to. You belong now to my husband, the Jarl." Craning her neck to try and look directly into Seera's face was a challenge from her shorter height and seemed to irritate her further. "You will never speak directly to him; only to me, and only when I give you permission."

Seera nodded even though she really wanted to scream her rage at this woman. She would not resort to such a tirade. It was beneath her to act in such a way. She was a Lady!

Gillaug's sharp gaze traveled the length of Seera in disgust. "You will undress now."

"What?" Seera took a step back as Gillaug's eyes narrowed.

"Do not speak again. This is my home and you are but a slave. Take your ruined clothes off or I will have the guard come in and do it for you."

Seera sensed she would indeed call the guard if she didn't obey. So Seera unhooked the bronze broaches that held the blue linen of her apron-dress and slipped it off. Next she unlaced the ribbons on her short goatskin boots. Finally she pulled off her woolen smock until she stood naked in front of Guillag, who continued to study her with loathing.

Guillag threw a brown coarse woolen smock at her. Seera caught it and slipped it on over her head. The woman offered no other article of clothing or footwear. Guillag collected the ruins of the well tailored clothes that Seera had taken off and studied them for a moment before asking.

"You are a noble woman?"

"Yes," she replied.

"You will not be treated as such here. You'll be worked until your hands bleed and you will spread your legs when Drenger asks it."

Seera's eyes widened at the last comment. She had known it would happen, but hearing it so plainly told made her wince. There was no escape. That was the truth that she could not accept.

The door was flung open and crashed against the wall. Drenger stood in the doorway. He had a fur lined woolen jacket draped over his shoulders that he took off and tossed on to a wooden chest beside the door.

"Leave us wife," he ordered. Guillag scurried out. The door swung shut behind her.

Drenger visually inspected her from head to foot. Seera looked around in search an escape. His lips parted to reveal yellowed teeth. Enjoying her sudden fear he grabbed her. Before she could stop him he yanked the smock over her head and threw it beside the hearth.

Terror seized her. She would not escape. Overwhelmed by this reality she didn't fight when he lifted her and carried her to the bed. Her breath was forced from her when he threw her down on her back. She gasped in a desperate need for air.

"No." Her scream tore from her. She found strength enough to launch herself off the other side of the bed. She hit the floor hard. Her knees bruised as she scrambled for balance and lost. She found herself cornered before she found her feet.

Drenger hit her hard across the face. His jaw was clenched in anger. "Don't speak, or defy me again." His hand struck the other side of her face. Before she could fall backwards he grabbed her by her braid and dragged her back to the bed.

He held her down with his heavy legs as he lashed her wrists one by one to the bed post. He would not give her the opportunity to move again. Satisfied she couldn't get free he stepped back onto the floor. She watched in horror as he stripped off his clothes to reveal a chest so hairy it seemed he wore a fur. His arms were thick and bore many pinkish scars. Seera opened her mouth to scream again, to fight for all she was worth, but managed to choke it back down. Nothing she could do would prevent the nightmare that descended on her.

The only defense she had was to close her eyes as his rough hands reached for her. She trembled as his weight pressed down on her. She clenched her teeth to stop the cry lodged in her throat at his violation. There was pain as her flesh tore.

It didn't last long, which was her only blessing, before he pushed her aside and climbed from the bed. Reaching for his discarded clothes he dressed and disappeared, leaving her tied to the bed, naked and vulnerable.

Tears leaked out despite her determination not to give into the humiliation. The cold air, which first caused goose-bumps, gave way to a weary numbness. She was unaware of how much time past before Guillag came back and untied her. Only then did her senses return and Seera scrambled off the bed to find the brown smock and pull it back on. She wrapped her arms around herself to keep from shaking.

"You will sleep on the floor." Guillag indicated a spot at the foot of the bed. Seera did not argue but curled in a ball on the bare floor. She refused to shed any more tears, even though her maidenhood had been taken from her in such a brutal way. She refused to cry because she had been taken from her home. She would not cry for the family she would never see again. She would not cry!

Somehow Seera fell asleep, wrapped in a cloud of denial.

CHAPTER 2

Rafn stood on a cliff overlooking the town of Skiringssal. He drew in a breath of the chill morning air as he admired the large trading center that had grown since that fated day so long ago. Under the leadership of his eldest brother Valr, their home in the district of Vestfold thrived.

A hint of the sun appeared on the horizon, bringing its promise of a new day. Below, a few early risers were setting up shop. In the walled compound behind the village, where the ruling family had built their homes, Rafn caught sight of Orn heading for the stables.

The day Rafn had first picked up a sword and been chosen by Thor, a violent storm had flared to life inside him. It was there in his eyes if you dared to look. Nicknamed the Raven by his men, Rafn called the power of the storm in battle and used it to fight with a deadly precision. His men felt the thunder when they fought by the Raven's side and it was why they had come to respect him as their warlord.

Rafn clenched his fist by his side and struggled to fight the darkness that would claim him. His jaw clenched in his ever present scowl as he watched Orn's progress across the courtyard.

The sun crept higher to reflect off Orn's golden hair. He was as different from Rafn as any man could be. Rafn's dark hair and strong body was in stark contrast to Orn's fairness and his lanky limbs. Rafn felt his tension ease as he concentrated on his brother. Orn did not have the heart of a warrior. Nor was he like the diplomat his older brother had become.

Orn's interests were in reading and writing, which he learned from a monk who lived within the village.

Orn glanced up at the sky, rewarding Rafn with the tranquility that had captured Orn's angelic face. His brother's smile touched something deep inside Rafn that could be reached by no other. A buried place that remained unmarred by his parent's death.

It gave him a rare sense of peace to glimpse the beauty inside his brother and was grateful that Orn did not hold violence in him as he did. Rafn remembered the day he had stood on the riverbank and watched while Father Duncun baptized his younger brother.

Rafn's loyalty still lay in the Norse gods Thor and Odin of Asgard, but he didn't discourage Orn's preference in the new Christian faith. He never tried to dissuade Orn from following the path he took. A man must choose his own gods. Thor and Odin were gods of war and were not meant for Orn. He accepted his brother for the man he was, as did everyone in the village. There was not a person within Skiringssal that did not love Orn. His kindness reached out to encompass all.

Orn disappeared through the stable doors. Perhaps the darkness inside Rafn was why he felt so protective of his brother, even more so than their sister Kata.

Rafn took the steep path back to the compound and stepped through the gate. The warrior on guard nodded in greeting. He found Orn in the stable putting a saddle on his horse, Night. Rafn ran a hand over the black coat of the stallion. His brother had already brushed down the horse and was gifting him with an apple for his patience. Orn turned and smiled.

"Going to visit that girl of yours?" Rafn offered his own awkward smile.

"I am." Orn threw his saddle bag over Night's flanks and secured it.

"Her father going to allow you to marry her?"

"He has agreed." Orn looked up at Rafn with a look of a man in love. Rafn couldn't help but be happy for him.

"I am pleased for you. I will have Kata prepare for the marriage to be held here in seven days…if her father obliges."

Orn laughed at Rafn's command. "I will make sure he does."

"You do have that way about you." Orn's laughter filled Rafn with contentment. He craved the peace he saw reflected in his brother's soul that he could not find in the turmoil of his own.

"I will return with my betrothed in two days time." Orn led the horse outside and climbed up into the saddle. Rafn admired the graceful control Orn had over his horse. Rafn knew he was a far better horseman than he, who preferred the feel of the sea to riding across the land.

"Two days time." Rafn stepped back as Orn gave the horse a kick.

Rafn climbed a ladder that led to the walkway on wooden defense wall, where he watched Orn ride out through the gate and head southwest along the coast.

Rafn looked forward to seeing his brother married. It didn't mattered that he was older and had yet to take a bride. Though he had enjoyed the arms of many women, he had found none that enticed him towards a union.

When he did, it would not be for love as it was with Orn. It would be for a joining of families, a strengthening of ties. But it would be to a strong woman. He could not stand to be trapped by a sniveling, harping shrew. He'd seen it happen too often to wish it on himself.

He blamed his inability to form such an intimate bond with another on the violence in his soul that never quieted. He'd seen too much death in his twenty five years. He'd taken a good deal of those lives with the blade of his sword. Like his father, Rafn was bred to be a warrior, ready to defend and to fight if needed. Only a strong woman could withstand that sort of life.

Thankfully Orn took after their mother and sister and didn't desire battle. Rafn had steered him from it as best he could, allowing Orn to become a scholar, studying from a Christian monk. Rafn was filled with pride to see Orn become such a man.

And in that was Rafn's peace.

Rafn crossed to the Great Hall to find Valr in a meeting with the family heads of the surrounding farms. Rafn waited patiently as they spoke of crops and livestock, and taxes that would go to King Harald.

He didn't have much interest in such domestic matters, so he found his mind wandering to other thoughts. He would go to sea again soon. It was where he longed to be. As his brother's second in command, and warlord, he went into the world to keep the trade open with other villages.

Rafn didn't look for battle the way many Viking warriors did. He fought viciously and remorselessly when he needed to in defense of his home and his people. But, he did not see himself as a conqueror or a raider. He found no joy in taking from others and leaving behind mourning families.

"It has been a pleasure, my lord," said one of the men as he rose, bringing Rafn's attention back to the group. The man was mostly grey with a thin face and yellow teeth.

The others, all of varying shapes, sizes and age, rose and bid their farewells to the Jarl and nodded to Rafn before leaving.

"Have I ever told you how grateful I am, that you are the oldest and the one the people chose to lead them." Rafn lifted an eyebrow in amusement at how well his brother handled the temperaments of those in his charge.

Valr chuckled as he reached for some bread and cheese off a platter that had been set on the wooden table before him. "Often."

"It goes well?"

"Indeed," Valr replied. "Has Orn left?"

"He has."

"Good. That boy is so giddy with love I couldn't take much more of it."

Rafn raised an eyebrow. "Were you not beaming with happiness before your wedding day?" Rafn gripped the ale a serving wench placed before him and took a seat across from his brother.

Valr bit into his bread as he frowned. "Perhaps I felt it, but I was more controlled." Rafn raised his horn of ale and drank deeply. The honeyed flavor was satisfying.

"You are always more controlled. Let Orn enjoy his happiness."

"At least it will be over soon." Valr sampled his own ale.

Rafn shook his head. He knew Valr loved his wife in his own way, but the two were so formal together. Rafn wanted to just once see Valr let his guard down. To grab Geira to him and plant a kiss on her mouth, not caring who saw. That would be worth many gold coins to see.

But that was not Valr.

Orn came to the fishing village and brought his horse into the small stable at its edge before looking for his intended bride. The wooden structure was in need of repair and from the stench, a good cleaning. Leaving Night with the young stable boy he continued on foot to the other side of the village.

"Welcome son." Edmundr clasped hand to arm with his future son-in-law as soon as he reached the man's cottage.

"Greetings Edmundr," Orn replied. "May I inquire to the whereabouts of your beautiful daughter?" A smile passed between them. Orn did not consider himself better than a fisherman because of his own noble birth. He spoke to him as an equal and a friend.

Edmundr nodded towards a small out-building. "She is in the cooking shed with her mother. Supper will be served in a few minutes. Please come clean up and join us for our humble meal."

"I would be most honored." Orn followed the older man into the dwelling that sat on the edge of town. Edmundr claimed he'd built his home upwind so that the smell of fish was not so overwhelming. Orn couldn't help but agree with the older man.

Orn ducked into the small dwelling and was greeted by Edmundr's fourteen year old son, Fox. Orn ruffled the boy's hair as his brothers had so often done to him.

"You have grown in the month since I was last here."

Fox smiled at the compliment, puffing his chest out in pride. "Mama complains that she always has to make me a new tunic."

"I'm sure she does."

Orn looked up as the women joined them. His future mother in law, Una, came forward and he greeted her briefly before turning his eyes to Ranka. She was a small woman with golden hair that had stubbornly stopped growing just past her shoulders. He had laughed often over her complaints that it did not sweep her hips the way other girls' hair did, but Orn had never cared. He loved the silkiness of the blond strands that framed her pretty face.

"My lord," she greeted formally with a slight bow, but Orn saw the intimacy of her gaze before she glanced away. He felt the warmth spread through him at its heated promise.

"Let us eat." Una beckoned to the table.

Orn took a stool next to Fox and showed no displeasure at the lack of elbow room. It was nothing compared to the elegant wooden table he was used to dining at, but it mattered not. The simple meal was a pleasant rabbit stew and grilled fish. The company was good and the food tasty. Orn felt blessed to have such people become family.

After they finished eating, he gave Una a gift of salt and other exotic spices that Rafn had acquired in trade. She beamed in delight at the rare treasure, and he was amused as he watched his future mother-in law opening each of the containers to smell and sample. He caught a glimpse of the tears in her eyes before she turned away.

"Thank you, milord. Your gift is most generous."

"My brother has requested that our marriage take place in Skiringssal." Orn spoke to Edmundr, but kept glancing at Ranka as he spoke. "In seven days time if it would not inconvenience you."

Una looked up in surprise. "Seven days. I have not even started sewing Ranka's dress. Certainly you can give me more time."

"There is no need. My sister has hired a seamstress to make the dress as a wedding gift. She is not one to say no to." He had to stifle a laugh at Una's stunned expression. "I hope this won't rob you of the joy of making it yourself."

"It is not an offer one can easily refuse."

"Ranka is my betrothed. My sister will insist on spoiling her." Orn looked at the woman he loved and was rewarded with one of her radiant smiles. Color rose on her cheeks that Orn found endearing.

Edmundr nodded. "Well then, it is settled. Seven days."

"I wish to take her back with me in two days so that the seamstress has time to make the dress."

Una glanced to her daughter. "I will agree to that as long as I may accompany you."

"You are always welcome."

The women rose and began to clear the meal away while Orn and Edmundr spoke of the successful fishing season. Much of what they caught was sailed down river to trade in Skiringssal. That is how Orn had first met Ranka, when she'd accompanied her father to the village six months before.

The day had been overcast and drizzling, but a ray of light had filtered through to shine down on an approaching boat. Orn had been caught by the innocent beauty who rode in its stern.

It was then that he knew he had to have her.

Later that night, Orn met Ranka outside the settlement within a hidden cleft between two large rocks on the beach. It hid them from anyone who might happen to come by. They had used this place before.

As soon as they were hidden, Orn embraced Ranka and placed his mouth on hers and was pleased by her response to his kiss. They had not seen each other in a month's time and they were anxious for each others touch.

They made love cushioned by a layer of sand that had blown into the hollow. Seven days could not come fast enough for him. Then he wouldn't have to steal such moments with her, he would have her in his bed always.

"It seems such a grand thing, marrying in Skiringssal." Ranka wiggled deeper into his arms. Orn cradled her close and kissed the top of her head before he replied.

"As my wife, you will have to get used to such excesses. My sister would have it no other way."

Ranka sighed wistfully. "Lady Kata is so beautiful."

"As you are beautiful, my love." Orn smiled down at her. His eyes reflected the truth of his words, but Ranka still could not believe them. How could she compare to the Lady Kata, or even Lady Geira, the Mistress of Skiringssal?

"You are beautiful," he repeated as he pulled her up so that he could kiss her. His lips were tender against hers, and she couldn't deny that he loved her, as much as she did him.

They made love again, this time with more care. More time to savior each other. Ranka knew that he was the best man in all the world and he had chosen her. Others might argue that Rafn was far more stunningly handsome, but Orn appealed to her. Rafn was strong, hard and rugged from the life he'd been born to lead, but Orn was sweet and kind, gentle and sharing. Even when he joined his body with hers, he did so with such tenderness as if he was afraid he might hurt her.

From what Ranka had seen of Rafn, she could not imagine him being so with any woman. She imagined lying with him would be intense and wild, like he was. He was too much like one of the Aesir gods of Asgard. Like the mighty Thor of storms and thunder that had lain claim to him long ago.

She glanced tenderly at Orn who lay back with his eyes closed, a look of satisfaction smoothing his face. He had chosen the Christian God, the way of peace. Ranka was glad for it.

They dressed quickly, her in her smock and yellow apron-dress, he in his tunic and tight fitting trousers. They did not want to be gone too long and be missed by her parents. They came from the cleft to walk hand in hand down the beach. So lost were they in one another that they were startled when a scream broke the silence of the night.

Memory of another night shattered by a scream seized hold of Orn; one so long ago he was surprised by the intensity of the feelings that reached for him. His parents' faces flashed before him and he gripped Ranka's hand hard in panic.

Together they ran towards the settlement to find many of the dwellings on fire. Two long-ships had been pulled up on the beach and many warriors swarmed the village.

The parallels to that long gone night were obvious; warriors attacking when they would find the people most vulnerable, and their use of fire to destroy and trap and kill.

"Run into the trees and hide," Orn yelled to Ranka, who started to cry. "I will find you there." He pushed her when she failed to move. Reluctantly she ran away from the burning village. He remembered how Rafn had looked at the age of twelve, thunder and blood apart of him.

Orn cursed himself for not having his spear on him. Rafn would be displeased by his forgetfulness. His brother never went anywhere without at least one weapon strapped to him. It was something that was not second nature to Orn and he often forgot his vulnerability. He knew first hand how violent the world could be if you were not paying attention to it.

He ran for Edmundr's dwelling. It had yet to catch fire. He'd find his sword and spear there amongst his things.

His steps faltered when Ranka's scream reached him. He turned to find a warrior with only one eye. His hand was tangled in Ranka's hair as he dragged her closer to the village. His vision shimmered with an image of his mother replacing that of Ranka's terrified face.

He reacted without thought, heading for her as their eyes met. She fought the giant's hold. Time slowed to a trickle. Nothing else existed but the moment the one eyed man brought his knife across her throat and laughed at Orn's startled cry.

He stood motionless for what felt like an eternity as he watched her gasping desperately for air. Everything went out of focus, except for Ranka's eyes as her life left them. His heart clenched with such wrenching agony he could not move. Unable to stop the man, Orn watched him toss her limp form on the ground and sneer in pleasure.

Again he was watching his mother die, caught in the fear of a young boy. Then it was Ranka whose life was gone. The man he was felt as helpless as the boy had been.

He felt the tip of a sword pushing into his spine. He felt his death and welcomed it, but it did not come.

Instead, Orn was forced to turn and face the man who owned the sword. Drenger, Jarl of Ribe, known for killing needlessly, he enjoyed preying on helpless villages just to wreck as much havoc as he could. Orn was grateful that Ranka was already gone, for Drenger's men would rape the women before gutting them.

Drenger snarled as he gripped his captive's face in a hand filthy with blood. "Orn Vakrson, what brings you to this little hovel?"

Orn could not answer. Drenger had only to push his sword through his chest and it would be ended. He waited, even prayed for it to come, but the pain came from a hard hit to his head and not the merciful blade. His vision blurred and unconsciousness claimed him.

Fox hid within the high branches of a tree and tried not cry out as he watched his sister killed. His mother and father lay dead outside their hut. The boy felt the tears sting his eyes, but he fought not to make a sound. He knew if he was discovered, he would be killed as well.

The Jarl of Ribe never left survivors, save for those he took as slaves back to Jutland.

The one eyed man who'd killed his sister, hit Lord Orn on the back of the head with the hilt of a dagger. He'd slumped forward and appeared as lifeless as the rest who'd been killed, but the giant grabbed him up and flung him over his shoulder. He took him to one of the long-ships and tossed him in.

Fox hugged the trunk of the tree and kept himself as silent as the animal he was named for. He waited until the killing and raping had stopped and the warriors had headed back out to sea before he slipped from the tree. He kept to the shadows until he reached the barn. It was in ruins but a few of the horse had remained within the trees behind the village.

Fox found Night, Orn's beautiful stallion that was fit for one only of noble blood and jumped up. He rode the animal bareback and barefooted, gripping onto the black mane and let Night run as fast as he could all the way to Skiringssal.

To unleash the Raven's anger!

CHAPTER 3

Seera knelt by the river among the other woman. Some were slaves, others maids and wives. In a basket by her side was a pile of soggy clothes. In her hands she scrubbed the last of the laundry Gillaug had forced on her. Her hands were puckered from the tedious task, but Seera knew better than to voice a complaint.

She'd wiped her stringy unwashed hair from her forehead. Sweat trickled down the sides of her face from both the labor and the hot sun. She longed to dive into the cool water and rinse the grime from her body.

Seera had learned greater respect for those who served. If ever she walked the halls of Dun'O'Tir again, she would not dismiss so easily those who labored for her.

She sat back on her heels to wring out the shirt. Her back ached and her legs cramped from kneeling. Even her hands throbbed in pain. She glanced at the others and saw an equal weariness.

A silent signal must have been given because the women began collecting their things. Seera tossed the shirt on top of the large basket and stood to join them.

She moved-in beside the other slaves and free women as they headed back to the village and compound beyond. As they passed the harbor Seera spotted a large drekar pulling up to the dock.

She tried not to panic as she recognized the mark on the sail that announced its owner. A knot tightened in her stomach.

She had been expecting his return with dread. That morning she had learned of the feast and knew the Jarl would return for it. She had scrubbed the dirt from the floor in the Great Hall with the horrible knowledge he would come for her again soon.

As she walked among the women, she tried her best to blend in. It was a pointless task, trying to be invisible. He would find her when he chose, but she needed time to grab her courage around her. She felt a shiver travel through her at the memory of his touch. Her trembling increased when she spotted the one-eyed giant.

Hwal disembarked first with a bound captive, who he dragged behind him. The man's golden hair was matted with blood on one side. The hollow eyed captive walked without resistance. He grieved, her heart felt in an instant. She observed him closely.

He was dressed in finely made clothing, marking him of noble blood. The sun picked up the glitter of a gold cloak pin clasping his blue cloak closed. She could just make out a black, or perhaps dark brown, tunic as the cloak parted.

Seera wondered where he'd come from. She felt drawn to him, as if he was a kindred spirit in a sea of sharks. She almost walked to him, before the reality of where she was came back to her.

Hwal had him. The giant scared her far more than Drenger did. It somehow made her grateful that the Jarl had wanted her, for she wouldn't have survived the one-eyed man.

Seera kept in time with the group of women returning to the fortified compound that encased the Jarl's home as well as those of his most valued warriors. Within its walls were also stables, the great hall, kitchens and field used for the men to practice and train on.

Seera discovered as she watched the captive that in one corner of the high walls was a cell. Hwal brought the man to the cell and shoved him inside. The man moved to stare out the grated window, which was parallel to a person's feet.

A chill went through Seera as premonition of why the man had been taken seized her.

The cell, which had been dug into the ground, was damp and cold. Water leaked down the outside wall and a large spider had taken up residence in one corner of the roof. Orn was alone in this dark coffin that had held little light when the sun was still out, but now that night had closed on them, the darkness was almost consuming. A faint almost indiscernible glow from the full moon could be seen through the bars that were his only window to the outside world.

Except for the brief glance through them he'd taken when he first arrived, he had no desire to look out beyond the muddy walls of his prison. He was already dead. Only the physical confines of a body that still breathed held him to this world. But that would end soon.

Hwal had gloated how he was to be sacrificed to the god Odin. A man of noble blood was a prize for the Aesir god.

Orn prayed to his God, to the son and savior, Jesus Christ. He did not pray to live, but that he would be with Ranka again soon.

He felt not the hunger that gnawed his empty stomach, or the thirst that dried his throat. He was beyond such cares. He did not fear death.

He would miss his brothers and sister. A small ache threatened to betray his conviction to die. He did not think of home, of which he would not see again. Home was where the almighty Lord would take him, when Hwal came to end his life.

A spider crawled across his leg, and Orn watched it with detached interest. He chose not to sleep, but to wait through the long hours for morning to come. He prayed without pause and felt that he was not so alone after all.

Every nine years there was a great feast to honor the god Odin, he who was leader of all the gods in Asgard, the world in which the gods lived. In the Norse religion, people lived in Midgard, the world which was created for them.

The day of celebration was upon them. Many people had come from the outlying farms to join in the feast. Seera was made to work in the kitchens with the other slaves, to produce the food needed to feed so many. They prepared fish, bread, and a variety of vegetables, fruit, berries, nuts and even gruel.

Seera had heard of such pagan ceremonies, but she had never been witness to one. Her life had always been directed by the monks who preached the words of Jesus. Seera worked with fear in her heart, for she'd heard the guards talking of the sacrifices that would be made to Odin. Not only the animal sacrifices that were so commonly made, but human sacrifices would be offered up to their god.

"They have captured one of noble blood." One of the slave women whispered to Seera. She recalled that the woman was named Kolla.

"To be killed in the sacrifice?" Since the man had been thrown into the cell, Seera had feared the worst.

"Aye," Kolla replied.

"Who is he?"

"I know not his name, but I have heard it said that he is the brother of a great Viking Warlord from the district of Vestfold."

"Does Drenger not fear retaliation?"

"The Jarl fears no one," Kolla answered.

Seera nodded, for she knew it to be true. Not even Hwal the giant stood against him, though in a fair fight, the one-eyed man would win.

Much ale and mead were distributed among the crowd. The sacrifices were to be held in a grove just outside of town. Gillaug forced Seera to accompany her to the ritual. Her mistress found glee in making a Christian woman witness the violent act that was met with excitement by Odin's followers. Seera remained rigid and refused to allow Gillaug to find the joy she sought. She would stand and watch, but she would not cower from the sight as the Jarl's wife expected.

The animal sacrifices were made first. Hwal took a spear and brought it down through the throat of a squealing pig as others held it. His eye widened in madness as he drew pleasure from killing. Another pig was brought forward and Hwal's spear ended its squeals. Blood spurt up from the wound as Hwal tore out his spear, he met Seera's gaze. A sneer turned up the corner of his mouth. Seera felt herself shutter at the hate reflected on his face. She looked away from him, only to meet Gillaug's satisfied smile.

Curse them both. She would not be the coward they wanted. She defiantly watched the rest of the animal slaughters without closing her eyes.

There were a dozen boars, a half dozen sheep and five horses that died by Odin's sacrificial spear. They wouldn't be consumed by the people, but burned in a fire to send to the halls where Odin waited.

Seera waited as a bloodthirsty cheer rose through the crowd. Nine human sacrifices were being led forward. Seera caught a glimpse of the man in the lead, the captive with the golden hair. His hands were tied behind his back, but he kept his head held high. For a moment their eyes met and she saw a terrible pain reflected back. This man had suffered greatly and welcomed his death. She was shocked by this revelation.

Orn was already dead. The moment he had watched Ranka die, he had not wanted to go on living, but they had not killed him. They had taken him to Jutland instead.

He had spent the last two days locked in a dirty cell, waiting. He had been given nothing to eat or drink until that morning, a last meal before sending him to Odin.

He was not a warrior, to be granted access to the great Halls of Valhalla. He was sure that Drenger was unaware that he was not like his brothers. He was a scholar and a Christian. A man of peace, not war!

Rafn was known throughout the Norse world as the Raven, and spoken of with fear among the people. Orn had never wanted the life as a Viking. He had turned from the belief in such gods as Odin and knew beyond doubt only the one true God would receive his soul. In heaven he would see Ranka again, for she'd followed him in his faith and been baptized. They were to have been married by the monk in his village.

He felt the tug of tears, but he forced them back. He would not show weakness in front of these people. He would not dishonor the names of his brothers.

His eyes met that of a beautiful woman dressed as a slave. Her face was bruised and her clothing soiled, but she held her head proudly. She had not been a slave long he realized. They have not broken her spirit yet. A defiant part of him hoped they never would.

He looked away from her as they led him to stand on a raised platform in front of the noisy crowd. He was ready to die. He quietly began to recite the Lord's Prayer, which had been taught by Jesus to his disciples.

Though Seera was unable to hear the young man's silent words, she knew what he spoke. It was the Lord's Prayer. How many times had she said those words? She stared harder at this Christian with surprise. She had assumed he would be a warrior, like the brother the other slaves spoke of.

Seera watched the tranquility descend over the man's face and realized she was quietly repeating the prayer along with him. His gaze shifted to look at her, though it was not possible her voice had reached him. He spoke the final words but his sight remained fixed on her…a sentinel of understanding amongst the ravening wolves that would devour him.

"Let it be done." Drenger's voice rose, silencing those around him. Seera felt a shiver travel up her spine and wrapped her arms tight across her chest to keep from trembling.

An eerie quiet froze everyone in anticipation. The men sneered with pleasure and the women's eyes were hungry for blood.

Seera had never felt more alone, but for that small connection to the man who was about to die. She wanted to scream out how wrong this was. Tears formed and she blinked them away so her vision would not blur. She was afraid to look away. Afraid to break the thin strand binding her to this man she would never know beyond these few precious moments. They seemed important somehow.

Seera concentrated on keeping her breath steady. Her heart skipped a beat as she watched the golden man forced upon a horse and a rope placed around his neck. Even then his eyes remained on Seera.

"Go with God." Seera whispered and the man smiled in gratitude. In that moment the bond between them strengthened. Seera tried not to cry out. Her heart ached as if she were seeing her own brother going to his death.

Then Drenger walked up and the man looked to him and spoke loud enough for all to hear. This young man's voice was enchanting as if he'd descended from the heavens to decree an important message.

"My brother will come for you." The captive's voice rang out loud and clear. He showed no fear as he spoke to the Jarl. If Seera were not mistaken a flash of fear shimmered across Drenger's face.

"He can try." Drenger laughed and the crowd cheered in response, but it did not fool Seera. Her captor was wary of this brother.

The man looked back at Seera and smiled. He seemed transformed into an angelic figure of such golden beauty that she was stunned. He was at once old and young…timeless. Soft white light surrounded him and Seera felt the presence of God with them both.

Drenger poked the horse with a sharp stick that sent it sailing forward. The rope around the man's neck was tied to a sturdy branch overhead, and with the horse no longer underneath him, he was left to swing in the air.

She felt it happen in slow motion, while the others faded into the background. The man's eyes remained on her until the light from them dimmed and their fragile connection was broken.

She could have sworn she felt his soul touch hers in comfort and understanding before it was gone, and the world around her returned in a rush of noise that assaulted her senses. A stab of pain shot through her heart at his loss. If he could evoke such grief in someone who did not know him, what agony those who loved would feel when they learned of his death.

Eight more people were brought forward. There were six men and two women, all of who were slaves. Seera continued to watch in numb silence.

"Lord Orn is of noble blood." Drenger shouted for all to hear. "It is befitting that he have slaves to accompany him." The crowd cheered loudly as the eight slaves were first killed with spears then strung up beside Orn in the trees.

"Orn," Seera mouthed his name. A name she would not forget.

Seera stared down at her hands. The blisters had calloused over, taking away some of the pain. She rubbed her thumb over the roughened skin of his fingers. They were the hands of a stranger.

Pushing the strands of her hair behind her ears, she stiffened her back. She worked beside the slave girl Yrsa. They were cleaning the mess left from the feast that had lasted for days before the vast majority of the people filtered back to their country homes.

"The men were savage the way they consumed the food." Seera tried once again to start a conversation with the traumatized girl, who she judged to be around fourteen years. Seera having passed her twentieth birthday felt for the child. "And the slobbering way they drank. Most are still drunk and unconscious…including the Jarl."

Yrsa gave no reply, only stared back out of eyes that held no more life than a corpse. Seera mourned the poor girl's fate. She had learned from Kolla that Yrsa had been taken at the age of twelve by Hwal.

The soul in Yrsa was so sick, that she had shut herself from the world that had offered her nothing but pain. She could not cope with the reality that had befallen her at such a young age. Seera prayed daily that Yrsa find her way back. Then again, she wondered if for Yrsa's sake it were not best to remain numb to everything Hwal did to her.

If Seera ever found a way to escape, she would bring the girl with her. If only a way could be found.

With the kitchen done, Yrsa followed Seera down to the river where they washed the clothes that Gillaug had given them. Hwal did not have a wife, so Gillaug took charge of Yrsa upon the warrior's request. Seera thought the woman enjoyed her dominance too much.

The day was cloudy, bringing a chill to the air. All too soon Seera's hands became numb. Yrsa worked silent beside her. Seera wished the girl would at least make a complaint against the cold.

The sun was getting low when Seera made it back to Drenger's dwelling. She was so tired she felt she could fall asleep while standing. There proved to be no peace when she pushed open the door to find Gillaug waiting. She pushed a leather bucket into Seera's hands. "Fill it from the well and wash the floor. The Jarl will return soon."

Stifling a groan, she reached for the bucket, barely grasping it in time. She scrambled to keep from dropping it. Gillaug snickered, but Seera was learning to ignore the miserable woman. She refrained from mentioning she had just washed the floor the day before. If it was not that task, it would be another.

With weariness like none she'd ever known, Seera worked her way through another day. Only when Gillaug was beneath her blankets, and only then, was Seera allowed to curl up on the bare floor at the end of the bed and go to sleep. In two weeks, she had not been offered a blanket.

At least she knew the floor was clean.

Seera was woken in the middle of the night by rough hands grabbing her. She cried out in shock, as she was forced to her feet. Drenger stared at her out of red rimmed eyes and the stench of ale strong on his breath.

Gillaug was no longer in the dwelling and she realized Drenger must have sent her away. Her mouth went dry. Her fists clenched by her side, ready for a fight.

Seera was still dazed at being woken so abruptly and instinct told her not to succumb. She fought against his power, even as he threw her on the bed. She squirmed in his grip, which only caused him to tighten his hold. She tried to kick him, but he held her legs between his own.

She cried out in dismay. That she could be so forced with no way of stopping it made her feel small and weak, and she hated that.

Drenger ignored the tears that sprang unwillingly to her eyes and turned her onto her stomach. He forced up the bottom of the brown shapeless smock, until she was exposed and vulnerable to him. He pushed his way into her. She clenched her teeth together to keep from screaming. She would not give him that satisfaction.

When he was done, he dragged her from the bed and gave her a good beating for her insolence. By the time he was done her face was a bloody mess. Her equally bruised ribs ached, but she did not think they were broken. She wobbled on legs that failed to hold her and she crumbled in a heap on the floor.

Drenger, having forgotten her, slumped on to the bed and was snoring soon after. Through blurry eyes she watched his chest rise and fall. A snort escaped as he sank deeper into sleep. A trail of drool seeped out the corner of his mouth.

Gillaug came back into the lodge and sneered at Seera. "I thought you were smarter than that girl."

She pointed to Seera's spot on the floor. "Go to sleep." Seera crawled to it with great care and curled herself into a ball, despite the pain of her ribs. She swiped at the moisture leaking from her eyes in annoyance.

She vowed he would not break her. She would not become like Yrsa, no matter what he did to her. The pain she felt was a sign that she was still alive.

Seera felt sleep claim her with a strong comforting presence. Orn appeared in her dreams, telling her to be strong. She was comforted by his words and drew them around her like a shield against the anguish.

CHAPTER 4

Rafn remembered the day his parents died with sharp clarity. Anger had caused him to pick up the dead man's sword. Anger had directed his actions, even before the god had touched him. In truth, it had not been Thor alone who had given him strength that day. Fury had played a hand as well.

"Thor chose you boy, because you showed courage." His uncle Gamal's words had echoed in the boy's memory, but it was the man who remembered the rage.

Reaching for his metal armor, Rafn recalled how he had nourished and honed the thunder within as he became a man. Once again he let the tempest in. He let the anger seize him.

The walls of his dwelling seemed to close in around him.

Only moments before, Fox had ridden into Skiringssal on Orn's black stallion and spoke words meant to draw forth the Raven. Rafn would become the warlord. His jaw clenched as he fought to keep his need for vengeance from showing its ugly face too soon.

"You ready to lead us into battle?" Dagstyrr asked, interrupting his thoughts. Rafn continued putting on his armor. He stuffed his head into his helmet and strapped his sword to his back, a double edged blade with a groove down the middle. Taking a knife from the table he sheathed it to his lower leg. The knife's handle felt oddly warm to his touch, as if it spoke a premonition.

"Aye." He growled. Dagstyrr, being his closet friend, did not step back where a lesser man would.

"My blade will taste Drenger's blood for daring to take Orn from us." Rafn's oath rang true as a distant thunder rumbled through him. He accepted it as Thor's acknowledgement to his promise. He knew Dagstyrr had not heard the god's voice.

Rafn grabbed a finely carved axe, covered with an intricate design of snakes twined together, and stuck it through his belt. This was meant as an additional weapon, for only the poorest of warriors used an axe. It was the sword, designed for hacking instead of thrusting, that was a warrior's most treasured possession and the wealth of owning such a weapon spoke of the nobility of the warrior class.

At the last he grabbed his spear. The weapon was used for thrusting as well as throwing, and had a sharp blade that was three feet long, and attached to a shaft five times longer. Rafn's spear was as finely made as his other weapons, each carrying the carefully carved designs of a talented craftsman.

"The men wait," said Dagstyrr.

"Good. I will have my brother back." Rafn's heart clenched in fear he would not admit, for he feared the worst. He tried to find the calmness that Orn brought to him. He failed.

His anger demanded release. He clenched his jaw against the sizzle of power he was barely able to contain. He drew in a sharp breath that caused Dagstyrr to look. The darkness threatened to devour, but Rafn refused to give into it…yet.

"It's time." Rafn walked from his lodge, forcing Dagstyrr to follow him to the ships. His sister waited. Over her shoulder she saw his men readying themselves for battle, each savage in appearance with the lust of blood in their eyes. Kata stood next to Valr. Rafn joined them to ease her worry.

"You will find him," Kata said. She placed her hand soothingly upon his arm.

She tried to meet his eyes, but he avoided hers. If hope lay within them, it would be his undoing. As Rafn boarded the drekar, her concern followed him. A cold smile tightened the corners of his mouth. She need not worry. He had no plans to die. He would be sending another to Vahalla's halls.

Rafn looked to his warriors. Sixty men went with him out to sea, sixty men who loved Orn and would see Drenger dead.

Seera had planned to wait. She had noticed in passing that the small fishing boats were never guarded as the large ships were. No sentry was ever posted at the small dock where the boats were kept. If she could get to one of the boats, she would head north to Hordaland, and get someone there to take her home. It was a risky plan, but the only one she had.

Logic told her she should wait until Drenger left the village again, but after her beating the night before, she had to leave. To stay meant giving him the chance to take her again. She'd prefer death.

Seera's hands shook. Drenger and his men were seated at supper. The slaves were not permitted to enter the hall until the meal was done. She waited in the kitchen with the others. Gillaug would not search her out for some time. It was her chance.

Clamping her hands together to keep them still, she searched the clammy room for Yrsa. The girl sat not far from the door. Pushing her way through the group of women standing in her way, she reached her.

"Come with me." She had to lean over so she could whisper to Yrsa and the girl followed her out into the night. It was already darkening as they slipped into the shadows. Seera retrieved a couple of cloaks hidden near the kitchen. Yrsa accepted one of the cloaks and donned it. Seera put the other on. If they were seen, hopefully they would be mistaken as women from the village on their way home.

Yrsa followed Seera's instructions without question. The girl had no mind left to think independently. Seera checked that their path was safe and led Yrsa between the buildings to the main gate. Seera sighed with relief on finding it still open. Keeping to the shadows, they waited for the sentry to turn and march down the wall the other way before slipping through.

They made their way down the hill to the dock just north of the village. Seera expected an alarm to go up with each step they took. With relief, the boats came into view. They were going to make it. Her heart sped up in anticipation.

She allowed a smile to convey her pleasure to the girl. Yrsa's eyes remained hollow, but Seera had hope that she understood what they had accomplished. She squeezed Yrsa's hand and walked down the path to the trees.

The cluster of trees stood ahead as a beacon. Their thickness offered protection. Her heart quickened with excitement. They would make it.

"Halt." Her blood turned cold at the dreaded voice that came out of the darkness behind her.

"Run." She pushed Yrsa in front of her, glad when the girl ran swiftly into the trees close to the small dock. Seera raced in her wake, had only to take a few more steps to reach the trees.

She started to shake from the feel of the horse's breath on her neck. She screamed as she was snatched up. Her feet dangled in the air as she struggled against strong arms. Drenger stared down at her. She had never seen him angrier.

His fingers dug into the bruises on her arms. Instead of fighting, as she knew she should, she froze. Still aching from his last beating she succumbed to defeat.

Drenger turned the horse back to the compound and sped towards it. He turned from the trees without a backwards glance. Seera looked to see Yrsa was hidden. She prayed that the girl would find freedom.

A shimmer of warmth traveled through her and wrapped around her like a cloak. She felt him then...Orn, his spirit was with her and hope stirred.

The horse passed through the gate and was pulled to a halt. Drenger leapt from the horse, dragging Seera with her. She glanced out the open gate to the sea that she had almost made it to. She glimpsed the dark shape of a ship hidden just north of the dock she'd been trying for.

Not a fishing boat, but a large drekar.

"Take the girl to the ship," Rafn ordered Hamr who held the young slave girl who'd escaped. She had not screamed when Hamr had grabbed her. Drenger had been close and the girl could have ruined things for them. Rafn watched Hamr lead her to the ship. The girl offered no resistance.

Rafn clenched his fists. If Drenger had not caught the other woman before she'd made it to the tree line, the Jarl would have ridden straight into them.

Rafn stiffened as Dagstyrr returned from his search of the area. Rafn's gut tightened at the anger on his friends face. Something was wrong.

"You must come," Dagstyrr whispered.

The ground was dry with brittle twigs and leaves. Rafn stepped carefully to avoid making a sound. A well trained warrior would hear the slightest noise.

The clearing came into view and bodies hanged from the trees. A blinding rage flared within him as he saw the body of his brother swing from the closest tree. His heart froze in anguish, even as a fire of pure rage flared to life. He struggled to hold back the storm.

He would have screamed his wrath, but for the fact he was a trained warrior and knew that silence was his ally. His finger nails drew blood he clenched them so tight.

"Cut him down." He spoke through gritted teeth, unable to trust himself to move, lest he betray their cover by charging straight into the town and pushing his sword through Drenger. Dagstyrr and two of the other men carefully cut Orn down while Rafn watched on with disbelief. Orn was dead, sacrificed to a god he did not follow.

He closed his eyes for a moment and let the fury consume him. He dare not breathe until he had control of it. Only once he was sure he wouldn't give in to the anger did he open his eyes.

"Thor, lend me your strength so I can avenge my brother's death. Let my hand be true, and my sword not falter."

The warrior, Hachet, carried Orn's body back to the ship. The men watched in grim silence. Rafn walked behind and more than one man stepped out of his way. A chaotic storm emanated from the warlord…the Raven. His power shone from his eyes as he met their grim faces.

All loved Orn. All wanted revenge. Rafn watched each man draw his sword, finger his axe, clutch his spear all in silent summons that death would be dealt swiftly and without remorse. Many would die on their blades. Pride in his men encouraged him. They would not let him down.

But it would be Rafn who would kill the Jarl of Ribe. He tore the helmet from his head and threw it to Hachet. He would have nothing obstructing his view that night.

All flocked to the Raven. They were his best warriors. Well trained and needing nothing more than a nod of his head to know what they must do.

Rafn watched the guards until sometime in the night, when each turned their eyes inside the compound. Whatever distracted the guards made them blind to the serpent slithering its way towards them.

Rafn and his men crept forward through the grass. The Raven's eyes fixed on a weak board in the compound's defenses.

He saw his chance and took it.

Seera waited in the same damp cell that had held Orn only days before. There was a wooden bench to sit on but no blanket and Seera shivered. She watched through the small window grate. The sun had already left the sky and stole what little light she'd had.

She tried not to feel the fear that spread through her. She tried to pray, wanted to pray, but she could not bring the words to her mind. She felt lonelier than she'd ever felt. She was so far away from any friendly face or loving arms that she felt forsaken.

She would die. Knew that was the inevitable outcome to her failed escape. She'd seen it clearly in Drenger's cold eyes. One did not anger the Jarl and live. Had Gillaug not warned her?

She did not want to die. She wanted to live free again, without the pain these last few weeks had brought her. She'd hoped that perhaps Peder would somehow find her, but he didn't know where she'd been taken. Jutland was not the only land where Vikings hailed from.

How would he know where to search?

She thought of her father's laugh when she did something amusing. Like when she was ten and wandered into the dyeing tent to help the women making the colored dyes from lichens, woad, weld and walnut shells. Her mother had still been alive and sat among them.

Seera had been so eager to learn. She'd pictured how the wool would become dresses, tunics, trousers, cloaks and jackets that were worn by all.

The women had been busy and had not noticed her at first. Not until she'd managed to trip over a trough that held a bright indigo dye and spill it all over herself. Her mother had been upset, in her quiet way, as she hauled Seera out of the tent and out through the castle wall to a stream beyond.

Her father had watched from the stone wall, and she could hear his laughter echoing. He'd been amused because his daughter had turned herself blue. Even the guards had snickered at the sight.

Tears came to her at the memory. She was hopelessly lost in a place that held no warmth or comfort. There was no reason left to keep going. Perhaps death was the only answer. She couldn't go back to Drenger's dwelling. The thought of him taking her again made her cringe.

If that happened, would she end up like Yrsa? Perhaps it was the hunger and fear that ate at her courage, or the cold that wove its way deep into her bones that made it hard for her to push aside her terror.

"Do not give into despair," a voice whispered. She squinted to see through the darkness, but no one was there. She was only hearing things.

Her head spun as she tried to make sense of what she felt. Something touched her shoulder and she jumped. Her eyes widened in horror for there was no one there.

"Cling on to hope. It will not forsake you." She heard the voice again which seemed to come from all around her.

Incredible warmth encompassed her. It eased her fear and she felt renewed. The voice was comforting and she clung to it.

Light grew in the space in front of her. Standing in the golden softness was a man and Seera opened her mouth in amazement at what she saw.

Orn...his smile was a comfort.

"Courage Seera," he said. "This night brings many surprises."

A croak came out when she tried to speak. What she saw was not a figment of her imagination. The truth of Orn's presence was hard to deny. She felt it deep within and welcomed it.

Words escaped her so instead she smiled and seeing that she had heard him he disappeared.

She felt a sudden punch in the stomach at his departure and wanted to scream for him to come back, but just then she heard a key being inserted into the iron lock that secured the door to her cell.

The door creaked open and Hwal stepped down. A chill traveled over her skin. She made it to her feet before he grabbed her and dragged her outside. She welcomed the fresh air after the cell's staleness.

Fear and courage warred with each other. She was not sure which would win.

CHAPTER 5

The guards near the gate watched with amusement as Seera was dragged into the courtyard and passed into Drenger's hands. He forced her to continue. She stepped on a sharp rock, cutting her foot, but the Jarl did not stop. Drenger came to a large wooden pole that stood in the center of the courtyard. On it hung a metal ring from which a rope was looped through.

Drenger forced Seera onto her knees with her face pushed into the post and tied her wrists so they hung above her head to the metal ring. His men came forward to gawk and laugh and cheer on their Jarl. Even the guards on the wall turned from their lookout to watch.

"You'll not disobey me again." Drenger ripped open the back of her smock to expose her skin.

"Just kill me." Seera screamed at him. She shifted so that she could stare into his eyes. There was no hint of kindness behind them. Drenger narrowed his eyes in disgust. She refused to turn her gaze away, unwilling to give him the satisfaction of seeing her cower. What could only be described as madness claimed her and gave strength to her weakened body and mind.

Since Orn had come to her, she felt his strength renewing her, giving her courage when she should have had none. This defiance must have shown on her face because Drenger's scowl deepened at her insolence.

His foot struck out and caught her in the stomach. She gagged desperately, not wanting to throw up in front of him. He searched her face for any weakness. She would show him none.

"Your wish may come, but not yet," Drenger replied. He stepped away from her and called to Hwal.

"Bring your whip." He did not look away as he shouted his order to Hwal.

The one-eyed giant appeared next to Drenger. Dwarfing the Jarl, Hwal was almost twice as wide. Seera was forced to stare up at him over her shoulder. He was a monster out of a nightmare making her cringe as his shadow descended over her. Hating the fact she feared him, she tried to hold his gaze. She gritted her teeth together to keep the tears from betraying her further, but she was all too aware that he knew his affect on her.

"Show my slave what happens when one tries to escape," Drenger ordered. Hwal sneered in excitement.

Seera turned her head away to fix her sight on a smooth rock not far from where she was bound. She heard him crack the whip in the air to test it and tensed her body in anticipation. But nothing could prepare her for the pain of the first strike across her back. She ground her teeth together against the sting, and the need to cry out.

She heard the snap of the whip before the next lash struck. She clamped her teeth harder. She must not give him the satisfaction of hearing her whimper.

Hwal continued to bring the whip across her flesh. Burning pain spread across her back until it was consumed. Her thoughts became muddled and she could concentrate on nothing but her fiery skin. She drew comfort from the fact she would die soon, and the agony would be gone. A part of her prayed for such a relief, but the rest of her stubbornly held onto the pain that kept her locked to a life she was not willing to part with.

Her vision was beginning to blur and she was afraid she going to pass out. She fought against that escape. Her defiance took control and demanded she show no vulnerability. She sought to allow the fire to become a part of her instead of fighting its consumption. The whip descended.

Eight, nine, ten…

Orn came to her. She felt his presence, just as she needed his strength the most.

Thor's blood that woman was brave, Rafn thought. He watched from his hiding place alongside his men. It was late in the night when all but the guards would be asleep, but there proved to be more warriors about than they expected. Many crowded together on the wall.

He noticed Drenger standing off to the side smiling with satisfaction as the woman was flogged. Rafn's hand tightened on the hilt of his sword and he had to breathe deeply to fight the urge not to act.

He needed control.

Rafn studied the crowd. They would not deter him. His nostrils flared in anger as silently swore he would draw blood that night in restitution for his brother's death. He vowed in Thor's name and felt the brewing storm as he shuddered in anticipation from the thunder echoing through him.

He let thoughts of his brother surface. Orn's smile flashed before him…eyes that held nothing but kindness. Orn had not been like Rafn, had not been a warrior. He'd been a man who longed for peace. A man looking forward to marriage to a woman he deeply loved.

Sparks traveled down Rafn's fingers. He flexed them with eagerness. Drenger would pay for taking such a man from the world. He would feel the hard steel of Rafn's blade in his gut. That was a promise he would see fulfilled before the moon disappeared from the sky.

The commotion in the courtyard had been the perfect distraction for Rafn and his men to sneak into the compound and position themselves between the buildings. In a good location to see what was happening, he waited for the right moment as he watched the woman tied to the post. He had counted ten lashes so far and still she had not cried out. He was impressed by her bravery.

Seera concentrated on counting the lashes to keep her mind focused against the pain that threatened to take control of her, she counted ten, but no more came. She waited but Hwal had walked away and Drenger was coming forward again. Seera's blurry vision sharpened on a shadow beside one of the buildings that had not been there earlier. The shadow turned into the shape of a man. A hard savage face stared back at her.

Surprise rippled through Rafn when the woman looked directly at him. She did not react to give him away, but continued to stare at him. She was a mess. Her face was bruised and swollen, her hair half out of its braid and tangled nastily, and the pain was not entirely concealed on her face. But her eyes held a fire that told him that Drenger had not succeeded in taming her. Rafn smiled in pleasure.

"Cut her down wife." Gillaug came forward to remove the ropes from her wrist. Seera fell to the ground. As she lay there she saw the man in the shadow move.

The night exploded into chaos as warriors materialized from between the buildings. Men began fighting, sword to sword. Drenger yelled as he locked blades with a man with fiery red hair.

Rafn was almost to Drenger, but first he had to dispose of the warrior who dared to stop him. The warrior was nothing, inconsequential to the man in his sights. He reddened his blade with ease and did not bother to watch the man fall. He was almost to Drenger who had managed to engage Dagstyrr. Rafn forced his way forward knowing Dagstyrr would do no more than delay the enemy Jarl. The honor of killing was for Rafn—and Rafn alone.

Gillaug ran off as soon as the fighting started, leaving Seera at the post. Seera struggled to sit up. Ignoring the stinging rawness of her back she turned to watch the warriors fighting each other. The man she'd seen in the shadows stepped in front of her, but he did not spare her a glance. He glared at Drenger. Rage boiled in him and his eyes reflected hatred that she understood all too well.

"Drenger," Rahn yelled. Dagstyrr stepped back from the fight so that Drenger could turn to face Rafn.

Drenger's brow drew down into a scowl. "Rafn Vakrson."

"Valhalla waits." Rafn referred to Odin's hall that awaited any warrior who died in battle. "Your life for my brother's."

"That wisp of a boy. He was a fine offering for Odin."

Rafn reached inside to the gathered storm and let it explode from him. He screamed as he swung his sword down towards Drenger. His enemy reacted quickly to stop it with his own.

"Now you die."

They fought back and forth, moving closer to the center of the courtyard with each lunge.

The air sizzled around Rafn as he fought with vicious strength. The men closest to the duo stepped back. None dared to step between the Jarl and the Raven.

Gasps rose from the Jarl's men as they gawked at the warrior of myth. They'd all heard of him, but many had believed the skalds' stories exaggerated. How could a man be touched by a god and live? Thor's own lightning bolt had struck him, when he was but a boy and all he bore was a scar on his right shoulder. It unnerved them to see the man of legend was real.

There was no doubt about the truth of the tales. Rafn's arm was strong and certain, his reflexes quick. He hacked with his sword in a continuous fluid movement. Relentless, he kept Drenger on the defense. The Jarl was breathing heavily in his attempt to stay alive.

All of Drenger's effort focused on keeping Rafn's blade from finding his flesh. In desperation he sought to find a hole in Rafn's offense in which to change the inevitable outcome. He snarled in contempt and foolish frustration.

Drenger seethed with anger as he made an attempt to turn the fight in his favor, but Rafn had anticipated his move. Rafn brought his blade against the other man's sword. Rafn felt the strength of Drenger's arm as metal pushed against metal.

Rafn had no doubt he would win this battle.

Thunder rumbled in the sky above and caused more than one warrior to pause in their own fight to stare up at the black clouds. Drenger's eyes flicked but a second upwards, enough for Rafn to lunge at him hard, causing his enemy to take a step back.

"No." Drenger screamed. Finding at last a weak moment he turned Rafn to the defensive. The Raven did not panic at the sudden change of direction. An eerie smile appeared on his face, warning the Jarl that he was still in control. Rafn stepped forward to stop each lunge, and back in the next step to avoid the full impact of blade on blade.

The Raven was baiting a trap, but Drenger could not find it. Sweat beaded on Drenger's forehead and his hands shook with weariness. His moves became desperate and lacked skill.

Power surged through Rafn as he prepared to strike.

Another step back and the man Drenger had called Rafn, would be on top of her. Seera prayed that he would succeed in killing Drenger, but she feared his failure. She watched the man's muscles bunching through his trousers and knew she was not being logical. Her stomach tightened in panic as they moved closer to her.

Seera's gaze swept down the young warlord's leg until she noticed a knife sheathed to his calf. Without thinking she grabbed it.

Rahn was aware of the woman's presence directly behind him, but he couldn't look at her as he moved to block Drenger's blade. He felt her take his knife and was surprised by her daring, but he couldn't afford to look at her.

He went for Drenger who faltered and barely stumbled back in time. The Jarl sidestepped and twisted as Rafn came at him, until their positions were reversed. Over Drenger's shoulder Rafn could see the girl had managed to stand. She was looking at Drenger with a hate that mirrored his own.

Thunder rumbled closer and Thor's chariot shot across the sky in a bright streak of lightning that did not reach for the earth. He felt his god's approval.

Rafn turned his full attention to Drenger as their blades collided, locking their hilts together. Rafn and Drenger were eye to eye, each furious and ready to kill. Rafn had no doubt of the outcome. The thunder was roaring in him, guiding his hand. He pushed back hard, unhooking his sword. He raised his arm for the killing thrust. An electrical charge traveled down his arm as he prepared to end it.

Reacting to something on his opponents face, he managed to stop his swing in midair.

Drenger's eyes froze in shock and blood bubbled from his mouth. Confused Rafn stepped back as the Jarl fell, cheating him of his kill. His gaze shot to the girl who was standing there with his knife in her hand. It was dripping with blood. She had rammed it through Drenger's back and into his heart.

Their eyes met and Rafn saw the satisfaction reflected in their green depths, the satisfaction that should have been his. He grunted in frustration and was barely able to contain his anger.

The woman's eyes filled with tears that trickled down her cheeks unaware. He had to force his arm into stillness so he would not give in to the temptation to push his blade through her chest.

"Rafn, we need to fall back." Dagstyrr spoke from behind him.

Rafn drew in a strangled breath, forcing the killing rage deep where it would do no harm. He held the woman's gaze for a moment longer, and something in them made him temper his anger. The woman did not move, or seem to be aware of the danger she had placed herself in by stealing the Raven's kill.

"Lord." Dagstyrr called again and Rafn assessed the situation quickly. The surprise was gone and more men were coming from the village. Many of Drenger's men lay dead at his feet. He kicked at Drenger's body and knew nothing else could be done.

"To the ship." Rafn's men responded to his call and began to slip out through the hole they had made in a weak spot of the wall.

Rafn turned to melt back into the shadows, but something made him look back at the woman. She appeared ready to topple, but somehow remained standing.

"Rafn?" Dagstyrr's face reflected a question he was not ready to answer.

Rafn approached the woman. The scowl on his face would have been enough to scare most people, but she remained unaffected. Growling he grabbed her and threw her over his shoulder. Dagstyrr raised an eyebrow at him, but Rafn ignored it.

They slipped into the night.

Hwal stood in the courtyard and stared down at his dead Jarl and the rest of the men who'd fought poorly that night. Hwal ordered the men on the walls to keep their positions, but those that had been in the courtyard had been unprepared and died too easily, all but Hwal. Pathetic! Life was wasted on such pitiable men.

Hwal glared down at Drenger. What a stupid fool, he thought. He would not even go to Vahalla in honor. A woman had taken his life. What a disgrace. He spit on Drenger's corpse. Hwal vowed he would not rule with such weakness.

"Should we go after them?" A warrior who'd just arrived through the gate approached him with wariness.

"Let them go," Hwal replied. "We will take care of them another day."

Hwal looked to the shadows where Rafn had disappeared with the woman. He would find her again, and the pain he would inflict on her would make the whipping she'd just received seem like nothing.

CHAPTER 6

The men said nothing as their warlord carried the battered woman onto the ship and lay her down close to Orn's blanket wrapped body. The young girl Hamr had caught scurried closer. Dagstyrr had managed to get her to tell him her name, but she would say nothing more. She just sat with her arms wrapped around her legs watching. Rafn had a feeling the girl, Yrsa, was evaluating him.

The men started rowing them out onto the dark waters. Rafn placed the wounded woman down on her side, being careful to avoid touching her back too much. Yrsa's eyes widened.

The woman watched him out of unfocused eyes. Her gaze turned to the bundle that held his brother's body. It was close enough for her to touch and he was shocked when she reached out her hand and tenderly placed it on top of him.

"Orn," she said. Rafn was shocked at the tenderness her voice held and was about to ask her how she knew his brother's name. Before he could demand an answer, her eyes rolled back in her head and she passed out.

Rafn stared at the woman in wonder, before gently turning her onto her stomach so that he might inspect the welts on her back. They were red and many were bleeding. Her skin was raw and swollen and Rafn was grateful she was unconscious, for even a warrior would find such wounds painful. He shook his head and rubbed a hand across his stubble. A warrior was trained to ignore such discomfort, but she was just a woman.

No, he thought. She was not just any woman. He had watched from the shadows as she was flogged. He had seen her bear the pain well.

Why had he taken her? She had taken his victory from him. He should have killed her for interference. He drew his knife from the hilt on his leg and looked at the blood on it. Drenger's blood!

He had promised that Drenger would die by his blade, he pondered, and this was his blade. Even if it had not been his hand that had wielded it, the man had died by it. His blood stained it.

Yrsa watched him warily as he twisted the dagger in his hand, contemplating what he would do next. Dagstyrr came up beside him.

"What are you going to do with her?"

"I don't know." Rafn shrugged as he slipped the knife back into its sheath and rose to stand beside his friend.

"Why did you take her?"

"I wanted her." Rafn admitted his desire to the only man he would ever tell such a thing to. He knew that Yrsa also listened, but he doubted she would repeat his words to anyone.

"She's not so good to look at." Dagstyrr frowned down at the woman who was a swollen and bloody mess.

"I liked her strength," Rafn answered.

"She was brave." Dagstyrr ran a hand through his red hair. "But she stole your kill. How does that make you feel?"

"Furious." His nostrils flared while he fought down the sudden surge of violent emotions. It took a moment to push back the darkness before he really considered the woman he knelt over. "Looking at her though has made me think...perhaps she had a stronger need to kill him."

"That is enough for you?"

Rafn glimpse up at Dagstyrr, the sun directly behind his friend caused him to squint. "I'm unsure. She took something from me, now her life is mine."

"A just trade."

Rafn stared at the unconscious woman and wondered who she was.

They traveled north until they came to the land of water called the Skagerrak, across which they sailed until reaching The Vik, whose tide carried them to Vestfold, and the town of Skiringssal. A few days passed without the woman waking. The welts on her back had begun to swell and a fever had taken control of her body. Rafn began to wonder if she would even live.

The young girl stayed by her side the entire time. When Rafn came to check on the woman, Yrsa watched him closely. She never spoke, but he sensed that she was standing guard over the woman. He recalled they had been trying to escape together. Perhaps there was a special bond between them.

Skiringssal came into view. Rafn stood to greet the sight with trepidation. They pulled into port and were greeted with cheers from the villagers as they noticed the emblem of the raven that marked the sail. It was the symbol of the war leader. It was Rafn's mark. Skiringssal was his town, his people and they were welcoming him home.

A mourning cry rose through the crowd as Rafn disembarked, carrying the wrapped body of his brother. The cry rushed beyond him and by the time he reached Valr's dwelling, the Jarl was waiting for him.

"Let me relieve you of your burden." Valr reached for Orn, but Rafn shook him off.

Rafn pulled Orn's body closer to his chest. His grip tightened and his face hardened with too much emotion. In his arms he held the one person who offered him the light to push back the darkness. That light was gone now and he was teetering on the edge. He clenched his jaw in a desperate attempt at control. "No—he has never been a burden."

Valr watched him closely, seeing the turmoil he was in. "Let us lay him to rest then," Valr said. "We shall feast in honor of his life."

"To honor him," Rafn agreed.

"What would you have me do with her." Dagstyrr appeared beside him with the woman in his arms. "Her fever worsens."

Valr's eyes widened in surprise at the stranger cradled in Dagstyrr's arms. "What is this?"

"She is mine!" Valr and Dagstyrr exchanged a look of amusement and Rafn glared at them both, daring one of them to say something. Valr did nothing more than hold his gaze, while Dagstyrr repositioned the woman.

"Let me take our brother." Valr tried again and for a moment Rafn was about to protest, but he released his bundle into the care of the only other man he trusted with Orn.

"Give her to me." Free of Orn's weight he needed to fill his empty arms with the woman. Her breathing was shallow and Rafn sensed she was close to death. His gut tightened in panic. A desperate need flared to life within him.

His gaze flicked over Yrsa, who was hanging back, watching out of solemn eyes. He did not acknowledging her as he turned and headed for his sister's dwelling.

A door opened and Kata stepped outside. Rafn's stride lengthened to bring him to her. Shock shimmered across her face and he realized he must look a mess. His gaze traveled to the battered female in his arms. He felt oddly protective of her and it made him edgy. He needed this woman to live.

Surprise registered on Kata's face as she studied the injured woman. "Inside," Kata said. She pushed open the door and let her brother carry the woman in. Yrsa followed him in. Rafn placed the woman on the bed that was centered on the far wall.

"Will you care for her?" Rafn asked. "I must see to Orn."

"What of Orn?" Kata stared at him in alarm. Realizing that she had not yet heard, Rafn drew her into his arms. He felt her stiffen.

"He is with us no longer." A sob escaped her and she buried her face in his shoulder and cried. He allowed Kata her moment of grief. He could offer her no more.

"You brought him home?" She spoke into his shoulder.

"I did." His arms tightened around her.

"Good." She pushed from his arms and used her hands to straighten her skirt. She tucked her long dark hair behind her ears and stiffened her back in determination to be brave. "Ask Father Duncun to give him a Christian burial."

"I will speak with him." It was what his little brother would want. Rafn stepped closer to the bed to stare down at the woman. He was reluctant to leave her. He gripped his fingers in his hair, while trying to calm the urgency he felt where she was concerned. It was illogical. It was unnerving.

He looked up to find Kata watching him. "I can leave her?"

Kata must have seen his trembling hands for she took them in her own. "Yes, go. She will be in good hands."

"I trust no other healer."

"Enough." She pushed him towards the door. "From the look of her I must see to her right away."

The young girl remained in the shadows behind Kata. He nodded towards her. "This girl is Yrsa. We haven't been able to get her to say anything more. She doesn't seem inclined to leave the injured one."

"I will have Esja look after her."

He was having trouble leaving and he didn't know why. With a final glance to the woman on the bed, he left.

Once outside he headed towards the hall in the center of the compound. Before he reached the doors he hesitated. There was somewhere else he needed to go first. He veered towards the chapel.

Kata wiped away her tears and studied the woman. She was in bad shape. Her back had been whipped raw. Kata looked to the door Rafn had exited. Why had he brought her back with him? When had her brother ever shown concern for a woman beside her?

Kata wondered about this woman who could make her brother act in such an uncharacteristic way. She shook her head. Later would be time enough for answers. First she had to keep her from dying.

She cut away the rest of the woman's smock, before placing a hand on her patient's forehead to feel the fever that burned her skin. She reached into a basin of cool water and withdrew a saturated cloth. She squeezed out the excess before placing it on the side of the woman's forehead.

Kata turned her attention to the pus filled wounds on her back. With a sharp knife she carefully cut open those that were infected to let the yellowish substance ooze out. Taking another damp cloth she gently wiped the pus free of the cuts and was pleased when clean blood began to flow.

She had Yrsa boil some water in a pot suspended over the hearth. The girl didn't speak, but she followed orders quickly, telling Kata she had been a slave for some time.

When she finished cleaning the wounds, she crushed up some dried willow bark that would be good for the fever. She set it to steep in the heated water. When the tea was done she poured it into a cup and set in beside the bed for when the woman woke.

Wanting to be thorough, Kata checked over the rest of her body. The woman had a bruised rib, and a cut on her left foot that was deep, but the blood was already crusted over and showed no infection. Her face was a mess. She had bruises on both sides of her face, but only the right side had swollen across the cheek bone. She traced a small cut that disappeared into the hair line.

Further investigation showed evidence of rape, for her opening had been torn. The man had not been gentle, making Kata angry. She knew such things happened all the time, but it was not how Kata would want her maidenhood taken. She trembled at the thought.

Feeling exhausted she turned her focus to the young girl, who had stayed close to the bed, never taking her eyes off the injured woman. The hollow look in Yrsa's eyes spoke of severe trauma. Kata had seen it before, in women after their villages had been attacked and they had somehow survived the men's assaults on them. She forced her voice to be gentle as she reached a hand out to the girl.

"You must be hungry."

Yrsa reached for her offered hand without hesitation. Together they walked to the kitchen, where Kata found Esja, the head servant who was in charge of seeing that the work got done.

She led the girl to an older woman. "Esja...this is Yrsa. She is a new servant and in need of your guidance." A look passed between them that said more than her words. She could trust Esja to know what the girl needed in the way of solace. "But, first she needs to eat."

She beckoned to the girl. "I will see that you are safe."

Kata returned to her patient's side. After checking on her, she settled in a wooden chair close to the bed, feeling exhaustion claiming her. She was just beginning to nod off in her chair when the woman stirred. Her eyes fluttered open to reveal a beautiful green. She mumbled something incoherent but Kata managed to get her to sit up long enough to drink the medicine. Easing her back onto her stomach the woman drifted off. Returning to her chair, Kata placed her head on the foot of the bed and fell asleep, not waking until morning.

Seera was trapped in a feverish dream that had no end. Pain gave way to warmth and comfort as Orn's face came and went. His musical voice spoke soothing words that kept her locked away from the agony that floated at the edges of her consciousness. The pain would filter in once in awhile, making her wish for death, but he would always return to ease her back into the light.

She dreamed of a far shore she had left behind and a brother who had often teased with relentlessness. She would hear her father's laughter and turned to catch a glimpse of him standing in a corridor before he faded away. Memory of her friend Jakob filtered in bringing her joy one moment and sorrow the next as she recalled that he was dead.

Around her colors appeared more vivid and sounds hollow in the ever changing world of her mind. A feathery breeze swept past her and around her, embracing her in warmth.

Her heart beat oddly loud to her ears.

An image of a man cloaked in the shadows formed. His dark possessing eyes stared at her from the darkness and sparked with power. She felt at once drawn to him and frightened by him.

Lightning shot from the heavens to rip up the earth behind him. The air pulse with searing power as it caressed his skin. It appeared to be apart of him and he did not flinched at the painful fingers that reached for him. Shadows moved across his eyes as if something lived behind them.

Thunder reverberated above, beneath her…through her. She drifted endlessly, further from reality.

A whip cracked and she cringed in fear of the pain it brought. Agony washed over forcing her to leave behind the light.

Seera woke with an intense headache and a desperate need for water. A chill shivered over her bare back, followed by a dull ache. Finding her limbs weak, it was difficult to roll over, which she soon found to be a mistake. She yelped at the sudden assault of pain.

"Stay off your back. It is still tender." A startled woman appeared beside her, helping her to her side.

Seera looked at the woman and seeing that it was not Gillaug managed a weak smile. "It does hurt a bit," she replied.

"Just a bit?"

"Alright, maybe more, but I will not admit that to anyone else." Seera attempted to sit but her head began to spin.

"Let me help you." The young woman assisted her up. "Don't lean against anything, and if you feel weak lay back down."

"Thank you." The woman moved behind Seera to examine her back. She was obviously some kind of healer, she thought.

"My name is Lady Kata Vakradottir of Skiringssal," she introduced, Vakradottir meaning that she was the daughter of Vakr. "This is my home." She indicated the dwelling they were in and it caused Seera to stare harder at her surroundings.

"Skiringssal?" Seera was astonished. "In Vestfold? I am not in Ribe?"

"Nay," Kata said. "You are in Skiringssal. My brother brought you here."

"Your brother?"

Kata pressed a wet cool cloth against her back, causing her to gasp. "Rafn Vakrson." The Vakrson meant he was the son of Vakr. "I am sorry to cause you pain, but I must keep your wounds clean so that infection does not return."

"He was the warrior that came into Ribe when I was tied to the post?"

"He didn't tell me what happened, he just left you here." Moving to Seera's side she placed her hand on her forehead and obviously pleased, she smiled. "Your fever is gone."

"Orn vowed he would come." Seera whispered, not realizing she had spoken.

"You knew Orn?"

Startled Seera met the woman's inquiry. She was not sure how to explain what had happened. Kata clasped her hands together as if to keep control of her emotions. The grief in the woman's eyes affected Seera deeply. She needed to make her understood.

"I was there when he died." Seera started to explain, but tears sprang into Kata's eyes and she refrained from saying more. Perhaps it was best that she not speak the details.

"Why did Lord Rafn bring me here?" She watched as Kata went to a wooden table and filled a cup from a clay pitcher.

"He didn't tell me that either." The woman returned to help Seera drink the water. She had never tasted anything so refreshing. Too soon Kata took the water away, barely leaving her thirst quenched. "You mustn't drink too much at first."

Seera nodded at the healer's advice. Weariness was settling in and she would need to lie down again soon. But first it would only be polite to offer a proper introduction.

"I am Lady Seera of Dun'O'Tir."

"The Fortress by the Sea?" Kata looked at her with new fascination as she reached for a small wooden container and began applying a soothing paste on her welts. Even such a small relief was welcome.

"Aye." Feeling a chill, Seera pulled the blanket up to cover her chest and tried to remain prone while Kata worked on her back. Her eyelids grew heavy and the headache stronger.

"How did you come to be in Ribe?" Kata's question pulled her back from the haze she'd been falling into.

"I would like to hear that answer myself." A new voice intruded into their conversation. Seera looked up to see Rafn in the doorway. She was suddenly glad she had pulled up the blanket to cover her nakedness. She met his gaze and felt a tremor ripple through her. His dark eyes demanded an answer.

"Drenger and his men came to Pictland when I was on my way home to Dun'O'Tir. They killed my maid and my squire, as well as the rest of my escort." She swallowed in an attempt to keep her voice from shaking. She accepted a drink from Kata before continuing. "They tied me and took me with them to Ribe where I was told I would be Drenger's slave."

"You are from the fortress on the cliff by the ocean. I have heard it is impenetrable." His face clearly showed his skepticism.

"She is the Lady Seera, my brother." Kata stepped closer to her brother as if to scold him.

"A Lady, not a slave then." He ignored his sister and continued to study her.

"Aye." The pounding in her head became louder. Sharp stabs of pain shot across her temple. She pressed her fingers into the right side of her head to still the throbbing.

"And you were punished for trying to escape?" He kept at her, unaware of her agony. She tried to stay focused on his words. She glanced up abruptly as she realized he must have seen her failed attempt at freedom.

"Brother, she has been through enough. Do not interrogate her." Kata was staring at her with concern. Her interruption was a blessing, for Seera had nothing further to say to the man who'd risen from the shadows to save her.

"You presume to tell me what to do." He looked to his sister, but there was no harness in his voice. "I am your warlord and I give the orders."

"You are a fierce warrior, but I am your sister and your love for me keeps me safe enough." There was no fear in her eyes when she returned her brother's fierce glare.

"I allow you too much freedom is what my warriors would say." He glanced back at Seera and must have realized the pain she was fighting to hold back. He took a step towards her and her vision blurred. Before she could fall backwards onto her wounds, he caught her arms and eased her down on her side. His fingers brushed over her hair as he pulled his hand away.

He had seen her try to escape?

"There was a young girl with me, did you see her," Seera asked. "Do you know what happened to her?" He held her imprisoned in tumultuous eyes, but he did not reply. Kata was the one to supply the answer.

"Yrsa is here. She is being cared for."

"That is good. She has suffered far too much for one so young."

Rafn raised an eyebrow. "Yet it was you who was tied to the post."

"I didn't have to endure years as Hwal's slave." She snapped at him as if her suffering had been nothing. That only confirmed what he'd already learned, that she did indeed have courage. He smiled in pleasure at the knowledge, and watched the suspicion grow in the green depths of her eyes.

"Why did you bring me here?"

Rafn pushed a lock of his raven hair from his face and studied her for a moment before answering. Because you are mine, he thought, and felt a resounding wave pulse through him at the truth of the silent declaration. To her, he simply said. "You killed Drenger. For that you now belong to me." He hid the smile from his face when he saw the spark of defiance in her eyes. To her credit she remained silent.

"You killed Drenger?" Kata asked in shock. "With your injuries, how did you find the strength?"

"He took something from me that did not belong to him." Seera answered Kata, but her words were meant for Rafn.

He did not have to be told that she'd been raped. With all the pain that had been inflicted on her, that was the most personal. It was no surprise she would want to see the man dead. She was a lady and she would have been protected by her father from any man touching her. Any who dared would have to die. Seera had understood that. He understood it as well.

"I will speak with you later sister." Rafn didn't say anything more to Seera before he left.

"What will he expect of me?"

"I am unsure." Kata answered honestly. "First he must bury our brother."

Seera looked at her with sympathy and wished she could explain how connected she still felt to Orn. How while she lay unconscious he was with her, giving her his strength. It made no sense that someone she had not known in life had become so close in death.

Tears burned her eyes as she finally gave into the need to close them. As she drifted into sleep she heard the cawing of a raven, followed by a distant rumbling.

CHAPTER 7

It was expected that *a vehement storm* would have grown to dangerous proportions within Rafn. Since returning from Jutland with his brother's body, everyone had been keeping their distance. They understood his anger, but no one wanted to stand too close in case it could no longer be contained.

He felt their distance as he stood out on the training field shooting arrows into one of the hay stuffed targets with such force the hay was spilling out onto the ground through gapping holes. He had already gone through a series of training exercises with both sword and spear, but it was not enough to burn the fire away.

Dagstyrr approached him and to his credit did not flinch when Rafn glared at him with burning rage.

"Shall we practice with our swords?" Rafn thought him brave to make such a request, because the warlord was not sure if he would be able to stop himself from killing anyone he fought, even in practice.

"It would not be wise on your part." He clenched his fists by his side as he fought to keep sane.

"I will carry my shield to protect myself." Dagstyrr lifted the leather bound shield up. "Let me worry about my own safety. You need to vent some of that anger before someone truly does get hurt."

Rafn's nostrils flared, but he did see the wisdom in what Dagstyrr was saying. The warlord let out a challenging cry as he grabbed his spear from the scabbard on his back. He brought it down with all his strength, to be stopped just in time by Dagstyrr. The resounding clang of metal against metal echoed around them.

The men parried back as an explosive agitation claimed Rafn. A crowd formed to watch. They all understood the seriousness of the fight, and admired Dagsytrr's bravery for putting himself in the path of Rafn's madness.

Rafn went at him again and again as the crowd watched in hushed silence. Again and again Dagstyrr was driven back, using his shield to block the most forceful blows.

Rafn twisted around and swung his sword with him, slicing it through the air with a downward momentum and found it shattering the blade of his friend's sword.

He snapped back to awareness and took note of the crowd as they all took an intake of breath at their warlord's strength. It caused Rafn to stop. Sweat poured off his head and down his bare chest. The scar on his shoulder itched and he fought the urge to scratch at it in irritation.

Dagstyrr's hand still shook from the violent impact and Rafn gritted his teeth as he realized he could have really killed him. That upset him to discover he'd been so close to the edge.

"You shouldn't have endangered yourself like that." Rafn fought to steady his breathing.

Dagstyrr remained his humorous self and observed Rafn with a smile. "Do you feel better?"

"Some."

"Let us find some mead then." Dagstyrr slapped him on the back. Rafn nodded at his friend's attempt to lighten the mood and followed him to the Great Hall.

The sound of thunder followed in his wake.

Rafn stood beside Valr and Kata on a hill behind the town which had a beautiful view of the ocean that stretched wide before them. He had picked the place for Orn's grave with great care, knowing his brother would approve his choice. Father Duncun stood over the mound of dirt, speaking words of his God and his heaven.

The priest's voice rang out in its foreign words; words of eternal peace without further suffering. Rafn fidgeted at such declarations, the continual turmoil bubbling with restlessness inside him.

Rafn would have preferred to place his brother's body on a pyre and burn it. But Orn was not a Viking and such a ceremony was reserved for those meant for Odin's hall.

Movement drew his attention to the Lady Seera. She stood next to the servant Esja, who was helping her to stay on her feet. Rafn felt his jaw clench in anger. She should not be out of bed. Even so thin a dress, as she wore, must hurt against her back.

Tears glistened in Seera's eyes and he speculated at her strange response. He recalled how she had spoken his name on the ship, as if they had been friends. His eyes narrowed in suspicion.

She had withheld something from him about Orn, he surmised at once. Fury took hold and he had to fight it back.

As he watched Seera reached out for a nearby tree as she faltered. Esja gripped her other arm to help keep her steady. Seera's face was pale through her purple bruises. He shouldn't have allowed her to come. As soon as the monk finished, he went to her.

"You must return to bed." Rafn snapped his order causing her to look at him in surprise, as if she had not seen him approach. Moisture still glistened in her eyes and he saw that she was trembling.

"I will go," she said, "in just a moment."

The others began down the hill and started towards the Great Hall, where they would feast and celebrate Orn's life, to tell stories about him while they drank ale and mead. He knew they would stay there until the sun rose, only then returning to their lives.

He dismissed Esja with a stern command that had been unnecessary, but his nerves were on edge. He made no apology to the servant woman and was thankful when she disappeared with the others. "Why do you cry for my brother?" He demanded to know.

Her shaking grew worse and with a grunt of frustration he reached for her.

"I don't feel him anymore." She spoke softly as if to herself and not to him. She looked down at the cross that marked his grave. Her legs gave way beneath her and he cursed silently as he lowered her to the ground. The foolish woman had yet to regain her strength and should not be on the hill, despite the warm day.

"Sit," he ordered.

He sat beside the grave and searched Seera's face for answers to why she felt his brother's death so deeply. Rafn's eyes remained hard upon her.

"I was forced to watch the sacrifice." He stiffened at her words. "Your brother was led through the crowd and he noticed me." She shifted so she could look up into Rafn's face.

"When he was led upon the platform he began to chant the Lord's Prayer and I knew him to be a Christian, like myself. So I spoke the words with him, though I was too far away for him to hear me, he knew I recited them." Her eyes glazed over and took on a distant look as if she were back at that horrible moment. Fear and sorrow washed across her face.

He had to stop his hand from touching her in comfort.

A tear trickled down her face and she met his eyes once again. "He told Drenger that you would come."

"I was not fast enough." Rafn growled in furious pain for having failed Orn so completely.

Seera searched his face before continuing. "He was very brave, your brother. His eyes remained on me as he accepted his death." She looked deep into Rafn's eyes and he had the feeling she saw too deeply. He glanced away.

She reached out and placed her hand on Rafn's. "When I was tied to that pole his spirit was with me, and again on the ship while I lay unconscious. He would not let my strength fail. He would not let me die."

Rafn stood suddenly, and pulled away from her. This woman had been with Orn as he died, and Rafn had not. He hadn't been there to stop it from happening.

"Go back to Kata's!"

Rafn didn't wait to see if she would obey him, but stormed off down the hill. Seera watched him go and felt his pain.

"Orn," she turned to the grave. "Thank you for being with me, and giving me your strength. Find your peace." She glanced to the path Rafn had taken.

"I pray also for your brother, that he find his."

Rafn stood at his favorite spot on the cliff that over looked the sea. The waves crashed against the rocks below sending up a spray of water. To his left he could see the edges of the town that slopped down to met the harbor. The dock stretched out into the bay with many ships anchored on either side. A cool wind blew passed him, soothing his hot skin.

Rafn felt movement as Dagstyrr joined him. "How is the woman?"

"She'll live." Rafn disguised the relief that brought him. He kept his voice hard and even as he spoke.

Dagstyrr observed him closely. "You look troubled."

His emotions surfaced in a rush, causing him to suck in a deep breath. A scowl contorted his face as unwanted feelings bombarded him. What was the woman doing to him? "I need to decide what to do with her?" He could hear the exasperation in his voice and cringed at it.

Dagstyrr snapped off a flower that grew along the edge of the cliff and twirled it in his fingers. "She is a slave."

His voice lowered. "No. She is a Lady."

"A Lady?" Dagstyrr smiled at the implication. His friend's gaze sharpened too keenly on him. He knew what Dagstyrr was thinking for it had entered his mind as well. He growled in response, causing a smirk to appear on Dagstyrr's face.

"She was taken only weeks ago from Pictland," Rafn continued. "She is the daughter of Eorl Airic of Dun'O'Tir."

"The Eorl is friends with King David." Dagstyrr's smile widened. "An alliance between Pictland and Vestfold would be good."

Rafn grimaced at his friend's words even as his heart beat faster. "What is it you propose?"

"You can make the Lady your slave, or you can make her wife." Dagstyrr spoke plainly, but Rafn hesitated at the stark statement.

"Wife?" His pulse raced at the idea, but he was not sure he wanted a wife. What did he really know about her?

Then again what more was there to know. He had seen her spirit clearly. She possessed strength that was admirable by anyone's standards. He closed his eyes as an image of Orn snapped before them. His brother's spirit had found her worthy enough to see her safely into Rafn's care, but that was something he would not tell anyone.

"Think on it." Dagstyrr's hand slapped Rafn's shoulder over the mark Thor had left on him. A slight jolt shot across the scar, causing Dagstyrr to yank back his hand in alarm.

"With Thor's guidance shall I find the answer," Rafn said. Thor was the god that Rafn worshipped. He was the son of Odin, the leader of the gods that lived in Asgard. Thor was the god of thunder and it was from his courage that Rafn drew strength. His brand was a constant reminder of his allegiance.

Of course the god of storms would not be so interested in the matters of the heart. Perhaps he should pray to the goddess, Freyja of the Vanir, who was known for her beauty and passion; She who was the goddess of love.

"Eorl Airic is a Christian, as is King David." Dagstyrr stared down at his throbbing hand but spoke nothing of it.

"As is my lady." And she was his...though he was reluctant to admit. Rafn felt the pull of the sea. The call to follow its currents was strong.

"Does that bother you?"

Rafn's only reply was a deepening of his scowl. He knew the Norse gods, he knew not of the Christian Deity that Father Duncun had tried to tell him of. He had not wanted to listen. His little brother had embraced the Christian God and his son Jesus Christ, who seemed to only want peace and love.

In a world as harsh as the one he lived, love would not stop the violence. Warriors were needed to protect and to punish. That was the reality of a Norseman, a Viking.

"The ship is loaded." Dagstyrr changed the subject realizing Rafn was not going to answer. "We are ready to go on your command."

"You trade to the north?" Rafn watched the waves with longing. It offered an escape that Dagstyrr must have sensed he needed.

"Come with us."

"It would be good to be out on the water." What he chose not to say was it would good to put a needed distance between him and the Lady Seera who consumed far too much of his thoughts. He drew in the salty scent of the ocean and enjoyed the taste on his tongue.

"I will meet you at the ships," Rafn said. He turned back for the compound and made his way down the path.

The thunder trembled inside him with each determined step he took.

"Rafn has gone with the trade ships to the north. Be at ease while he is gone. Come with me to town and we will buy some material to make you some new dresses." Kata informed Seera of her brother's absence as she combed the lady's golden brown hair.

"You have already shown me enough kindness by giving me this exquisite dress I now wear. You needn't offer more." Seera ran her hands over the silken blue of her skirt.

"Hush. You are a lady. I will see you have the finest wardrobe befitting your rank." Kata laughed lightly at Seera's protests. "We have a wonderful seamstress in the village and she will be more than pleased to be kept busy."

Seera clung to the warmth of Kata's offer of friendship. Her voice cracked with emotion as she spoke. "Thank you for all you have done for me."

Kata put down the comb to take Seera's hands in hers. "You have nothing to thank me for. Your friendship is enough."

The two ladies walked into the village and found the shop that sold textiles. They bought wool and linens of the finest qualities. There was even silk brought to the large trading village from a foreign land. From the shoe maker they bought Seera some dear-skin ankle shoes tied with leather lacing. Before returning to the compound they also made an appointment for the seamstress to come to Kata's on the morrow.

Seera felt the exhaustion in each of her muscles as she slumped down in one of the wooden chairs at the table. A headache was beginning behind her eyes and her weakness frustrated her. She looked up to Kata. "You have bought too much."

"It is my brother's money." Kata laughed at the look of horror on Seera's face.

Rafn's glowering face popped into Seera's mind and caused a shiver. "He will not be mad?"

Kata sat down in the adjoining chair. "Nay, he leaves me in charge of his domestic things." A servant had left hot tea and she took a sip.

Seera reached for her own tea and thought of the pleasant day. The people had greeted her kindly and tried not to notice that her face was purple and blue. If they wondered about her they refrained from asking. Perhaps it was simply because she shared the company of the Jarl's sister.

A nervous idea caught her off guard. Had it anything to do with Rafn's claim on her?

When night came and Kata insisted they go to the Great Hall for supper, Seera fidgeted nervously. She wanted to object but she could not decline when Kata had been so kind to her. Seera was still unclear as to what her status was among the people of Skiringssal. She had assumed she would be a slave, but Kata treated her as the lady she had always been. Would these people allow her to go home? She feared to ask, despite their obvious welcome.

From Kata's dwelling they walked across an open courtyard to the Great Hall where they were greeted by Esja, the servant woman she had met at Orn's funeral.

"Esja, the smell coming from the kitchen is mouth watering." Kata greeted the woman with obvious affection. The woman smiled with pride.

"Thank you, my lady. I have been keeping the cooks under strict watch today, seeing as we are to have a guest." Esja glanced to Seera and nodded.

Seera returned the older woman's smile and tried to hide her surprise. She was considered a guest? That made no sense. Rafn had told her that she now belonged to him, she had been afraid that meant she was not free to leave. Certainly a guest would have that right. She was more than confused, and wonder if she should ask about returning to Dun'O'Tir. She bit her tongue before she could. It was not the time for such inquiries.

"How is Yrsa?" Seera looked around for the girl.

"She is in my care," Esja replied. "Upon Lady Kata's request, Yrsa is one of my servants, not a slave." Once again surprised she looked to Kata with gratitude.

"No man will be allowed to use her again, unless she gives her consent." Kata's words spoke understanding that put Seera at ease.

"I thank you for that. She was taken when she was twelve and has known no peace in the two years since."

"I will see that she has it." After making her promise the servant woman bid her goodbye and returned to work.

People began to fill up the long tables that were set around the large room. Kata led her to the raised table at the head of the hall. She could see that it was the table reserved for the Jarl's family, and their closest companions. Certainly she wasn't supposed to eat there. She glanced to Kata in question. Her new friend answered by indicating a chair to her right.

Before Seera could sit, a chiefly looking man walked in with a woman by his side. Those around them rose and greeted the man and his wife as they made their way to the head table. This was the Jarl, Seera realized, and Rafn's older brother. She had seen him at the funeral. He approached her and eyed her with curiosity, as did his wife.

"Brother," Kata stepped forward. "This is Lady Seera of Dun'O'Tir."

"Rafn told me that you are Eorl Airic's daughter," Valr said. "I am Valr Vakrson, the Jarl of Skiringssal and this is my wife Lady Geira of Vestfold." The introduction was formal.

Seera had been around noble men all her life, and bowed politely in response to his introduction. When she rose he took her hand and bent over it for a moment. "I welcome you to my home."

Geira dipped a polite bow. "I welcome you also."

"I thank you both for your hospitality."

Seera took her seat with reservations. She noticed that to her right the chair was left empty. It was Rafn's chair she realized. Placing her to his left implied a relationship that did not exist. Certainly Kata was aware of what people would think.

She leaned towards Kata to whisper her concern. "I'm not sure Rafn would wish me to sit in such a place of honor."

"You are Rafn's. It is where he would want you to be."

Seera felt panicked and searched for a valid argument but could find none. Rafn was not there to set things right. She wanted to argue that the place she sat was reserved for a wife, and that no such intimate relationship existed between them. She sensed her words would fall on deaf ears so she kept her silence.

As she ate she tried not to notice the glances her way from the curious people. She could read their interest as they tried to figure out the significance of where she sat. Rafn should be there to clear up the confusion. Until his return she would be forced to play along.

After the meal was completed, a skald came forward to tell stories of the gods in Asgard, both the Aesir and the lesser Vanir. He spoke eloquently of the gods. Though Seera was raised a Christian, she was aware of some of these stories. She enjoyed the stories of the fertility goddess, Freyja. She had strength that Seera admired. And the ones of Loki the mischief maker she found to be funny.

By the time the evening was coming to a close, she had relaxed. She was so tired and content that when Kata bid Valr goodnight and rose, Seera was eager for the warmth of a bed. Kata and Seera made their way outside, where they were approached by a short balding man wearing a brown robe.

"My Lady." He bowed to Seera. "I am Father Duncun."

"I saw you speak at Orn's funeral," Seera said. "I had hoped that I would have a chance to meet you."

He stared at her with kind eyes that put Seera at ease. "You are a daughter of Christ?"

"I am Father." A breeze blew off the water and tugged at her unbound hair. She absently pushed it away to clear her vision.

He was pleased by her response. "Then you must come see me so that we may talk."

"I will Father." She felt comforted by his presence. He reminded her vaguely of the priest at Dun'O'Tir. He was far younger than the monk at home, but his manner was much the same. She felt a twinge of homesickness.

"Good," he answered. He started to leave but turned back to say one more thing. "I have heard the men speak of your bravery."

Shocked she looked between the monk and Kata. "My bravery?"

"Aye. They say that is why Lord Rafn took you. That he admired your courage." Father Duncun sauntered off towards his chapel and Seera could only stare after him in amazement.

She turned to Kata. "Is it true?"

"I don't know. He has not spoken to me of it."

Seera shook her head. "The men have it wrong. He took me because I was Drenger's slave." A strong gust of wind reached her. She grabbed her skirt to keep it down. Kata fought to do the same.

"Perhaps that is all it is," Kata said. "But, we don't know what he was thinking. Maybe to him it was more." They continued walking as the wind kept up its assault.

Seera opened her mouth to answer, but snapped it closed again. Her feelings became jumbled. She tried to make sense of why she kept thinking of him. He had rescued her, she thought. It only made sense for him to creep into her mind. A flutter tickled her senses. She refused to admit her attraction for the mysterious, handsome stranger that had taken her from hell. Forcing her thoughts to still she followed Kata through the compound and almost missed when she stopped in front of an unfamiliar dwelling.

Seera looked up at her with a question reflected in her eyes. A smile streaked across Kata's face as she opened the door. A fire had been started in the hearth and candle lanterns lit around the room. Seera remembered that Kata had left her briefly to go speak with Esja. It must have been the older woman who'd lit them. She was urged inside.

"You are healing nicely. You have no need to remain in my place."

"I have no need for a house that is so elegant. I had expected to stay with the servants." Panic gripped her as she stammered to speak. Her suspicions began to grow about whose place this was.

Kata chuckled, unfazed by Seera's growing fear. "It is a room fit for a lord. It is my brother's and it is here that you are to stay."

"There is only one bed." The words slipped from Seera before she could stop. She clamped a hand over her mouth to keep from saying more.

"He is not here, and will not be back for a few weeks." Kata sought to ease her worries. "When Rafn returns. He will tell you were he wants you to be."

"Aye, he will fix it." Seera nodded. Kata bid her goodnight and left her alone in Rafn's dwelling. Seera repeated over and over that he was not the same as Drenger. Rafn was a Viking, but he had the respect and love of his people. She had not seen that among Drenger's own. Certainly that spoke well of a man's character. She wrapped her arms around her own body to still the trembling. She took a deep breath to keep from remembering.

Rafn was different…he was different.

Exhaustion swept over her, pushing away the nerves. He was not there. She slipped off her dress, leaving on the smock she wore beneath. She refused to sleep naked in his bed.

With thoughts of the man whose blankets kept her warm, she fell asleep.

CHAPTER 8

Rafn sat staring out across the large expanse of rough water that stretched before him. His hand rested on the single oar, mounted on the starboard side, used for steering the wooden vessel. He scanned the fjords to his left, beautiful in their wildness. An eagle soared high above the tree tops into the clear blue sky. A strong wind blew from the south, making the long-ship, called a drekar, glide smoothly. It allowed them to use the sail instead of the rows of oars meant for rowing in still weather.

The salty air stung his face causing him to squint. Still the freedom was a relief. Rafn was a master of the sea, as most Vikings were, and it gave the warlord a sense of power to find harmony with such an unpredictable beast.

He felt the drekar, with its double prows, shift beneath his feet. The rocking rhythm was soothing to his turbulent soul.

He loved his ship, having put many days of labor into its construction. He glanced around at the sixty men who traveled with him on board, though the drekar was capable of holding a hundred. Off his port was a smaller ship, manned by Hamr and twenty five other men. The smaller ship rode the waves higher than Rafn's, yet both were built for shallow water, making it possible to take them inland along the rivers.

The warlord glanced at the other ship, noting the identical twin dragon heads that mirrored those carved into his own prows. He knew from a distance the ships would look like sea serpents riding the waves.

Having already spent time trading in the territories of Hordaland and Sogn, Rafn directed the ships further north along the western coast to a place called Trondelag, where there was a large trading center. Rafn was looking forward to seeing the Jarl Kobbi. His wife was Dagstyrr's sister. She was an extremely beautiful woman and many men in Skiringssal had mourned her loss to the Jarl in Trondelag.

Rafn's memories of Kobbi were that of a good man. He smiled with the knowledge that Auga was happy with the marriage that allied Trondelag and Vestfold. The cold spray continued up off the water, but Rafn didn't mind that his tunic had long since clung to him with dampness. The high sun kept him warm enough, as did thoughts of the waiting ale that Kobbi would offer him when he arrived.

"My lord, the village has shown on the horizon." The warrior Leikr informed.

"Take us into port Hachet." Rafn stood to allow Hachet to take his place at the oar. Hachet's steady hand made him the best for taking the drekar through the shallow waters off the shore.

People filtered out from the wooden buildings that followed the coastline and gathered to watch the drekars pull up to the harbor. Kobbi waited on the wooden dock with a smile on his face as his men helped to tie the ships to the posts.

Rafn and Dagstyrr disembarked together and each clasped hands to arms with Kobbi.

"It is good to see you again my friends," Kobbi greeted.

"We are most pleased to be here," Rafn replied.

"Where is my sister?" Dagstyrr looked around eager to see her again. A woman stepped from the crowd, bringing a grin to his face.

"Here brother." She walked towards them, the deep red of her hair making her stand out among the people. She was as beautiful as Rafn remembered and he looked at her with appreciation, for she glowed even more so because of the obvious swelling of her stomach.

"Sister, I am to be an uncle." Dagstyrr beamed with pride, as he reached for her and dragged her into an embrace.

"This winter." She glanced affectionately at her husband, who returned her smile with a look of tenderness that spoke of his obvious love for the woman.

"Let your men begin the trading, while we go to the Great Hall." Rafn gave orders to Hatchet to get the men settled and left him in charge of the trade. No man was a better haggler.

The three men, with Auga on Dagstyrr's arm, headed past the palisade walls and to the hall that stood close to the center. It was comparable in size to the one in Skiringssal, but more ornately decorated. A banner depicting a seal, Kobbi's sign, hung behind the head table, which was set close to a hearth made from stone and mortar. A large fire blazed in its center.

They were led to the large wooden head table, where Kobbi and his wife sat together in matching high backed chairs. The others sat on stools offered them.

"I heard about Orn, just this morning." Kobbi's somber voice spoke with sadness, as they each sat with drinking horns of ale in their hands. Rafn instantly sobered. His hand clenched the cattle horn and his knuckles whitened. Kobbi watched patiently as Rafn's face eased from the onslaught of pain.

Through clenched teeth he replied. "The Jarl of Ribe killed him."

"You have avenged his death?" Kobbi noted how Rafn's eyes narrowed.

"Drenger is dead, but it was not by my hands." Rafn replied with bitterness that was not lost on Kobbi. Rafn placed the drinking horn on the holder used for keeping the horn from tipping. He had yet to take a sip, which Kobbi also noticed.

"Will you share the story?"

Auga had grown concerned and Rafn met her eyes. He pushed the pain from him, to lock it away in a safe place deep inside. It was not the time to bring it forth. He took a long drink of his ale and felt himself relax.

Rafn looked to Dagstyrr who was having a hard time keeping a smile from his face. He scowled at his friend before relaying the story to Kobbi. He kept the anger from his voice and spoke as elegantly as any skald, ending with the briefest details of the Lady Seera. When he was finished Kobbi was also looking at him with merriment.

"You two seem to find great pleasure in my predicament." Rafn growled which caused the others to break out laughing. Though Auga's expression said clearly that she could not see what was so amusing.

"It was your right to take her," Kobbi agreed. "Her life is yours for denying you the fulfillment of your pledge."

"And, remember my lord," Dagstyrr added. "Drenger is dead."

"Aye…and you have yourself a woman." Kobbi's eyes twinkled and he chuckled when Auga shook her head at the men. Certainly her sympathy lay with the woman.

"To do what with?" Rafn looked at them in bewilderment.

"To have your way with." Kobbi roared with laughter, which earned him a fierce look from his wife. He raised her hand to his lips and kissed it, receiving a reluctant smile.

"She was raped." The words left his mouth unwittingly. It shouldn't have mattered. It was his right to lie with her if he chose.

Kobbi studied Rafn with surprise and startling understanding. The Raven valued the woman. Amusement danced in his eyes. "You care for her."

"I advised him take her as a wife. Form an alliance with Pictland." Dagstyrr spoke to Kobbi, ignoring Rafn's scowl at being discussed.

Kobbi rubbed his chin. "It would be a wise move."

"You both are finding way too much enjoyment in discussing my future." Rafn flung up his hands in exasperation. The feelings coursing through him were unnerving. To have others see such emotions in him made him edgy. He fiddled with his drinking horn.

"You must think beyond your own needs, to those of your people. An alliance with King David would be of benefit against the warriors of Jutland."

"It would." Rafn sighed in reluctance. Both men looked at him expectantly, but it was Auga's softer expression that forced him to answer. "Aye."

"A wife then?" Dagstyrr asked.

Rafn again caught Auga's gaze and though she'd remained silent, not wanting to intrude on the men's conversation, he had known her exact feelings. She seemed content that Seera would be a wife and not a slave. He nodded in acknowledgement.

"A wife." Relief coursed through him as he voiced his decision. The darkness in his soul wavered and trembled, allowing Rafn to find the strength to push it deeper.

Normally Rafn loved the noise of people gathered in festivities, but that first night in Trondelag, with the Great Hall filled to bursting, brought him no joy. He wanted nothing more than to escape the laughter and the skalds endless stories. Even his ale went untouched. He poked at the pork and beef with his knife on the platter in front of him, but found he was not hungry. He declined the fish, having eaten his fill on the journey.

Kobbi and Auga slipped out early, the pregnancy making her tire quickly. Dagstyrr missed their departure; he was too busy flirting with a petite brunette with doe-like eyes.

"I'm going to check on the ships." Rafn spoke to Dagstyrr as he rose to leave, and received only the slightest nod. Rafn smiled in amusement as he slipped into the cool night. The wind that had seen them through the day had died off.

Rafn walked down to the docks, nodding a greeting to the warriors on guard duty. Hamr and Hachet had remained with the drekars to watch over the trade goods. Rafn spoke to each of them briefly before heading for a walk along the shore.

He strode along the rocky beach until he came to a large boulder on its edge. Leaning his back against it he stared out to the black waters. The moon's light reflected off the ripples that traveled towards the horizon. He drank in the solitude, enjoying the echoes of the insects in the trees. An owl screeched somewhere behind him as it swooped in to snatch up its prey.

He was glad to be away from the constant questions and the women trying to win his affection. All had been beautiful in one way or another, but he had been drawn to none of them. He thought only of the battered face of a woman with startling green eyes that drew him in.

She was not even there with him and he felt an inexplicable peace reaching inside him. It caught him by surprise. No one but Orn had ever managed to still the angry storm in him. And even his brother only managed that feat while in Rafn's presence. Seera was many days travel away, yet he felt her light becoming apart of him.

The thunder rumbled in protest, causing a flare of fury. Sucking in a deep breath, he pictured Seera's face and managed to find his control.

Kobbi took Dagstyrr and Rafn out into the hills the next day to do some hunting. They left behind their swords, but took with them bows and arrows, as well as javelins, which were shorter than their spears and meant for throwing.

Kobbi gave them each a horse from his own stables to ride. Rafn was given a light brown mare that reminded him of the color of Seera's hair. The horse was even tempered and well groomed. This told him her owner cared for her.

They rode for about an hour before leaving their mounts to continue on foot down a path that was too narrow. They continued on in silence, placing their feet carefully and quietly as they followed in the tracks of several deer.

Kobbi took the lead, as was expected, and the other two men eagerly followed. They had not gone far when Kobbi raised a hand to signal them to stop. Carefully he beckoned them forward. Seven deer were in a clearing ahead, drinking from a lake that had formed from a waterfall higher up in the hills. Rafn could hear its power, but it was not within their sight.

Both Dagstyrr and Kobbi took out their bows and fitted it with an arrow. Rafn chose instead his three javelins. Kobbi led them upwind from the animals, until they were close enough, but were yet unseen.

They waited patiently as the deer moved from the lake into the clearing and began eating the grass that grew across it. Satisfied Kobbi gave a quick hand sign to the other men and sent his arrow sailing to the largest of the deer.

Rafn was quick to react and soon threw a javelin in a perfect arch to the nearest animal. The young buck dropped with the javelin through his left eye. Dagstyrr also brought down one of the deer, by sending his arrows in quick succession, until the deer was dead.

Startled, the other deer turned to run on their surefooted feet into the cover of the trees. Not seeing Rafn, one of them ran very close, and Rafn had a javelin in him before he could pass. The animal fell, but was not dead. Rafn grabbed the knife from his leg and brought it across the deer's throat to end its suffering.

"Always have to be better than the rest of us." Kobbi rolled his eyes and chuckled as he came to stand next to Rafn.

"It's a curse, nothing I can do about it." Rafn shrugged his shoulders, but soon he was laughing also.

Dagstyrr came to join them and met Kobbi's amused gaze. "Try being around him all the time."

"Am I so bad?"

"Always." Laughing Dagstyrr smacked him on the back.

They made makeshift sleds to pull the deer back to the horses, and secured them to the backs of their mounts. On their way back to the village they passed a farmer who was bringing his cattle back down out of the mountains to his farm in a valley not far from the village. This was the practice of many farmers, to transfer their cattle to the high pasturelands during the summer months, then to bring them back to winter in the stables known as byres.

Kobbi greeted the man who he was obviously acquainted with. They spoke pleasantly for a few minutes before the Jarl guided his guests back to his village and another night of feasting.

They spent five days in Trondelag, enjoying Kobbi's hospitality and procuring a fair trade for their goods. Dagstyrr spent time with his sister, making her promise to bring the baby to Skiringssal after it was born.

For reasons Rafn could not explain, he convinced Kobbi to trade him the hazel colored mare that he'd used on the hunt. He had a bay stallion that he'd left in Skiringssal, but he wanted the mare for Seera. He didn't explain his true reasons for wanting the mare to Kobbi and the man did not question him.

The morning they left, Rafn rose to find a sharp chill on the air. The summer was ending and fall was already on the wind. Rafn pulled a thick cloak around his shoulders before walking to the docks. All his men were already boarded and waiting for him to join them.

"I will see you soon," Kobbi promised.

"As will I brother," Auga added as she reached up to embrace the man who was her sibling. Tears came to her eyes that she stubbornly wiped away.

"I thank you for your generosity," Rafn said. "And will see you in Skiringssal when winter has released its hold on the waterways."

"Aye." Kobbi embraced hands to arms with Rafn, before stepping to his wife's side.

Rafn and Dagstyrr boarded the large drekar, and ordered Hachet to take the ship out to sea. The wind was strong and soon caught the sail, which would prove to bring them home all the quicker.

And to the Lady Seera, who would be his wife. He tried not to admit how much that pleased him.

To the south the day had turned gray. The same chill was on the air. Many stayed in doors as the wind howled outside making it miserable to even walk from one building to the other.

Hwal sat in his new place at the head of the table. He had been made Jarl, not out of respect, but of fear. Those of Ribe knew that Drenger had been a merciless leader, but Hwal was proving to be much worse. None dared cross him in hopes of avoiding his vicious temper.

If he'd kept himself controlled because of Drenger, he did so no longer. He took to his bed any he wanted; slaves, other's wives and maiden daughters. He did so for his pleasure and to make those under his rule understand he could do whatever he desired. His word was the ultimate law.

He'd also taken for a wife, Gillaug. The woman who'd found such joy in Seera's humiliation. She had once been cruel and spiteful, but no longer. Hwal used her brutally, if not often. He treated her no better than a slave and she soon retreated into herself, afraid at any moment he would choose to end her life.

She sat then at his side because he demanded it of her. She was dressed in her finest clothes, necklaces, arm bands and broaches that told those around them of her husband's riches.

The one-eyed giant drank mead from a goblet made of gold that once belonged to a king. He was drunk, as he often was, but that only made him more dangerous. His warriors boasted and laughed at the table around him. To keep their loyalty, Hwal gave them many gifts and women.

They raided often. Taking what they wanted from other villages, as well as the monasteries of the monks, who offered no resistance. The priests did not carry weapons, or have any knowledge of defending themselves. They died easily on their spears as they prayed to their god to save them.

Hwal laughed loudly. "Continue with your story, son of Feggi." He raised his goblet to a young man who sat close to the fire.

The man was too skinny and had eyes like an owl. He continued because he was too afraid not to. Hwal found delight in this, even when the skald's voice began to shake.

At the end of the night Hwal stumbled back to the dwelling that had once belonged to Drenger and now belonged to him.

Gillaug was forced to go with him. His hand on her arm was as strong as iron. There was no escape for her even if she'd had the courage to try, and she did not. Sometimes she thought it would have been better if Hwal had just killed her and thrown her body into Drenger's grave as a sacrifice to the gods.

Mostly she was afraid of death by Hwal's hands. He was known to make his victims suffer cruelly before granting them an end to the pain. She feared what such pain would feel like. She had seen warrior's near madness by the time Hwal was done with them.

Once inside their dwelling, Hwal ordered her to strip and get into bed. He used her quickly for which she was thankful.

At his climax, he thought of Seera, as he always did. When his hold on his people was firm and undeniable, he would seek her out…when the Raven had grown complacent in his guard.

CHAPTER 9

The cold that had touched the land was suddenly replaced by an unordinary heat for the time of year. The people were able to go out without cloaks for warmth and the wind was so still that the heat on their faces made them believe summer was not at its end.

Seera sat at Orn's grave. It wasn't the first time in Rafn's absence that she had found herself there. She went to the hill when she needed to speak about the things she couldn't with the others. Somehow she felt Orn was listening.

"I feel a stranger to myself," she told him. "From that girl I was back in Pictland at the King's court."

She pictured in her mind the large hall in the Keep where many had gathered. She remembered the noise and the laughter and the Queen's smile as she spoke with Seera. The delight she had felt about being in such regal company.

She frowned as another memory surfaced. Of a brash young lad who sought her fancy. "How I hated the way Lord Kent watched me. I was Eorl Airic's daughter. He had no right."

"Perhaps I thought myself his better, but I found him pompous and conceited. He was more in love with himself than any other."

She crinkled her nose at how he'd catch the eye of every woman in the room, even when speaking to her. "If my brother, Peder, had been there, he would have taken the lord aside and set him in his place."

She smiled at the sight that would have made. Peder would have said very little, but his stance and his reputation with a sword would have spoken volumes. Only a word or two would have been needed to send Lord Kent away.

"Maybe I thought myself more deserving than a man who would stray from his bridal bed. I had romantic notions of a man who would love me and no other. I forgot my duty to King and land."

Seera laughed even as tears misted her eyes. Fear seized her as other memories pushed their way to the surface. Too fresh was the hurt and humiliation.

"I did not once imagine that my maidenhood would be taken in such a way, by such a man." Seera felt a comforting hand touched her shoulder, though she knew no one was there. It was her imagination only, but it made her feel better. It made her feel renewed and hopeful.

Weeks had passed since Rafn had left to trade in the north. Weeks since Seera had moved into his home. She tried not to leave a trace of her presence in his dwelling, but it was impossible. Kata had insisted on a whole wardrobe for Seera. She had two trunks full of clothing and accessories that she kept under the window.

She had become too comfortable in Rafn's house and had begun placing vases of flowers to cheer up the starkly male room. She made no other changes, but she loved the smell of fresh flowers, which she knew would not be around much longer.

Skiringssal had been a welcoming place. She was still having a hard time accepting that. Each day she spent time with Father Duncun in prayer, before Kata would come and get her. The two of them were already friends, and Seera felt blessed for that. She also enjoyed Esja's company. The older woman was tough and spoke her mind. She often had Seera laughing.

Rafn's brother Valr had also sought her out two days after Rafn had sailed away. He was a serious man, but he gave her his respect. The people followed his example and always called her lady.

Feeling restless, Seera rose and headed down the hill, away from the grave. At the bottom she ran into Valr. She accepted an invitation to walk with him to the cliff that overlooked the ocean. It was a beautiful spot to peer down on the town and the dock below.

"The crops are all in," Valr said. "Just in time I think. The wind may be still today, but it will turn cold again soon enough."

"Fall will soon be upon us."

"The women tell me you have been a big help in storing the crops in the storage sheds. That you offer your assistance willingly in all things," Valr looked at her with appreciation.

"I eat the meat your men bring in, and the food your women prepare," Seera said. "It would be wrong for me not to help."

"It is not expected." Valr studied her from a face that was always stern and serious. His eye remained unreadable.

"I don't understand that." Seera looked at him seriously. "Why should I not be expected to do my share of work?"

"You are a lady, but that is not the reason. It is because you are Rafn's woman." The corner of his mouth lifted at the look of distress on her face. Even the wrinkles beside his eyes deepened. It was the closest to a laugh she had seen from him. She sensed a depth to him he kept hidden.

"I am afraid that people have come to a wrong conclusion about us," Seera said. "He claims I belong to him, but I am treated as though I am his wife. That is not right."

"Rafn will clear up any misunderstanding when he returns. You needn't worry about it."

"You are right. He will set them straight." Seera looked out over the choppy waters below and to the horizon.

Seera took a sudden intake of breath when the drekar first appeared on the horizon. It was too far away to tell for sure, but somehow she knew it was Rafn's ship. A sudden nervousness shivered through her. She had been living an unreal existence, teetering on the edge that she knew would crumple once the warlord returned.

Silently Seera and Valr watched the longships coming closer, until the largest one began pulling up to the dock below. Seera couldn't stop herself from searching out Rafn. She found him standing in the stern and she stared at him foolishly. Her face heated when he turned, looked up the cliff and spotted her.

Rafn was astounded. The beautiful woman standing on the cliff with his brother couldn't be the battered girl he'd left in his sister's care. The woman who stared down at him was the most exquisite creature he'd ever laid eyes on. Her light brown hair was left unhindered and fell to her waist. The soft curls were caught by the wind and blown around her in a silky veil.

She pushed it from her face and looked down at him again. There was no mistake. This was his woman.

Dagstyrr came up beside him and drew his attention away from the vision on the cliffs.

"It would seem that your sacrifice will not be without its benefits." Dagstyrr chuckled. "Perhaps I should offer to marry her in your place."

"I would not try it." Rafn growled as he fingered the hilt of his sword. Dagstyrr laughed harder.

Rafn looked back up the cliff, but Seera was gone. Assuming she was making her way down to the docks with the rest of the village, Rafn turned back to the task of making sure all the trade goods were unloaded and brought up to the compound for storage.

He gave into Leikr's care the mare to bring to the stables. He'd watched over her like she was a prized treasure or a favorite child as they'd made their way along the coast to Skiringssal. She was as pleasantly tempered as Rafn had first assessed and was pleased by it. She would make a good mount for a lady.

He watched absently as Leikr led her up to the compound and through the gates to the stable where Rafn and Valr kept their other horses. He turned to find Dagstyrr waiting for him.

"Give this to her." Dagstyrr placed a gold necklace in his hands. The center pendent was an emerald, of a green to rival Seera's eyes. It was obviously acquired from a distant land. Rafn looked up at him in alarm.

"What is this for?" Rafn scowled.

"To let her know you were thinking of her when you were gone."

"It appears it was you who did all the thinking."

"Only in regards to the alliance," Dagstyrr said. "And don't tell me she was not in your thoughts the entire time. I know you better than that my friend."

Rafn shot him a look that would have had most men backing off, but Dagstyrr held his ground. Rafn grabbed the necklace and stuffed it into his tunic, before storming off the ship.

Dagstyrr's smile widened.

Lady Seera didn't show up at the docks. Instead he was met only by Valr and Kata. He did not want to appear too anxious to see her so he did not ask where she was. Instead he went with Valr to the Great Hall to discuss the success of the trade. Valr was pleased, as he knew his brother would, to hear things had gone smoothly.

Still he did not ask about Seera.

The servants began setting up for supper, making him realize how hungry he was. "I need to clean up before I eat brother." Rafn stood to leave.

"Of course, you've had a long trip." Valr also rose and followed him outside where they each went separate ways.

Rafn went to his dwelling and pushed the door open. The first thing he noticed was the smell of the flowers before seeing them placed around the room. Under the window were two trunks he had never seen before. He lifted one to see that it held women's clothing. Seera's?

Yes, he smelled her essence in the room, but she was not there and he was beginning to be concerned about where she was?

There was a knock on the door.

"Enter." He was disappointed when it was just a maid bringing him a pail of heated water.

"My mistress thought you would like to wash up." The girl bowed slightly as she informed him.

"Your mistress?" The maid poured the water into a large water basin he kept on a small table in the corner. He preferred to bath frequently as any good Norseman did.

"The Lady Seera, my lord." The girl, whose name he recalled was Agata, told him.

"I see." His sister had given her a maid, and apparently plenty of clothing. It would seem that Seera was not being treated as a servant in his absence. It pleased him that his sister had been so insightful.

"Thank you, you may go." Rafn dismissed the maid who nodded as she backed out the door.

He stripped out of his soiled tunic and used the water and a bar of soap to freshen himself. He donned a new tunic of deep blue wool and walnut colored trousers. He replaced his belt and slipped his knife into his leg sheath, never going anywhere without at least one weapon. He tied his wet hair at the back of his neck.

He stored his sword in the corner by the door, along with his shield and bow and arrows, axe, as well as his spears and javelins.

Feeling better he looked around his room once again. There was not much evidence of Seera, but she'd been there, slept in his bed. How had Kata known his thoughts so well that she'd been astute enough to move the woman into his place?

Thor, where was she? He wondered with exasperation.

Seera was hiding at Kata's. She was too nervous to meet him face to face. It was silly really. She had taken one of her gowns from the trunk and fled to Kata's while he was still unloading the ships. She couldn't avoid him forever, but she would put it off as long as possible.

"That dress is perfect." Kata helped Seera dress in the green silk dress, with gold lacing. "It matches your eyes."

"It's not too much. I just grabbed the dress that was on top." She smoothed it down with her hands and adjusted the twin broaches that held the dress together at her shoulders. The smock she wore underneath was a pale yellow and complimented the dress nicely.

"Now for your hair." Kata made her sit in a chair and grabbed a comb from the table. Kata began to brush the tangles from Seera's long hair.

"I think we should just tie it back with a single ribbon and let it flow down your back."

Seera nodded her agreement, for she was not able to make such an important decision.

When Kata had finished, she stepped back and smiled. "He won't be able to take his eyes off you." Kata commented, bringing a blush to Seera.

Did she want Rafn to stare at her? Would it be better not to draw attention to her? If he was attracted to her he would want to lie with her.

She shivered at the memory of Drenger forcing her. Kata must have understood.

"Rafn is known to be a strong and sometimes violent warrior. He has taken lives when he has needed and his fierceness in a battle is known through out the Viking world, and beyond." Kata's words brought a fresh wave of fear to Seera. "But, he is not unkind. He treats the women he has bedded with great tenderness."

"How do you know this?" She felt only slightly embarrassed to discuss such a subject with Kata.

"Women talk amongst themselves. Many would love to lay claim to him." She explained patiently. "There are going to be many disappointed women."

Seera looked at Kata and wondered what she meant by that. Before she could ask, Kata was ushering her out the door and they were on their way to the Great Hall, where Rafn was sure to already be.

He was sitting in his high back chair at the head table, twirling a goblet of ale between his fingers. His patience was beginning to grow thin. If she did not show herself soon, he would be forced to find her. He was not inclined to do that. Valr sat to his right, speaking as if he knew nothing of his discomfort. Dagstyrr sat across the table from Rafn in equal oblivion.

A hushed silence went over the hall forcing Rafn to look up in time to see Kata enter with Seera at her side. If he thought she'd been beautiful on the cliff, she was even more so now. He stumbled to his feet and watched her cross the room to him.

The warriors who had been with him and had not yet seen his lady without her injuries also watched in stunned appreciation and a bit of envy. He disregarded them. His full attention was on Seera.

Seera started shaking at Rafn's intense stare. It surprised her that he gave her the honor of rising and waiting for her to join him. She glimpsed to Kata, who gave her a push towards the head table.

Silence held the crowd as they watched Seera glide across the hall to Rafn. Blushing she offered her hand. "My lord." Her voice was soft, with a slight tremble as she took a small bow.

"My lady." His eyes stayed on her as he accepted her hand and held it to his lips for a moment before releasing it. He stepped back to pull out her chair.

Seera took the seat with relief, feeling her legs were much too weak. Kata slipped into the chair on her left as Rafn lowered to the seat on her right. His dark eyes shimmered with far too many emotions before they released her from their hold.

"You look exquisite tonight." Valr's words echoed Rafn's thoughts. The look on his brother's face told him clearly that he held Seera in high regard. That was good. It would not be hard to win his support when he took Seera as his bride.

As Seera looked up, Rafn caught her gaze. A smile tugged at his lips. Her eyes could hold anyone entranced. She twisted the material of her dress nervously in her hands. He reached out to still them.

A crash of thunder boomed outside causing Seera to jump. It was followed closely by a second, in the same instant that rain began to pelt the roof.

Are you giving me your approval Thor? Rafn wondered. His hand remained on hers. They were warm and smooth in contrast to the roughness of his.

His god answered with another crash of thunder that sounded astonishingly close. Rafn couldn't help but smile.

CHAPTER 10

The rain continued as Seera picked at her meal. Her stomach was tied in knots and she couldn't bring herself to eat. She rode a wave of conflicting emotions. When the evening came to an end she was unsure if she felt fear or relief.

Rafn had left sometime before to speak with the guards on duty. She kept glancing around watching for his return, but he never came back. She was disappointed.

"I'll walk with you." She quickly rose at Kata's offer to escape and the two women left the crowded hall. She felt many eyes watching them as they made their way to the door. A heavy weight lifted from her as the large wooden door closed behind them.

Rain drizzled from dark clouds sprinkling her with a light spray, as Kata accompanied her back to Rafn's dwelling. She lifted her skirt so the hem wouldn't become caked with mud, but her shoes were a mess by the time they crossed the courtyard.

"Should I be here, now that he's back?" Seera stopped at the door, reluctant to cross its threshold.

"He will expect you to be here."

"Are you sure? He didn't even speak to me all through supper."

"He would prefer to speak in private." Kata held her skirt higher to avoid a puddle.

"Go, you are getting wet." Seera ordered Kata to leave, even though she wanted to scream for her to stay.

She watched Kata until she disappeared into the dark before entering the dwelling alone. Agata had already been there to light the fire and the candles. Seera searched the shadows, but Rafn was not there.

Why did this man cause her such discomfort?

She slipped off her muddy shoes and left them by the door, not wanting to soil the floor. From one of her trunks she took a pair of slippers and eased her feet into them. She paced the floor not able to sit on the fur covered bed. When she grew tired she chose instead to sit at the wooden table. She rubbed her eyes knowing she should get ready for bed.

"No," she thought. "That wouldn't be good." She did not want him thinking of the bed.

She could brush her hair. That would do no harm. She pulled off the ribbon, but she didn't move to get the comb. She looked at the door and knew she was being silly. He wasn't coming. He had found somewhere else to spend the night.

Perhaps he was with a woman, she considered. That made her jump to her feet. She felt a stab of jealousy at the possibility he was with someone else.

Thunder rumbled threatening in the sky, causing Seera to jump in fright. The rain began pelting at the shutter that covered the window and on the roof over her head. Her heart was beating rapidly at having been so frightened by the sound of the storm. She couldn't stop herself from laughing.

Rafn opened the door to find Seera standing in the center of the room, hands over her mouth trying to suppress the laugh that came bubbling from her. Her damp hair flowed around her as she turned her green eyes to him. They sparkled with something indescribable.

Seera tried to compose herself as she saw Rafn standing in the doorway. A flash of lightning lit up the sky behind him, washing him for just an instant in a yellowish glow. He was an extremely handsome man. She laughed even harder when he raised an eyebrow at her.

Rafn stepped into the room, allowing the door to swing shut behind him. "Should I worry that you apparently find me so hilarious?"

Seera took in a breath and looked to him with seriousness. "I do not laugh at you, my lord. I was just feeling too many things at once and I needed to release the tension."

"So it had nothing to do with me?" He watched her consider his question before she answered.

"It has everything to do with you." Her eyes widened at her admission. Her hands once again found her skirt and began kneading the material with her fingers.

Rafn took a step towards her and was pleased that she did not move away. He looked down at her and wanted nothing more than to kiss her. But, he didn't. Her eyes flicked up to his but refused to hold his gaze. He already knew her strength, but her shyness was equally appealing.

"We have yet to get to know each other, you and I," he said.

"Aye." Her fingers twined nervously in her dress. He grabbed them into his own. They were cold and he sought to warm them.

"It is important I think, for us to do so before we wed." Rafn watched as her eyes narrowed in confusion.

"My lord." She started to object, but he wouldn't let her voice her reservations.

"Call me Rafn." He touched his hand to her smooth face. No trace of the bruises remained.

"Rafn," she spoke his name for the first time and he liked how it sounded on her lips.

"You understand that you are mine?" He removed his hand to search her eyes and saw her nervousness.

"You have told me it is so. But, you did not say I would be your wife." Her thoughts turned inward so that he couldn't tell what she was thinking.

"You would rather be my slave?" A tremor shifted in him, calling to the darkness. His nostrils flared.

"No." Her reply was honest for it did not displease her to think of him as a husband and her as a wife.

"That is good," he said. "I want you for a wife."

"Why?" Confusion still gripped her face. She had no concept of how she made him feel. That he'd wanted her even when she was battered, before he'd seen her outer beauty, for he liked her courage.

"I would see an alliance between Vestfold and Pictland," he answered, for he was not ready for her to know the effect she had on him.

"I see your logic." She replied as diplomatically. It was not the romantic declaration a young woman dreamed of hearing, but she was the daughter of an Eorl and she knew duty came first. "My father will be pleased."

"Will he?"

"He will see the benefits in such a union." She boldly met his dark expression. "Besides, you have rescued me and he would honor you for that."

Rafn studied her closer and saw something settle in her eyes. A glimpse of the trauma she'd suffered at the hands of Drenger. Rafn growled in anger. If the man were not already dead, he would treat him to days of torture.

Seera stepped back at the anger radiating from him. She didn't know what she'd done to upset him, but her defenses went up and she looked to the door to assess if she could make an escape.

Rafn saw her reaction and cursed himself.

"I am tired." He forced his voice to calm. "I don't wish to frighten you."

"I'm not frightened." Her chin rose as she spoke. She would not have him believing she was a coward.

His heart eased at her gesture. She stood with hands fisted by her side as if ready to do battle. "You just don't wish to be here with me."

The lines of his face smoothed, making him appear younger. The fierce scowl that was often on his face softened and he seemed more approachable.

"You are wrong." She took a step towards him without thought. She moved on instinct that she would be safe with him.

"Am I?" He saw the heat in her eyes and knew she felt as he did.

Rafn grabbed her hand and pulled her to him. He had dreamed often while away, of being with her, and he knew exactly how he wanted to get to know her. His hands sought the broaches at her shoulders and undid them. He believed she would protest, but instead she stood still. He felt her tremble beneath his hands as Rafn slipped the gown from her shoulders and pushed it over her hips until it lay crumpled at her feet.

Standing now, in only her smock, she looked up at him. He wanted to kiss her, to consume her. But he tempered his need at the look on her face.

She was bravely trying to hide her terror from him and that brought an instant urge to protect her, even from him. She was trying so hard to give him her trust. He could not betray it when things between them were still so fragile.

Seera swallowed her fear, determined not to run screaming into the night. He was not Drenger. He was Rafn. She was to be his wife, and a wife had a duty to please her husband. It would be right with him. Kata said he was tender. She tried to concentrate instead on the tremor of excitement he evoked in her.

She let him lead her to the bed and coaxed her into sitting on the edge as he took her feet one by one and removed her slippers and stockings. Taking her hands he stood her up again so that he could pull back the blankets. He helped her beneath them and then did the most amazing thing. He covered her without getting under.

Rafn walked around to the other side of the bed and lay down on top of the covers. Her back was to him and he simply wrapped his arm around her and held her while he drifted into sleep. It was not the erotic fantasy he'd had of their first night together, but somehow it seemed right.

Seera fell asleep with tears in her eyes. For the first time in many nights, she did not have nightmares.

It was barely dawn when Dagstyrr wandered from the longhouse used by the unmarried warriors. Sleep eluded him, so he decided to go out and clear his head instead. He walked through the dead village and realized it was earlier than he'd assumed.

Dagstyrr took a trail that led behind the compound to a pool of water that he often used for bathing. Not many came to this place, it was considered a private spot for the Jarl and his family, but Dagstyrr had been given permission to use it and often did in the early mornings before the others awakened.

Even with the night's storm, the morning was already warm and promised another hot day. Summer was not going to leave without a fight, he thought. He knew many would take advantage of this last hot spell before winter had them confided inside their homes.

Dagstyrr was reaching the end of the trail. His thoughts fled to their recent trading venture and his visit with his sister. So distracted was he that he almost failed to notice that someone was already ahead of him.

The warrior managed to stop just inside the trees, before his presence was detected, but he was unable to turn and walk away. All thoughts left him when he realized that the person using the pool was Kata.

Believing she was alone she stripped from her clothes and entered the water slowly, letting herself adjust to its coldness. Blessedly and regretfully she sank beneath the water, hiding her from his view. He eased himself between two trees to get a better look, but making sure she would not see him.

Kata dunked her dark hair and come up sputtering water, but looking as gleeful as a child enjoying a swim on a hot day.

He knew he had to turn away. If Rafn caught him watching his sister in such a way, he would likely impale him on the end of his spear. He had to leave, but his feet would not obey the command his mind was shouting at it. How could any man turn from such a beautiful sight?

If there was a man who possessed such strength, it was not him.

The sun climbed higher, washing the pool with its light and warmth, as the woman swam leisurely beneath its welcoming fingers. Dagstyrr was a man as good as dead, if he stayed there. If Rafn came upon him hiding like a young boy then things would get ugly.

Just as he was about to regain control of his body, Kata rose from the pool, and no force on earth would have been able to move him from his spot. She stood for a time on the edge of the pool and lathered soap over her body and through her hair. Only once she had rinsed and wrapped a drying cloth around her could Dagstyrr breathe again.

Dagstyrr thought she was the most beautiful woman. He had always believed so. He had more than once dreamt of her in the night when he shouldn't have, but one could not control the course of dreams. Even so, he found himself thinking of her while fully awake, and had tried his best to hide such feelings from those around him.

Especially from the friend that was as close as any brother. He had not dared even question if Rafn would approve of such a match. He may have found the courage to do so if he believed that Kata returned his feelings, but she had never given him any reason to believe she did.

They had spoken many times, for they'd grown up together in Skiringssal and he had always been included into her family. But she treated him no differently than one of her brothers. If she was not attracted to him, then there was no reason to anger her brother needlessly.

Still he would very much like to step from his hiding place and walk up to her, to have her look at him with a much deeper feeling than a sister to a brother.

Sighing silently he slipped back carefully until he was once again on the trail. Turning his back he left her behind with regret.

Many days northwest, deep within the mountains, a wolf howled. The day had waned and the moon was full, the air still and touched with warmth. Within the mountains, high and hidden was a meadow of exquisite beauty, even by the light of the moon.

Two women had just entered its tranquility. The first, shorter and the older of the two stopped.

"Home shall be within this place," she said to the other. Her eyes were touched by a bit of madness, or knowledge that others did not understand.

"I will build us a cottage in the far corner," the other, her warrior sister proclaimed.

"Aye, where the moon's light may touch us," the older one said. "Where magic find us, and sight not withheld. Wait we will for the one we must."

"As you have seen, sister," the warrior woman agreed.

Again the wolf howled, speaking to the fullness of the moon. The warrior held a spear and kept a sharp eye to the surrounding trees. Nothing would threaten them long.

But the other had no concerns. She walked radiant in the night's glow as she led the way to the far side of the meadow. She stopped not far from the sharp wall of a cliff.

"Build beneath my feet and the goddess will bless it."

"With the day's first light, I will begin," the warrior woman answered. And the wolf sang again, this time far away.

The older woman lifted her hands to the moon and chanted a song of ancient words.

CHAPTER 11

Seera woke to find Rafn gone. She ran her hand over his side of the bed to find it was still warm. She stretched to clear the sluggishness from her body and smiled at how safe she'd felt sleeping in his arms.

Something glittered on Rafn's pillow and caught Seera's attention. She reached over and picked up a beautiful gold torc necklace with an emerald embedded in the center. She lifted it so that the light from the window reflected off the perfect stone. Was it for her?

She was afraid to be mistaken, but why else would he have left a woman's necklace on his pillow if it were not meant for her. Perhaps it was a gift to honor their pending union? Certainly it was not one of love. Rafn barely knew her, so she decided it must be an engagement gift, acquired on his trading venture.

Did that mean he had thought of her while he was gone?

Only in concerns of the treaty he hoped to get from a marriage to her. She really needed to remind herself what the true nature of their union would be.

A wonderful smell drew her attention to a meal that had been left for her on the table and realized she was famished. She felt rejuvenated after the best sleep she'd had since being taken from her home. She felt giddy with warmth as she remembered Rafn's arm wrapped around her.

Seera went to the table and tore apart the fresh bread that was still warm. It melted in her mouth it was so good. There were eggs and milk, and apples from the last harvest. She knew none were left on the trees and felt sad that they would not be able to enjoy fresh fruit much longer.

The door creaked opened and Kata entered. She laughed at Seera shoveling the food into her mouth in a very un-lady like fashion. Seera allowed a guilty smile.

"Has my brother worked up your appetite?" Kata raised her eyebrows, causing Seera to blush.

"He did not lay with me if that is what you are implying." Seera grinned at the confused look on Kata's face.

"He didn't?"

"He did nothing more than hold me while he slept." The feel of his embrace was still imprinted on her. She felt the blush deepen on her face and assumed it had turned a bright red.

"I see." Kata was struck by a new insight. Her brother was in love with this woman. If he were not, he would not have shown such honor as considering her feelings. But this she didn't say to Seera.

"Do you know where he is?" Seera looked up with expectancy.

"I saw him just a few minutes ago ordering the servants to prepare a feast in celebration of his betrothal?"

The heat on Seera's face traveled down her neck and she felt foolish at such a reaction. She must look as flighty as a young girl with her first crush.

"He wants us married, so he can form an alliance with King David." Seera told her plainly, determined to squash any romantic assumptions. "I am just the instrument in which he will achieve his treaty."

"That is what you think?" Kata wondered what her brother had told the poor girl. Apparently nothing of love was mentioned.

"It is what it is." Seera nodded. "I can accept my duty."

"What are your feelings towards Rafn?"

"Feelings?" She was surprised by the question. What did feelings have to do with any thing?

"Will a marriage to my brother make you happy?" Kata watched the confusion cross Seera's face as she contemplated the best way to answer the question.

In the end she could only speak the truth. "Yes."

Seera tried to help with the work for the feast, but Esja wouldn't allow it. She pushed her out the door with a firm no. Yrsa was there and Seera was surprised when the girl offered a tentative smile. It was the first time she had ever seen one on the girl's face. She'd been told by the others that she was beginning to speak a little and Seera was pleased.

Feeling restless she walked the path to the cliff where she loved to look out at the sea. As she came to the top of the path she noticed someone was already there. She was about to turn around and leave, when she realized it was Rafn.

He turned to look at her before she could decide what she should do. He held his hand out to her.

"Come." He beckoned in a strong command, but his eyes reflected his need.

Seera went to him without hesitation. She seemed to want to do what this man asked. It was disconcerting yet comforting at the same time. Dear Lord she was a mess of warring emotions.

She let him take her hand in his and decided she like the way the rough skin of his hand felt against the softness of her own. His hand was warm, as his arm had been as he'd held her in the night.

They stood together, hand in hand, staring down at the waves that crashed against the reef below.

"I love this spot." Seera spoke first. He looked down at her and studied her for a moment before replying.

"You do?"

"Yes, it is my favorite." Her gaze remained on the sea, but she sensed his had turned to her.

"It is mine also." It pleased him that she had come to him, that they shared a fondness for the view.

"They wouldn't let me help." Seera sighed.

"What?"

"The women..." She nodded towards the compound. "They wouldn't let me help with the feast." Rafn smiled as he understood her concern.

"They were right to send you away." He turned so that he faced her. She had such beautiful eyes.

Seera's heart began to race at the way he was looking at her. There was no mistaking his desire. And perhaps a bit of the same confusion that she was feeling. It shocked her, for she had not expected to see it in him.

She couldn't look away. She knew she should, but he locked her in his gaze and she wanted…

Rafn leaned down and kissed her. His mouth was warm and light on hers and it sent a shiver of excitement through her. His mouth pressed harder and made her forget how to breathe.

She had responded to his kiss. That was good. He had been unsure what her reaction would be, but he had felt something from her and acted upon it. He pulled her against him and left his hand pressed against the small of her back as if to lay claim to her.

She placed her hands against his chest and felt his muscles flex against her palms, and knew the strength he possessed. But, she did not push him away. Somehow she managed to breathe between his kisses and when he pulled away she was left feeling flushed.

"Come." He took her hand once more and let him lead her down the path, back to the village. Many people were out and wandering the streets when they made their way through town. Everyone called greetings as they headed back to the compound. Rafn simply nodded to each as he passed, but did not stop to speak with any of them. They must be used to this kind of response from him, for nobody minded and continued to smile pleasantly as they moved on.

Once in the compound, Rafn led her to the stable that she had learned was the one belonging to his family. Seera had never been inside it, but she'd heard the horses daily as she'd walked past it.

He didn't speak to her again until they came to the last stall in the stables and to a beautiful mare whose coat was light brown with a soft peppering of dark brown spots along her flanks.

"What a beautiful animal," Seera said. She stroked the horse's nose, and the mare brought her head down.

"You like her?" Rafn watched her reaction closely and how comfortable she was around the horse.

"She is exquisite," Seera replied. She looked around and noticing a barrel of apples that bore too many bruises to be sent to the kitchens, she grabbed one and held it out for the mare. The horse took it in her teeth and ate the offered treasure.

"You like horses?"

"I've ridden almost every day since I was a small child. When we were old enough, my brother and I would race across any open space we could find." Seera's eyes held pleasure and sadness at the memory. Rafn could see that she missed her home and family. Seera remained unaware of his evaluation of her as she continued to speak. "Since we've been grown, duty has kept my brother busy and we do not race so anymore, except on occasion when we wish to feel like children once again."

She loved her brother, as surely as he'd loved Orn. They were as close as he was to Valr and Kata. Yet she had not once asked him to take her home. Did she believe that she couldn't? He refrained from speaking of it.

"She is yours." Rafn felt a surge of pleasure at the gleeful surprise that came to her face.

"Mine," she said. "Such a magnificent animal, and you would give her to me."

"She is worthy of a lady such as yourself."

Seera's smile spread across her face as she returned to stroking the mare's coat. He felt her eagerness to ride the horse, but she did not voice it. He would give to her, her silent wish.

"If you want, we can take her for a ride and see how she handles for you."

"I would very much like that. Is there a saddle I could use?"

He found pleasure in bringing her joy and simply studied her expression of pure delight that shone on her face.

Rafn turned from her to find the saddle that Kata used and helped Seera to secure it to the horse's back. Once done he went to another horse that was mid way down the stalls and offered it an apple.

The stallion grabbed it in its teeth and Rafn reflected a touch of sadness that made Seera wonder. She looked at the horse, which was a beautiful black stallion, and watched as it tossed his head restlessly, as if it had been cooped up too long.

"His name is Night," Rafn said before she could ask. "He belonged to my brother." Seera nodded in understanding of the pain that Rafn still felt for Orn's loss.

"He has not been ridden since Orn's death." Moving away from Night he approached a roan stallion. The animal snorted when Rafn stroked him. Opening the stall he led his horse out.

She stood patiently until Rafn was ready to leave. They led the horses out and away from the village before climbing on their backs.

They rode until mid day when they came to a cove with large rocks strewn along the shore. Rafn helped her from her horse and led her to a flat topped boulder that they could sit on. They sat and watched the waves crashing against the large water smoothed rocks that jutted out from beneath the water.

Rafn remained quiet and Seera was reluctant to intrude into his private thoughts. Instead she enjoyed the fact that they could be together without the need to talk.

They sat there for about an hour before Rafn finally jumped from the boulder and held out his hand to her. "We must head back now or we'll be late for our own feast. Esja would have my head if that happened."

"I didn't think such a mighty warrior as you would fear a servant woman," she teased.

"You have never seen her angry." He glanced over his shoulder as if he were about to be descended on by a sea monster.

Seera chuckled at his mock fear. She enjoyed seeing him so relaxed and she had an urge to stay instead of returning to the crowd which was awaiting them.

Kata, Geira and Agata would not leave her be. They had shown up in Rafn's dwelling as soon as they'd returned and begun fussing over her to the point where she wanted to beat them off. Seera fingered the beads on the chestnut colored gown Kata had chosen as she brushed her hair and twined in tiny white flowers. When their pampering was complete, Kata placed the emerald necklace around her neck.

Kata held up a mirror so Seera could inspect the outcome. She had to admit they'd performed magic.

Agata was sent ahead to let Rafn know she was on her way, while Kata and Geira walked with her through the still night, which had been surprisingly warm since Rafn's return.

Rafn met her at the door. He was dressed in a short sleeved wool tunic, dyed a deep red that was shocking against his black hair. On each arm was clasped a gold arm band, etched with entwined snakes and matched the buckle on his belt. Around his neck hung an iron replica of Thor's hammer, Mjollnir, which was said to come back to the god after being thrown. Seera had heard it said it was his personal amulet, symbolizing his chosen god.

When Seera met Rafn's dark eyes she could see in them a storm. As if the rumors she'd heard of Thor choosing him were true. Oddly she heard an echoing thunder, yet the sky remained clear.

Geira and Kata hurried on ahead so that the couple could enter together. Seera took the arm that Rafn offered her and allowed him to lead her to the head table. The women had gone to an extra effort and decorated everything with the last of the flowers from the fields. It was the last of summer brought in for one final evening of enjoyment before everything became withered and brown.

Byzantine wine was served to everyone and once each person in the hall had a goblet filled with it, the Jarl rose to speak.

"I welcome you all in celebration of my brother's betrothal." Valr spoke loudly so all could hear. A roar rolled over the crowd. "You have all heard by now, that he plans to take the Lady Seera of Dun'O'Tir, to be his bride." Even louder cheers filled the hall.

Rafn stood to speak. "In a few days time, we will be heading to the fortress castle on the cliff in Pictland. It will be there that we will marry, with her father's blessing."

That he would win the Eorl's blessing, no one doubted. Rafn was a very persuasive man. Rafn raised his goblet and drank deeply from it, as everyone cheered and did the same.

Before Seera could bring her own goblet to her mouth, Rafn sat beside her and offered her a drink from his. He tilted it and gave her a taste of his wine.

Through all the cheering and innuendos shouted out from the gathered men and women, Seera could focus on only one thing.

That Rafn intended to bring her home.

One man in the crowd clung to the shadows and watched the couple closely. A sneer crossed his face. He was a trader from Jutland and had recently left Ribe. Hwal had sent him to Skiringssal to find out where the slave girl had been taken.

The new Jarl cared not for Yrsa that had been his slave, but for the one who'd been slave to Drenger. He had been angry when Rafn had taken her, and he wanted her returned to Ribe.

Hwal had boasted that he would not be as easy on her as Drenger had been. This he'd promised as he'd slipped many coins into the trader's hand. He wanted information on what was happening with the Lady Seera.

That Rafn planned to marry her would not be received well. The next morning the trader left to sail for Ribe with his news.

He went straight to Hwal in the hall when he arrived in port. The one-eyed giant had been waiting for him.

"They may have already left Skiringssal, my lord," the trader told him. "They head for Dun'O'Tir to marry."

"He is taking her for his wife?" Hwal snarled in disbelief.

"Aye, my lord."

"Then I will have to get her back before she arrives home."

"I know someone who would be good at sneaking past the many warriors who are sure to be accompanying them."

Hwal smirked. "To find her in a weak moment."

"Aye, my lord." The man stepped back from the hatred that seized Hwal's face.

"Let it be done," Hwal waved the man away, and turned his thoughts to the lustful pleasures he would force upon the Lady of Dun'O'Tir.

CHAPTER 12

A boy of about fourteen showed up to take Seera's trunks. He was strong for his age and Seera told him so. He gave her an awkward smile. Seera sensed the boy's sadness. It made her wonder what had happened to him. He should be happily teasing the girls, as the other boys his age were doing. She watched him disappear towards the dock with her trunk.

"His name is Fox," Kata said as she joined Seera. Her voice carried a note of the same sadness when she spoke the boy's name.

"Has something happened to him?" Seera asked, causing Kata to look away and breathe in to control some strong emotion that was gripping her. When she turned back to Seera, she saw the wetness in her eyes.

"Come inside." Kata led her into the dwelling and they each took a seat at the table. Seera gave her time to compose herself before speaking.

"Fox is the brother of the woman that Orn was to marry." Kata fumbled with her hands. "Orn was visiting the village of his betrothed, to make the final arrangements. They were to wed seven days later."

Tears leaked from the corner of Kata's eyes. Seera felt her own misting as she watched her friend's tears. Kata's focus was not on her or anything in the room, but on something deep inside. Seera reached out and grabbed her hand.

"While he was there, they were attacked by warriors from Jutland. As you know they took Orn, but everyone else was killed, including Orn's future wife."

Seera drew in a deep breath as she recalled the grief in Orn's eyes, and understood better how it had gotten there. She saw the deep effect it had on Kata and wondered how Rafn felt?

"Rafn became angrier than anyone had ever seen him before. His rage was barely contained," she answered as if hearing Seera's silent question. "He went to Ribe to get Orn back."

"And when he found him dead, he vowed to take Drenger's life." Seera began to see clearly the mistake she had made, and the implications of it.

"Aye."

"And I foolishly denied it to him."

"Aye."

"And the boy?" Seera returned to questions of Fox.

"He was the only survivor. He waited until it was safe and then rode here to tell the Jarl what had happened." Kata used the sleeve of her dress to wipe her tears away.

A shadow filled the door and they both looked up to see Rafn standing framed within the opening. Seera met his eyes and saw the anger in them. He was not pleased.

"Kata, go." He snapped his order. Kata nervously slipped past him, looking to Seera as she left. Rafn's gaze stayed on his intended bride, who lifted from the chair to come before him.

"I am sorry, I should have realized."

"She shouldn't have spoken of such things to you." Rafn's nostrils flared as he looked down at her. For some reason this made Seera angry.

"Why not?"

"It was not her business." A growl rumbled from his throat. He felt the darkness in him respond to his rising temper. It sank its talon's sharply into his anger, making him shudder.

Seera saw dark shadows move across his eyes. She dared herself to look deeper and glimpsed the storm that was brewing. She felt the power reach for her. Its sharp fingers teased her skin.

Gripping her defiance against it she snapped. "He was her brother also. And she knows I was witness to Orn's death. You didn't believe it important to discuss with me why you claimed me?"

"No." A spark of energy sizzled in the air between them. He clenched his fist urging the tempest back.

"Why?" Seera drew her strength forward. Reacting to the look on his face, her anger flared.

"You are mine, I have need of you." He shook his head to clear it. "Nothing else matters."

"It's that simple?" Her eyes narrowed. "I am but your tool in forming a diplomatic relation with my father!"

"Aye." He spat his reply.

"No it isn't." She studied him closely, searching for something. "It is more."

"You think so?" His eyes widened in challenge.

"Yes," she screamed. "I took your kill. You wanted me to suffer for that."

"Suffer," he yelled. "You have been treated as a princess since you've been here. Perhaps you would prefer the same treatment you got from Drenger."

She moved closer to him, meeting his furious eyes, unafraid to look into them. "It must have crossed your mind, that you should have just killed me." She had come to learn much of the Viking code of honor since coming to Skiringssal.

She was staring at him, daring him to do it. Damn that woman! He exploded and before he could stop himself he reach out and gripped her throat. She didn't even flinch at his threat, but continued to stare defiantly at him.

"I should have killed you," he said with more control than he felt. "Things would have been simpler."

Still she did not react. She trusted that he would not harm her. Thor's thunder, it irritated him! Mostly because she was right, he couldn't harm her. His hand eased its hold and he stepped away from her.

Saying nothing more Rafn stormed out of the dwelling. Seera watched him go. She rubbed the welt he'd left on her throat. Her anger fled quickly, as she understood the extent of his pain. He had loved his brother and was a long way from accepting his death.

When he finally released the full force of that anger, God help whoever was standing in his way.

They sailed for Pictland late in the morning. Kata and Agata were accompanying her, for which she was grateful. Ten drekar left the port of Skiringssal. The largest was the warlord's ship. The other nine accompanied him in case the Eorl did not welcome Rafn as he had planned.

Rafn's mood did not improved once on board and he avoided Seera. As soon as Hachet had taken them out to sea, Rafn took a place at one of the oars and began rowing madly. The other warriors had to struggle to keep pace, but they all knew better than to complain.

Dagsytrr kept glancing between Rafn and the Lady Seera, trying to assess the problem, but the woman was calm. If the trouble was between them, than she hid it well, though Kata didn't look so at ease. Rafn had never fought with his sister. Certainly he would not do so now. He shook his head. It was not for him to worry over.

They sailed until it was dark, at which point Rafn ordered the ships to drop anchor. Rafn's ship alone was brought close to shore so that the women could get out and stretch their legs.

Hachet started a fire and Agata prepared the fish that Leikr had caught, into an evening meal.

The three women sat apart from the men, and Rafn made no attempt at joining them. He sat silent and scowling beside Dagstyrr as he picked at the fish on his plate. After a time he tossed the remains of the fish into the fire and walked to the beach where he began throwing stones out into the water.

"You going to tell me what troubles you?" Dagstyrr approached with caution.

"It concerns you not." Rafn's face pinched in an ire he really didn't understand. It was bubbling in him, almost to the point of boiling over and he wasn't even clear what had set it off. Deep within he knew it hadn't been Kata's words, or Seera's defiance that irked him.

Dagstyrr stood his ground against Rafn's snarling. "It does when you push us so hard that we have to row like mad to keep up." Dagstyrr casually pointed out as he lifted a stone and tossed it across the moving water.

"A warrior does not complain." He snapped louder than he intended and whipped a rock as hard as he could into the inky black sea.

"I'm not complaining." Dagstyrr fingered a smooth stone in his hand. "I am concerned."

"Don't be!"

"If that is what you wish." Dagstyrr tossed the stone to Rafn, before going to find a soft spot to lay his blankets.

As Dagstyrr was adjusting his blankets he looked over and noticed Kata watching him. He raised his eyebrows in question to the look on her face. She had obviously seen his attempt to speak with Rafn, and his failure. What did she know that he didn't?

He turned his gaze to the stars and lay with his hands behind his head. He had felt the power radiating from his warlord, his friend.

Rafn was going to erupt…and soon.

"I am going to clean up in the stream on the other side of those bushes," Seera pointed as she spoke to Kata. Agata was already fast asleep and Seera wished she could succumb so easily.

Rafn was still pacing on the beach and from the icy look in his eyes he had not worked through his anger yet. She wished there was something she could do to help him. She knew that it was futile, she was partly to blame. If he'd vented his anger on Drenger as he'd needed to do, it wouldn't still be eating away at him.

"Alright." Kata was upset too. She was taking the blame for how Rafn was acting, but Seera knew it had nothing to do with her. She had only released the rage that was already there.

"Get some sleep. He will just have to work through it on his own."

Kata looked up at her and nodded, but said nothing. Seera placed a hand on her shoulder before following the path through the trees to the stream they had found earlier.

She missed how Rafn's gaze moved swiftly to her when she'd gotten up and walked off, or noticed him following her. He was determined to keep her in his sights.

Seera undid her hair from its braid and brushed her fingers through it before tying it back. She knelt by the stream and rinsed her face with the cold water. It was refreshing. She glanced around and satisfied that she was alone she took off her cloak and pulled off her shoes. She stripped off her dress so she only had her smock left on. She pushed up the sleeves and washed her arms then she pulled the smock up to her thighs and entered the water to splash it on her legs.

After washing she stepped back on the rock strewn shore and knelt to pick up her dress and cloak when she was suddenly yanked back. A hand clasped over her mouth. Foul breath drifted to her, as if the man had a rotten tooth. She realized the mistake she had made, by leaving camp alone. She had left herself vulnerable. Stupid!

"Hwal wants you back." The man spoke into her ear. She tried to struggle, but that had never gotten her anywhere. It was so frustrating to be overpowered, but it always seemed she was.

"No point in fighting," he said. "You will be coming with me."

"No she won't," another voice penetrated the night. Relief flooded her at the sound of Rafn's voice.

The man let go of her and turned to find the tip of a sword pushed up against his chest. Before he could say anything, Rafn raised the axe in his other hand and knocked him unconscious with the handle.

"Get dressed," he told her as he flung the man over his shoulder without effort. He watched while she pulled on her dress, cloak and shoes and then made her walk before him to camp.

Seera realized that he must have been watching her. She peered over her shoulder at him, but his face was hard and unreadable.

Warriors woke instantly and alert as their warlord walked back into camp and threw the man onto the ground.

"Tie him." He shouted his order to Hachet. He stood back to watch his warrior secure the man's hands behind his back.

"Who is he?" Dagstyrr joined him and scowled down at the unconscious man.

"I don't know, but I will enjoy finding out." His anger was on the verge of bursting forth. He heard the resounding thunder moving in him, preparing its power. The air crackled, drawing a sharp look from Dagstyrr. His friend nodded in understanding.

Dagstyrr took the hardened leather pail of water that Leikr had filled from the ocean and threw it in the man's face.

The man came awake sputtering to find himself surrounded by a dozen warriors. They looked fierce and ready to kill, but it was Rafn who made him shutter. He could almost hear the thunder that lived inside the warlord.

Before he asked a single question of the prisoner, Rafn had him brought to his feet. His fist found the man's gut quickly. Having failed to knock him off his feet, Rafn sent a blow to his face. Another and another found the man. He drew blood from the man's mouth, the corner of his eye and the side of his head. He felt satisfaction when he heard the crack of rib.

Seera had rejoined Kata. The women huddled together, watching in horror the act of violence. Somehow Agata remained sleeping and Seera envied her oblivion. Kata raised her hands to her mouth to stifle a cry. Seera understood her fear to utter a sound.

But Seera watched Rafn closely. She knew each time the vein in his temple pulsed. She witnessed a full range of expressions cross his face. And still the rage came. His men stayed back, letting him vent his fury.

Her gut tightened in worry, but she kept focused on him, only him. She was able see him more clearly than anyone else did. She saw past the anger to the rawness of his pain. She saw that if he could not release it, it would consume him.

She knew that she should pity the man that was receiving his beating, but her only concern was for Rafn. She despised the prisoner. He'd wanted to take her back to Ribe, to the brutal giant who would suck the life from her—bit by bit until she were but a shell.

Rafn's explosion had ripped from him with such force he'd been unable to stop his reaction. Only when the man finally succumbed and fell to his knees, did he feel the rippling wave wash away. With his control regained, Rafn brought his axe beneath the man's throat.

"You will bring a message to Hwal."

"What would you have me say?" The man managed to ask as he choked on a tooth that he'd swallowed. Blood filled his mouth from the gap.

"That, I will enjoy killing him." He beckoned to Dagstyrr who dragged the man to his feet. "Come after my woman again and your life with be forfeit."

The man nodded his understanding before Dagstyrr and Hachet forced him down the beach to the boat he'd hidden.

Rafn felt Seera watching him. He drew in a calming breath before turning to her. He stared at her for a long moment before walking to her side. He felt apprehensive at having her witness him when the darkness fully claimed him.

"Go to sleep." He ordered and lowered beside her, where he intended to stay through the night.

Seera simply nodded and did as he expected.

In the hidden meadow sat the woman who many believed was a witch because of her ability to see things that she should not have been able to. To know when things would happen before they did. She looked up as the warrior woman came towards her, a deer over her shoulder.

"The deer will feed our hunger, as the dwelling keeps us warm," she spoke in her strange way.

"The mountains are full of life to sustain us sister, if one knows how to survive." Her sister did not smile, for it was not an expression she was comfortable with. She'd led a harsh life, one that had taught her strength and independence from men who had represented nothing but cruelty for them both. For their mother who now lay dead.

"The spear is alive in your hand, as is the arrow. Soon the sword you have taken to be yours will become as one with your soul."

"I will practice until it is so."

"The goddess will give you strength."

"One thing men have taught me is how to wield a sword. Ever have I watched them closely when they were unaware. Soon I vow…none will stand against me."

"Your cunning will be needed, and your arm will prove true. When the time has been caught, your worth you will prove."

CHAPTER 13

Everyone rowed in silence the next day. Rafn was much calmer and eased up on their speed. If the men were grateful they said nothing of it. Seera watched from where she sat huddled with the other women.

Since morning the sky had been overcast and they'd been sprinkled by a light rain that had worked its way right down to their bones. It did not seem to bother the tough exterior of the warriors, but the women were miserable. They huddled beneath the hide tent that had been erected on the ships deck for them.

Rafn had turned sullen, Seera decided. He'd expelled what he'd needed to and now he could do nothing more than remember. When their eyes had met, she saw it.

They were now on the North Sea, far from land, so when night came they huddled on deck in their blankets, except for the women who were given the tent. Kata and Agata slept close to each other for warmth, but Rafn insisted that Seera sleep close to him.

Two days out from shore, the wind calmed and the rain eased up, giving them a pleasant day. That night Rafn decided Kata and Agata could sleep on deck and be just as warm. He wanted time alone with Seera and said as much to Kata, who nodded her understanding.

Rafn took her within the tent and lowered the side panels to offer them privacy. He sat leaning against a cargo box that had been brought inside to use as a backrest. He dragged her into his arms and held her against him.

They sat quietly for some time, feeling the rocking of the ship, before he finally broke the silence.

"I don't want to be angry," he said softly so his voice did not carry to his men.

"I know." She leaned her head back against his chest.

"I'm sorry you had to see me like that," referring to what he'd done to Hwal's man. Seera pulled from his arms so that she could turn and face him.

"Do not." She spoke with absolute seriousness. "It was what you had to do."

"It did not scare you?" He should have known that it wouldn't. Not this woman who didn't even cry out as she was whipped repeatedly. Not the woman who had stared him straight in the eye without flinching when he'd lashed out at her.

"If he'd taken me back to Hwal," she simply stated. "It would have been me on the receiving end of a beating, and most assuredly rape."

Cold terror clenched his heart. "I will never let that happen."

She watched the hardness leave his face to be replaced by his desire and she responded to it. Without thinking she leaned into him and found his mouth with hers. She kissed him tentatively, a bit unsure of what she was doing. His arms came around her back and pulled her closer, kissing her deeper.

Rafn gave in to his desire for only a moment. He fought the urge to push her beneath him and lay his final claim to her. He wanted to feel her body open to him, wanted to show her exactly how she made him feel, but he forced himself to pull back.

Seera looked up at him with hurt confusion as he pulled from her. He had felt how strongly her heart beat for him and knew she was close to being ready for him. Instinct warned that she needed more time.

"Not yet." He ran a cool hand over her heated face and smiled as her lips eased from a pout. She nodded in acceptance.

Seera wanted to argue with him, tell him not to stop, but he was honoring her by waiting. How could she not honor him by accepting?

Seera allowed him to lay her down and was pleased when he stretched out against her and wrapped her in his arms. She fell asleep to the gentle rocking of the ship, and the strong heart beat of the man who she wanted as she never had another.

Kata stayed awake long after Agata fell asleep in her blankets. She was restless and tired at the same time, yet unsure which to give into. She was sick of being on the ship. She wanted to see land again, and feel solid ground under her feet. She'd never much liked the feel of the sea beneath her, or how it unsettled her stomach.

Her brothers would stare at her in confusion were she to ever tell them such a thing. Both of them took to the sea easily and longed for it when they kept too long at home. Rafn had more freedom to come and go than did Valr, but her eldest brother never voiced his complaint.

Then again, did Valr ever complain? His feelings were always kept close to his chest and never revealed to those around him, even his own family.

So different from Rafn in so many ways, she thought. One brother was too controlled, while the other fought desperately each day to keep his emotions from ruling him.

Kata hugged her blanket tighter around herself and looked to the men who stayed awake through the night to keep the wind in the sail and the ship headed in the right direction. She glanced around and was surprised to see Dagstyrr standing looking out at the ocean that lay before them.

Above shone a thin sliver of a moon, and the night reflected only a few stars. The water lapped black against the ship's side. What he looked at she could only guess, for she could see nothing in the darkness. As she continued to study him she realized he was simply lost in his thoughts.

In the darkness his red hair was washed out and hard to see. She pictured its color in her mind. It was not as bright as that of his sister Auga, Kata recalled, but more of a reddish brown. Auga on the other hand had hair that looked coppery in the light.

Kata realized she liked the color of his hair. For someone who had hair that was considered so dark it was mistaken for black, she would have loved to have some other color. Even Seera's hair if you looked at it was not simply light brown, but was mixed with shades both darker and lighter, giving it a textured look.

For whatever reason that possessed her, Kata continued to stare at Dagstyrr. She studied not only his hair, but how his shoulders stretched the fabric of his tunic. If she allowed, which some impish creature seemed to make her do, she let her eyes drift lower. She blushed as she realized she was enjoying looking at his finely shaped buttocks and legs.

Foolish thoughts, she told herself. He thought of her as his sister only. She warmed at the feelings that were stirring in her. He was a fine man to look at. What harm was there in it?

Dagstyrr moved and went to speak with the man working the steering oar on the stern side of the ship. It was a good thing. Who knew what dangerous things would have entered her mind had he stayed there a moment longer?

Seera woke suddenly to the ship violently tilting back and forth. Rafn was already on his feet and helped her to hers. He pushed out of the tent to the deck and they found that the world had turned to madness. Rain came crashing down on top of them and the wind was whipping them back and forth.

The men had taken in the sail and were rushing around trying to make sure everything was tied down securely to the deck. Kata and Agata clung helplessly to the side not far off.

"Sister, over here," he yelled to them and watched them teeter towards him. Seera had to grab his arm to keep from falling.

"I want you three inside the tent," he ordered over the howl of the storm.

Seera tried to protest, even as Kata and Agata ducked into the tent that was threateningly close to being claimed by the wind.

"Don't argue." The look on his face told her he would throw her inside if he needed to. She turned and pushed into the tent.

The three women sat close together and away from the hide walls that were amazingly waterproof. They clung together to ride out the storm. Each wrapped in their blanket for what warmth it could offer.

"Is he is still angry with you?" Kata asked over the noise of the storm. She'd been feeling so guilty for causing him to be upset with Seera.

"He was never really angry with me. It was not something that you caused, please believe that."

"I saw how angry he was," Kata said. "That rage was real."

"It was something that was simmering in him for a while," she said. "It needed to come out so it wasn't trapped inside."

"You believe that to be true?"

"I do. He lost a brother, as have you. It is not something that anyone should accept easily." Seera moved further away from the tent's side as the wind batted at it.

"You understand him so well?"

"I only try." She didn't want to give too much of her heart away. "A wife should get to know her husband."

The ship tilted sharply, causing Kata to fall into Seera. She helped steady the other woman and felt how she shook. She wrapped an arm around Kata to keep her warm. Agata moved in closer on her other side.

"I am glad that you desire to, especially after he blew up at you." Kata pulled her blanket over head and buried deeply in its warmth.

"I did not let him intimidate me," she chuckled to lighten the mood.

"How could you not be scared of him?" Agata asked "He is the fiercest of warriors."

"One thing my mother told me when she was still alive, is that you can't give them too much power. That a husband can order all he wants, but if he wants a happy marriage, he can't expect his wife to always listen."

"Is that true?" Agata was surprised at such words.

"That is how it was for my parents," Seera said. "They had a great love." The door flap whipped open, spraying the women with icy rain, before falling back into place. Seera wiped the cold moisture from her face with her hand.

"I'd like to marry for love." Kata sighed, trying to keep them from thinking too much about the storm.

"Can you not?" Seera adjusted her blanket and pulled her knees in closer to her chest.

"I can hope, but it will be up to Valr and Rafn to choose my husband."

"My brother, Peder, was to have chosen mine." Seera began to wonder what reception they would receive when they reached Dun'O'Tir.

"Will he accept your betrothal?"

Seera laughed to ease the growing tension. "I will see that he does. He will see the logic in forming a union between Pictland and Vestfold. It has nothing to do with love." Seera wondered why she added the last part. She wouldn't be the first woman to have a husband that did not love her, yet something in her longed for it all the same.

Seera was soggy and cold, hating the miserable weather that threatened outside. Nothing but a thin protection separated the storm from the women, and it was more than a little frightening.

Through it though was a ray of hope. Soon she would be home.

The squall didn't last long. The men were experts on the water and had not been overly concerned about the storm. It was not as bad as some they'd had to endure. Rafn was standing in the front prow when land first came into view. It was nothing more than a dark blur on the horizon, but it was a welcomed sight.

"You figured out what you are going to say to the Eorl yet?" Dagstyrr asked from beside him.

"That Seera and I are to marry."

"You are not going to ask his permission first?" Dagstyrr tried to suppress a smile at his friend's audacity.

"No."

Dagstyrr laughed. "What has that woman done to you?"

"She has done nothing." Rafn scowled at his friend and dared him to suggest he was weak minded towards the fairer sex.

"What if the Eorl tells you, you can't have his daughter?"

Rafn placed his hand on the hilt of his knife and gripped it. "I will not be giving him a choice."

"You could have married her in Skiringssal and just sent him word of the marriage, but you didn't."

"I want this alliance, and as a gesture of good faith I thought the wedding should take place at Dun'O'Tir." A cool breeze blew off the water to tug at his unbound hair.

"And it had nothing to do with Seera?" Dagstyrr asked. "Perhaps you thought she would prefer it."

"I did not ask." Rafn looked at his friend and tried to figure out what his friend was saying. Why was it Dagstyrr seemed to see his heart so clearly?

"She has a brother," Dagstyrr bent to tie a rope that had loosened in the night. Securing the cargo it held with a strong knot, he glanced up to Rafn.

"Lord Peder," Rafn's eyes narrowed at the expectant battle which awaited him.

"He is said to be quick with the sword and unafraid to face down any foe." Satisfied the rope would hold, he stood up.

"I have heard that." Rafn grabbed the side rail and leaned into it. Salty moisture caught in the wind washed his face.

"Yet you are still determined not to ask?"

"She is mine," Rafn said. "I will fight to keep her if I must, but I hope for their cooperation." The land before them began to take form. Sharp cliffs rose from the sea to meet a land rich with trees.

"For the sake of the alliance?"

"No, for Seera's," Rafn admitted. He did not turn to see the smile on Dagstyrr's face, but he knew it was there.

Hachet turned the ship so they could follow the coastline north. The other ships followed close behind. It was afternoon by the time Dun'O'Tir appeared.

Seera had believed she would never see home again, so when the castle came into view she felt an overwhelming sense of relief. Rafn came to stand beside her.

"You are happy to be back?" He peered at her closely watching her reaction. It amused her.

"I have missed my family. I have also missed this place. Its beauty has long spoken to me."

Rafn had to admit it was a magnificent site. A fortified castle of stone, built on the flat top of a large rock that was connected to the main land by a narrow strip of land. The sides of the rock were sheer and impossible to climb. The only way into the fortress was through the main gate which was heavily guarded.

Rafn could see the guards walking the wall that surrounded the castle. Many spotted them and stopped to watch the ten Viking ships that were approaching from the sea.

"There is a bay up ahead. It is the only place there is to pull in the ships," she told him.

Rafn ordered Hachet to head for the bay, while Seera kept her sight focused on her home. She could just make out the shape of Peder on the fortress wall, but he was too far away to see his expression. She felt a sense of unease.

Would Peder allow this marriage?

CHAPTER 14

Peder stared down at the Viking ships that dropped anchor. Only one proceeded to the beach where three women and two men disembarked. Peder clenched his teeth.

"Father," Peder called to the man climbing the ladder up to the wall where he stood.

"What do you see?" Airic stepped off the ladder onto the battlement.

"Ten Viking ships." Peder shifted his feet, scraping his soft leather boots against the loose bits of rock.

Airic looked down at the drekars anchored below and scowled in anger at the sight of them. He grabbed the stone wall, his knuckles turning white.

Peder pointed to the five people at the bottom of the path that led up the hill. The Eorl's eyes narrowed. "They have Seera with them."

Peder's thoughts turned dangerous. Since the day he had learned of Seera's abductions he had been sending out his soldiers to look for any signs of where she might have been taken. Those who had returned had failed to discover who had taken her. Peder had not been able to find much rest. Sleep eluded him in the nights and the servants had learned to walk carefully in his presence.

They understood, for everyone who dwelled within the castle walls loved Seera and had prayed daily for her safe return. Peder couldn't prevent the anger. Taking his sister had not been a wise move. His hand sought the hilt of the sword attached to his belt. His cloak fluttered behind him in the breeze as he sought to tame his fury.

Father and son met the warriors and the women at the main gate. Airic ordered the gate opened so that Peder and he, with a dozen guards could step through to wait his daughter and the men with her.

Seera walked ahead with a dark haired man, who wore arrogance wrapped as comfortably around him as a cloak. Peder's suspicions arose. The Norseman met him eye to eye, each drawing conclusions about the other without a single word being spoken.

Seera did not see the silent battle that went on between Rafn and Peder. She saw only that her father was standing there waiting. She ran forward and threw her arms around him and was encompassed by his embrace.

Father and daughter stood there in each other's arms for a moment as she fought to keep the tears from spilling over. She had not realized until that instant just how much she had missed him.

"You are alright?" He looked at her with the tenderness of a father who loved his daughter.

"I am." Seera took a step back and looked to her brother.

Her first impression was that he was haggard. His eyes bore dark circles beneath them, and he needed a good shave. Even his hair had grown longer than Peder usually wore it, as if he'd forgotten to keep it trimmed. She met his eyes and saw his fatigue. She wondered if he'd slept in all the time she'd been away.

"I am relieved to see you alive." Peder's voice broke through her speculations. She stepped into his arms and was comforted by the quiver of emotion that vibrated from him.

"My men did not have luck in finding you."

"I am here now."

"He is the one who took you?" Peder broke the embrace and turned his glare to Rafn. Seera saw the challenge on his face.

"Nay," she quickly said. "He is the one who rescued me." She took an involuntary step towards Rafn.

Airic's keen gaze narrowed on Rafn before Peder could reply. "Then I am grateful to you, for she is my only daughter and I have a soft spot for her." His hard features smoothed as he looked to Seera.

Peder, who was not so easily mollified, continued to stare at Rafn who made no appearance of being intimidated. She knew how head strong both these men could be and impulsively stepped between them.

"We are tired and hungry brother," she said to him. "Will you allow us in?"

"You don't need permission to enter your home," Airic said to his daughter. "And your friends are welcome."

"The four that are with you may enter," Peder added. "The others will remain with their ships until an understanding has been reached."

"They have already been ordered to do so," Rafn said.

Seera moved towards Rafn, meeting his gaze only briefly. "Brother, Papa, I would like to introduce you to the warlord and brother to the Jarl of Skiringssal, Rafn Vakrson."

Peder's eyes widened in recognition and again found his hand pushing aside his cloak to reach for his sword. Rafn's eyes narrowed on the action but made no move towards a weapon of his own.

"I have heard your name, and know of your reputation."

"As I have heard of yours, Lord Peder of Dun'O'Tir," Rafn replied.

Peder's eyes fixed on Rafn as his fingers rubbed the leather bound hilt he grasped. The air seemed to thicken between the two men and Peder could feel the sizzling power rise. Goosebumps rose on his flesh. His teeth clenched. "Do they not call you the Raven?"

"It is who I am in battle, not who I am standing before you now." They again took each others measure and Seera again stepped between them, catching her brother's suspicious attention.

"I must wonder sister, why you feel you must keep placing yourself between us?"

"Come, we can speak inside," the Eorl said, saving Seera from having to answer. From the way Peder watched her, she knew he would expect an answer soon. She fought the urge to join Rafn and instead drifted to her father.

Seera slipped her hand around the Eorl's arm and allowed him to lead her through the gate. Kata and Agata followed next, as Dagstyrr walked with Rafn behind. Peder brought up the rear, to keep an eye on his guests.

They entered the Keep and Seera was glad to be home, but she felt a detachment she had never felt within these stone walls. She couldn't explain it, but the connection with this place that she'd always felt had somehow diminished. She was tired, she told herself.

"These women are your maids?" Peder asked once they were inside.

"Agata is my maid," she told her brother, pointing to the blond woman who was hanging back. Indicating the other she introduced, "this is Lady Kata Vakradottir, and sister to Lord Rafn."

Peder looked at her with appreciation, until Rafn stepped to his sister's side with a scowl on his face. Peder nodded to him, understanding his protectiveness. Turning his attention to his own sister he spoke firmly.

"Sister, show Lady Kata to one of the guest chambers, and your maid where she might sleep."

Seera looked to Rafn, who smiled and nodded. Peder noticed the exchange and narrowed his eyes. "Go," Peder's voice had a sharp edge to it that was normally so controlled. "I have things to discuss with Lord Rafn."

His tone startled Seera and her gaze snapped to him. He met her inquiry with a hard stare that offered no room for disobedience. She was the first to look away and he waited for her to leave before beckoning the men to follow.

Rafn went with Peder and the Eorl to the Great Hall, where they took seats at a long table close to the hearth. A large window was on the wall close to the table and Rafn could see the blue sky beyond it. Dagstyrr lowered to the seat beside him and he felt grateful for the lone presence of support.

"What is it you want?" Peder got right to the point. Rafn felt the tug of a smile at the man's straight forwardness.

"I will gladly reward you for bringing my daughter home," the Eorl offered before Rafn could reply. He looked to Seera's father to discover the man's study of him. He was not as at ease as he would like Rafn to believe.

"I do not want your riches, my lord."

"What then?" Peder demanded and leaned across the table towards the one he believed to be a threat.

Rafn did not react to the hardness in his eyes, though he felt the thinness of the path he walked on. He kept his tone even as he spoke the words he'd come to say. "We have come here, so that Seera and I can be married." He held Peder's eye, daring him to refute his right.

The Eorl's eyes sharpened at Rafn's casual insolence and Peder stood so fast his chair toppled over. It hit the floor and echoed across the chamber. A servant just entering the room stopped abruptly, afraid to move any closer.

Rafn who was across the table from Peder, stood as well and the two men faced each other with deadly intent. Dagstyrr got to his feet, ready to defend his leader if needed. Airic rose as well, not wanting to be the only one left sitting.

A sharp wind blew with a sudden gust through the window to reach for Rafn's hair, lifting it to frame his face in a flurry. It carried on it a surge of power that crackled loudly as the wind died away.

"I have not given her to you, outlander." Peder glared at the stranger who presumed too much.

Rafn was not cowed by the man's anger and met it with equal gruffness. "I do not ask your permission."

Airic laid a hand on his son's arm and drew Rafn into his commanding gaze. "Let us sit and discuss this like gentleman." Only the Eorl's blue eyes betrayed his fury. Airic was a man of control, much as Valr was. The similarity pleased Rafn and he bowed to the man's request.

"The Eorl speaks wisely." Dagstyrr spoke to ease the growing tension and eased into his chair beside Rafn.

Peder grabbed his chair and set it up right, before sitting. An uneasy silence descended. The Eorl pinned Rafn with irritation.

"You are an arrogant man, coming in here and telling us that you are going to marry Seera, instead of requesting her hand as is right," Airic said.

Rafn opened his mouth to speak, but Airic cut him off.

"I am grateful to you for saving my daughter," Airic continued. "But do not think that I will simply give her to you as a reward."

"My lord," Dagstyrr spoke up before Rafn had a chance to reply. Rafn shot him a nasty look which he ignored. "Rafn and I have discussed what a union between our countries could mean. We are here to propose an alliance between us, through a marriage between the Lady Seera and Lord Rafn."

"You are a Norse man," Dagstyrr continued before anyone else could comment, "As is King David. A treaty between us would be a good thing."

"Is this true," Airic asked Rafn. "You want peace between us?"

"Aye." Rafn tried hard to keep his face passive and his voice from seething with impatience.

"Then I will reflect upon it."

Peder sat very silent, watching Rafn with eyes as keen as a hawk. Rafn sensed the man had guessed it was more than peace he wanted. He would be judged before Peder would bless a marriage.

He shivered in anticipation at the challenge, as an answering boom quake through him.

Seera was in her bed chamber, soaking in a warm bath. The heat eased the tension from her tight muscles, even as the soapy water cleaned away the dirt. It was hard to still the worry about what went on between Rafn and her brother. Her father was better at listening, but Peder was a soldier and always on the defensive. He and Rafn were much alike she realized. Two strong headed bulls. Things could get nasty between them if she let it.

She sighed at what she would need to do. She would tell her brother that she was going along with this alliance, even if he didn't give his blessing. He would bluster with disapproval and demand her compliance, but she would be as stubborn as he.

She could tell Peder that she had fallen in love with Rafn. It would not be a lie. Her feelings for the man had only deepened on the voyage from Vestfold, but they were still too new, too raw to be spoken to anyone. Such feelings left her vulnerable and she thought it best that Rafn knew nothing of them.

Seera wanted this marriage. Laying in the bath she remembered how Rafn's mouth had felt against her. It had just been a kiss, but it had promised something more. Something that Seera wanted.

She stepped from the bath as the water turned cold and wrapped a drying sheet around her. There was a knock on the door and Agata entered.

"Mistress," she said as she closed the door behind her. "Supper will be served shortly. We must get you ready."

Using a second drying cloth she wrapped her wet hair. "I am hungry. It would also be good to make sure the men have not killed each other." She settled at her vanity and let Agata use the cloth to dry most of the moisture from her hair.

Smiling Agata began to pin up Seera's damp hair. "They are still in the Great Hall, my lady. No blood has been spilled yet, but the servants are whispering about the tension between the Warlord and your brother."

"Then I had best get down there."

Agata helped Seera into a dark blue dress. She slipped her feet into soft ankle shoes. As a final touch she put on the emerald necklace that Rafn had given her. Let her brother see that Rafn cared for her.

Kata entered into the room. She was wearing a red dress that was a stark contrast to her dark hair. She had pinned her hair back from her face, but left it loose down her back. As Seera's it was still damp. Seera thought she was beautiful.

"We had best be off," Seera said to her. "Our brothers need our supervision."

"A woman's touch might be called for." Kata laughed in agreement.

They made their way down the stairs to the Great Hall. People had yet to arrive. The only ones present were the four men.

Dagstyrr and her father were speaking amicably but Peder and Rafn just sat there in silent battle, with matching scowls and crossed arms.

It was time for intervention.

Peder was not sure he liked this warlord of Skiringssal. He was far too confident. He questioned the real motive behind a marriage to his sister. What did Rafn gain? It had to be more than just a treaty. An alliance didn't need a marriage to fortify it. Other compensations could be made. Warriors traded. Secrets shared.

Marriages had been made for such things before. It was always a good thing to unite countries through ties of family. It made the union stronger. But was that really the reasoning behind his wish…no his demand, for a marriage.

The man was egotistical to be sure. Arrogant and cocky, to think he could make such a demand and live. He would gladly like to test his strength on the training field. First chance they got. He could see that Rafn was studying him just as intently. It would be a good match.

As Peder watched Rafn, the iciness in his eyes melted and his gaze shifted to something over his shoulder. He stood with years of practice grace and Peder turned to see the women coming across the room.

He looked back at Rafn with surprise to see the way he watched Seera. The man desired his sister. That was no surprise, many men did. What was a shock was that there was more than desire reflected in his gaze.

It was love?

Peder had not considered that as a possibility. He rose from the table as the other men did and waited for the ladies to join them. Rafn went to Seera and took her hand. He brought it to his mouth and gave it a kiss.

"You look lovely, my lady," he said softly.

Peder watched Seera's reaction and saw the slight blush that came to her cheeks, but she was unafraid to meet the warrior's eyes. She had feelings for him as well, Peder assessed. He would need to find out more about what has happened to his sister while she'd been away. Peder tightened his hands into fists. Rafn had better have the right answers.

Dagstyrr came and took Kata's hand and led her to the chair beside him. He smiled in appreciation of her beauty as he held the chair back from him. Kata blushed at the look he gave her as he sat next to her.

She leaned towards him so that she might whisper. "How are things?" She watched Rafn hold out the seat next to the Eorl, and Seera sat between father and brother, while Rafn returned to sit beside Dagstyrr. It was a good sign that he'd not insisted on Seera sitting beside him.

Dagstyrr chuckled quietly. "Lord Peder hasn't thrown him in the dungeon yet."

"Let's hope it doesn't come to that."

The servants came and served them. It seemed that supper was to be a private affair that evening. They ate in relative silence save for the occasional question, usually between Dagstyrr and the Eorl.

When the food was cleared away and night had turned black, Peder finally rose and looked to Rafn.

"Now we talk in private," he demanded.

"Let it be." Rafn joined him.

"Brother!" Seera tried to stop him, but Peder gave her a stern look.

"If you have any hope of a wedding," he said. "Do not interfere."

Seera could only watch them leave, hoping that the talk didn't include weapons of any kind. She glanced at Kata who watched in sympathy.

CHAPTER 15

Peder led Rafn to a room that looked to be a library. There were a few shelves containing books set beside a stone hearth in the center of the room, where a fire had been lit. A servant entered with mugs of ale, which he placed on a desk before ducking out.

"You have books." Rafn ran his hand over the leather bound tomes.

"Seera loves to read." Peder informed him and was pleased by Rafn's surprise.

"I did not know that about her." Rafn lowered to one of the two high backed chairs set before the hearth.

"Our mother was a Saxon, from King Alfred's court in Wessex. He has many scribes working to produce books for him. He encourages those around him to learn to read. My mother was one of them. Seera gets the interest from her."

"You do not read?" Rafn accepted one of the mugs from Peder before the man took a seat.

"I know how, but I do not care to spend my time doing so," Peder answered. "I prefer a more vigorous pastime." This was something Rafn understood.

"I will have to get her to teach me," Rafn said. He looked up to find Peder regarding him closely. He sampled the ale in his hand, but fought the urge to drink deeply.

"You love her?" Peder's direct and very personal question surprised Rafn.

He choked on the ale, coughing to dislodge the liquid from his lungs. His shock dissipated and he realized Peder expected an honest answer. He shrugged, deciding to offer complete honesty.

"Aye."

Peder's ale remained untouched as he twirled it in his hand. His jaw tightened before his next question. "You have lain with her?"

"Nay."

Peder watched him for a moment before continuing. "Why not, if you claim she is already yours."

"You want the truth," Rafn asked, turning to face him. "It may be hard for a brother to hear."

"I demand it," Peder said. Rafn nodded in reply.

"A man named Drenger, who was the Jarl of Ribe in Jutland, is the one who took your sister. He was not kind. He took Seera as his slave and he raped her." Peder's eyes flared with anger and he tossed the mug of ale aside, uncaring that it splashed across the hard floor and dented the iron mug as it smashed against the stone wall. He motioned for Rafn to finish.

"She is a courageous woman," the warlord told him, and Peder did not mistake the look of admiration in Rafn's eyes. He added that to his assessment of the man. "She fought back and was badly beaten. She tried to escape from the village but Drenger caught her and tied her to the punishment post and had her whipped."

Peder's rage grew as the story continued. Vengeance for his sister's pain was foremost in his mind, but he forced himself to listen.

"I was there that night, hidden in the shadows with my warriors."

"Why were you there?" Peder caught the pain that reflected for an instant on Rafn's face. Another bit of information.

Rafn growled and Peder could have sworn he heard a crash of thunder, yet the night remained clear out the small window in the library. "Drenger killed my younger brother. I was there to plunge my sword through his gut and watch him die."

"Then my sister has been avenged as well," Peder said. "I owe you for ending the bastard's life."

"It was not by my hand that he died." Rafn scowled and made no attempt to hide how that still upset him. "Seera took the knife I had strapped to my leg and while I fought him, she put it through his back."

Peder stared at him in shock. "My sister killed him?"

His nostrils flared dangerously. "Aye."

"And that is why you claimed her?" Peder was a Christian and did not follow the same code of honor that those who followed the Norse gods did, yet he understood fully how a Viking would view the circumstances. "She is a Christian woman and does not share your beliefs."

"She understands fully why I took her."

"I want to hear now, why it is you have not lain with her." Peder wanted him to say it.

"She has been taken forcibly once already. When she comes to my bed it shall be as my wife and she will be willing."

"Then you honor her." Peder was beginning to see things clearly. This warrior from Skiringssal, honored and respected Seera, he admired her courage and strength. And she had taken his heart.

"Perhaps my first impression of you was wrong, Rafn Vakrson," Peder admitted. "If you place such value on Seera, then maybe I will bless your marriage."

"There is one more thing you should know," Rafn said.

"What is that?" Peder's suspicion was raised again.

"On the way here, we stopped for a night and a dozen of us took the women ashore so they could have a break from the ship," Rafn said. "Seera had gone to wash by a stream and was attacked by a man claiming to have been sent by Hwal. He was second in command to Drenger, therefore probably the current Jarl."

"And the man?"

"I sent him back to Ribe severely beaten with a message to Hwal."

"And what was the message," Peder asked.

"That I would see him dead," Rafn replied as Peder nodded in understanding and agreement.

Seera went down to the Great Hall in search of Peder. She had risen early in hopes of catching him still at breakfast. To her dismay she found the hall empty. Her brother needed to hear her out, he'd interrogated Rafn long enough.

She dismissed a maid who tried to offer something to eat. She would think about food later, after she'd obtained Peder's blessing.

Movement from a small doorway drew her attention. Shock coursed through her as a man stepped into the hall. She was seeing a ghost. It was the only explanation, for the man standing before her was dead. She saw him killed by a deadly blade and left to die among the others.

"Jakob," Seera said. She approached the man with caution, still reluctant to credit her eyes with what she saw. A genuine smile of joy crept across her face.

"Lady Seera," he bowed slightly, a look of adoration washing his face. "I am glad to see you returned safely. It has haunted me that I was unable to protect you."

"We were overpowered by men who'd been trained to kill. I do not blame you." She brought her hands to her mouth and suppressed the need to laugh with sheer pleasure. "I am happy that you are alive."

"It is a surprise to my own self," Jakob said. "If Peder hadn't found me in time, I would have bled to death. As it was it took weeks of recovery."

Seera spontaneously hugged him, causing the man to blush. He hugged her in return, for a moment giving into the need to hold her in his arms. He had loved her for many years. Since they were first leaving childhood behind and growing into the adults they would become. She had no idea and he planned never to tell her.

"Have you seen my brother?" Seera stepped away from him and smoothed out her skirts.

"He is on the training field with the Vikings that you brought home with you." Jakob's voice tightened with disapproval and weariness. A look of fear crossed his face, and Seera was sensitive to it.

"They are not like the others."

"I beg your pardon?" Jakob lost the distant look that had come to his eyes to focus on her.

"They are not like the Jutland warriors who attacked us. Fierce they are, but they are also honorable."

"You have gotten to know them so well?" Jakob studied her closely, searching for the truth behind her words. He noticed the redness that rose on her cheeks and the way she fidgeted with the gold torc around her neck. It was one he'd not seen before.

"Aye, Lord Rafn is to be my husband, and I would very much like your good wishes."

Jakob stared at her in shock for a moment, before he recovered his voice. Even then he had to clear it before he could speak. A stab of jealousy hit him that he'd been unprepared for. He had known someday she would marry another, but to marry a Viking after he'd been so viciously attacked was more than he could take.

"Your brother has allowed a marriage to that man?" His surprise caused him to speak too frankly. "He would give you to such a violent man?"

"He is not violent," Seera snapped at him, feeling rather defensive of the man she was coming to love. "He is courageous, and he is strong. He fights his enemies with deadly force, but only when he needs to. He is not like Drenger or Hwal, who kill for the pleasure of it. Who hurt and rape, and sacrifice good decent people. He is kind enough to rescue a battered woman from a hell not of her making, and make her his wife."

Seera's face grew hot with anger. Jakob took a step back having realized too late that he had overstepped his boundaries. A look of contrition seized his face.

"I am sorry. I did not mean…" Seera was embarrassed by her outburst.

Jakob held up a hand to stop her apology. "It is I that am sorry. That day still grips me. I could not save you. I couldn't stop them. I am not a warrior like your betrothed. I…"

"Hush," she cut him off. "You don't need to be. You have always been a loyal companion and friend. That you live is all that is important."

"And that you are home and safe. If Lord Rafn is the reason why, then he has my gratitude, for you have ever been my friend. If a marriage will bring you happiness, then I can only give you my fondest hope that it will continue to do so."

"Thank you." She hugged him again, needing to know their friendship was still intact.

This time he did not hesitate, but allowed himself to feel her body pressed against his, for it would never happen again.

Seera left Jakob and hurried off to the area set aside for soldier training. What was Peder trying to prove? He was done interrogating so now he needed to prove Rafn's strength. She shook her head in frustration.

She came upon them parrying back and forth with their longswords. They were both shirtless and sweating despite the chill in the air. There was no question that both these men were powerful warriors.

Their swords clanked together, back and forth. Their feet moving in a perfectly timed danced as they stepped first one way than the other. Seera stopped to admire the perfection of Rafn's solid body, marred only by a scar on his left shoulder. Where her brother had hair growing on his chest, Rafn had none to hide his molded muscles. She forgot for a moment how to breathe and had to suck in a deep breath.

Dagstyrr appeared beside her and she spared a brief glance in his direction. He had a smile on his face that told her plain enough that he knew what she'd been thinking.

"Your brother is determined to prove Rafn's worth," Dagstyrr spoke what Seera had already realized.

"And is Rafn holding his own?"

"I would not doubt that Rafn will measure up," he said. "Lord Peder will be left with no illusions of his strength."

"Good." She turned red when Dagstyrr chucked.

The men stopped when they noticed her and walked over to join her. Seera scowled at her brother before turning her attention to Rafn.

"I am glad to see that Peder has left you whole."

Rafn raised an eyebrow before bowing his head briefly. "He has tried admirably, but he can't touch me."

"He has no modesty this man of yours." Peder shook his head, but he was smiling and that was encouragement…and about Rafn being hers…

"And do you brother?" She rolled her eyes at him, causing him to roar with laughter.

"I suppose not."

Seera stared at him with a threat in her eyes. "Are you finished with him yet? Can you release him so that I might show him around?"

Peder's face reflected amusement. He regarded her as she stood with hands on hips, ready to fight him. "He is yours sister." He waved his hand in surrender. "Come Dagstyrr, let us find ourselves something to eat."

"It would be my pleasure." Dagstyrr followed her brother across the courtyard, leaving her alone with Rafn. She felt a tingle of nerves at having been so bold.

"My lady, what would you like to show me?" Rafn met her eyes and their darkness shimmered, then seemed somehow lighter, more a dark grey than the midnight color they usually were. His face held a smug pleasure that she'd demanded his presence.

"I'd like to take you riding." Her mouth went dry, but she spoke her wish before she lost her nerve.

"I would enjoy that." He touched light fingers to her face.

"Good," she said. At least she thought she spoke, as his fingers brushed her lips.

"Would I be permitted to wash first?" A devastating smile streaked his face and she almost failed to answer.

"Of course, I'll meet you in the barn when you are done."

Not waiting for him to reply, she walked across the courtyard. She felt his eyes watching her the entire way.

Peder led Dagstyrr into the Great Hall and summoned one of the servants to bring them something to eat. The Eorl was already there and they went to join him.

"Good morning," Airic said as the young men joined him.

"Morning Father."

"Greetings," Dagstyrr said and sat down opposite the Eorl and beside Peder.

"What do you think of the Warlord of Skiringssal," Airic asked without delay, unconcerned about talking so freely in front of Rafn's second in command.

"So far he has proved worthy." Peder spoke honestly and smiled at Dagstyrr's intent gaze. "I have yet to test his hunting skills, but his warrior's skill is as good as mine, perhaps better."

"You are generous in your praise," Dagstyrr said.

"I am honest. I would expect no less from a man who is to be my brother-in law."

"So you believe we should let the wedding proceed," Airic asked.

"Rafn has shown her respect. He has honored her by not lying with." Peder wouldn't speak of the rape. It was something a father should not have to hear, even if he suspected it might be true.

"He has also told me he loves her." Peder noted the surprise on Dagstyrr's face as he shifted beside him. The man chuckled.

"How did you get to him to admit such a thing? I have seen the truth, but couldn't wrestle a confession from him."

Peder's laugh joined the Vikings. "I can be persuasive."

"You will have to tell me your secret." Dagstyrr shrugged his shoulders as he sat back in his chair.

A serving girl appeared to slide a tray of cold meats and cheese on the table. Another placed a tray with hot tea. She poured them each a cup before leaving.

"Then we have a wedding to plan." Airic announced as he sipped the bitter brew.

"A wedding," Dagstyrr echoed.

In the land of secret beauty, the warrior woman danced and spun as the power of the goddess filled her. Though Freyja was known as the goddess of love and not one sought by warriors, it mattered not.

The warrior woman was one of her followers as was her sister. They were part of a group called the Disir, who worshipped the goddess.

So as the warrior woman practiced with the sword she had taken off the one she'd slain before their escape, she knew the goddess blessed her. It pleased her that the sword was newly forged and had yet to be used in battle. When she had first seen it, she had known it was hers.

Through each sun she had practiced with bow and arrow, spear and axe. Finally it was time for the sword, the weapon of the elite warrior class, noble men who were born to fight. She was neither noble nor a man, but it did not stop her from learning how to use the powerful blade.

Its hilt was finely etched and its blade was forged by an expert wielder. It was perhaps too large for a woman, but that would not stop her from making it her own.

She felt the magic touch her feet as she stepped lightly and moved as she'd seen countless warriors do.

If the men had been amazing to watch, then she could only be described as elegant. Her feet barely left a mark where they touched, and the whirring of the blade through the air was like a song born on the wind.

She had but to imagine the enemy she would face, feel the goddess fill her and her arm was true and swift.

The sword had only to meet the flesh of another and then it would be complete.

CHAPTER 16

Rafn met Seera in the stables. She was just brushing down a pair of horses and saddling them. They were beautiful animals with coats the color of wet dirt. The only difference between them was that one had a streak of white down its forehead.

"I had a lunch packed for us." Seera peered over her shoulder at him as she finished securing a sack to her saddle.

"Then we are set." Rafn studied her with a deep appreciation as he accepted the reins she held out for him. He gripped the leather in his hands without thought as she turned from him and headed for the stable doors. His eyes didn't leave her as he followed...for there was nothing he wished to do more.

They led the horses out through the gate and walked them across the narrow piece of land that served as a bridge from the rock to the mainland. Rafn looked down at the parallel cliffs that fell straight down on either side of him. It was an impressive sight.

Once on the other side they mounted and Seera led him down a path that led along the top of one of the cliffs. The trees of the forest had already been touched with the turning of the season. Instead of thick green foliage they traveled through a canopy of reds and yellows. Occasionally a leaf would fall in front of them. It reminded Rafn that soon the waters would be impassable. He needed to be back in Skiringssal before that happened.

They rode until the sun was high in the sky, at which time Seera led her horse into a small clearing beside a sharp cliff. Before them was a clear view of the sea. It was one of those places that she had come often before her innocence had been harshly taken. She hoped to capture again the peace the place had always brought.

They tied the horses by a green patch of wild grasses so they might have their own feast. Seera reached into a bag attached to her horse's saddle and brought out a blanket which she spread for them to sit on. She then took out a meal of bread, cheese, fruit and small apple cakes baked fresh that morning. Rafn enjoyed just watching her as she arranged the food on the blanket. Only once she settled herself did he move to join her.

At first Seera was very quiet as they each sat and enjoyed the food. She didn't look at him, but out at the vista that spread before them to the ocean in the distance. Occasionally a line would form before her brows as if her thoughts were troubling her. He wanted to reach out and smooth them, to put her mind at ease.

Finally when their meal was done, she broke the silence.

"Tell me something about yourself?" Seera asked him and when he looked at her she had to force herself not to look away from the intensity of his stare.

"What would you know?"

"Tell me something you would never tell your warriors." Her eyes sparkled with a dare as he considered her question. "Something truthful."

His face became smooth and youthful with the corners of his lips raised just a bit. He rubbed at his cleanly shaven chin. "I love the rain. I love the sound of it, the smell of it and the feel of it on my skin. I love the thunder and lightning that charge the world with its energy." He was seeing something in his mind that made him smile.

He shifted to see her better. "Now you," the challenge was written clearly on his face and she had the urge to shock him.

"I like your eyes," she said before she thought better of saying something so intimate. "I like how they gleam when you laugh, and how they crinkle at the corners."

Rafn was so stunned by her admission that he couldn't stop himself from roaring out in laughter. A smile washed across her face that turned her from beautiful to enchanting.

"I never know what to expect with you." His hand found the back of her neck as he leaned over to brush her lips with a soft kiss.

A mischievous imp took control of her words. "I hate being predictable." A giggle bubbled forth at her confession. He was leaning in to kiss her again when the expression on his face changed. It went from smooth to hard so quickly that she was startled by his sudden alertness.

His gaze shifted to the horses. One of them had become spooked, which had triggered him to be on the alert. The horse was pulling against the rope that held him in place. The other one began to fidget as well. Rafn was on his feet the next moment and trying to place the danger.

"Stay here," Rafn ordered after she'd risen. Satisfied that she would obey him, he made his way cautiously to the stallion closest to him.

"Whoa there boy," he held out his hand and approached slowly. He placed a hand on the horses flank and started to sooth him.

In a blur something tore out of the bush nearby, brushing by Rafn and heading straight for Seera. Instinctively Rafn grabbed the axe he'd left attached to the horses saddle.

Seera stared in stunned silence as a large boar with very large tusks came tearing out of the bush towards her. It charged her, forcing her to step backwards, until the ground beneath disappeared and she felt herself falling. She let out a scream.

"Seera," Rafn yelled as he saw her go over the cliff. The boar snorted in frustration at its lost prey and turned towards Rafn just as he released the axe with deadly accuracy.

He didn't wait to see if his aim was true before he ran for the cliff's edge. His heart was clenched in terror and he was sure that she was dead. He dropped to the ground and peered over the edge.

Sitting on a ledge about six feet down was Seera. Relief flooded him as he called out to her.

"Are you alright?" She looked up at his bellow with a stunned expression.

"Aye." She scrambled to her feet, using the cliff wall to steady her. "But I would like off this ledge if you wouldn't mind."

"Be right back," he replied with a laugh born from the release of his tension.

He yanked the axe from the skull of the boar and chopped down a young tree. He stripped it of its branches then returned to the ledge. Seera was leaning against the cliff wall, staring down the steep drop that would have killed her if she'd missed the ledge. Thank Thor that she hadn't.

"Grab on." She turned and gripped the tree sapling. "Don't let go."

Rafn pulled with all his strength until she crested the edge and he pulled her to him. He landed on his back with her on top of him. Their eyes met, their hearts pounded, and there was only one thing Rafn could do. He put his hand on the back of her head and pulled her down, until her mouth was on his.

Seera responded to his kiss. While his mouth still claimed hers, he rolled them away from the edge, ending with her beneath him. Her mouth opened to him and his tongue sought hers. She felt a tingling sensation deep within her.

"I was so afraid," he mumbled, between kisses, "that I had lost you." Lips crushed together in desperation. A fire rose between them, locking them in a moment of selfish need.

"Don't you ever," he said breathlessly before claiming her mouth again, then pulling back enough to finish "do that again!"

Seera heard the rawness in his voice and wondered where it came from. She had not expected such emotion from him.

Rafn managed to stop kissing her long enough to look into her eyes. He saw confusion and a question in their green depths.

"Don't you know how much I love you woman," he answered her silent plea to understand. Her eyes widened with surprise

"You love me?"

He simply smiled and answered with a kiss. One that left no doubt as to how he felt. He gave into the sensation of her, melting to her warmth. One moment, then another passed, before he broke free.

"They will be awaiting our return." Rafn pried himself from her and helped her up.

Seera was breathing in rapid gasps, her pulse racing, but she knew he was right to stop. "Aye, we should be getting back."

Rafn had said he loved her. The unbelievable words echoed through her. She knew she was smiling like a fool, but each time she looked at him he was staring at her. She had to look somewhere else...anywhere else. Her attention was drawn to the boar.

"How are we going to get it home?"

Rafn smiled. "I have an idea."

He dragged the boar to the horses and threw it on the back of Seera's mount. He lashed the boar to the saddle, making sure it would be secure for the ride back. He turned to Seera who was looking at him with a frown.

"What am I suppose to ride?"

Rafn jumped on to the back of the stallion and held out his hand to her. She took it and he swung her up in front of him. He wrapped one of his arms around her waist and held her against him.

"Comfortable?" He spoke softly into her ear. She peeked over her shoulder to see his teasing grin.

They rode up to the land bridge and dismounted so they could lead the animals across on foot. The guards nodded to them as the passed through the gate. They were met on the other side by Peder. He examined the boar before saying anything to them.

"How did you kill this pig?" He studied it with interest. "The wound was not made by a spear."

"It was made by an axe," Rafn said.

"An axe? Bringing an axe down into its skull is an interesting technique. You must have been close to the animal." Peder looked at him astonishment.

"I was across the clearing." Peder looked at him in confusion, before Rafn clarified. "I threw the axe."

"It was thrown?" Peder was surprised. "I have heard of such a thing, but have never met anyone who could actually throw an axe with any accuracy."

"Now you have." Rafn smirked with arrogance.

"Why did you not use a bow and arrow?"

"I didn't bring them with me," Rafn looked to Seera and shook his head. "Besides it was an instant reaction to a threat. The boar had just run Seera off a cliff."

"What!" Peder stared at Seera in shock. "Must I lock you away to keep you from harm?"

"Nay brother," Seera said. "I am fine as you can see, thanks to Rafn."

"It would seem that you are always around to save my sister," Peder said to the warrior.

"Enough," Seera complained. "I am tired and would like to clean up before supper." Both men turned to her with mocking smiles. Sighing in exasperation she walked off. Their laughter trailed behind.

After Seera had bathed and dressed, and the tub had been cleared away, Kata arrived in her room. It was evident she was upset as soon as she stepped into the chamber.

"Are you alright?"

"I am fine." Seera took a seat at the vanity to finish her hair.

"I heard you were almost killed?"

Seera laughed lightly, as she pinned a strand away from her face. "Almost might be a bit of an exaggeration. I wasn't even hurt."

"But you fell over a cliff!"

"And landed on a ledge directly below me," Seera said. "It was not even that far down."

Kata shook her head. "But a boar charged you."

She glanced to Kata. "It didn't even touch me. Besides, your brother took care of that nasty beast. We will probably be getting it for supper."

"I heard it was going to be part of your wedding feast." It was Kata's turn to smile at the shocked look on Seera's face.

"My brother has yet to agree."

On cue there was a knock at the door and both women turned to see Peder enter the chamber. Kata excused herself and Seera was left to face her brother.

"Is there something you wish to say?" Seera got right to the point. She had no desire to dance around the issue.

Peder laughed. "It would seem you already know why I am here."

"I want to hear it from you." Seera felt suddenly nervous and had to take a seat on the edge of her bed.

Peder sat down next to her, studying her for a moment before he continued. "I give your marriage my blessing."

"He has measured up to all your tests?" Her tone was disapproving and she was frustrated from all the male boasting. Peder flicked a finger beneath her chin in a familiar gesture from as far back as she could remember.

"He is worthy." His face pinched with seriousness as he searched her eyes. "Is this what you want sister? Rafn may claim you are his, but I will not see it come to pass, if it is not your wish."

"You would fight him?"

"I would." Peder took her hand. "You are a sister to make any brother proud and I would see you happy."

Seera was deeply touched by Peder's affection for her. She squeezed the hands that held hers. "He makes me happy. Trust that I know my own heart."

"You have my trust."

"Then I will be a wife?" A smile crept across Seera's face. Peder pulled her against him and held her tightly for a moment.

"You will, but if he does you wrong, does not keep you safe, I will kill him."

"I love you Peder." Seera touched her hand to his face. "You have always been someone I could count on. I am honored by that."

"I love you also sister," Peder rose and headed for the door. Before he pulled it open he turned to Seera. "The wedding will be the day after tomorrow."

Seera's heart leapt and she found she had no voice to reply. She felt the excitement bubble up inside of her. It was not so long to wait, but it seemed like a lifetime. She wanted it done. She wanted to go to Rafn's bed and feel no fear. Feel only the love that was between them.

The day after tomorrow! It was too long to wait.

That night Seera was restless. She tossed first one way then the other, until her blankets were a rumpled mess. She was first too hot and had to throw the blankets from her, than she was too cold and was dragging them back on.

Moonlight worked its way past the shutters on the window. She found herself watching the way it reflected on the walls. In those moments of wakefulness, she went over the days events. She remembered most vividly the way Rafn had looked at her after the boar attacked. His eyes had been naked and vulnerable, open to her sight. She had felt his emotions touch deep inside her. Touch her heart in a way she had never thought another could.

Two days was so long to wait to be in his arms, and to feel his warmth against her. She stood suddenly and pulled a cloak around her in case she ran into another. Barefoot she crept into the hallway and made her way down to the floor beneath her own. The bed chamber given Rafn was on the far end.

The hall was dimly lit by candle sconces on the wall. It was also empty and quiet. Before her courage failed, she boldly went to his door. She took a calming breath, but it did nothing to slow the beat of her heart.

She eased the door open slowly, not wanting him to wake just yet. She saw him within the shadows of the bed. His blanket was pushed down to his waist and the moonlight from the open window washed over his chest.

Rafn had heard the door open, bringing him instantly awake and alert. His first instinct was to reach for his dagger that he always kept close at hand, until the next moment had brought Seera into the door frame.

He closed his eyes and feigned sleep, unsure of her intentions. He heard her soft slow steps approach until she was beside him. Her cloak fell to the floor.

He had been dreaming of her…and now she was by his bed. He had only to reach out his hand. His jaw tightened. She should not be in his chamber.

He opened his eyes and she stared in shock at their clarity. No dregs of sleep showed in them. But, he was of course a trained warrior. He could come fully awake in a moment.

She heard him grumble and was afraid she had angered him. She knew the instant he lost his battle for self control. He reached out and grabbed her.

Seera landed on top of him, but not for long. He shifted her beneath him and pressed himself against her. His mouth was on hers, hot and demanding. Belatedly she became aware of his nakedness and the hardness between his legs.

She gasped to catch her breath and he pulled back from her to pierce her with his gaze.

"Why are you here Seera?"

"I couldn't sleep," she answered innocently, though if he could feel the pounding of her heart he would know her thoughts were not so.

"So you thought to disturb mine?" He tried to keep the pleasure from his face at her boldness.

"I believed you would not mind." She held his gaze and there was no mistaking the invitation in them.

"Now is not the time Seera," He drew a breath in an attempt to still the rising temptation her nearness brought.

"We are to wed," she argued. Rafn's fingers tangled in her hair. He brought their knotted locks to his nose to breath in their scent. A hint of something flowery still lingered.

"Two days. Then I will give you what you seek."

"And now!" Her temper flared. How dare he turn her away! Did he presume to tell her, her own mind?

"Go Seera, before my control is gone."

"But…"

"I promised your brother, would you see me ruin the trust we have built?" Her anger dissolved at the logic of his words. His head lowered to offer another kiss.

"Nay." She answered his question after he pulled from her. Rafn moved to sit on the edge of the bed.

Seera reluctantly climbed from the bed and reached to pick up her cloak. She looked at him and found that he was watching. He took her hand and brought it to his lips, his eyes remaining on her.

"Soon, my love," he said as he stood to pull her into his arms, and leave her with a final kiss. It spoke a promise of his tenderness and the passion that would burn between them.

She left then, because if she stayed he would break his vow and she could not let him do so.

Rafn was relieved when the door closed behind her. He knew sleep was lost to him that night as he lay back down. Even so a smile crept across his face.

She had come to him.

CHAPTER 17

Rafn waited with impatience as he stood at the front of the stone chapel. He fidgeted with the belt on his black tunic. His equally black trousers hugged his legs comfortably. He had tied his hair back with a leather thong to keep from his face, which he'd freshly shaven when first rising.

Around his neck hung the symbol of his god, Thor's hammer, that he never took off. The Priest scowled openly at its presence in a house of God. The monk had also objected to the jeweled dagger that rested on his hip.

He ignored the man's arguments. Rafn would not be left vulnerable, or the woman he loved left unsafe.

The chapel door had been left open to the clear day beyond. The wind was still, but the air remained crisp to redden the faces of the guests filtering in from the bailey.

Dagstyrr sat in the pew closest to him, dressed in similar attire, though his long sleeved tunic was a deep brown, with lighter trousers. He also carried a dagger on his belt. Rafn glanced to his closest companion as he tugged at the collar of his tunic.

Finally the endless stream of people settled on the pews and a hush descended over them. Rafn focused on the doorway, willing Seera to fill it.

Kata stepped through first, her raven hair bound up at the back of her head, giving her a decidedly mature look. She smiled at him before accepting Peder's arm. Seera's brother led her to the front bench and she took the spot beside Dagstyrr that had been reserved for family. Peder took his seat on the bench across the thin aisle.

Rafn watched the door again and Seera entered on her father's arm. She was a sight to behold in a cream colored gown that flowed to the floor with shimmering beads. The sleeves of her dress hung to her wrists, where they widened with a trailing length of silk.

Her brown hair, naturally highlighted with golden strands, hung freely to her waist and was pinned only on top where it held a thin veil of lace that trailed down her back. Her neckline was squared, creating a perfect view of the torc that encircled her ivory neck. The emerald caught the candlelight as she walked towards him.

The matching color of her eyes sparkled when they met his. A peaceful light, that none could see, reached out to encompass him, pushing deep the dark storm.

Rafn could not take his eyes from her, this woman who was about to become his wife. Freyja was certainly responsible for placing this woman in his path. For Thor would not trouble himself with such an emotion as love.

Seera reached out her hand and Rafn closed his own around it. With hands clasped they turned towards Father Albert. The Priest spoke words of love and fidelity, honor and protection. They spoke words that bound them together as one and made solemn vows to love one another until death separated them.

And the thunder inside of Rafn stayed quiet through it all.

It was a happiness that Seera had not expected to find, and in a Viking warrior from a land not her own. He married her in a Christian ceremony, though he was not, and this told her that he respected her.

A feast was held in the Great Hall and the boar was indeed served as part of the ceremonial dinner.

"I would like to bless Lord Rafn and Lady Seera," Dagstyrr rose with a mug of ale and lifted it to the couple. "To a strong marriage!" he lifted the mug and downed the ale to the cheers of the assembled people.

"To my sister and new brother-in law," Peder said, bringing another loud response from the feasters.

Airic, not wanting to be left out of the toast, stood also. "And to the many grandchildren they shall bring me." This caused laughter from the gathers, a smile from Rafn and a blush from Seera.

Many dishes were brought before the couple, but Seera found she could only sample a small portion of each. Her stomach was tied in knots of anticipation as the feast came to an end and their first step as a married couple was to be taken.

They went not to the bed chamber that had always been Seera's, but to a larger room given to them by her father. It was more appropriate for a couple than the girlish room that had seen Seera grow from a child into a woman.

Seera was stunned to find that the chamber had been decorated with many candles and flower petals strewn on the bed, preserved from the last flowers of the season. The fire had been lit, and by the warmth of the room, had been for some time.

Rafn shut the door and Seera was absorbed by a sudden shyness to this inevitable moment. He took her hand and led her further inside, until nothing stood between them and the bed. The time that Seera had both longed for and feared was upon them and she had only to trust it.

Rafn saw her hesitation and knew the reason. He felt for her. For the trauma she'd been through, but she was now his wife and it was their wedding night. He would wait no more to lay his final claim.

"Trust in me, my love," he said as he turned her to face him.

She saw in his eyes the desire that consumed him and felt her body react to it. This was the man she loved, the man she trusted. She did not move away when he pulled her to him and kissed her.

He worked at the ribbons that held her dress closed, until he had it off and thrown somewhere close to the hearth.

He lifted her in his arms swiftly and brought her down onto the bed. Her nakedness did not concern her as he too stripped himself of his clothing.

She was feeling so many different things at once that she felt drunk, though she'd had but a little wine. He towered above her, with the light of the fire softening his skin to orange.

It did nothing to hide the stark maleness of his hard body. The strength in his muscles could overpower her easily, but she did not fear him, or what he was about to do. Thoughts of Drenger vanished as if they never were and she thanked God for taking the memories from her so she could be a good wife.

They came together, gentle at first and then with an overpowering desire that neither could control. When Rafn filled her it was not with pain, but with a fervor that Seera didn't know that she could feel.

Their bodies molded together, and a healing light encompassed them both. Rafn knew beyond doubt that he'd found the missing part of his soul in his delicate wife.

A languid happiness kept Seera sleeping far into the morning. The warmth of Rafn's body lay up next to her. She squirmed closer to him and let the dreamy sensation control her awhile longer.

It was mid day before Rafn finally stirred and stared at her with unveiled contentment that she had never seen in his eyes before. His fierceness was always reflected in them to some degree, whether it was full blown or just simmering beneath the surface. Never had it be absent before. It made him seem so much younger.

"What is it you are smiling at?" Rafn questioned the strange look upon her face.

"Just that I like seeing you like this?" Her eyes reflected the truth of her words.

"And how is that?"

"Happy." She laughed at the puzzled look on his face.

"And why should I not be happy, wife?"

"I never said you shouldn't." Seera shook her head. "I am just glad that you are so."

His expression turned serious. "I am happy." He reached out his hand to her and traced the smoothness of her face, the fullness of her lips.

At the touch of his fingers against her face, she felt her body spark with wanting and wondered at his effect on her. Certainly she was tired from their long night of lovemaking. How could her traitorous body want more?

Rafn almost responded to the invitation in her eyes, but he held himself back. He'd been unable to control himself through the long night, wanting her over and over again. He must give her rest, and something to eat.

"I am hungry." He sprang from the bed, his voice booming to the rafters. Seera laughed at her fierce warrior as he stood naked and demanding before her.

"Agata should have left food in the corridor," Seera said.

Rafn peered through the door to confirm no one was about and lifted the tray that had been left them. Taking it into to bed with them, they ate as if they hadn't in a fortnight. Only once their appetite for food was fulfilled did they turn to satisfying a more pleasurable hunger.

And Rafn found his peace.

Rafn and Seera stayed in their chamber for three days before anyone finally saw them. Rafn found Dagstyrr and Peder on the practice ground when he ventured outside for some fresh air.

"Well brother-in law," Peder raised his eyebrow at the extremely contented man. "It would seem that being a husband agrees with you."

"It would appear so." Dagstyrr grinned mockingly at his friend.

"As two who are yet unwed, you can't know the satisfaction I feel," Rafn smiled in reply.

"I can imagine." Dagstyrr rolled his eyes.

"It is best you not explain to thoroughly," Peder warned. "She is still my sister."

"It would be best," Rafn agreed, causing Dagstyrr to laugh.

"What now my lord," Dagstyrr asked. "Now that you have done what you came here to do."

"Now we go to see the King," Peder answered for him. "For an alliance is still to be discussed."

"I look forward to meeting with King David. I have a message from King Harald to give him."

"We should leave at once. I will inform my father of our departure."

"I will inform my wife." Rafn nodded to Peder as he left.

"I will get my things," Dagstyrr said. He turned to go, but Rafn stopped him with a sharp command. He looked to his warlord in disbelief.

"You are to stay here to watch my wife and sister. There is still a threat to Seera and I will have her watched by someone I trust."

"My lord," Dagstyrr started to protest.

Rafn cut off his argument. "I will not be challenged in this."

Dagstyrr relented. "Then I will see it done."

Seera was even less pleased to be left behind than Dagstyrr. She had pleaded with him to allow her to ride by his side, but she was thwarted by not only Rafn but Peder as well. Neither man wanted her to leave the protection of the Fortress.

"How could harm come to me in the presence of two such warriors as my husband and brother?" Seera complained to Kata as they stood on the battlements, watching the two men crossing the thin land bridge.

All too soon the trees consumed the men and she could no longer see them. She had not expected to be parted so soon from her new husband. Already she missed his arms around her. Her bed would be cold that night. She sighed in frustration.

"His absence will not be so long," Kata tried to comfort the new bride.

Seera pouted. "It will feel so."

"Come, let us go amuse ourselves in his absence." Her friend pulled her from her vigil on the wall.

"What trouble shall we find?"

"I would like a walk outside the walls. I have yet to venture past the courtyard."

"Then I will get lunch from the cook to bring with us." Seera's mood brightened with the idea of getting out.

"Make sure you get enough for three."

She stopped to look at Kata in surprise. "Why?"

"Because Dagstyrr has been appointed our bodyguard and will certainly not allow us far from his sight."

"He didn't?" Seera was shocked.

"You might as well get used to a shadow." She chuckled at her brother's audacity for not informing his wife. "We will not lose him."

"Then three it is." Seera shook her head. She would have a talk with Rafn when he returned.

True to Kata's words, as soon as they stepped out through the gate, Dagstyrr was behind them. He kept back to give them their privacy, but he made no secret of his presence.

Kata felt sorry for Dagstyrr. It was beneath his rank as Rafn's second in command, to be stuck babysitting two women. Though when she looked at him, he only smiled in greeting, showing none of the anger he must be feeling at such a post.

As a warrior he wouldn't complain, even if he didn't like his task. Kata knew that Rafn had only assigned him as bodyguard, because he trusted that man more than any other. No one else would be worthy enough to guard his new bride.

Kata suppressed her smile at Rafn's protectiveness of Seera. Then her face dropped in sadness. Orn would have been pleased to see Rafn find such a love. To see that there was someone that could reach past Rafn's hard exterior to the man on the inside.

Kata looked at her new sister-in law. Did Seera understand how special she was? No other woman had ever been able to get close to the mighty Viking warrior of Skiringssal.

And plenty had tried.

Later in the day the women went to see Father Albert. He was new to Dun'O'Tir. The Eorl had invited him to this posting for more than a need for a new priest. It was because he'd been trained at the scriptorium in Wessex to be a scribe.

Airic had commissioned him to make books to expand his small library. He had selected one to give to Seera as a wedding gift and is why she went to see him on her father's request.

"Greetings ladies," Father Albert bowed as they entered the small room he used to make his books. A large window was along one wall and gave adequate lighting.

The priest was in the process of making ink when they arrived and his hands were black with it.

"May we watch?" Seera had always wanted to see how it was done.

"It would be a pleasure."

Seera and Kata kept silent as they watched the monk crushing something into a fine powder.

"What is that?" Seera inquired.

"It is guals, which are growths caused by insects in oak trees. I scrap them from the tree and then when they're dried out, I must crush them to powder, as you have seen."

"Then what do you do," Kata asked.

"I will add it to boiling water until I have a mixture that resembles tea. When the ink is ready, I use it on parchment made from smoothed animal skin, which I bind into books."

When he was done he handed Seera a wrapped package, which contained the new tome her father wanted her to have. Tears came to her eyes when she realized the book was about Dun'O'Tir, with hand drawn pictures and text of the castle and surrounding lands.

"To remember your home," her father said as he entered the room.

"It is wonderful." She hugged him. "I will treasure it always." When she was far from this place, beginning her new life in Skiringssal with her Viking husband, she thought.

CHAPTER 18

Seera and Kata had taken a walk on the beach and then sat down on some boulders to simply watch the waves rolling in. Seera was trying to hide a smile when she glanced at Kata, and found her trying to stare at Dagstyrr without him seeing her.

Dagstyrr had followed them each time they left the castle. He stayed at a distance, so as not to intrude on their privacy, but he watched them closely. It was on the second day they had ventured outside the wall that Seera realized Kata's attraction to Rafn's second in command.

Dagstyrr was a handsome man. Not in the same roguish way as her husband, but he was pleasant to look at with his auburn hair and infectious smile that appeared so easily on his face. Rafn did not smile so. He was far more serious and private.

"You should invite him to join us." Seera's suggestion caused Kata to look at her nervously.

"I couldn't."

"Then I will." Seera rose and went to him before Kata could stop her.

Dagstyrr watched her approaching and kept his eyes fixed on her. His gaze slid past her to Kata, who'd followed, as Seera hoped she would.

Seera saw his eyes light with delight. The feelings went both ways, she was happy to discover. Kata stood silently before her, and Seera wondered why she should suddenly be so quiet with a man she'd know all her life. They had spoken many times. What had changed?

Kata and Dagstyrr continued to stare at each other and Seera realized that neither would speak first. Rolling her eyes, she broke the silence.

"We would like to know if you would join us while we eat," Seera asked him and caught the surprise cross briefly across his face. "There is no need for you to sit here alone."

"It would be my pleasure to join the company of two fine ladies as you." Dagstyrr spoke not to her but to Kata.

He chose to sit next to Kata and Seera began to feel like she should perhaps leave them alone. They didn't speak of anything personal, but there was something unspoken between them. It made her smile to see Kata caught in the same web that had trapped her.

Love was an odd emotion. It could make you feel safe and vulnerable all at the same time. But she would not want to give it up.

She sighed silently as she felt the ache of loneliness. She missed Rafn. She knew he would be back in a few days time, but she found the waiting hard.

A wind picked up off the water and brought with it an icy chill that forced them to head back to the protection of the castle. A storm came with it and was coming in hard. They had not even made it off the beach before the wind blew so hard they could barely walk.

Dagstyrr walked with them, instead of trailing behind this time, helping them up the steep incline when the blustery weather threatened to blow them over.

They reached the Keep before the worst of the storm hit, bringing with it the first snow. Seera stared at the white flakes as they fell from the thickening clouds overhead.

She knew this storm was a warning that they needed to leave soon if they were to make it back to Skiringssal safely. Rafn would want to sail as soon as he returned. She would need to be ready.

"It came in fast," Kata said to her when they began to climb to their bed chambers. Dagstyrr had left them, but not without a long glance at Kata, that left her feeling off balance.

"This time of year they often do," Seera said. "I think I will go for a nap, I am feeling somewhat tired."

"Yes, of course." Kata watched Seera head up to her chamber. Once she was sure her sister-in law was out of sight, she snuck back down the stairs and was surprised to see that Dagstyrr was still standing at the bottom as if waiting for her.

He turned and smiled at her and she was convinced he had expected her to return. Had she been so obvious with her feelings?

"Once Rafn returns, I will advise him that we should start for home," Dagstyrr told her. "This storm will not last, but winter will soon lay claim to the land, and then we will not make it back."

"I had not thought of that." Kata wasn't sure she was capable of thinking of anything other than him. It was disconcerting.

"Where is Seera?" He looked towards the stairs.

"She was tired and went to lie down."

"And you have no need to rest?"

"I do not." A smile spread across his face that held her prisoner. Why was he affecting her so oddly? This man who'd she'd known forever.

"Let us find some hot tea." Dagstyrr held out his hand to her and she took it without hesitation.

They found a maid in the hall and sent her to fetch the tea. Finding the fire lit in the Great Hall they took a seat in front of it and waited until the servant girl returned with not only tea, but some loaf cake as well.

"Thank you," Kata dismissed the girl and sat silently with Dagstyrr letting the hot drink and the fire warm her.

"Rafn will return soon," Dagstyrr said without looking at her and Kata wondered why he mentioned it.

"Aye, he will."

Kata returned to her bed chamber that night and lay wondering what Rafn would think of the interest she'd developed in his best friend. Would he approve of a relationship between the two?

A rebelliousness rose in Kata, and she realized she didn't care what her brother thought. She wrapped a blanket around her shoulders and crept from her chamber.

She did not knock when she approached his door, but pushed it open with more boldness than she felt. He was standing by the hearth and turned to look at her in surprise when she closed the door behind her.

For a moment she feared he would tell her to leave, but instead he came to her and pulled her towards him. He lifted her into his arms and carried her to his bed. If either thought of what Rafn would do if he caught them together, they did not voice it.

The storm blew itself out by the next morning and the sun returned to fill the sky as Rafn and Peder made their way back to Dun'O'Tir.

"Things went well," Peder said as they rode along a well traveled path.

"I have no complaints," Rafn agreed. "King Harald and my brother should both be pleased with the alliance between us."

"As is King David, he rewarded me with a fine sword for bringing you before him."

Rafn turned a serious gaze on Peder. "I should thank you brother, for not stopping me from marrying your sister."

Peder laughed. "You we're not so inclined to give me a choice."

"It is so, but you could have still refused." Rafn's smile was smug with satisfaction at having won the battle.

Peder's smile faded. "I almost did, but you changed my mind."

"I did my best to do so."

"You are a good man. I know that you will protect my sister with your life."

Rafn's nostrils flared as fierce talons gripped his heart. "I will."

"Then let us get you home to her." Peder kicked his stallion to move faster and Rafn worked hard to catch up. He was not as good on a horse as he was at sea. It would not be good to let Peder know that.

It was late at night when Rafn returned to Dun'O'Tir. Only the guards were still awake. He was tired from the long ride, but he would give his wife a proper greeting all the same.

He found her asleep when he entered their chamber. He stripped his soiled clothing and climbed underneath the blankets to warm his cold skin against her. She stirred.

Her eyes opened sleepily and she turned to him. A smile touched her lips as she came awake.

"I am happy to see you." She snuggled closer to him.

"I have missed you." Rafn kissed her. She responded instantly to his touch and that pleased him.

He made love to her deep into the night, wanting to make up for all the nights he'd had to sleep alone. Finally sated he closed his arms around her and slept more soundly than he had in along time.

Morning came sooner than he'd have liked and he did not want to rise too quickly. But when he reached over to Seera he found her gone. He sat and searched the room, but she was not there. His eyes hardened at her absence. He didn't like that she was not within his reach.

He made to rise from the bed when the door opened. Seera walked in carrying a tray of hot tea and what was probably their breakfast.

"I did not want Agata coming in and disturbing us, so I went to get the tray before she could bring it," Seera smiled at him and his expression eased.

"It was good of you to think of it."

She set the tray on the table by the hearth. "Your trip went well?"

"As I had hoped it would," he replied. "The snow kept us trapped a day longer than I had wanted, but it retreated."

"We had the snow here as well."

"It makes me realize that we should be leaving for Skiringssal," he warned her. "The water will be treacherous if we wait much longer."

"I had thought you would say that," Seera said. "I have our trunks already packed and ready."

"You are a good wife." Rafn smiled and leaned over to kiss her as she came to sit beside him on the bed.

"I hope you will always think so."

They ate in silence each thinking of what must be done to hasten their departure. Seera would miss her father and brother. She would have to convince Rafn to bring her back in the spring so that she might see them again.

"I should find Dagstyrr," Rafn said when he finished his meal. "Did you see him while you were getting our breakfast?"

"Nay, but I did not linger." With a teasing smile she added without thought to what her words would do. "Perhaps you should check your sister's bed chamber."

Rafn rose from his chair, knocking the remainder of his tea onto the table. "Why would you say such a thing?"

Seera was shocked by the anger in his voice and stood to face him. "It was but a joke, husband. I have noticed while you were gone that Kata seemed to have feelings for Dagstyrr."

"Feelings?" His voice boomed loudly.

"She has not admitted so to me, I may have misinterpreted." Seera tried to explain, but Rafn was no longer listening. She immediately regretted her words. She had failed to anticipate his reaction.

"Stay here." He grabbed his sword from where he'd left it beside the door.

"But…" she tried to stop him.

"Do not interfere." He stormed through the door and Seera was alarmed and feeling guilty. What made her say such a thing?

Rafn reached Kata's chamber and didn't bother to knock. He threw opened the door, his anger barely in check. His suspicion was not misplaced for Kata was not alone.

Kata and Dagstyrr woke at once, his sister pulling the blanket against her for protection. But his second in command, his friend, jumped from the bed regardless of his nakedness.

"My lord, I can explain." Dagstyrr faced him fearlessly, when no other man would have dared.

Rafn snapped at Kata. "Leave us. Go to my wife."

"Brother, please," she tried to calm him. He pinned her with an angry look and she knew there was no reasoning with him.

"Do not disobey me." His growls had her grabbing the blanket more firmly around her before fleeing out the door.

Dagstyrr had not moved to put on his clothing, but stood vulnerable and weaponless before his warlord.

Rafn raised his sword and pressed the tip of into Dagstyrr's chest. A trickle of blood ran down the man's skin, but he did not flinch. It took all of Rafn's will power not to push the blade into his flesh.

"Did you think I would not find out?"

"I had not intended to keep it from you," Dagstyrr replied.

"She is my sister." He spoke through clenched teeth, fighting the thunder that was responding to his anger.

Dagstyrr did not let fear show on his face. This was a man who was like a brother and he placed his trust in their friendship. "I am in love with her."

Rafn's face softened into disbelief and he lowered the sword and turned his back on Dagstyrr as he thought about his friend's words. Dagstyrr took this opportunity to grab his trousers and pull them on. He didn't like being quite so vulnerable.

"You love her?" Rafn looked back at him, his emotions pulled precariously under control.

"If anyone can understand the effect that has on a man, I thought it would be you."

"I did not expect this." His fingers caught in his hair as he began to pace the width of the chamber.

"I have had feelings for Kata for a long time."

Rafn watched him closely, looking for signs that his words were false. He saw at once they were not. "You have never mentioned it."

"I believed she would never return my affection so I did not see any reason to speak of it."

"But she does. At least that is what Seera has concluded." He looked towards the bed and the anger flashed again in his eyes. He raised the sword again but did not approach Dagstyrr.

"You will wed. The moment we are back in Skiringssal, I will see it done."

"I will marry her," Dagstyrr said. "It is what I want."

"That is good, but even if it were not so, I would make you marry her. You have taken her innocence and you will give her your protection in return."

"Aye, my lord."

Rafn lowered his sword. "Finish getting dressed. We have much to do before we depart for home."

Dagstyrr nodded and only when Rafn had left did he sit on the bed and sigh in relief. That could have gone a lot worse, he thought.

Then he smiled.

The dream had come again in the night, the one that had brought the Seer and her warrior sister to this place. She rose early, even before the sun had yet to claim the sky. She looked to her sister's bed and found it empty. She'd gone on the hunting trail already. It did not surprise her.

The Seer stepped outside and saw the snow that had fallen in the night. A clear trail of prints cut across its perfection.

"Freyja, goddess, hear my prayer. Keep land and life in your care until its release at winter's end."

She raised her hands above her and let the visions of the night clear in her mind. "When time has come, bring son and mother into our protection. By the goddess' name thy will be safe."

She breathed in the crisp air and smiled as a few flakes began to fall from the cloudy sky. The air was still and the beauty of the whitened world could not be ignored. The Seer stepped out into the early winter day and spun herself around as the snow began to fall thickly.

The cold flakes fell on her warm skin as she twirled and danced with her arms stretched wide and her face turned towards the sky. She marveled at the dizzying affect of the motion and the falling snow that seemed to be endless. Her already pale hair turned even whiter and snow melted on her eyelashes.

She laughed in childish glee, becoming one with the moment, embracing the now, even as echoes of the future slipped from her.

CHAPTER 19

Peder helped Rafn with the loading of the many bridal gifts that the Eorl had insisted on giving the couple, even as Rafn protested that it was too much. Airic waved off his complaints and gave them anyway. Rafn's ship was loaded down as if he was just returning from a trading voyage, yet he'd given nothing in return.

Seera laughed at the expression of disbelief on her new husband's face and the joy that her father had in disconcerting him so. He had found a way to take the control from the arrogant man who'd come demanding his daughter's hand. It was more effective than a confrontation of strength, Seera thought. Her husband did not seek wealth the way other men did and he seemed uncomfortable with it simply being given to him. He felt it wasn't earned.

This spoke strongly to the Eorl of his character and he decided among other reasons, that he liked this man of the north. He was a man with honor and that was all a father could ask of the man who would care for his daughter.

Airic embraced Seera. "I had not thought to lose you so soon. After months of worrying and missing you it would have been nice for you to be here longer."

"I know Papa, but the seas must be crossed now before it becomes too dangerous."

"And there is no hope that you can convince him to stay for the winter?" Airic voiced his hope.

"Nay, he is expected home."

"Then go my daughter and know that my thoughts remain with you." He smiled and touched his hand to her face. "Your mother would be so proud."

Seera went then, before the tears started, turning only once to wave to him standing on the outer wall.

Peder was on the beach waiting for her. Rafn had ordered his men to secure the cargo and was coming to stand beside him.

"I will see you again soon," Peder promised and hugged her affectionately. "It is not so far between us that we will not travel to each other often."

"You are right," Seera said as she stepped from his embrace. "But I will miss you still."

"Take care of her," Peder said to Rafn. "I expect to find her safe and happy the next time I see her."

"I vow it will be so."

Seera boarded the ship with Rafn's assistance and she stood to watch her brother until distance made it impossible to see him. She went to join Kata beneath the tent. She sat quietly, glancing now and then to Dagstyrr where she could see him through the rolled up side of the tent.

"We now have your wedding to look forward to." Seera smiled. Kata looked at her and blushed, but she couldn't have looked more pleased.

They arrived back in Skiringssal without incident and Seera was glad to be off the ship. It had been a cold journey, with icy winds and a scattering of snow on their last day of the voyage. They were close enough to home that the warriors knew where they were going and were able to row on and keep close to the shoreline.

A crowd waited when they pulled up to the dock. Valr stood with his wife and were the first to greet Rafn and Seera when they disembarked.

"It is too cold to stand here," Valr said. "Let us go to the Great Hall and you can tell us of your wedding."

"A drink of mead would not be turned down," Rafn replied. "We have much to discuss."

They went to the hall, followed by Dagstyrr and Kata who glanced nervously at the Jarl. Rafn would inform him, as was his duty. Seera felt for Kata. She knew what it felt like to want the approval of a brother so that you could wed the man you loved.

Once seated before the hearth in the Great Hall, the men began to discuss what had happened with King David. Valr was pleased with the news that Rafn brought home, that an alliance was welcomed and sealed by their marriage.

"So what of the wedding," Geira finally asked. "My husband may not want to hear such pleasantries, but I do."

"And how do you know they were pleasant wife?"

"The smile on her face tells me so."

Seera watched their banter for a moment before speaking up. "It was a beautiful ceremony."

Valr turned to her, his face held as serious as it always was. "And your brother had no objections?"

Seera laughed before admitting. "He did not like Rafn's arrogance, but your brother's charm soon won him over."

"Not before he tested my skills at everything he could think of," Rafn said. "I still have bruises to prove it."

"I like him already." Just the corner of his mouth lifted to betray his enjoyment.

"Which brings me to another matter that must be settled," Rafn looked to Kata as he spoke, which caused her to squirm. Valr was instantly alerted by the action and his eyes narrowed suspiciously.

"What would that be brother?"

"Another wedding will take place before this week is done."

"And who will wed?" Valr looked at Kata as if he already knew the answer. She smiled in reply.

"Kata is to wed Dagstyrr. Neither one are to be given a choice. The decision is mine and will not be refuted."

"Is that so brother?" Valr turned a cold stare on Dagstyrr, who met it without flinching. "And why would that be?"

"Kata is already his and he will abide by our laws and take care of her and any child that she may carry." Rafn's declaration caused Kata to redden in embarrassment. Seera took her hand in comfort. Certainly Rafn didn't have to so publicly scold her.

But then it was not so public. It was just family, and Valr as the eldest brother and head of the family had every right to know what had transpired between his sister and one of his warriors.

"Then there will be no delay," Valr said to Kata. "You have two days to make the arrangements and then it will be done."

Dagstyrr smiled at Kata and Valr's expression eased at the obvious love he saw in the other man's eyes.

Two days later a ceremony was held in the Great Hall. It was done according to Norse law. It differed from the Christian ceremony that had been Rafn and Seera's, but it was beautiful all the same.

Dagstyrr moved into the home that Kata lived in for he did not have a dwelling of his own. He'd always slept in the warriors lodging.

All was good. Seera adjusted to her new life with surprise that she could feel at home someplace other than Dun'O'Tir. Rafn was gone with his warriors during the day, but evening always found him home with her. They made love deep into the nights and woke in each others arms.

Seera was blissfully happy as was Kata. They spent their days together while their husbands were off teaching the young boys the art of being a warrior, and honed their skills with their men when they had time.

Geira sometimes joined them in their chores. She enjoyed showing Seera how things were done. Seera was willing to work hard and Geira was impressed by this Christian bride that had stolen the heart of the fierce warlord.

"I can see why Rafn fell in love with you," Geira told her one day.

"You can?" Seera was surprised at the older woman's statement.

"You have strength and intelligence that were lacking in the women who were constantly trying to tame him," she said with a frown as if she scorned such women.

"I do not wish to tame him."

"That is good, for he was born to be a warrior, and he is a Viking like no other. It is not for him to change." She glanced at Seera in seriousness.

"But you have brought out that side of him that only Orn had ever been able to touch. That is how I know you are special."

Seera shifted uncomfortably. "I am nothing special."

"You are."

Seera was touched by Geira's praise. She had realized when first meeting Valr's wife, that she was a serious woman who did not show her emotions easily. That she would pay Seera such a compliment was surprising and it made the young woman feel the Jarl's wife had accepted her into her family.

That night after supper had been cleared away they remained in the Great Hall to listen to a skald that had arrived on a trading vessel that afternoon. He was a robust man with more facial hair than anyone she had ever met, but he was a jovial man who smiled easily and enjoyed a good tale.

"The god Heimdall was bored," the man, whose name was Unr began. "So disguising himself as a human, he came to Midgard."

"First he came to a peasant's cottage, where he was invited to spend the night. The couple let him share their bed. Nine months later, the woman gave birth to a son. He was sturdy but coarse and was given the name Thrall, which meant Slave."

Seera listened with interest.

"Heimdall next spent the night at a farmer's house, and again a son was born nine months later. He was named Karl, which meant Free Man."

"Finally he came to a nobleman's house and he was given hospitality and a night with the man's wife. A third son was sired by him, this time a strapping young boy who became skilled with the use of a spear and the bow. His name was Jarl and his descendants became warriors, fighting men. That is why the warrior class is made up of men of noble blood."

Cheers went up from the warriors that filled the Great Hall and many drinking horns of mead were raised.

Rafn pulled Seera's chair closer to him so he could whisper into her ear. "Come wife, I have tired of this crowd."

When Seera looked at him, she found it hard to breathe. Even after three weeks as his wife, he still managed to cause her heart to skip a beat when he looked at her thus. A smile touched her lips in anticipation as they slipped from the noisy hall into the chill night.

Rafn made his way to the forge located at the far edge of the village. The smith was a man named Gormer. He was a fourth generation blacksmith. Rafn didn't know him well, but knew he had a wife and a dozen children. Rafn had heard it said that it was why he spent so much time in the forge.

He ducked into the stone building and was hit by a rush of heat. A fire burned hot in special hearths used for heating the metal.

Rafn watched silently as Gormer was pouring liquid iron into a mould set close to the fires. From what Rafn could make out through the rising steam, was that he was casting spearheads.

The blacksmith looked up and saw Rafn. He set his mould aside and reached for a sword that had been stuck into the heat of the fire. "A moment if you would not mind," he said.

"Go ahead, I'm in no hurry," the warlord replied.

The man took the sword to a stone table and pounded out any imperfections that it had until it appeared smooth. He then stuck it into a trough of water, causing a hiss of steam to engulf him. Coughing slightly he turned to Rafn.

"I have it ready," Gormer told him.

"I am anxious to see it."

Gormer took something that was wrapped in a soft leather cloth and brought it to Rafn to inspect. He carefully folded back the cloth so that the warlord could see the newly finished sword.

Rafn took the sword and tested it in his hand. He ran his fingers down the smooth blade that had been finely etched with markings along both edges. The hilt was wrapped with hard leather, and etched only on the ball of the handle.

"It is excellent Gormer," Rafn told him even as he continued to inspect the weapon, testing its sharpness.

"I am honored by your words, my lord." The man lowered his eyes in embarrassment of the praise.

Rafn slipped the man a few gold coins that lit the man's eyes up. For work well done Rafn felt generous and also gave him one of the bands of gold he wore on his own arm. The man was speechless at such generosity as he accepted the treasure made for one of noble blood.

"He will be pleased." Rafn ducked back out the door and the freshness that welcomed him. The cold air was pleasant after the intense heat of the forge. How Gormer worked all day in such a place, he couldn't image.

Rafn went in search of Dagstyrr and found him still lounging in his dwelling. He teased his new brother-in law about such laziness, but his friend only smiled a reply.

"I have something for you," Rafn told him as he joined Dagstyrr at the wooden table inside the dwelling.

"And what would that be?" Dagstyrr's curiosity was piqued as Rafn lifted the wrapped sword and handed it to him.

Dagstyrr unfolded the cloth and held up the perfectly balanced blade, his eyes wide with excitement, though he was confused. "Why?"

"Not so long ago I broke the blade of your best sword and I have noticed you have yet to replace it."

"I had not expected you to do so." Dagstyrr grinned in pleasure at the gift.

"It was the least I could do. You stood by me when I needed you, for that I am truly grateful."

Dagstyrr grew equally serious. "I will always stand by you. You are my closest friend. The brother I never had."

Rafn nodded in acknowledgement of the other man's loyalty. It was good that he married his sister.

Snow kept Hwal locked in the village, and those around him soon learned that it was much better for their Jarl to be out raiding than in Ribe. He grew restless easily and soon his temper grew short. Servants and slaves alike stayed out of his way as best they could.

He rode his warriors hard when gone from the village, but let them spend their time drinking and bedding the village women when not. Many fights broke out amongst them, which Hwal found entertaining.

Let the strong wean out the weak, he thought.

As for the women of Ribe, it was not a happy existence. Even those who were married found themselves often traded for a night to another man. Traders that came to the village were always given their choice.

The freewomen found themselves no better off than the slaves. They were worked and used at will, and if they'd had any courage they would have fled back to their families. But all understood that were they to escape, their families would suffer for it.

Hwal had a tight hold on all the land that fell in his control, and with winter setting in and closing off the shipping lines, he would have to turn inland and expand his boundaries.

They could take the horses and attack when the farmsteads and villages believed themselves safe. He would sacrifice to Odin and seek the god's pleasure. When spring came and the sea was free of ice, he would strike into Vestfold.

Rafn will have thought him no longer interested in his wife. Thinking that his reputation was enough to keep the giant away, but the whale would rise from the sea when the raven was looking to the sky.

CHAPTER 20

Time passed quickly until Seera found it was the middle of winter and preparations for the mid-winter festival were underway. Many people had begun arriving for the celebration from the outlying farms and villages. It was promising to be a large event.

Even Seera couldn't help but get caught up in the excitement, even after weeks of feeling sick. She had been staying long in bed, when she should have been out helping Kata and Geira, but both women insisted she get her rest.

Her suspicions were confirmed when she realized she had not bled since she'd returned to Skiringssal as Rafn's wife. She went to Kata's house and was glad her sister-in law had yet to leave.

"What is it?" Kata noticed the shocked look upon Seera's face.

"I'm pregnant," Seera blurted.

Kata smiled. "I was wondering how long it would take you to notice."

"You knew!" Her eyes widened in surprise.

"I admit, Geira and I both have suspected for awhile," she replied. "But we felt that it was for you to discover on your own."

Seera shook her head. "And I suppose that is why you both wouldn't allow me out of bed."

"Geira said the morning sickness would pass eventually, but that we shouldn't overwork you in the meantime."

"I feel a lot better this morning. In fact I feel very energetic and am looking forward to the festivities."

"I am glad to hear it," Kata said. "But I still do not want you overdoing it."

"I promise." Seera gazed became unfocused as she turned her thoughts inward. She looked back at Kata with wide eyes. "I have to tell Rafn!"

She turned to walk out the door but Kata stopped her. "You will need your winter mantle before you go."

"I will indeed." Seera blushed at her obvious absentmindedness.

Seera went to the training field, where she found Rafn and Dagstyrr with a group of boys who looked no more than ten years of age. They seemed so young, but they had powerful thrusts behind their lunges and Seera could see that this was not their first time at the training field. Seera wondered how old they had been when their training had started.

Seera stood to the side, not wanting to interrupt her husband. She realized she should have waited for night when they could be alone. The cold air was beginning to seep beneath her mantle and her exposed face was feeling quite chilled. She envied the men's ability to ignore the elements. Rafn didn't even bother with a cloak.

Hard to the core, others would say, but she knew that it was not so...she who had felt his tender hands upon her and knew the love in his heart. She was about to turn and leave when Rafn approached her, leaving Dagstyrr to the boys.

"You need something wife?" He raised an eyebrow in question when she failed to answer immediately.

"I wanted to tell you something," Seera said. "But I shouldn't have interrupted you, I am sorry."

Rafn realized Seera was agitated about something, "Dagstyrr continue without me." He grabbed Seera's hand and led her to their dwelling.

Agata had recently built up the fire and Seera was glad for its warmth. Seera removed her cloak and went to warm her hands over the hearth.

Rafn watched his wife with growing suspicion. He remained silent, choosing instead to let her tell him in her own time what was troubling her.

Rafn studied her as she busied herself straightening the bed, even though it had already been done. He sat down at the table and used the time to rub down the blade of his sword until it shined anew.

Finally Seera sat on the edge of the bed and looked at him. Joining her, he took her hands in his and simply said, "Just tell me."

"I am going to have your baby," she replied with a mix of shock and giddiness.

It took a moment for her words to become clear, but when they did Rafn stood so suddenly it stunned Seera.

"You are not pleased?" She felt a moment of irrational fear.

He turned to face her and pulled her to feet. "I could not be more so," he said before claiming her mouth.

Seera responded to his kiss and went into his arms. He lowered her to the bed and his kisses moved to her neck and back to her mouth, before he pulled back in sudden worry.

"Will it hurt the baby," his eyes filled with concern that touched Seera. If others only knew how her fierce Viking could be so tender. She was sure it was not something that he would want his enemies ever knowing.

"It will not," Seera replied, before pulling his head back down to hers.

Sometime later, Agata showed up to return the clothing she had taken to wash and was surprised to find Rafn there.

"I will go," she said nervously as she turned for the door. Rafn, who'd been standing before the fire in only a short tunic, turned to Agata with a smile.

This stunned Agata even further, for she had never seen the warlord with such a look of contentment on his face. It seemed strange. She looked to her mistress asleep in the bed and was sure she was the reason for Lord Rafn's change.

"Come in," Rafn beckoned her. Agata quickly went about her business of returning Seera's clothes to her trunk. She turned to leave, when Rafn stopped her.

"Go tell my sister-in law to have a feast prepared. Tonight we celebrate." His gaze shifted to Seera as he spoke.

"Aye, my lord."

Geira having suspected the reason for the impromptu feast, made sure it was a lavish one. The hunters had brought in a fresh kill of deer that she confiscated.

"What is all of this, wife," Valr asked when he showed up for dinner to find the Great Hall prepared for a celebration.

"Your brother requested a feast to celebrate."

"He did? And his reason, when many days of feasting for the midwinter festival begin tomorrow."

"I'm sure he will tell you at supper, my lord."

"He had better." Valr frowned.

The hall was packed that night when word had spread that Rafn had an announcement to make. To make a dramatic entrance, Rafn made sure he and Seera were the last to arrive.

Valr watched them approach the head table and shook his head in response to Rafn's behavior.

A smile came easily to Rafn's face as he came to stand next to his brother. Valr was quick to notice the way he was beaming and narrowed his eyes.

"Do not frown," Rafn said. "It is a time to give thanks."

"And what are we thanking?"

Rafn turned to Seera and took her hand. "That my wife carries my child," he said only loud enough for Valr to hear.

Valr's eyes opened in surprise and then he too smiled. He turned to the expectant diners and raised his mug of ale. "I am to be an uncle," he yelled.

A cheer went up and congratulations were bellowed and the feast began.

They sat and ate in relish the dishes brought before them, Rafn insisting Seera eat more than her usual portion. For his son he told her. So that he would grow strong.

"It could be a daughter," she whispered to him, earning a smile from him.

"And she would need to have the strength of her mother," he reasoned. Giving in to his demand, she made sure she filled herself to bursting.

Life was indeed good.

The holy women of the Disir, those allied to the goddess Freyja, led the sacrifices that would be made to honor her and her brother Freyr, who was the fertility god. They went out as a group into the forest, and with the hunters chosen to select the beasts that would be offered up in sacrifice.

Freyr who was associated with sunshine and rain, prosperity and fruitfulness was always worshipped at the winter solstice, for he would bring the spring back when it was time.

Boars and stallions were offered to the goddess and her twin as the sun began to disappear behind the mountains. This was done by the holy women and the chosen away from the crowd of feasters. It was done at a spot selected by the women, known only to those that were present for the sacrifice.

Rafn and Dagstyrr were among the hunters. Rafn himself sacrificed the first animal in Freyr's name. When the squealing of the beast had died away, the group left their sacrifices, for they were not to be consumed by the people. They were for the gods and the gods alone.

When Rafn and Dagstyrr arrived in the Great Hall, the festivities had already begun. Not everyone would fit within the building, so tents had been erected outside and were also filled to bursting. Much laughter filled the night as Rafn went in search of his wife.

In one of the tents, the boy Fox sat silent and alone. He had not made any friends since coming to Skiringssal. Valr had offered him a home and warriors training. It was an honor he knew, but he felt so utterly alone. He missed his parents and his sister, the friends of his childhood.

He often thought that he should have died that night as well. To be left to such loneliness was unbearable. He accepted a mug of ale from a drunken farmer who wandered by and had noticed him. The man wandered off a moment later and Fox was relieved.

Fox sipped at the drink in his hand, watching the people come and go around him. Would he ever feel like he belonged in this place? Would he ever find someone who understood the torment in his heart?

The servant woman Esja came into the tent then with trays full of food that she brought to the tables. Following behind her was a doe eyed girl that he'd seen occasionally around the village and working with the other women. She was small, with blond hair and very sad eyes.

She looked at him then, perhaps sensing his study of her. Her brown eyes reflected the same hollowness he felt inside himself. It stunned him. He had not thought that anyone's soul could reflect his own.

She quickly looked away from him, but not before he sensed her own loneliness.

Later that night Fox searched out the girl and found her alone in the Great Hall in a corner. She was holding a plate of food and picking at its contents and did not see him approach until he sat down beside her.

A startled look crossed her face and he thought she would run from him.

"You don't need to fear me," he said before she could leave. "I am Fox."

The girl studied him for a long moment and he was sure that she was not going to reply. She seemed to come to a decision and spoke softly, "I am Yrsa."

"I am glad to meet you Yrsa. Would you be my friend?"

Something reflected in his eyes that the girl was drawn to. Realizing she didn't fear this stranger she found herself answering, "I will be your friend."

For the first time since the night his village was destroyed, Fox smiled.

Time moved ever closer, the Seer knew, even as she threw the bird bones and studied their meaning.

The seid magic would be needed to wrap a net of confusion around the man. She saw this clearly in the placement of the bones, understood that when the time came that it would protect the woman, keep her safe within a hidden cocoon. The Seer's spells and the warrior woman's sword would be enough.

This she had seen. This it would be. Ever closer did it come...when spring once again came.

She moved across the cave she had selected for the winter solstice. She waited only for her sister to return with the offering. While she waited she sang and danced to the goddess and the brother.

The warrior woman entered the cold cave that was only dimly lit by a low burning fire that had been set by the entrance.

The warrior woman had a rope around the neck of a wild goat she'd led into a trap. She brought the animal forward into the circle that the Seer had drawn on the cave floor.

The Seer's eyes widened with a wild look as she held a knife in her hand. Chanting to the goddess she brought the blade across the goat's throat, killing it quickly. Blood spurted from the wound and the Seer held her hands to it.

With bloody hands she first smeared it on her sister's face, before doing the same to her own.

"Goddess, accept what is offered." She raised her hands and the blood ran down her arms.

The sisters looked at each other and each felt the power of the night.

CHAPTER 21

Spring's warm breath filtered back into the land, bringing with it milder winds and sunnier days. Everyone's spirits lifted as they were able to enjoy the feel of warm air on their faces again. Activity around the village increased and people began to spend more time outside.

Through the winter months Seera's stomach had grown and she could now feel the baby moving. It was a thrilling time for her, of expectation and joy as she planned for the baby.

Not long after Rafn and Seera had made their announcement, Geira had also found out she was with child, but her pregnancy was not going as well. She was sick and spotting blood when she should not have been. Kata put her on bed rest, which didn't please Geira but she couldn't fault Kata's logic in forcing her to stay off her feet. It had taken her years to conceive a child and her body was not willingly accepting it now.

Valr worried for his wife and it showed in the dark circles beneath his eyes. He had become a silent brooding man waiting and praying that things wouldn't end up badly. A premonition hung over his head that he tried desperately to ignore, but each time he looked into Geira's pale face and saw the strain the pregnancy was having on her he couldn't quiet the worry in his heart.

There were times when he believed it would have been better if she had never conceived a child. He never spoke these words aloud. It would not help Geira through this trial to know her husband harbored such thoughts.

It didn't take much insight from his family to understand his unspoken words. They saw how torn up he was. He had wanted a child for so long, had prayed and sacrificed to the gods so that it might happen. Had he doomed his wife?

Rafn tried his best not to show the joy he himself felt about his pending fatherhood, when he understood how precarious Geira's pregnancy was. Seera had spoken to him in the nights of her concern and he wouldn't flaunt his own happiness in the face of his brother.

Yet Valr had gifted them with a beautiful wooden cradle he'd bought from a trader passing through. Rafn was forced to accept the gift and not ask him why he didn't keep it for his own child. It was then Rafn realized that Valr believed the child would not live.

If the child should die, then Rafn would need to be there for Valr. The women he knew would comfort Geira, but only a brother could share the pain of a man. Only a brother could sit silently beside him and grieve with him.

And a brother could sacrifice to the gods in hopes that they would hear his prayers and allow the child to draw its first breath.

It was early one afternoon when a drekar from the northern territory of Trondelag came into view on the Vik. It flew the flag of Jarl Kobbi and many people went down to the harbor to meet them. Dagstyrr waited anxiously on the dock, for he expected his sister to be on board, with the babe that would have been born during the winter.

As the ship pulled up to the dock, Seera spotted a woman with shocking red hair an even brighter shade than Dagstyrr's. There was no mistaking her as the warrior's sister.

As soon as the drekar was secured, Kobbi helped his wife climb off the ship. She was followed by a second woman, carrying a child bundled in a blanket. Seera assumed her to be the baby's nurse.

"Sister." Dagstyrr pushed his way forward to drag the woman into his arms. Seera could tell the siblings were close. It made her long to see Peder again. Perhaps she could convince Rafn to take her to Dun'O'Tir after the baby was born.

"It is good to see you brother." The red haired woman spoke to Dagstyrr. She turned to the nurse and beckoned her forward. "Hildr, please show my brother his niece."

"A daughter," Dagstyrr smiled as he looked down into Hildr's arms to see a very alert baby girl looking back at him. A soft chuckle escaped him when he noticed the mop of red hair. "She is hideous."

Auga punched him in the arm. "Hush, you know she is exquisite."

Laughing, Dagstyrr rubbed the sore spot on his arm while making a pained expression. His attention returned to the gurgling baby. "She is."

Kata appeared next to him to get a better peek at the little girl. "She is beautiful, Auga. You must be very proud."

Auga beamed with maternal pride. "I am. It is good to see you again Lady Kata."

"As it is to see you, but no need for such formality, we are family."

Auga looked in confusion at her brother who was grinning like a man with a well kept secret. "Sister, Kata and I are wed."

"She's your wife." Auga looked from one to the other. "Much has changed since we last saw one another."

"Congratulations," Kobbi clapped his hand on Dagstyrr's shoulder. Then he took Kata's hand. "Lady, it is a pleasure."

"Lord," she replied in kind.

Rafn came forward and clasped his hands to Kobbi's arms in greeting. "Come my friend let us find you something soothing to drink. My brother waits in the Great Hall."

"And where is your wife, Warlord?" Kobbi raised his eyebrows and made a pretense of searching the crowd, though he had no idea what she looked like.

Rafn reached for Seera's hand where she stood behind Kata and pulled her forward. "I would like to present Lady Seera, formally of Dun'O'Tir, now of Skiringssal."

To Seera he said, "Wife, I would like you to meet Kobbi, a dear friend and brother-in law to Dagstyrr."

Kobbi's eyes grew wide in appreciation, which caused Rafn to scowl. Kobbi laughed at his protectiveness as he noticed her expanded stomach.

"It is a pleasure." Kobbi took her hand and bowed slightly over it.

"As it is mine," Seera replied.

Kobbi's face lit with delight as he turned once again to face Rafn. "You are to be a father! Let us drink to that."

Rafn's face soothed at the mention of the baby. Kobbi noted how easily the smile came to the warlord's face and looked to the woman in wonder. He would never have believed any woman could tame the beast.

The men walked on ahead and Kata introduced her to Auga. Seera was fascinated by the baby. Soon she too would be a mother and she wondered if she would look as at ease as Auga did.

They went to the Great Hall to find Valr already there. He greeted Kobbi more formally than had Rafn and Seera realized their relationship was not the same. They had obviously met before but did not share the camaraderie as Rafn and Kobbi.

The men sat down to discuss things, while servants brought them ewers of mead and horns to drink from. Kata led the women to a table on the other side of the room where they could talk of things that mattered to them.

Kobbi placed on the table a leather wrapped object that he'd brought with him from the ship. All the men eyed it with interest, but it was Rafn's gaze he held. "I have for you, something I expect you to trade a fortune for."

Rafn watched in anticipation as Kobbi opened the cloth to reveal a longsword of extreme beauty. The metal blade was double edged, with a groove along the center. The dark gray metal of the hilt was elaborately decorated with images of ravens and snakes, the eyes of the largest serpent were inlaid with small rubies. Rafn's eyes lit up as he reached out and took hold of it.

An electric pulse traveled up his arm at first contact, calling to the thunder in his soul. He sucked in a gasp and fought to calm the rapid beating of his heart.

Standing he tested the blade by slicing it through the air to judge its balance and weight. A sharp crack split the air and the essence of the sword sung a song that called only to him. He grunted his approval. It was as if the sword had been made for his hand alone. It was a part of him, and he knew he had to have it.

Dagstyrr and Valr exchanged a look that spoke of envy and awe. They met Rafn's gaze and saw a renewed power sharpening his eyes.

"It is a Frankish sword." He rubbed his hand reverently down the blade, expecting it to be cool, but instead he felt the heat locked within it. A smile slowly emerged on his face.

"Its name is Serpent," Kobbi said. "And when I saw the ravens etched onto the hilt, I knew it was for you."

"And it will be mine." Rafn knew he would pay a hefty price for its possession, but he cared not.

"As I hoped you would say." Kobbi's grin was one of triumph.

Kobbi and Auga stayed a week before heading home, but not before they'd come to an agreeable trade for the sword, which Rafn paid a fortune for. Many gold coins left with Kobbi in exchange for the serpent sword, but he'd have done anything to claim it.

The morning after Kobbi left, Rafn headed out early to the practice field to learn the feel of the Serpent. He felt on the edge of possession when he swung it. The men were awed by the power the sword gave to their warlord. Vikings were a superstitious lot about their weapons and they could clearly see the spirit of the sword had called out to Rafn.

The sword was one of beauty. Frankish swords were envied by those without them and cherished by those who owned them. The Franks used a pattern wielding technique in making their swords that involved combining strips of iron of different hardness for increased suppleness and flexibility.

And Rafn had never seen one finer made. It was a sword made for a King and Rafn felt very protective of it. Even his men were not allowed to touch it and only had the opportunity to see it when sparring with their warlord.

After acquiring it, Rafn made a sacrifice to Thor. He wetted the sword in two deer and then offered them to his god. The thunder echoed loudly inside him, increasing his power, renewing his strength.

And the god spoke from the world above by sending a bolt of lightning streaking across the sky.

Seera let the door to her dwelling swing closed behind her as she stepped out to greet the pleasant day. She heard the musical voices of the birds which had returned to the trees and smelled the budding leaves. The farmers had already begun to turn the earth in their fields in anticipation of planting the new crop.

It spoke of life and rebirth, causing Seera to place a hand to her bulging stomach. She was blessed with a kick from her unborn child. Though she would have liked a girl, Seera had secretly begun to think of the baby as a boy.

"Would you come with me to my brother's grave," Kata asked Seera as she came to join her.

"I will accompany you." It had been some time since she'd had the need to sit at Orn's grave and talk to him. Perhaps she should tell him of how happy she was, how at peace Rafn had become. These were things she was sure that Orn would want to hear.

They greeted those who were already awake and going about their daily chores as they passed through the village. They walked through the town and up the hill to the grave that Rafn had dug himself. Father Duncun had placed a wooden cross to mark the site and Kata had draped a pendant of an eagle on it. It was Norse superstition and the priest would most likely not approve, but Kata didn't care. The eagle had been Orn's talisman.

The women knelt down beside the raised mound of earth. Seera prayed to her God while Kata simply sat remembering Orn. How he smiled, and laughed, the look on his face when he spoke of his betrothed.

"I miss him so," Kata said.

Seera took her hand. "I know. I wish I could have known him."

"He would have liked you, and he would have been pleased to have seen the happiness on Rafn's face, to know that he had found love. Orn often worried that the storm inside of Rafn wouldn't allow him to enjoy such simple joy. I wish he could have seen the two of you together."

"He knows." Seera reassured her. She had never shared with Kata how Orn's spirit had come to her, but she remembered the feel of him when he'd been with her in spirit, the peace of the light that surrounded him.

"You believe so?" Kata looked hopeful.

"I do."

Seera was clutched by an uneasy feeling as the trees rustled behind her. She turned to peer into the forest and was unsettled by the dark shadows that seemed to move within. She felt the lurking threat that they hid. The happiness, the contentment, she had felt moments before was lost to an instinctive fear for survival.

She struggled with her weight to gain her feet, causing Kata to look at her with concern. She opened her mouth to shout a warning as she saw movement over Kata's shoulder.

A hand clasped over her mouth just as another man grabbed Kata, who yelped in surprise. Seera recognized him from Ribe. A tremor traveled up her spine as she realized it was Hwal who held her, even before he spun her around and forced her to look at him. With his hand still over her mouth and his other holding her tight, he glared down at her with pure hate.

"My lord, what of this one?" Another man indicated Kata, whose eyes had grown wide with horror. She looked to Seera in helplessness.

"Leave her, I want only this one." Hwal's one eye fixed on her, and she saw the spark of insanity simmering beneath the surface. That he lusted for her had always been obvious, that he wanted to possess her could not be mistaken and Seera knew fear like she'd never known before. For whatever Hwal did to her, would harm her child.

Kata began to struggle as two of the men carried her away and Seera feared they would rape her.

Kata was the sister of two fierce men, married to a warrior just as strong and she wouldn't simply succumb to these men. She fought for all she was worth, managing to sink her teeth into the one who held her, causing him to pull his hand from her mouth as he cursed.

Kata did not hesitate but screamed as loud as she could, in hopes that her voice would be heard.

The man called Lene suddenly had a knife in his hand and stuck it in her side to silence her, while the other man smashed her on the head to knock her out.

Shock numbed Seera. Kata lay unmoving on the ground and Seera prayed she was not dead. Tears of frustration and grief welled in her eyes as Hwal dragged her into the trees.

A glimmer of hope touched her when she saw the men reacting below, already headed in her direction.

Hwal cursed furiously. "We will not make it passed them now." He muttered as he dragged her deeper into the trees.

With Seera clutched in the giant's arms, the four men ran quickly into the thickest part of the forest. They moved with incredible speed, placing distance between them and Rafn's warriors, who would kill them without hesitation if they were caught.

Seera was helpless to do anything but stare at the passing landscape, until they came to a large cave in which Hwal immediately stopped in front of.

He called his three warriors to him. "I want you, Abiorn to scout our back trail and make sure we are not being pursued.

Abiorn fled into the trees. The other two were ordered to keep watch. An uneasy glance moved between them.

Terror rushed her at being left alone with the man of her nightmares. He dragged her into the dark cave, with the only light illuminating its interior coming from the fading sun.

Hwal loosened his hold on her so her feet slid to the floor of the cave. He turned her to face him. "I have waited a long time to reclaim you." He ran his a rough hand across her face to push her hair from it.

"I was never yours." She spat in his face, even knowing it was unwise to provoke him. "Drenger would not allow it."

A dangerous glint flashed in his eyes as he wiped the spit from his cheek. She flinched in anticipation of the pain, even before his hand came across her face. Tears stung her eyes, but she did not cry out. She stared back at him in contempt.

He snarled like a rapid wolf. "You will be mine! And you will learn your place."

"My husband will find you, and I will enjoy watching him kill you." She teetered backwards when he struck her again. She tasted blood on her lip.

"Silence!"

She obeyed as fear for her child robbed her of her courage. She would not look at him, but she could smell his fetid breath as he leaned over her. His hands began moving down her body in a violent need to claim every part of her at once.

Hwal stopped when he reached her stomach, his eye widening in shock at having discovered what her cloak had so effectively hidden.

"What is this?"

The venom in his voice made Seera shutter even as she boldly answered. "The Raven's child! A Viking whose name you should not forget, for he brings your death."

She thought she saw a slight hesitation before he howled in fury. "Let the Raven come. I will send him to the halls of Valhalla. You can be assured of that."

She knew Rafn's reputation, didn't doubt there was a reason he had earned it, but Hwal was the largest man Seera had ever seen. She had to believe Rafn would triumph, even over as hulking of a beast as Hwal. A protective hand moved to her stomach.

Her captor noticed the action and he pulled her hard against him. "It changes nothing woman."

His hand struck her against the side of her head and her vision swam as she tried to maintain her balance, but her footing was lost as Hwal kicked her feet out from under her and she landed hard on her back. His foot found her side and sent her sideways until she was curled into a ball, wrapping herself around her child in protection.

While she lay there, too afraid to move, she heard a sound that brought shivers. A terrible memory of being tied to the punishment post was fast upon her as she heard Hwal snap his whip in the air.

She dared to peak up at him to find that he was sneering at her with satisfaction.

"You remember this, don't you?" Drool trailed from the corner of his mouth. "Your punishment is far from over."

"Don't," she whispered in desperation, knowing Rafn would not save her this time.

He snagged her cloak and brought her back to her feet, which threatened to fail her. Her eyes widened in horror as he yanked the mantle from her. She heard the metal pin that had clasped it closed hit the hard floor. She couldn't keep herself from trembling.

With the whip still clutched in his right hand, he turned and pressed her up against the rock wall.

"Stay still and I will consider allowing you to keep your child," he said. "Fight me and I will end its life with the tip of my knife."

Seera managed to nod that she would not move. But her legs shook so badly that she was afraid she would fall. If she could not stay standing, he would kill her child. She closed her eyes and prayed liked she'd never done before.

The tearing of her dress brought her back to the moment and even the ability to pray was lost. A numb acceptance clouded her thoughts as she waited for the first strike of the whip.

The courage she'd had when she'd been flogged while tied to the punishment pole would not come this time. Defiance had fueled her anger then and this time she had none to lend to courage. Stark and primal fear was all that remained and she cried out as the whip found flesh again and again.

She lost track of how many lashes tore up her skin. Tears flowed unchecked down her cheeks and her sobs were met with satisfaction by the giant.

The baby's kicks were frantic and she wanted to soothe it with a gentle touch, but if she let go of her precarious hold on the stone wall, she would not be able to remain upright.

Tired of his punishment on her back, he pushed her to the ground which caused her to yelp in surprise at the raw burn that tore up her back. He climbed on top of her. There was nothing she could do to prevent him claiming her body. She shuttered at her lack of courage and was glad that Rafn could not see her cowardice. Tears clouded her eyes as Hwal pushed up her dress and smock, and forced himself into her.

She lay as still as she could, fighting the urge to struggle against him. She must not. Must not allow harm to come to her baby…

He took her violently, to the point where she could feel herself tearing, and she felt blood between her legs.

Her baby!

The tears did not come again. She separated herself from the pain by wrapping a cocoon around her heart and mind and endured until he was finished. When he was done she feigned unconsciousness and he shoved her from him.

He growled his frustration. "That babe makes you weak. At first light I will rid your body of it."

Seera forced herself not to react to his declaration, but lay silent and unmoving until Hwal succumbed to his own exhaustion and slept.

When his snoring reached her she opened her eyes and moved slow and silent. He remained asleep and unaware of her movements. He was well satisfied and confident that his men kept watch. She would have to be careful. It was her only chance and she did not hesitate to take it.

Under the cover of darkness she crept on silent feet out through the cave opening, making sure to hug the wall so as not to be seen and slipped into the forest…with what strength God had granted her.

CHAPTER 22

Dagstyrr knelt, clutching Kata in his arms. He'd found her unconscious and bleeding when he'd reached the top of the hill after hearing her tortured scream. His heart stopped in his chest as it seized with fear. The men who'd followed him up to Orn's grave stood at a distance, giving him space as he leaned over his wife.

His hands became frantic, checking each inch of her body until he found the source of the blood. There was a cut in her side that could only have been made by a knife. Panicked and outraged he snapped an order for Leikr to search out the one who had harmed Kata.

He lifted her and carried her to the compound as fast as he could. Her breathing was shallow and he was afraid that it would cease altogether. He went through the gates and was at a loss what to do. Those who were injured were always taken to Kata. Who else knew of healing?

He knew there must be others but he didn't know who. Dagstyrr grunted in frustration. Across the courtyard he could see Father Duncun hurrying towards him. The monk reacted to the look of hopelessness on his face.

"Bring her to her dwelling. I have some knowledge of healing. I am not as well versed as your wife, but please allow me to see what I can do."

"Of course Father," Dagstyrr answered with relief born from panic.

Just as Dagstyrr lay Kata on the bed, Rafn came bursting in with Valr on his heals. "What has happened?" He took in his sister's condition.

"I was outside the compound with Leikr when I heard her scream. It came from the hill where Orn's grave is and I ran as fast as I could to get to her. Others followed me, but we were too late." Dagstyrr stared helplessly at Kata as Father Duncun checked the wound on her side and held a cloth against it to staunch the blood.

Valr placed a comforting hand on his shoulder, but Rafn turn angry. "Did you see who did this?"

"Nay," Dagstyrr shook his head. "There was no one else there when I arrived. I sent Leikr to search for any sign of the assailant."

Rafn looked to the door and his face turned as hard as stone. His gaze was drawn back to Kata and then he met Dagstyrr's eyes. "Has anyone seen Seera?"

"Kata was alone."

Rafn raced out the door and to his own dwelling. He threw open the wooden door, startling Agata who was folding Seera's dresses into her trunk. "My lord?" A touch of fear laced her voice.

"Has my wife been here?"

"Nay, my lord, she is with Lady Kata," she said. Her words caused Rafn's face to harden even further and a deadly fire flared to life in his eyes. Agata took a defensive step away from him.

Rafn stormed back out and met Valr halfway across the courtyard. He pushed aside his panic and seized the rage that was building deep in the core of him. He clenched his fists in a struggle to contain it. "He has taken her"

"Who?" Valr stared at him with concern.

"Hwal…he has Seera."

Rafn was furious. Valr soon realized that everything that happened was about Seera even as Rafn ordered his men into action. His men were quick to carry out his orders, angry at the insult done to their warlord. Their loyalty was without question as they searched rapidly the area around the village, for the evidence of who had taken Seera and where.

But Rafn knew who'd taken her, even without waiting for Kata to regain consciousness so that she could confirm. He stopped by her dwelling long enough to find her stabilized. Father Duncun had cauterized the wound shut to stop the bleeding, after ascertaining that the damaged was not severe.

The monk told him he was more worried about the lump on her head and vowed to stay with her to make sure pressure did not build in her skull.

Dagstyrr was quick to assess Rafn's mood. He recognized the storm at once building in his friend. Dagstyrr had stayed by Kata's side as the other men had searched, but he would not be left behind when Rafn went to Ribe. The warlord called to him an army of men. A thousand warriors answered his call and their shouts called for vengeance and blood.

Valr was waiting at the dock when Rafn arrived and insisted on going with them when they launched from port. Kata was his sister as well and he demanded action.

Rafn nodded once and jumped into his drekar. Valr followed because he was a known warrior in his own right. Though, he went also because he worried for his brother. Rafn was barely keeping his rage contained as it was, but if they found Seera and her child harmed in anyway, no one would be able to hold Rafn back. Valr feared when that happened Rafn would not fight wisely. The Jarl would defend his brother's back, whether he welcomed it or not.

"Be safe husband," Geira had said to him before they boarded the ship. She looked at him with fear in her eyes, but he couldn't answer her plea to remain. His place was with his brother.

A fog descended upon them when the stars should have filled the sky, but Valr could see that Rafn would not be deterred. He would have his wife back.

As for Hwal! He would endure days of torture before his life was ended.

With each step Seera took deeper into the trees the mist thickened around her, hiding her from her enemy's eyes. She prayed even as the pain in her abdomen increased. She was all but numbed to the other injures claiming her body.

She kept moving because she could not stop. Though she had no idea where she was going, she had to keep walking until she found safety for her baby.

A moan of despair clogged her throat as she pushed aside branch after branch. She'd left any kind of trail behind, thinking it safer to melt into the thick foliage of the forest.

She stumbled on. The branches tearing at her arms and legs, even as the fog grew thick and heavy. It was more a blessing than a curse. Seera didn't know where she was going anyway, so seeing the path she took was not so important. Hiding her trail from Hwal on the other hand was.

Pain centered in her abdomen and she worried for the child within her, Rafn's child. How would he handle it if she lost the life he so desperately needed to fill his heart with peace?

Tears stung her eyes from the pain as she continued to move forward. She clutched her dress to her chest to keep it from falling off. Her bare back remained exposed to the cold, but Seera knew even if she'd remembered to take her cloak, it would hurt too much to place it over the welts on her back.

The tree trunks became so thick that she had to weave carefully through them, climbing as best she could over their large roots.

Her energy had long seeped from her, and her legs were nothing more than numb limbs that she no longer commanded. Her head spun and her eyes blurred from the deepening pain and she knew that she would go no further. She stumbled against a large tree and seeing that it had a hollow beneath it where the roots had made a natural burrow, she crawled within it.

She gasped in the thick air and felt a chill settle in her bones. She brought her knees up and wrapped her arms around them in a desperate attempt to stop the shaking that consumed her body.

She sobbed out of frustration and desperation. The tears streaked down her dirty face, leaving a clear track of their path. She would lose the baby. No part of her could deny that utter truth. It would die and most likely take her with it.

"Rafn," Seera cried out his name, even knowing that he couldn't hear her. That she was so far away that she had no hope of him ever finding her. She was lost and alone in a dark, featureless world.

How was she to fight? It was not within her to escape this time. She was being hunted by a madman. When the fog cleared, he would find her, and he would kill her. She had no doubt of that.

Snow came then, an early spring blizzard to block out all else but the huge wet flakes that fell in front of her. With luck the snow would hide what trail she had left and leave Hwal blind to her whereabouts.

She was so cold. She hugged herself and thought of the warmth of her husband's arms. At thoughts of him, the tears flowed and she choked on her sobs, until her eyes stung and had grown puffy.

When the tears would no longer come, her eyes were so heavy with fatigue that she no longer had the strength to fight their pull. Sleep took her from the pain of her body and of her heart.

With luck, God would find her and take her home to his kingdom, where she could live without fear and the hurt of loss.

Without…Rafn…the thought echoed into her unconsciousness, bringing with it a terrible ache of hopelessness. It was too hard to think of never seeing him again. She welcomed the darkness that took her.

A soft light grew at the edge of her vision. It entered her dream with familiar warmth that Seera reached for.

A man appeared and knelt down beside her and she had to squint to make out his features. She was not surprised to recognize Orn. His face held such peace that she wept to look upon it.

"You can't die Seera." He reached out a hand and touched it to her face. With his touch her fear disappeared and she wondered how he had done such a thing.

"Am I not already dead, my husband's brother?"

"Nay, you are not." His smile was beautiful as it spread across his face. His blond hair reflected the light, causing it to glitter like a chest full of gold.

"Then how am I here with you?"

"You are simply between worlds and I am here to plead with you to fight to stay alive."

"Why should I not follow you to paradise?" As Orn shifted in the light, a trail of colors shimmered around him as if he stood inside a rainbow.

"You saw how losing me affected Rafn." Orn's words reached deep into her soul, causing her to wince in despair.

"It tore him apart."

"Think what would happen if he lost you, lost his son. He would not be able to recover." Orn moved his hand to place it over her swollen belly and the child moved in response. Relief flooded her that he still lived.

"Son?" She wept sobs of joy and weariness.

"He will live, as you will, if you are strong enough to fight."

"My strength leaves me." She searched for residual energy to do what he asked, to choose life over death, to find a way to see Rafn again. There was nothing left inside her but emptiness.

"Then I give you mine, as you once gave me yours. And stay with you as I did before."

"You will stay with me?" He gave her hope as his arms wrapped around her. She felt pure power encompass her.

"I will not leave."

"Damn that insufferable woman." Hwal screamed into the night and his two warriors fought not to step away from his rage. They each understood that they had failed him in not seeing her escape. They were lucky he had not already killed them.

Hwal's anger had nearly led his sword to take their lives, but he had need of them yet. He would deal their deaths when their usefulness was gone.

They stood silent while he vented his wrath upon them, each understanding that their lives were being spared, and that they must not fail him again.

He spoke to the younger of the two. "Lene, find Abiorn and tell him I go after the woman, the two of you blend into Skiringssal so that you may stay apprised of what their warlord does."

"Aye, lord." He left before Hwal changed his mind on the death sentence, and was soon swallowed by the storm.

"Klintr, you will come with me." He stared out into the spring blizzard that prevented him from seeing any kind of trail. He yelled into the storm in fury.

"I will find you Seera. Make no mistake that your death will be painful when I do."

Klintr thought it foolish to go chasing after a mere woman, but he was wise enough not to speak such words aloud. He looked with longing towards the path Lene had taken and envied the man's escape.

The blizzard did not reach the low lands or the men out on the water. Rafn rowed like a man gone crazy. His warriors had a hard time keeping pace, but they would not admit to it, understanding what fueled their Warlord. The need to kill had seized each of them in turn, until all were ready.

Valr tried to remain the one man with a clear head. He stayed at the steering oar of his brother's ship. He had appointed Maurr to captain his own drekar, so that he might stay near his brother. Rafn had scowled when Valr boarded, but had said nothing. Valr was not only his brother, but his Jarl as well, and his word was law.

Though the days were long, Rafn refused to stop and the men were allowed no rest. He was insane with fear for Seera and guilt that he had not already dwelt with Hwal. He had known of the man's obsession for his wife, yet he had done nothing but make an idle threat. So consumed was he in his happiness that he had become complacent in his duties.

It was a mistake he would render. Hwal's death would not be quick. He vowed to Thor and to the all the Aesir gods as well as the Vanir. The Jute would cry out for mercy before he was done.

Thunder roared through him.

It was early morning when the ships appeared on the horizon and the warriors in Ribe stood at alert.

It was a bloody scene as a thousand men spilled from the ships to tear the village apart. Women ran into the hills with the children, while the men stayed to hold off the angry men who had come for their deaths.

Many cursed Hwal's name for bringing death upon them…for what, his obsession over a woman. Only a fool would try and steal the Raven's wife. The warlord fought with the strength of Thor. What man could stand against the man chosen by the gods themselves?

Rafn held the serpent in his hand and he felt the magic in the sword unleashed as he plunged it deep into the flesh of men who dared to stand between him and his wife. He pushed his way through the fortified walls, tearing the gate apart with only an axe, the men on the walls unable to stop his wrath.

Valr stayed close to him and he growled in resentment at having his big brother watching him so. Nothing was going to stop him. Not until he had Seera and the child within her, back in his arms.

He came to Hwal's dwelling and kicked in the door to find a scared woman huddled in the corner. She looked upon the blood drenched madman and screamed.

"Shut up woman, or I will silence you," Rafn threatened as he tore the place apart. She was not there.

"Where is your master?" When she failed to answer him he grabbed her arms and dragged her to her feet. "Speak."

"He has not returned my lord." Her voice shook when she spoke and she trembled beneath his grip.

"You lie." He shoved her back and pressed his sword to her chest, making sure she understood what he meant to do to her. "Tell me where my wife is?"

Sobs choked her and tears clouded her eyes as she pleaded with him. "I don't know."

"Brother." Valr laid a hand on his shoulders and did not flinch when Rafn turned cold eyes upon him. "The woman does not lie. We have not been able to find Hwal."

Grunting in frustration Rafn tossed the woman to the floor and ignored her whimpering retreat to the corner.

"Then where is he?"

"I don't know, but we will find him."

"You can be assured of that, if I have to tear all of Jutland apart to do so."

"Set fire to the compound's walls," he ordered his men. "Plunder the village until nothing of value remains. I don't want Hwal to have anything left when he does show his cowardly face."

The men bellowed in agreement and the killing of Hwal's warriors continued, as the shops and homes were rampaged, and the fortified walls destroyed by fire and axe. Those who had escaped and hid within the forest shook with fear at what reached their ears.

Even the children were too afraid to cry.

CHAPTER 23

Seera drifted on the verge of consciousness and oblivion. Orn was with her as he promised, but there was someone else as well. She'd been lifted from the dark and lonely place and carried to somewhere warm.

A soft healing hand touched her with gentleness and concern, and she could almost make out someone speaking to her in a motherly voice. She yielded herself. Felt safe.

Time seemed to move in slow motion. There were moments when she was so hot she squirmed to try and escape the heat that would consume. And pain. It was there, but she was oddly disconnected from it.

And through what must have been many days, Orn did not leave. Many times she reached out to him and always he filled her with hope.

Then the delirium left as her fever broke and she became aware of the warmth that enveloped her in a thick wrapped fur. A soft pillow cushioned her head.

Had it been a dream? Did she again lie in her husband's bed? She was too afraid to open her eyes and discover she was wrong, that she was still crouched beneath the tree.

A hand touched her head and she jumped in surprise to find an unknown woman staring down at her.

"Be at ease," the woman said as she smiled oddly at her. Seera tried to sit but the woman eased her back onto her side with a gentle push.

"Where am I?" she looked around the strange dwelling. It was small, holding two beds and drying racks filled with a variety of plants.

"In my home you are." The woman spoke as if she were addressing a child, and that made Seera feel uneasy.

"My baby," she remembered and fought the covers back to see her stomach.

"Hush you now," the woman said. "Son is safe, as are you. Fret you not."

"I am not a weak child to be talked to so." Seera's irritation grew.

"Mother and child are safe," the woman continued as if Seera had said nothing. She stood and walked around the crowded house as she muttered.

"Just as I have seen," she spoke as if she was alone. "Come I knew she would. Shown by the goddess was I…by the goddess." She turned her gaze back on Seera and for an instant seemed surprised to see her there.

"Son is strong."

"I will not lose him?" Seera asked, not knowing if this woman had such knowledge as to answer her.

"Favored by Thor he is."

The door opened and in walked another woman, but one unlike any Seera had ever met. She was dressed in a tunic and tight trousers, as a warrior would dress. Her hair was braided and wrapped tight around her head. She glanced at Seera with a hard look.

"You are awake."

"Aye," Seera replied. She was unsure what to make of such a woman. "I would know where I am?" She tried to move but the various pains of her body protested and she lay back on her side with a grunt.

The woman studied her for a moment as if she were being evaluated before she answered. "You are deep in the mountains where no one will find you."

Seera felt a moments ease at the promise before she asked her next question. "Who are you?"

"I am Joka." The woman boasted, in perfect imitation of the way a warrior would speak. "This woman here is my sister. She is Systa."

"I am Seera. How did I get here?"

"I saw your coming, moons ago I did." Systa started ranting again. "I saw you stumble and fall. I saw you wrapped within a tree. You bled and you fevered."

Seera stared at her in astonishment. It was Joka who spoke next. "My sister is one of the Volvas, practitioners of seid."

Seera stared in confusion, bringing a studying gaze from Systa. Her eyes widened in surprise before she spoke next. "She is a Christian, ignorant of our ways my sister."

"A woman of Christ?" Joka looked at her with suspicion.

"Aye," Seera saw no reason to deny her faith. Her prayers had kept her safe.

"Then I shall have to explain," Joka removed a quiver of arrows and a bow from her back before sitting down in a chair that sat beside a wooden table.

"Seid is magic," Joka said. "A Volva is a woman seer, able to prophesize the future."

"Magic?" Seera stared at her in disbelief.

Joka was on her feet and leaning over her bed, knife clasped in her hand so fast Seera had not see her move. "How else do you think I found you while a blizzard raged in these mountains?"

Systa's calming voice cut the tension. "Joka, frighten our guest not. Lacks understanding." She turned her silver eyes on Seera. "Believe she will learn, she will."

Joka resumed her seat, but she scowled at Seera, who realized she would be wise not to anger her.

"I am sorry," Seera offered. "I know little of the old ways."

"Teach you what you need, we will," Systa promised, bringing a grunt from Joka. "Hush now. Rest you need."

Seera shook her head which brought only a blinding pain. "I am fine."

"Child needs it." Systa fussed with the covers until Seera was once again snug in her cocoon. Seera was too weak to resist.

"I need to return to my husband."

A low growl started in Joka's throat. "Husband, what need does a woman have of a husband?"

Seera's defenses rose and she met the warrior woman's hard stare. "I love my husband, and I would see him again."

Joka once again rose and came to stand beside the bed. "A husband to protect you? To keep you safe?" Her gaze roamed over Seera. "A woman would do better to know how to protect herself. Then a man could not do what has been done to you. Where was your husband when you were beaten and raped?"

Seera had no idea how to reply. A part of her wanted to agree that a woman should know how to defend herself. How many times had she been defenseless to a man? How much pain had her ignorance caused her? Rafn could not help when he knew not where she was. What if she'd been able to protect her own self?

Joka stared at her as if knowing her thoughts and this unnerved Seera. This woman knew nothing of her, of her problems, or her life. She returned the woman's disapproving expression with one of defiance. This won her an awkward smile from Joka.

"Joka will teach." Systa proclaimed, even as both the woman stared at her in disbelief. "It is the right thing." She stared at her sister until Joka nodded an assent.

"Just show me the way to Skiringssal, I would return to Rafn." Seera snapped her demand even though just attempting to sit was too much for her.

"The Raven!" Joka stared at her in surprise. "The legendary warlord, feared throughout the Viking world?"

"He is my husband." Seera filled with pride that they knew of him.

"You are wed to him!" Joka spat with a mix of awe and distain.

Seera smiled. "Aye…and he will be looking for me."

"To Jutland he looks," Systa said. Her eyes glazed over, seeing something the others did not. "Blood lays his path. The thunder brews, but his hammer is yet to fall. The god will show before the end."

Seera stared at the woman, sensing the truth of her words, but flinching all the same. Rafn would rip the world apart to find her. This she did not doubt, but she cringed in horror at the violence that would blaze his trail to her.

Joka met her gaze and sneered in contempt. "He does it for you and you would not honor him with your faith. This is a world of violence. To survive it one must embrace that fact."

Seera was unsure of her reaction, or Joka's sudden defense of a man she obviously disdained. "You would have me condone such cruelty?"

"I would have you accept that it is necessary."

She struggled to get free of the heavy hide trapping her. "I must return to my husband!"

Joka's expression tightened into one of anger and revulsion. Her fist flexed around the dagger she held in her hand. Seera saw it was still stained with blood. Joka's words were sharp when she spoke. "To be once again his property?"

"To be his wife." Seera stared at her with anger.

"It is the same thing." Pain shadowed Joka's eyes that made Seera wonder.

"He loves me, and I him," Seera said. Joka's nostrils flared as if to argue, but she kept silent.

Systa interrupted. "Strong your love is. Will be again, but here must you remain."

"Why?" She looked to the Seer.

"Find you he will, giant with one eye." She leaned in close to Seera so she was forced to look at her. "Safe you be here, but leave and hunt you he will. Within his grasp you be forced to see him cut from you the son. Scream for death you will then."

Seera shivered from her prophesy and though she did not believe in magic, she saw the truth of what Systa proclaimed deep in the silver shadows of her eyes. She saw something there that made her flinch and she shut her own eyes against it.

She had never been more afraid, and Rafn was so far away.

"You don't need him," Joka said as if she knew her thoughts. "I will show you how to fight for yourself. This I promise."

Seera stared at the two sisters as she felt the stirring of her son inside her. She placed her hand on her stomach to soothe him. Rafn would find them. He would. But perhaps she should heed Systa's warning and stay where Hwal could not find her.

Hwal and Klintr wandered the forest, deeper and deeper into its depths, searching for sign of Seera's passing. To his amazement, Hwal could find none.

"Did she sprout wings and fly out of here?" Hwal spat. "She is just a woman. An injured pregnant woman! Certainly there is some trace of her."

Klintr did not answer his master and lord for fear of receiving the man's wrath. He refrained from pointing out to Hwal that they had wandered aimlessly in the blizzard, losing any hope of finding such a trail. They were as lost as the girl was bound to be.

But Hwal was not a sane man. He sought with a one minded goal that made no sense to the younger man. Beautiful women could be found elsewhere. What was so important about this one? What power did she possess to cause a man to lose his mind? For he was sure that is what had happened.

Klintr believed she was a witch, and the sooner she died, the better in his opinion. Then would Hwal's sanity return.

The mountains stretched on forever and Klintr despaired in ever finding Seera in the vastness that stood before them.

Hwal would not be deterred. He would have his prize.

When they failed to find Seera in Ribe, Rafn ordered the men to scour the country side. They attacked village after village, searching without mercy for the warlord's wife. But wherever Hwal had taken her, it was not within his holdings. Each day the desperation and the anger grew in Rafn until even his men were afraid to get too close.

Only Valr and Dagstyrr dared tried. They spoke to deaf ears, for Rafn would not stop his war until his wife was found. News of their coming preceded them as they approached each settlement. A thousand Vikings from Vestfold, crashing through the countryside looking for the wife of their most feared warlord.

They left a path of destruction and many widowed women as each day Rafn pushed them forward. After two weeks searching with no answer, Valr finally pulled his brother aside.

"She is not here," Valr said and stood solid against the fury Rafn shot at him with a single glare. "Heed my advice brother. I will go to the ends of the world with you to get her back, but first we must have a plan. We must return to Skiringssal and organize ourselves. We are getting nowhere with this random attacking of the Jute's villages."

"She has to be somewhere," Rafn answered, losing the anger to let through the raw savage pain to his heart. Valr flinched more from that realization than if Rafn threatened him with his spear.

He had known that Rafn loved his Christian wife, but the extent of it was more than Valr had anticipated. Rafn would drive himself mad, until he ended up dead.

"Let us adjourn to our shores, to call more warriors to us. Send out men to find answers. Someone somewhere knows something. We must find that person."

Rafn remained silent, his voice would betray too much of inner turmoil, and he did not trust it. He nodded in agreement.

"Home then," Valr said.

"Home." He did not add that he had no home without Seera and his child.

The violence that surged forth from Rafn sent a ripple through the world. An imbalance had resulted, but Systa saw that it would have to run its course before it was set right again.

It was a path that Rafn must travel before he would be reunited with Seera. It was something that Systa could see, but she would not discuss it with the man's wife. She needed to stay in the meadow and if she worried for her husband than Systa would be unable to make her stay…and it was important for her to remain in the sisters' care.

Systa walked across the meadow and into the forest to follow a path that would take her along the cliff wall. From memory she crept along the narrow path until it led her to the entrance of a small cave. She had found this place the day before. She ducked in through the dark mouth which was lit only by the moonlight that filtered down through the trees.

Systa crawled inside on her hands and knees, feeling her way along the gravelly ground with the palms of her hands. She found the center of the cave floor and shifted to sit cross legged. The moon's light lent just enough light that Systa didn't bother with a fire.

She began to chant softly, calling to the goddess for strength. A feeling of calm descended over her as she finished with her song. She turned her thoughts to the injured woman lying in her bed. Of the first time the pregnant woman had entered her dreams.

It was the same night that Joka had found the courage to end their father's life, that she'd first had the dream of Seera and her son. As the vision swirled in her mind, her sister had taken a dagger to their sleeping father, freeing them once and for all from the nightmare that had always been their lives. They had run then from the pain and the death towards a hope that they would each find something more.

Systa had promised Joka that it was in this very meadow that they would find the beginning to a new life. It had been the right thing to do. To distance themselves from the place that had been nothing more than a prison to the women who dwelled within it. Systa had enjoyed watching Joka's strength grow as she found herself.

It was important that Joka teach Seera what she knew. To show her that there was a way to fight back against the violence. These things Systa had told Joka, but the Seer had seen far more than she had ever shared with her sister.

She had not explained to her that it was important that the Raven find his wife here, that both their futures were somehow connected to the man who had become a legend. Systa didn't know yet what that future was, only that it would be. Joka would not understand this. She trusted no man.

She heard the cawing of a raven in the trees beyond the cave and she peered out to catch a glimpse of it as it took flight. It flew swiftly through the night air to land on the ground just outside the cave.

His head swiveled back and forth as he stared at the silver eyed woman sitting within. A smile touched Systa's face. The raven lifted his wings wide and took to the sky.

Systa watched him disappear into the darkness with clear understanding.

CHAPTER 24

The cawing of a raven woke Seera from her scattered dreams. Longing for her husband still echoed within her. She ached to feel his warmth pressed up against her in the night. Through the small window, she could see that the moon was still high in the dark night.

Seera fought past the confusion of the unfamiliar cottage. The dull ache of her back seized her senses and she remembered where she was.

She squinted into the darkness, but the fire had gone out in the hearth and she could barely make out the sleeping form of Joka across from her. She did not see the other one, Systa. Her heavy eyelids closed as she shifted to find a position that was comfortable, while avoiding touching her back.

Her fusing ended and she fell back to sleep, not waking again until it was morning. The bright sunlight through the open window brought her awake. This time when she looked around she was where she expected to be. There was no illusion that she might be home in her husband's bed.

Even before she opened her eyes she knew the smell was not right. The air was crisper and didn't carry the smell of salt that she'd always been used to. It had been with her through her childhood at Dun'O'Tir and blowing off the sea in her new home in Skiringssal. Even Ribe had been close to the ocean.

The salty smell and the sound of the waves had always been the one constant in her life. Its absence was a sure sign that she was still so far from home.

Seera struggled to sit as voices outside the door carried into the empty cottage. The door ease open to admit Systa, who smiled pleasantly when she noticed Seera was up.

"Good morning," Seera said as the woman approached her.

"As well to you." Systa pushed a stool up beside the bed so that she could sit. "Look at back need I." She motioned for Seera to lie down on her side.

Seera was naked since Systa had removed her ruined clothing when Joka had first carried her in unconscious. Unfortunately Seera had nothing else to wear. She doubted either sister would have a dress that would fit over her expanded stomach.

She would worry about that later.

Seera let Systa remove the bandages from her back. As they peeled away, the air stung the tender sores and she tried not to wince from the discomfort.

"Beginning to scab are they," Systa said. "Not long and better will they feel."

"I know. This is not the first time he has whipped my back raw. Though I think it was worse this time." Seera let the words slip out. She turned her head to find Systa staring at her with surprise.

"Took you from your husband, I thought?" She began to apply a soothing ointment to the wounds that made them feel a lot better.

"Aye. This time he took me from my husband, but once before he took me from my father."

Seera told the tale of how Drenger and Hwal had come to Pictland and taken her, how she was made a slave. Joka entered the dwelling and sat on the other bed. She stared at her with a hard expression, but she made no attempt to interrupt.

"It was Rafn who rescued me from that place and took me back to his sister in Skiringssal to be healed." As she explained and she could have sworn she heard a grunt from Joka when she spoke her husband's name.

"Much have you endured," Systa said and placed her hand on Seera's shoulder.

"What woman hasn't?" Seera heard the bitterness in Joka's voice. She looked at her and saw Joka was surprised to have spoken aloud. Having drawn Seera's attention, her expression hardened, but not before she glimpsed a deep seeded pain. Seera sensed not to ask.

Speaking of the things that had happened to her, made Seera remember something she had almost forgotten in her delirium. Right before Hwal had taken her, one of his men had stabbed Kata. The last she had seen of her sister-in law, she was lying unconscious on the ground…she had not wanted to believe she was dead.

Systa's gaze shifted to her as if she sensed that Seera wanted to ask her something. "Be not afraid to ask questions of me."

"You have said that you can see things?" Seera looked to the woman with uncertainty.

"Aye, see many things I do."

"I need to know if my sister-in law, Kata, is alright. When I was taken she was injured badly. I need to know she did not die." She met the Seer's gaze with such hope.

"Tell you that I cannot," Systa said with regret. "Only you was I shown."

"I understand." Her fear grew in her from her disappointment. She had to accept that she would not know Kata's fate until she returned to Skiringssal. Tears blurred her vision, but she felt no embarrassment as they flowed down her face. Her friend might be dead, because of Hwal's obsession for her. That was a truth no one needed to tell her.

It was her guilt to bear.

Systa returned once again to her private cave to weave her magic; the net that would hold the one-eyed giant more effectively than a dozen strong men.

A cauldron burned over the fire she had built, suspended on a tripod. Many plants that had been specially prepared, as well as the heart and liver of a wolf, lay on the ground beside her.

One by one, she dropped her items into the pot, as she chanted words of binding. The cauldron hissed when the heart and liver were added, and a blue smoke rose up from the pot. It spun into the air above her.

She spoke more words, this time giving instruction to the smoke that held the spell. She gave it directions to search and it disappeared through the cave opening.

Systa smiled in satisfaction, knowing her trap would snare the man.

The blue smoke traveled the forest trails, unable to deviate from its course. Animals stepped out of the way, leaving the witch's snare to find its prey.

Hwal and Klintr wandered still. The younger man was ahead scouting the trail and could not see what came from behind.

The one-eyed giant turned as if sensing the danger. He stared at the blue smoke, not understanding its significance, but realizing it as a bad omen. He opened his mouth to call back Klintr, but by doing so he opened a path for the smoke to enter.

He choked as it slid into his body and his vision blurred. He swatted at an unseen foe and clawed at his neck in a sudden desperate instinct to be rid of it.

Klintr turned back to see the actions of his Jarl. A blue aura surrounded the man, but it soon dissipated.

Hwal looked at him and he shivered.

Summer's heat had come and Seera's stomach grew as her seventh month of pregnancy began. Her wounds were healing, but she stayed with the sisters, for her son's safety. Systa had made a dress for Seera and surprised her with it the first time she was able to get out of bed and venture outside.

It had surprised Seera to walk out through the wooden door to find she was in such a beautiful place. It was so peaceful and quiet. Seera was quick to appreciate the tranquility of the meadow that the sisters had made their home, and realized it was a good place to recover and wait for her husband to find her.

She had come to like Systa and Joka. It was not hard to admire their decision to leave the world of men behind them and fend for themselves.

Seera had learned that Systa had been feared by the town folk and was accused of being a witch. She didn't know Joka's story yet, but knew a painful one lay buried deep in the woman's soul to have hardened her so.

It had rained that morning and as the sky cleared to reveal a blue sky, a rainbow streaked across the heavens that took Seera's breath away. "It is so beautiful."

"Bridge it is," Systa said.

"A bridge?" She looked to the Seer for understanding.

"Aye, between us and the gods. Heimdall guards it, he does. Bifrost it is called." As Systa spoke she split long pieces of grass with her finger nail, placing them in a growing pile at her side.

Seera sat next to her. "I have never thought of a rainbow as anything other than a miracle of God."

"What is miracle? What is touched by the gods?" She handed a pile of un-split grass to Seera, who tried to follow the woman's example.

"The world was created by God. Many miracles, many beauties did he gift us, in everything that is around us."

"Interesting is this faith," Systa said. Her hands stopped in their action to look up at Seera.

"I suppose it is as strange to you as your beliefs are to me," Seera said.

"We of the old do not discount the existence of the new, as you of God are quick to." She resumed her task, making short work of splitting the grass until none were left. Seera quicken to keep pace.

"I don't discount them," Seera looked shocked at the accusation.

"Believe you not. Allow not that others are possible." She reached for a couple of separated strands and began to weave them together.

"My faith does not allow for us to acknowledge any god other than Our Holy Father."

"Why?" Her hands moved in a practiced pattern without her even looking down. Seera could see the shape of a basket emerging in Systa's lap.

"It is what is taught, and it is our place not to question." Seera split the last of her grass, but she had no idea how to weave anything.

"Should always question. Must question why gods do the things they do."

Seera did not answer for she had no argument against Systa's wisdom. Was it so wrong to want answers? Was it not right to seek them?

Systa smiled with kindness as she always did. Seera did not always understand the Seer, but she had grown to respect her.

Through the many days that followed, Seera learned much from Systa about the gods in Asgard, about the earth spirits; the giants, elves, trolls and dwarfs. She learned about the importance of the great ash tree, Yggdrasil, the World Tree. It was around this tree that all the various Norse worlds revolved.

The World Tree rose through the middle of Asgard where the gods regularly assembled within. The tree had three main roots; One that stretched down to Niflheim and Hvergelmin, the seething cauldron in which life had originated. Another grew in Midgard, and was nourished by the Well of Knowledge and guarded by the giant Mimir. The last root sprang in Asgard.

As a living entity, Yggdrasil was at continuous risk of decay. Four sacred deer nibbled on its leaves, while its lower root was gnawed by the serpent Nidhogg. Though even as it was threatened, it renewed itself and was a symbol of life and a symbol of endurance to the Norse.

Odin was the supreme deity, but not the only one to be worshipped and sacrificed to, as Seera already knew. Rafn had always chosen Thor as his god of worship. Never forgetting Odin in his sacrifices, but looking to Thor for guidance. Thor was known as the strongest of the gods and defender of both Asgard and Midgard, as well as the protector of chaos.

It was all so different than the words of the Lord spoken by the priests. She found the intricacies fascinating. Yet it was based on such violence that Seera knew she could never turn from her own God. No matter how interested she was in another people's beliefs.

Joka came to Seera as soon as she was satisfied that she'd healed enough to begin training. Joka's insistence pushed past any reservations Seera had.

"Do you want to always be a victim to the men who seek to harm you?"

"No, I don't." Too often had she been helpless to the will of a man, at their mercy.

"That is good." Joka smiled. She was quite attractive when the rare expression touched her face. Many men must have desired her.

Seera wondered about that. Perhaps it was not such a good thing to be desired. Look what trouble had befallen her because men wanted to possess her.

"Teach me Joka. Tell me how to survive when I find myself alone."

The warm wind rushed across the open meadow, creating a wave of colors as the flowers danced to its movement. It swept across Seera's face. She closed her eyes to enjoy the refreshing feel of it.

"You have a strong spirit Seera. Your strength will come if you call upon it." Seera opened her eyes to find Joka's stern study of her.

Seera felt a familiar sensation behind her. She sensed an otherworldly encouragement wash over her, bringing her support. Orn touched her shoulder in approval.

Seera glanced to her side to see Systa staring strangely at her, but by then Orn was gone.

She followed Joka to a field the woman used for training. A straw target was set up on the far end. She placed in Seera's hand a bow that she'd just finished making. It still carried the strong scent of a willow tree.

"This is your weapon," she said. "You must treat it with respect so that it will protect you when you need it to."

Seera ran her finger along the smooth wood and tested the tautness of the string. She felt a power surge through her.

"The bow is a good weapon for you. As long as you are with child, you can't learn the spear or sword. But the bow will give you the advantage of distance so you need not rely on strength."

Joka placed an arrow into her bow and pulled back on the string until her aim was steady and sure. The arrow sailed through the air with precision, landing in the center of the target. Seera was impressed and feared she would never be able to even come close.

Seera's first attempt was clumsy. She tried to imitate Joka's actions but when she tried to pull back the string, the arrow popped out and landed on the ground.

The next attempt was no better. The third the string snapped, cutting her finger and she somehow managed to break the arrow. Embarrassment replaced the excitement she'd been feeling only a short time before.

Joka stood behind her, but when Seera glanced over her shoulder, the woman's face was unreadable. "It is alright, it will come. Do not give up hope. Push past the frustration and you will succeed."

Seera turned back to face the target. "I pray you are right."

"I was not so coordinated when I began learning." Joka moved Seera's arms into the right position, and stood flush to her back.

"Truly," Seera asked.

"I broke many arrows." She surprised Seera with a laugh. "Keep your arms steady." She placed her hand over Seera's and helped her pull the arrow back, while the other assisted in steadying the bow.

With Joka's help the arrow flew forward, managing to hit the edge of the target. Now if she could only do so on her own, she thought.

"Thank you," Seera said.

Joka nodded in acknowledgment, looking away as she did so, as if receiving thanks was an embarrassment.

Rafn stood on the cliff overlooking the ocean. It had always been a favorite spot of his, and remembered how Seera had found the place on her own. He ground his teeth together as his memories tormented him with an image of how she had looked standing on this very cliff. He had just returned from the north and had not yet seen her beauty behind the bruises. She had been a vision from a dream…and he knew beyond doubt that she was his.

Kata startled him as she came to join him. He looked at her for a brief moment with eyes unveiled before they became distanced by the hardness that had taken hold of him.

"Brother." She laid a gentle hand on his arm, causing him to stiffen. He did not want to be touched by anyone. Not unless it was his wife's hand. Sensing this, Kata withdrew her hand.

"I miss her too," she said and regretted her words as he narrowed his eyes in disbelief at her mention of Seera. She took a step back from him. She had never been afraid of this brother, never had cause to walk lightly around him, but she was suddenly unsure. He did not welcome her counsel as he once had.

"You are healed," he asked her as his eyes drifted back to the rough waters that spread to the horizon.

"Aye," she could say no more.

"Go then sister," he said. "I am not good company and I have no wish to lash out at you."

Kata could only nod and leave him to his silent torture. Kata walked back through town, saddened by the loss of her friend and her brother's pain. Dagstyrr grabbed her hand and pulled her towards their dwelling.

"Would he speak to you?" Dagstyrr asked when they were alone.

"Nay." Kata shook her head as tears glistened in her brown eyes.

Dagstyrr drew her into his arms. "He won't talk to anyone, including me."

Kata sobbed into his shoulder. "I have never seen him this bad." Not even after Orn's death had he drawn so completely into the darkness.

Dagstyrr's embrace grew tighter as he sensed her need for comfort. "He has never loved this way before."

"Do you think she is still alive?" She pulled back so she could read the truth in her husband's eyes.

"I truly do not know." His words gripped her heart, for she could see in his expression that he believed the worst.

Klintr brought down a stag that they had happened upon. Thankfully Hwal had kept silent instead of continuing with the ranting he'd been doing as of late. He often spoke to himself as if he was having a conversation with another person. It was very unnerving.

Klintr pulled the stag to the river's side where he'd left Hwal sitting. The giant was still in the same spot, staring at the flow of the water in the river as if he expected something to rise up out of it.

He dragged the deer close to the water's edge and began skinning it with his belt knife. He was clumsy in his technique as he hacked away at the hide. It was not work he usually did and the cut he made from neck to anus was ragged at best. He tore the hide back, exposing entrails and organs. He had no use for the hide and planned to leave it for the wolves to fight over.

What motivated him was the hunger that had been gnawing at his stomach since their supplies had run out. He'd been catching fish and rabbits to keep them fed, but he craved for something more filling.

He made a mess out of butchering the stag, but he managed to cut out some decent sized hunks of meat that he suspended over the fire on a makeshift tripod. Hwal watched him through his one good eye, saying nothing, for which Klintr was grateful for.

Klintr moved closer to the fire to check the cooking meat and could hear that Hwal was mumbling under his breath. He couldn't make out the man's words, but the hairs on the back of his neck stood up as if he felt some evil presence. He did not doubt it. This forest gave him the creeps. Something unnatural dwelled within them and the sooner they left them the better he would feel.

Hwal reached out and grabbed one of the hunks off the tripod and began devouring it as if he were a wild beast. The half cooked meat dripped blood and grease down the giants chin. He did not bother asking for an eating knife, but tore away at the meat with his teeth as if they were fangs.

It was almost enough to make Klintr lose his appetite.

CHAPTER 25

With reluctance Rafn sent word to Peder, knowing his brother-in law would not forgive being kept from the truth. His message was sent swiftly and soon Peder, Lord of Dun'O'Tir arrived.

Valr met him on the dock, for Rafn was out again searching. The young lord was not pleased when he disembarked from the drekar and stood face to face with the Jarl.

"Has my sister been found?" There was an icy coldness to his blue eyes. A violent wind rocked the ship behind him as the clouds darkened overhead.

"Nay, but the search continues still."

"Where is my brother-in law?" His eyes scanned the port but did not find him. He ignored the merchants scurrying around to secure their stalls and pack away their supplies as the impending storm grew closer.

"He searches along the coast for any sign of the route Hwal took when he left here." The wind tore at his cloak and his eyes shifted to the black sky. "Let us speak more in the Great Hall and I will have the servants fetch some mead."

Peder looked back to his would be host and recalled his manners. "I am sorry for my rudeness," he said. "I am Peder of Dun'O'Tir, the Fortress by the Sea, and brother to the Lady Seera."

"Welcome Lord Peder, I am Valr Vakrson, Jarl of Skiringssal and brother to your sister's husband."

"It is a pleasure." Peder grew tired of the formalities and wanted to return to the topic of Seera's abduction.

"Let us talk in comfort." Valr led him through the dispersing crowd as the first drops of rain fell. Peder only glanced at the town he'd been so curious about. It did not hold any interest against the worry in his heart.

Valr had them seated with a drinking horn of mead in their hands before they spoke again. Peder's patience was growing thin. Valr sensing this was quick to tell him everything that had been done so far in finding Seera.

"Hwal seems to have vanished," Valr said. "We have left men in Ribe to wait his return, but he has made no attempt to return home."

"And the rest of his holdings?" Peder shifted with restlessness in his seat. He ignored the mead before him.

"We have found no trace that either Hwal or Seera has been anywhere in his lands." Valr waved off a serving girl before she could interrupt.

"They must be somewhere." Certainly his sister had not vanished into thin air. Where might a madman take her?

"Rafn will not stop until she is found," Valr promised. Peder face tightened at hearing the warlord's name. Valr would need to soothe the man's temper before Rafn returned.

"Have you returned again to Jutland since the first search?" The rain hit hard against the thatch roof and against the planks of the walls. The wind howled through the cracks in an eerie wailing.

"We tore the land apart for weeks before turning back," Valr explained. "We left no rock unturned." Valr lifted his drinking horn and sipped the fermented honeyed drink, allowing it to warm the chill that had come to him.

"You are satisfied she is not there?" Impatience infused his words.

"I will never be satisfied," Rafn said as he came up behind the two men.

Peder rose and lashed out at Rafn with no hesitation. "You vowed to keep her safe, when I gave her to you in marriage. Yet you did nothing to prevent this threat you knew was against her."

Rafn made no attempt to stop Peder's attack, even when the man shoved him hard in outrage. Valr was on his feet immediately, his hand going for his sword, but a swift look from Rafn stayed his hand.

"If my sister has come to harm...," the fierceness of the lord's voice cut deep into Rafn's pain.

Whether from fatigue, or the truth of Peder's words, Rafn flinched. If Peder had not been but inches from the other man's face, he would have missed it. At realization of the depth of rage and suffering he saw buried in the mighty warrior's eyes he backed off.

"I apologize." Peder felt his anger melt away.

"I head for Jutland in the morning," Rafn said as if nothing had happened. "I will take with me an army twice as large as before and I will not rest until they tell me where their Jarl has hidden."

"I am going with you." Peder demanded, refusing to be left behind. He was satisfied when Rafn did not argue.

"I welcome your strong hand. Rest tonight, for it will be your last." With that he left Valr to care for their guest.

"He does not look well." Peder was shocked at finding the fierce Viking warrior so vulnerable.

"Nay, he has been pushing himself and his men since Seera was first taken," the Jarl said. "His love for her goes deep."

"So it would seem." His gaze met Valr's and saw something unspoken in them. Peder waited for him to speak what troubled him.

"It would be good for you to know, that Seera is with child."

Peder stared in surprise at the Jarl of Skiringssal. Valr's words did nothing to ease his worry.

The sweet scent of pine rode the wind, touching Seera's skin with the warmth of the day. Her son stirred and she placed a gentle hand to soothe him. It wouldn't be long until he was born and still Rafn had not come.

Did he believe her dead?

The thought sparked a pang of dread. If he did not think she was alive, than he would never come. She would have to find him.

She inhaled deeply, determined that her strength would not fail her. It was what the sisters taught. That a woman had to look no further than herself to find the security she needed. No man need define her. No man was needed for protection.

She ran her hand along the wood grain of the bow she carried. It had been sanded smooth, not by a man's hand, but by a woman's. She felt the thrill quiver inside.

It was in her reach, to be self sufficient…and strong.

Fear did not have to rule her when she was caught in a situation not of her making. She knew all too well how suddenly the cruel world could push something upon her that she was unprepared for. She'd been struck more than once when complacent…but she could seize control, if she dared.

A light breeze tousled her hair as she took aim at the target on the other side of the field. She recalled Joka's words about seeing the center of the target in her mind and never taking her eyes from it.

Feel the power of the bow as the string is pulled taunt, Joka had said. With steady arms loose the arrow. When in combat, do not wait for the arrow to find its mark before loading another arrow.

But Seera did not feel the power the way Joka described it. As if the bow had its own spirit. Seera knew that it did not. It was too hard for her to accept what she believed to be pagan beliefs. Even with the knowledge that Joka believed without question.

What she did feel was the cramping of her muscles as she forced them to work in a way they never had before. Stifling the complaint that so easily rose in her mind, she pulled just a little further back on the string and kept her gaze locked on the center of the stuffed pad she was using for a target.

She released it, bringing with it a sigh of relief from the easing of her muscles. The arrow flew true, and Seera watched in stunned amazement as it tore into the hide bag. Not the exact center, but very close.

She couldn't stop the pride from claiming her. In a boastful way that would be frowned on by the monks in the monastery back home, she laughed and whooped with pleasure.

"A good shot." Joka appeared from a path that led deep into the trees. She was just returning from a successful hunt.

"Thank you." Seera was unable to hide her excitement. And why should she? She beckoned to the deer slung over Joka's shoulder. "Let me help."

"Nay, you are too far gone in your pregnancy to be doing any lifting."

"You are right." Seera frowned at having to admit that despite all, she still had limits.

"It will not be so long," Joka said as if she knew exactly what her thoughts had been. "After he is born, there will be no boundaries."

"It is what I hope for."

"You can still scrape the hide." Joka smiled at Seera's startled look.

When had she ever had to scrape a hide? "I will do my best." She did not want to admit to her lack of knowledge.

"I will teach you." She met Joka's knowing expression.

"You and Systa have been so kind to teach me so many things." She lost her smile and was overcome by such gratitude, that Joka looked away in embarrassment.

"It is only what all women should know." Joka quickened her pace.

As promised, after skinning the deer, Joka taught Seera how to scrape the tissue off the hide. It was awkward in the beginning, especially trying to work around her large stomach, but soon she caught on to the technique. Joka's smile encouraged her to continue.

Systa had joined them after having spent the afternoon collecting the plants she needed to restock her supply of medicines.

"How feel you today?" Systa bent down next to her.

"A bit sore, but nothing that gives me concern." She sat back and allowed Systa to take the hide from her and roll it up so she could carry it.

"I know of what will ease aches." Systa looked to Joka with an odd smile.

"You are right." Joka seemed to know exactly what her sister was suggesting and Seera looked from one to the other for an answer.

Having cleared away their work and stored the meat, Systa led them into the trees behind their dwelling. They came to a path that looked like it had been used often enough to have left a clear narrow path.

A strong sulfurous scent drifted on the air, but neither sister seemed concerned by it, so Seera followed without questioning it. She was curious when she saw steam rising above the trees from some place up ahead.

They came to a clearing with a large circular pool nestled up against a cliff wall. The strong smell was coming from the steaming water, and Seera understood. She'd heard about such places.

"It is a mineral pool." Seera stared at it with excitement.

"Healing waters it is," Systa said. "Its warmth will embrace you and aches will be soothed."

Seera smiled and undressed. With Systa's help she eased down into the water. She was able to submerge up to her neck and it was a most pleasant delight. Far better than the tubs she was used to bathing in, that barely covered her.

The heat that almost seemed too hot when she first stepped in soon became soothing and Seera felt relaxed in a way she hadn't in a long while.

A raven cawed in a tree overhead, drawing Seera's attention. It watched from its perch, swiveling its head back and forth. Seera felt drawn to the bird as it lifted into the sky.

That night Seera slept deep. For once she was not haunted by the dreams that too often crept into her sleep. Instead only a comforting light touched the edges of her mind. She welcomed it, for it was familiar.

Orn was with her, as he often was since she'd come to stay with the sisters. He was a guardian angel watching over her.

She had not shared with the sisters about her belief that Orn's spirit was with her, but she had seen Systa staring at her with suspicion more than once.

Orn came to her that night in her dreams, and she was glad to look upon his face. In some small way it made her feel closer to Rafn.

"I feel your soul strengthening each day." Orn took her hand and she felt a jolt shimmer through her.

"I am learning to defend myself," Seera said, even though Orn already knew this.

"Rafn would be proud."

"Would he?" Seera searched his eyes for answers and was stunned by the mystery that lay within them. She felt an impulse to reach out to that unknown which he had touched. "Or will he think it not the place of a woman to have such knowledge."

"You think he will not approve?" He frowned with worry.

"I would like to believe he would be pleased, but he is a warrior, and a man. In my experience men expect to control their woman."

"It is true." Orn sighed. "Most men Norse and Christian alike prefer to know they are the masters. But love has a way of softening even the mightiest man."

"Is that why you are here Orn? To tell me I should not stop."

"I have sensed your reluctance to accept the words of the Sisters completely. They will teach you what you need to know. Do not be afraid to embrace it."

Seera squeezed Orn's hand and his peace became apart of her. They sat in silence for a time, before he had to leave.

Orn placed a hand on her stomach and smiled. "It will not be so long now."

"Will Rafn find us before then?"

"I don't have that answer." With those words the light faded and she felt the same sense of loss she did each time their connection was broken.

She woke to find Systa staring at her. The woman hissed in fear of what she had felt. Of the presence that still lingered in the space around them.

"Who is this that comes to you?" Her face crunched up nastily, insanity shinning in her eyes.

Seera stared at her in fear. She had never seen Systa like this. She was on the defensive, ready to spring at the unseen enemy. Seera sat up and reached for Systa, who immediately backed up and crouched to the floor.

She crawled backward on the floor, sniffing the air as if it carried a deadly scent. "Tell me?"

Seera tried to put her at ease. "He is the spirit of my brother-in law. He watches over me only. He means no harm."

"A man?" She stood quickly and began turning in a slow circle, seeking the source of her discomfort.

"He was a good Christian man, killed far too young by the Jarl of Ribe." Seera reached a hand to the Seer who refused to take it. She took a step backwards.

"A Christian?" She was suspicious. "Raven is his brother?"

"He was Rafn's younger brother, and he was a good man." Seera let her hand drop back to her lap.

"Why comes he?" Another hiss escaped Systa as she remained ready to attack.

"He has been with me since I escaped Hwal's grasp and almost died." She tried to get the woman to understand. "I was there when he died, and we have a connection. I can't explain why or how. Yet it is so and he brings me comfort."

"His spirit you fear not?" Systa's voice softened.

"Nay, it is pure and gentle. He has been touched by God's grace and I do not fear him."

Understanding came to Systa and she began to relax. She moved to sit by Seera on the bed. "Much have I to learn of your god." Systa sprang to her feet, anxious for the conversation to end. "Breakfast I will make."

Seera began to rise. "I could help." Systa waved her off.

"Joka waits."

Systa left and Seera fought her way off the pallet that served as her bed. She moved with awkwardness to a basket near the wall and pulled out the dress Systa had made her. With difficulty she pulled it on.

As she was about to reach the latch on the door she felt Orn's presence. Her shoulder tingled with heat as it did each time he touched her. She sensed his unease.

"It will all be fine," she whispered to him.

CHAPTER 26

They followed the river inland and were upon the next settlement with swiftness. Rafn ordered the longships pulled to shore, and the warriors jumped from the crafts, eager for battle.

Rafn was the first onto land, the serpent held ready in his hand. He was armored and helmeted, a fierce expression pasted permanently on his face. He looked like a man out of a nightmare.

"Take everything you find and kill any who oppose." Rafn's men hollered in answer to his call.

Over the last week they had come upon one village after another, and in each case Rafn showed no mercy. He plundered everything that the settlers owned. He killed any man who stood ready to defend what was theirs.

Peder watched with a growing trepidation as the Raven was unleashed. Even as he understood Rafn's pain, he worried about the savagery of his actions. It was not for him to stop the man from what he must do, but Peder made sure that Rafn did not allow undue harm to come to the women or children, though it proved not to be a problem among the Raven's men. Rafn and his brother Valr followed an honorable code, and their warriors were well trained and respectful.

They approached the village as a violent storm descending upon a scarred land. The women screamed as they spotted the armed warrior. Men reached for whatever weapons they could, though they were not trained Vikings used to doing battle, but farmers. They held axes, scathes, knives and some even grabbed for their bows and arrows. None possessed a sword or spear.

"I look for Hwal." Rafn stood before the gathered men standing as a wall between them and their families. The women and children could be seen running from the village.

The Raven's men ignored them, allowing them their escape, but kept their fierce gazes locked on the unorganized men. More than one looked ready to faint on the spot.

One brave old man came forward. "He has not come here. He sends one of his men for the tribute. Never does he do it himself."

Rafn saw the truth of the man's words, and gave a nod to signal his men to advance forward.

"My men will take what they like. Fight and you will die. If you flee with your families we will not pursue."

One young man pulled back the arrow in his bow and sent it flying, but Rafn saw the action and sidestepped the deadly missile. Without hesitation his axe was thrown through the air and embedded in the man's skull. The others jumped back in surprise at the suddenness of the man's death and the accuracy of the axe.

"I am Rafn Vakrson, Warlord of Skiringssal." He paused to watch the reaction of his name as it rippled through the villagers. "Your Jarl has greatly insulted me." His eyes flared with his anger and held the village men captive with their fear. "Until he faces me like a man, I will decimate his people. Deliver my message to him."

Rafn ordered his warriors to enter the village and soon they were ripping apart the dwellings, pulling from them all they could find.

"Brother." Peder laid a hand on Rafn's shoulder as he chose to sit back and let his men tear through the village. Rafn deflated under his scrutiny. It was not obvious to the farmers who cowed before him, but to the man who had come to know the Raven's moods over the last many days. Peder could tell that Rafn had become paralyzed with the hopelessness of their fight.

"We go on." Rafn stated his simple need before Peder could voice his concerns.

"As you wish." If they did not find Seera soon, Rafn would destroy himself and Peder knew his sister would not want that. He had no wish to see Rafn lose his soul to this desperate quest.

Hwal and Klintr discovered a single family farm in their wandering. Hwal had begun acting paranoid, seeing danger in ever shadow they came upon. Klintr believed the Jarl had lost his hold on sanity, but the young warrior was too afraid to leave the man. A crazy Hwal could be more dangerous than a sane one.

So Klintr stayed with Hwal doubting his decision daily, but not having the courage to leave him. Hwal was sometimes lucid and at other times speaking in riddles that made no sense. It was a cloudy day when they came on the farm.

"They will have food," Klintr suggested when it seemed that Hwal would give him no direction.

"Aye they would keep their food from us. They would try and hide it."

"They would not deny one such as you, my lord."

"Deceitful they are." Hwal snarled as they drew closer to the dwelling that had been built close to the trees across the field they farmed. "They hide Seera from me even now."

"We don't know that Seera is here." Klintr tried to reason but Hwal would not listen.

A woman stepped from the dwelling with a basket in her arms. She noticed them and started to wave in a friendly gesture of welcome until she noticed Hwal and she stepped back.

Fear sprang in her eyes, as if she already knew what Hwal intended for her. Klintr understood. Hwal brought out that instinct in most people, even had he not drawn his sword and carried it as if he went into battled.

The woman turned to run, but Hwal had expected her action and stopped her retreat. He held her back against his chest and the woman started to whimper.

"Where is she?" The giant spoke into her ear.

"Who do you speak of?" The woman's voice trembled.

"Seera, where have you hidden her?" He held the sword up for her to see. A stream of light broke through the clouds and reflected off the iron.

Tears flowed freely down her face and the woman began to shake in fear.

"I know no Seera." She begged him to believe her, but he refused to. Klintr could see from the woman's face that she did not lie, but he was not about to voice his opinion. Hwal was as likely to use his blade on him, as the woman.

Hwal turned the woman so that she was forced to look into his ugly face. Her eyes grew wide with terror and she knew the moment he had lost his patience with her. She screamed as the sword was pushed between her ribs, puncturing one of her lungs. Blood bubbled to her mouth and her screaming stopped. Hwal pushed her away in disgust and kicked her body from him as if it were vermin.

"Mother!" Klintr turned to see a young man racing across the field towards them. He carried no weapon other than an axe as hurried in his anger.

He should have stopped to think, Klintr believed, but this young man was not a warrior. He would not have been trained from a young boy to be a Viking. He may have some skill, but he was nothing but an annoyance for the man who'd killed his mother.

"Where have you hidden my slave, boy?" Hwal howled in a voice that stopped the man in his tracks just out of the giant's reach. The boy looked at his mother and seeing that she was dead, he shouted in rage.

"She was my mother." The young man had courage, Klintr had to admit, but he was foolish all the same.

Hwal pointed his sword, blood dripping from the tip. "My slave, give her to me."

"I don't have your slave." He seemed to sense finally that the one-eyed giant was perhaps possessed, but certainly deadly.

Hwal moved towards him with casualness, as if the boy were a mere pest that was irritating him. He did not even lend his full strength to the swing of his bloody sword. The young man managed to stop it with his axe, but the weapon was just a simple tool used for chopping firewood, it had no real power.

It did not take Hwal long to add his body to the dirt beside the woman. A displeased grunt escaped him as he pushed his way into the dwelling.

No one else hid inside, but the father had to be around somewhere and Klintr kept a watch behind them while Hwal tore the place apart.

By the time the giant was done the place was a shambles. He'd overturned beds, emptied trunks, scattered herbs and dishes and anything else he could find. When he found no trace of Seera he became enraged and Klintr just stood out of his way and let him wreck what havoc he could.

They found a pantry of food, dug into the ground behind the cottage and Klintr filled their packs with supplies, while Hwal went back to the dwelling and using coals from the hearth he set it on fire.

It was not long before the flames engulfed the structure and as Klintr had expected, the man whose family Hwal had killed came running down a hill behind the house where he'd been up tending to his sheep.

He hurried towards his dwelling frantic to stop the fire, but he failed to notice the two strange men until he came around the cottage and saw the bodies of his wife and son. He stopped in shock before looking up to meet the madness of the one-eyed giant and knew his fate was sealed.

The next village Rafn came to was expecting him. Their women and children, even their elderly, had already been sent away. Waiting for them were not the simple farmers that had been allowing them to ransack their homes in exchange for their lives, but warriors. At least a thousand thick, they waited armored and ready with weapons to stop the Raven from going further.

But Rafn was not cowed. His force was easily twice as large, and he did not fear defeat.

As the Jutes began pounding their spears against their shields in intimidation and fury, Rafn's eyes flared in anticipation. Dagstyrr and Peder flanked him, and each was as prepared to fight as he. He had always trusted Dagstyrr and had come to respect Peder over the past weeks that he'd stayed loyally by his side. He fought as well as any of his men.

He was no coward.

Fight they would, fight until all lay dead. If Hwal would not show himself, than he would condemn his men to death.

Rafn's warriors took up the beat of pounding spears against shields and hollered a deadly cry that rose higher and fiercer than their enemies. To the Jutes eyes it was if the two thousand men before them had all suddenly turned into the legendary Beserkers. Men who worked themselves into a killing frenzy before going into battle, needing only to take life after life.

But Rafn knew they were not, for he'd trained his men to be in control at all times even in the heat of battle. A warrior was far more vulnerable when he let the killing lust claim him and disregarded all reason. A man must keep strategy to each motion of his sword, each swing, each lunge. One must always be able to see the next step, even before their opponent reacts.

So even as his men planted fear in the Jutes hearts, Rafn stood deadly still, his eyes fixed on the moment ahead of him. Peder was impressed at Rafn's sudden and absolute control. He was not intimidated by the enemy force that stood before him.

He whistled for his horse to be brought to him, and he was soon mounted along with Dagstyrr, Peder and about a hundred others. The rest of the men would go into battle on foot. They had not wanted to bring along too many horses to slow them down.

It would not matter. Their numbers worked for them, as did their training by the greatest warrior of their time.

Almost in unison, by some unseen signal, the two war parties charged each other. Swords clashed in a growing crescendo and soon each man was engaged in hand to hand combat.

Rafn felt the storm rise in him and he drew out the thunder…then he unleashed the Raven onto the battlefield. He brought down man after man without effort. He pushed further into the thick crowd, until his horse hindered him. He jumped from his mount so he could fight in closer quarters.

He hacked and he sliced and he faced one angry warrior after another. Blood drenched his tunic, smeared his skin, and spattered his legs, his shield and his helmet. Seera would not recognize him if she were to see him stabbing his way through Hwal's men in hopes that he would find her.

The blackness completely consumed him as each movement he made called forth more power. He continued until he stood face to face with Hwal's second in command. He matched Rafn equally in size and the determination on his face spoke of his courage. The two men circled as they judged and prepared for the fight.

He fought with a touch of insanity and found his strength begin to ebb as thoughts of Seera started to intrude in his mind, making him lose his needed concentration. Where was his wife? How many men did he have to kill to find her? Would she approve?

Would she understand?

The serpent grew hot in his hand and Rafn raised it as he screamed his pent up rage. Hani met him with strength that forced Rafn to concentrate and draw on the storm within.

Thoughts that did not belong on the battlefield and could ruin a man's stride, seeped into his mind all the same. Instinct told him that she would not want such needless death.

A cold weariness soaked into him as her loss sapped his will to continue. It broke his momentum and in that one instant of hesitation, the other man struck. Hani's sword found Rafn's flesh as it tore into his side. Rafn centered his concentration a second too late. Even as the serpent came alive in his hand and bore into the other man's chest, so did the steel of Hani's sword push through Rafn's right arm. The serpent fell from his hand as Rafn could no longer maintain his grip.

Pain threatened but was ignored as Rafn withdrew his knife with his left hand and sliced it across the other man's throat. Hani gagged as blood poured from his mouth. He pawed at his mangled throat in desperation before Rafn finished him off by pushing his knife through his heart.

Rafn fell to his knees even as the battle came to an end around him. He became deaf to the world around him. His eyes lost their focus but for a single stab of light that appeared before him. He stared in astonishment as an unarmed man stood within it.

"Orn," he whispered in shock as he recognized his little brother. "Orn," he repeated needlessly, but he could find no other words to explain what he was seeing.

Dagstyrr pushed the man he'd been fighting from him, and at once all swords, axes, spears and knives stopped their slaughter and all eyes turned to watch the Raven fall. He sat teetering on his knees, staring at something in front of him, before falling backwards.

Dagstyrr ran to his side and sighed in relief to see his lord's chest still rising and falling. Thank Thor and whatever other god had a hand in keeping him alive, he sent up a silent prayer.

"He lives." A ripple of relief went through the mass of Skiringssal's warriors. The Jutes having seen their commander dead, backed from the field of battle. By consensus they were done. The war was over. The Raven would do no more damage, and the Jutes would no longer fight.

"Get him back to the ships." Peder began to shout orders and no one questioned his command.

Once his wounds were tied off and Rafn was carried aboard his ship, they headed for home. Peder worked to keep the bleeding stopped while the others rowed like mad. No one would stop until Skiringssal was in sight.

Rafn teetered on the verge of unconsciousness before he allowed it to claim him. He could fight the pain in his heart no longer. The wounds of his flesh were inconsequential, but the rendering of his heart, his very soul sent him over the edge seeking oblivion.

He allowed the agony to swallow him as his mind wandered through his memories, until he was once again a twelve year old boy, standing in a ruined village, holding a bloody sword.

Valr, Orn and Kata stood staring at him in disbelief as the blood dripped from his arms and face. It wasn't his blood, but that of the men he had dared to kill. He still felt the anger that had claimed him…and the thunder rumbled through him as he teetered on the edge of sanity.

Smoke burned his nostril and the rain came harder as it worked to extinguish the flames that had destroyed the village. His father…his mother…both gone from him.

He grabbed the storm around him and allowed its final claim as he vowed that he would never rest. He had welcomed the god in, craving its strength…wanting it.

Gamal, his uncle came through the crowd to stand before him. He remembered looking up to meet his eyes. Vividly he recalled how his hand still shook with rage and how his uncle stood facing him.

"Give me the sword," Gamal had said.

"It is mine." Rafn gripped it tightly in his hand.

"I don't dispute your claim. You have earned the right to keep it. I simply want you to put it down until you learn to control the storm that is building within you."

Rafn's nostrils flared and he hadn't wanted to relinquish his weapon, to give up the fight. He had wanted to vent his anger…until he could drive the pain of his parent's loss from him.

Gamal had reached out his hand and Rafn knew that he must trust in him. So with reluctance he handed his uncle the sword. Over the years that followed Rafn had indeed learned to control the storm, to call upon it when he had need of it, to hide it deep inside when he did not. It had been a constant struggle to maintain and he'd lived on the brink of madness.

Seera…his wife…the one who had calmed the storm…he remembered her. Remembered her courage, her beauty…how she had felt in his arms. It had been in her that he'd found his way from the edge.

Then she'd been taken. Pain rushed inward so fast it threatened to choke him. In that inevitable moment, his soul began to collapse.

Those who met the ships were stunned and confused at seeing their warlord carried by his men off his ship and through the crowd. Valr barked an order that had the people scurrying away and a path opened up for them.

Rafn was brought to Kata who had to keep herself from crying out in alarm. Never had she thought to see her brother brought down. How could anyone have touched him? He was far too disciplined. She had always trusted in his invincibility.

"Can you repair him wife?" Dagstyrr laid a hand on her shoulder as Hachet and Leikr laid Rafn on the bed.

"I..." Kata began and looked up into the worried faces that were all staring at her. "I will make sure he does not die." She spoke with more confidence than she felt, but she could not let them down.

Esja pushed her way in to offer Kata assistance. Valr stepped out of her way and the woman went to Kata's side.

"I have faith in you sister," Valr said.

"Order these men out of here brother."

Valr nodded in understanding. "Give the women space. Let us meet in the hall and you can tell me how this happened."

Dagstyrr glanced at Kata before he left. He spoke nothing, but she had not missed the fear in his eyes. She looked down at Rafn.

"You fought foolishly brother." She scolded him even knowing he could not hear. "Your worry for Seera clouded you...and look what has happened. You are no good to her dead!" She choked back her tears.

Esja placed a hand on her arm. "He will live. I know of no greater healer than you."

"I hope you are right." She unbound his arm and cringed at the damage done. She cut away his tunic to find his body burning with fever. His pus filled wound was swollen with infection and she used her knife to cut it open so it could be drained.

His arm did not look good and she feared he would lose the use of it. What would happen to him then, if he could not fight?

The Raven had been wounded and could not soar with a clipped wing.

And his wife had not been found. It really could not get much worse than that.

CHAPTER 27

Kata was tired and wanted nothing more than to sleep, but when she was satisfied that Rafn was stable and would have succumbed to her need, Valr burst through the door.

Worry dug deep in the corner of his eyes. His self control was about to shatter and this more than anything had Kata instantly awake.

"He will live." Kata moved to reassure him. Valr's eyes shifted to the unconscious man but a moment.

"It is Geira, she is in great pain," he said. There was an edge of panic to his voice.

Kata began collecting her things. "I will see to her. Get Dagstyrr to sit with Rafn. Tell him if he wakes, to keep him in bed."

Valr nodded and went in search of Kata's husband, while she rushed to her brother's dwelling that stood closest to the Great Hall. She found Geira curled on the bed.

"Can you move?"

"Some." Geira looked up at Kata from a pale face tight with fear.

"Let us get you lying back on the pillow so I can see what is wrong."

Geira let her help her onto her back. Kata pushed up the bottom of her smock so that it was up past her abdomen, and spread her legs, instructing her to bend her knees. She placed a hand on the woman's stomach just as the muscles contracted and brought a gush between her legs.

"It is too soon," Geira said through clenched teeth.

Kata met her eyes. Both knew the truth of those words, as the waters of birth trickled out. The night was long as Geira's pain worsened. Kata gave her an infusion of willow bark to ease the pain, but it did not help and she was afraid to try anything stronger.

Geira's strength was failing her and she kept slipping unconscious. Kata was worried. Close to dawn, the boy child was born…but not alive. Geira watched with numb shock as Kata wrapped the tiny body into a blanket. Kata tried to keep from shaking as she placed the baby on the rug near the end of the bed.

She returned to Geira's side to find her cold and clammy. She wrapped a warm blanket around her to keep her warm.

Valr chose that moment to return. He met his sister's tear filled eyes and saw the lifeless bundle at her feet. Through the long night he'd accepted that the child he'd waited so long for was lost to him, but it still struck him like a knife to see that the child was dead.

"What was it?" He wanted—no…needed to know.

"Valr, please." Kata tried to stop him, but he picked up the baby and pulled back the blanket. He stood very still as he stared down at the blue form of the son he would have had.

"Brother." Kata placed a hand on his arm and flinched as tears came to his eyes. Valr was usually so controlled. He never gave in to his emotions the way Rafn did. To see his grasp on them slip, tore at Kata's heart.

Valr carefully wrapped the baby again and let Kata take the bundle from him. He looked to Geira then, who was barely holding onto consciousness. When he tried to meet her eyes, she would not look at him. She didn't even seem to notice that he was there. Valr knelt by the bed and took her hand and still she did not respond.

A knock on the door drew their attention. Kata went to open it and found Dagstyrr. He looked from her red eyes to the still form in her arms.

"Can you get Esja," she asked him before he had a chance to speak.

He hurried off and returned in a short time later with the servant woman.

"Esja, can you take the baby." Kata handed her the tiny body. "It would be best for them both not to have him near."

"Aye, my lady." Esja's eyes filled with tears. At her age she'd seen many babies die in childbirth, but the Jarl and his wife had wanted a child for so long.

Kata waited for her to leave before turning to Dagstyrr. "How is Rafn?"

"He has still not woken, but the fever has not worsened."

"Is he alone?" She teetered on her feet from the fatigue of too many sleepless hours.

Dagstyrr watched her with concern and reached to take her arm before she fell over. "Agata is with him. You must rest."

She glanced over her shoulder. "I still have to tend to Geira. I need you to take Valr with you."

"Why?" His concern deepened.

"It would be best while I examine her, incase there is any complications."

Dagstyrr understood her unspoken words and managed to coax Valr away from his wife side. Dagstyrr suggested they wait in his dwelling, where they could have the privacy they needed.

Kata returned to Geira and pulled back the blanket. She still needed to work the afterbirth out, but what she saw stopped her. Horrified and scared she stared down at the blood that soaked the bed beneath her. It was too much, too fast.

Kata tried to see what the cause was. Geira did not react to her examination and that worried her. The problem was too deep inside. There was no way to stop the bleeding.

Uncontrollable tears flowed from her eyes as she began to panic. What was she to do?

A hand touched her arm and she glanced up to see Geira looking at her. "It is alright." Her sister-in law spoke with far more calm than Kata felt.

"No," Kata said, but she had no further words to offer. What good were words in the face of death?

"Valr will need your strength. He will deny it, try and hold his pain where others can't see it."

It seemed somehow important to reassure Geira's concern. "I will not let him be alone."

Geira held her hand with a weak grip and managed a smile, but she could no longer speak. Her hand fell slack as the last of her life slipped from her.

Kata could only stare in disbelief. Blessed gods this was not happening. For a long moment she stared at Geira's lifeless face, free now of any pain. Sighing with resignation she pulled the blanket up to cover her and turned for the door. What would she tell her brother?

The morning was bright and people bustled around unaware that anything was wrong. To Kata everything looked gray.

After failing to find Valr at her place, she went to Rafn's. He sat at the table with Dagstyrr staring at their brother who still lay unconscious. Rafn would have to wait, Valr's need was greater.

Kata's face shone with her sorrow as she went to her eldest brother. He knew even before she spoke what she would say.

"I'm sorry," she said. He allowed her to embrace him, but he remained very stiff.

"I would be alone now." He pushed her from him and headed for the door.

"Brother…" She moved to follow but Dagstyrr stopped her.

"Let him be." Realizing Dagstyrr was right, that he would need time, she let Valr go.

She went instead to Rafn and felt his forehead. It was still hot, but perhaps not so much as earlier. She was too tired to say for sure.

"Go sleep wife. I will wake you if you are needed." Kata had no strength left to argue.

Rafn's fever broke and he regained consciousness, but he had lost something of his spirit and Kata mourned for its return. She saw him struggle each day, even as his wounds healed.

He did not have the strength in his arm and Kata feared it had healed wrong. She warned him that he would need to exercise it each day to regain its use, but he seemed not to hear her.

He had lost hope. There was nowhere left to look for Seera. No word had reached him of where Hwal had taken her. Without her he had no desire to keep living, and yet he still did. He wished his warriors would have left him on the battlefield, left him to the halls of Valhalla.

But Dagstyrr stubbornly would not let him die. He came to see him each day he lay in his bed, while the fever came and went. Even when the threat of death had past, he would not leave him be.

He went to see Valr before the Jarl left for his required visit to the King.

"Please send Dagstyrr out on the trade route," he said. "I can't stand his hovering over me."

"It is only out of concern." Valr raised his eyebrows.

"I do not want it, or his pity," Rafn snapped and there was a brief spark of his old self, but all too soon it was gone.

"I will send him on the next tide, but you must promise to build your strength. Kata says you won't listen to her."

Rafn had acknowledged Valr's own loss in the silent way that brothers did. They did not speak of it, but Rafn understood and it was a bond the two brothers shared.

He reluctantly agreed to Valr's request. He was a warrior and wanted no one's sympathy. "Fine if it will give me some peace."

Peace was not for Rafn. He had known that once, had accepted it as his fate, until Seera had come to him. He shut his eyes against the sting of pain that still clawed at his heart.

She had given to him something he had no right to. She gave him a contentment that did not belong to a warlord, a man whose greatest talent was killing. Curse the gods for ever letting him glimpse such a treasure. It was certainly Loki the trickster's doing, that had led her into his life.

How Loki must be laughing to see how far he'd fallen.

Rafn headed to the practice field once the sun had dipped over the horizon, when he could be sure that his warriors would not be around. He would regain his arm, but he would not have an audience judging his strength. He would not suffer the humiliation.

His hand wrapped around the serpent and he tried to raise his arm to swing it through the air, but it did not sail with grace, or coordination. He did not have the full range of his arm and it brought sweat to his face to try and raise it past his shoulder. He gritted his teeth in pain and frustration.

Peder watched unseeing from the shadows, his eyes reflecting his worry.

As Valr promised, Dagstyrr left with the morning tide, two ships trailing behind his own. He said a private goodbye to his wife before he left, but he said nothing to Rafn, for which the warlord was grateful.

Dagstyrr shared his concerns with Peder instead. The lord from the fortress by the sea had proven himself on their campaign through Hwal's lands. The men all boasted of his courage and calm in the fight, and had welcomed him into their ranks.

Peder tried to look at a situation from a distance, rather than allowing his emotions to take control. He did not understand the pull of love, so could not comprehend how deep the talons of such a feeling could sink. He had never given his heart to another, leaving him with such vulnerability.

He did not pity Rafn, for his brother-in law would resent it. Peder instead wondered at the effect his sister had on this legendary warrior. To have such passion for another as to prefer death as to life without the one you loved was beyond his imagining, but a part of him felt envy at such an emotion.

He had known many women, but none had enticed him to linger. He always snuck from their beds before the morning came, to avoid such awkward moments as conversation after intimacy.

But perhaps there was more to intimacy than he had yet experienced. Something he had glimpsed between Seera and Rafn.

Peder stayed on the docks until Dagstyrr and his ships had left port. He had turned down the man's offer to join him, preferring instead to stay in Skiringssal. He didn't know if there was any hope left of finding his sister, but the place she was taken was still the best place to look for clues.

There must have been something that was missed, perhaps a small insignificant clue that would mean nothing to another, but would to the Lord of Dun'O'Tir. It was remote, such hope, but he was yet unwilling to give it up.

Rafn's faith had failed him. Despair had robbed him of his will and so it was left to Peder to carry on.

Two weeks passed and even Peder began to lose heart. He went down to the beach to clear his mind of his frustration. The hot sun over head was in opposition to his dark mood.

"Lord Peder." Drawn from his thoughts, Peder looked down on a boy of about fifteen, with sandy hair and grey eyes. He was tall and lanky, with muscles that were just beginning to grow with the strength of a man.

"Is there something you want?" Peder tried to ask kindly but his voice came out sharper than he intended.

"I need to speak with you." He looked around as if not wanting to be heard. "Privately, if you would not mind."

Peder took note of the boy's nervousness and beckoned him to walk with him from the village to a cliff where they were sure to be left alone.

"What is your name boy?"

"It is Fox." The boy tried to puff up his chest in imitation of one of the warriors. At another time Peder would have found it amusing.

"You are free to speak now."

"I would have gone to Lord Rafn, but he has not welcomed visitors since his injury."

"He will understand. If it is important, I will bring him the information myself." Peder saw that this eased the boy's concerns. Relief washed over his youthful face.

"Tell me."

"There are these two men down in the village. They have been here awhile and I assumed them to be traders, but they don't seem to be from any of the ships. The trading vessels have come and gone, but they remain."

"And?"

"Last night I saw them leaving the tavern, and they were drunk. I followed them a bit and overheard them talking of Hwal and his obsession with Lady Seera."

Peder stood straighter. "Could you tell who they were?"

"I heard one of them complain about being ordered to remain in Skiringssal by Hwal." Fox shifted from one foot to the next. He stopped to push at a loose stone with his toe.

Peder considered the best way to deal with these men. He would enjoy beating the information from them, but more, it would give Rafn what he needed to continue his fight.

"Show me Fox, where these men are." Peder smiled for the first time since receiving word of his sister's abduction.

Lene and Abiorn had stayed in Skiringssal even as the Raven had flown in rage from the town to their homeland. The first time there had been a thousand, the second twice as many, and still Lene and Abiorn had stayed instead of fleeing home to protect their families.

Neither man had taken a wife and had no children that they had claimed as theirs, so perhaps they did not have the urgent need to die for their people. They each knew Rafn's reputation, had watched from a distance as his anger grew and saw how the warriors flocked to him.

Neither man wanted to face such a man in battle. They were not cowards. They had killed with ease when it was called for, but to fight a man such as Rafn was suicide.

"We have not heard from Hwal or Klintr," said Lene as he pulled his cloak tighter against the sudden chill that crept up his spin. It made no sense as the day was warm, but goose-bumps rose on his skin.

"You believe them dead?" Abiorn also peered into the shadows as if expecting something lurking beyond his sight.

"What are we to think, it has been months."

"I had expected to hear something by now. What could have happened?" Abiorn forced his gaze away from the shadows to look at his companion.

"We know that Lord Rafn's men did not find him, or he would have been gutted and hung by the walls." Lene pulled up the hood of his cloak as if it would offer him some protection against the hidden threat.

"Then the witch must have put a spell on him and he died an unnatural kind of death." Abiorn also pulled his cloak around him.

"It could be safe to return home. With the Raven's injures he no longer looks to Jutland's shores."

"But what happens when he has healed?" Again Abiorn searched the area around him suspiciously, searching for anything amiss.

"We will have melted into Jutland long before then. Besides, I am not sure we should risk ourselves much longer. When the Raven has taken flight again, I for one do not want to be in his line of sight."

"Aye, we have lingered for too long beneath the enemy's gaze. Our luck will not hold much longer."

"What keen insight you have." A voice from the dark alley behind them spoke. "Your luck has indeed expired."

Abiorn drew his sword only to have it snatched from his hand by Lord Peder, brother-in law of the man they were just discussing. This man would show them no mercy. He would take them to the warlord and each would die slowly.

Five warriors accompanied the lord. Abion and Lene were easily subdued, and Abiorn thought of the green hills of his home. He should have returned to them long ago, for now he would never again set eyes on them. He looked to Lene and knew the man had the same thoughts.

"Cooperate with us and I will make your deaths quick." Peder spoke quietly, but it did not hide the contempt behind his words.

Abiorn only nodded, for what words were there to speak.

Two punishment posts were raised and the prisoners were hung by iron bracelets to metal rings. The men were stripped and left vulnerable to any who passed by. Warriors called threats and the women threw rotting food at them, calling them whatever foul name they could think of.

Peder left them and felt no pity for the treatment they received. He had been unable to find Rafn in his dwelling, or the hall. The stable and the practice field also were empty. Thinking perhaps he had gone down to check on the docked ships, he headed in their direction.

No one he asked had seen Rafn since the previous night at supper. Peder did not know where else to look. Had Dagstyrr or Valr been in Skiringssal he could have consulted with either man. Instead he went to Kata.

He approached her dwelling and knocked on the wooden door as he called out. "Lady Kata."

The door swung open and Kata stepped out. "Lord Peder?"

"I am looking for Rafn with little success and thought perhaps you knew of a place where he might be hiding."

Kata considered his question. "There is a place east of the village, a little less than a half days ride where he sometimes goes when he wishes to be alone."

"Do you know where it is?"

"I know only that it is east, in a cove close to the sea. He has never permitted any but Seera to go with him." Kata pushed her unbound hair from her face.

"I thank you then, for your assistance." Peder went to bow, but her gaze shifted past him to the growing crowd. Lines appeared on the bridge of her nose.

"What has happened?" She took a few steps further from her dwelling, trying to see what the commotion was.

"Two men were discovered hiding in the village. We believed them to be Hwal's spies." Her head snapped back to stare at Peder. Her eyes grew round and her face pale. He became worried.

"I must see them." She lifted up the skirt of her dress enough to make walking easier. He offered her his arm. She hesitated before accepting. She laid her cold hand lightly on his arm and they made their way towards the center of the compound, the crowd parting as they proceeded.

The naked men were now covered in a colorful array of slime and liquids from a vast variety of food. If it were not for the seriousness of the situation, Peder may have laughed at how ridiculous they looked.

Kata however had become very still and silent beside him. A look crossed her face that told him she was remembering the day she'd nearly been killed. Her eyes were fixed on the prisoners, studying them closely.

"It is them," she said. Anger rose in her and her hand tightened on his arm.

"You are sure?"

"I will never forget their faces. How I managed to miss them amongst the people, I do not know. I should have." Her hand slipped from him as she took a tentative step forward, fists tight at her sides.

"They are warriors, trained to conceal themselves." Peder tried to reassure her that she had not failed and was not to blame.

Kata nodded but did not reply. Instead she quickened her pace towards the two men. People stepped away from her determined path and watched with silence as she approached the prisoners. Each man stared at her and sneered.

"Where is Hwal?" Her voice shrilled with anger and shocked those closest to her. Peder moved up behind her, ready to defend her.

"He could be just about anywhere." The skinny one with a beak nose laughed. Her face turned red with anger.

She slapped him hard across the face, bringing a cheer from the crowd. Lene growled in contempt at having been humiliated by a woman.

The other, shorter man with a puckered face stared at her in silent hatred. She glared at them both, but neither would look away. They had no fear of her.

Kata spat in the skinny one's face. "You may not answer me, but you will answer my brother. I promise you, you will beg for mercy by the time he is finished with you."

"From what I have seen of him lately, he has lost his edge. He is not the raven he once was."

Peder stepped out of Kata's shadow to stand next to her and when the man noticed him he lost the contemptuous grin. "Make no mistake. The Raven's talons are still sharp. When I bring him before you, that quick death I offered will be your greatest wish."

"Then kill us now," the short one spoke for the first time.

"Nay," Peder said. "It is for Lord Rafn to decide your fate. The insult was done to him, and you will pay for it. How long you suffer will be up to you. You will tell us where Hwal is before we end your torture."

"Perhaps we do not know," the skinny one said.

Peder turned his hard stare on him and Kata thought she saw him shake. Peder drew a dagger from his belt and stepped before the skinny one. Taking the blade he made a cut down his chest. It was not fatal, but deep enough to draw blood. The man ground his teeth.

The other looked on with understanding that it was only the beginning.

The Raven had yet to arrive.

CHAPTER 28

Rafn watched the waves crashing against the rocks. Soft laughter trickled through his memory and he almost turned at the sound. She would not be there if he looked, but the urge to peer over his shoulder almost overwhelmed him.

What did one do when hope was gone? How did they move forward as if their world had not lost focus? He welcomed the pain that gripped his heart. It told him that he still lived, was still connected to something. At least until he severed it, once and for all.

He drew the tunic over his head and tossed it onto a nearby rock. The hide trousers he wore were well worn and conformed to the shape of his muscles. It was if they'd become like a second skin so well did they hug him. He tied a band of cloth around his forehead to keep the hair and sweat from his eyes.

He held his sword, so poetically named the serpent, tightly in his hand. His knuckles became white he squeezed it so hard. He drew in a deep breath and willed himself to concentrate.

He would have to reclaim the warrior inside. His people expected no less from him. Anger would sustain him, if he could keep hold of it. Fury would fuel his actions and see him through to the end of his days. If the gods willed, it would not be so many.

Balance, his soul cried out as he placed his feet in a fighting stance. He sliced the serpent through the air and the whirring of the blade was welcome music.

The waves crashed loudly beside him, but he pushed the sound of them to the back of his mind. His focus was on the blade and the imaginary opponent he faced. He became the dancer as his movements turned fluid and fiercely beautiful.

Rafn's arm which had tensed at first, now moved freely and without restraint. The pain, if there was any was filtered out as the blade became his only focus. The serpents on the handle seemed almost animated as his motion became steady and precise.

A calm he had not felt in months flooded him as the sword sang to him. It was alive in his hand and centered him to the moment. In the now he could survive, where all memories of the past were gone and the future did not exist.

The wind that caressed his face and caught his hair was all that mattered. The dance that kept his feet moving and his arm in perfect motion, was all he felt. If he closed his eyes and denied himself even the sight of the familiar place, the associated memories fled without catching hold of him.

If he never stopped, never allowed a momentary thought to seize him then he could keep breathing without feeling the need for her. He could become once again the warlord he was destined to be. Once again become the Raven that others respected and enemies feared.

A distant rumble of thunder became louder as he heard it coming closer, closer. It was beside him, in him, a part of his very essence. He was a Viking warrior. He belonged to Thor. He knew it, accepted it—even welcomed it. It was who he was born to be.

Rafn opened his eyes as the thunder was replaced by the sound of a horse's hooves tearing up the ground beneath its feet. He stopped his dance, the serpent held ready in front of him as he turned in time to see the horse stop abruptly a few feet from him.

He did not move, but stared at Peder in irritation. Rafn felt the tranquility slip away, to be replaced by a hardness that centered him. His eyes betrayed the coldness that he'd wrapped around his heart.

"I am pleased to see that your arm is better," Peder said.

"You should not have doubted." Rafn shrugged as he reluctantly slid the sword back into its sheath. "What need have you to interrupt me?"

"Two of Hwal's men were found lurking in the village." Peder got right to the point. "They await you on the posts."

Rafn's eyes flared but he did not allow hope to spark. He would not sink back into the despair that had threatened to ground him. He would fly once again as they were all waiting for him to do. He would be the Raven, the man who brought death to those who opposed him. It's what was needed to survive.

Until he was ready to die!

Peder must have sensed his need, for he did not question the harshness in voice. "Let us ride then brother, and force from them what we need to know."

Rafn saddled his horse and they rode in silence back to Skiringssal and the duty that awaited him.

A raven flew overhead catching Seera's attention as she stepped from the trees beside the practice field. Clouds consumed the sky and added to Seera's foul mood. Her body ached and she had lost any grace she might have still possessed only a few days gone.

At least the clouds kept the sun's heat trapped behind it, allowing Seera that small escape as she turned back towards the small cottage. The sisters were out somewhere, which she couldn't recall. They had told her, but she hadn't really been listening. She was too tired, too sore to be able to think of much else.

The baby had dropped lower. She could feel his head pressing down between her legs in an almost painful grinding that would not ease. He had become less active recently she had noticed, as if he was saving his strength for the birth that would come soon. She both longed for its arrival and feared it.

Certainly after everything she'd survived, birthing her son was nothing to be scared of. It set her nerves on edge and she wanted so much to have Rafn there. The sisters would not hear of it. Even mentioning his name brought a scowl to Joka's face. She did not like hearing of Seera's Viking husband.

So Seera kept her longing deep inside. She was beginning to accept the dull ache that was constantly a part of her. It soothed her somehow to feel it. It was a small tangible tie to her husband.

The raven landed in a low branch of a nearby tree and cawed noisily. Seera stopped and stared at it. If she accepted Systa's teaching, the raven was a sign. The bird after all was Rafn's namesake. But she didn't have any idea what its possible meaning could be, even if she could readily accept its message.

A dull ache began in her back and by the time the sun began to dip in the evening sky, it had worsened into wrenching cramps.

Even as Seera began to recognize the contractions for what they were and worry that she was alone, the sisters returned. Systa approached her, an all knowing smile spread on her face.

"The time is upon us," Systa said. "Come, we have prepared."

"What?" Seera questioned just as another contraction had her doubled over. Joka moved beside her to help her stay on her feet.

Systa took hold of her hand. "Fear not our new sister. Awhile yet he'll be. Time we have."

"Time for what?" She struggled to stand up straight.

"To get you to where you need to be."

"What my sister means, is that we have prepared a special place for your son to be born." Joka added with impatience. She encouraged Seera to lean heavily on her.

Seera didn't have the strength to argue, so she allowed the sisters to lead her into the trees, to a place not far from the mineral pool. They had built a small tent out of animal hides. Joka helped her duck inside, where she found a fire had been started in a pit dug into the ground of the hard packed dirt floor.

A metal pot had already been set to boil and was beginning to bubble. Blankets had been set aside as well as the clothing that Seera had fashioned out of rabbit hides. The swaddling cloths she had sewn were also there. She had not even seen Systa take them from the cottage.

Seera needed no coaxing to sit on the fur that had been lain out on the floor. The contractions were coming one on top of the other now and she could barely stay on her feet. Before she sat down, Joka helped her out of her clothes so that she was left naked. It felt so much cooler and she was thankful for even so slight a release of her discomfort.

Sweat beaded her forehead as the contractions became more intense. She clenched her teeth to keep from screaming. Somehow she felt it would be weakness, and she did not want to be weak in front of these two women.

"Let me see." Systa eased her legs apart so that she could feel inside. Her fingers probed just as Seera's muscles clenched and her waters of birth broke, drenching Systa's arm. She wiped it off on the hide.

"He comes he does. He will wait no more." Systa smiled at Seera who could only groan in relief at knowing it was almost over.

They had her move to a kneeling position, which they told her would make birthing him easier. With Systa's instructions Joka supported her as Seera was encouraged to shift so that her elbows touched her knees.

Systa sat behind her to receive the child. Seera could not remember women giving birth this way before, but Systa told her it was the Norse way, and her son was a Norse child.

"Muscles you must use to push him out," Systa said and began a chant in a language that made no sense to Seera but soothed her all the same.

"That is it, good you are doing."

Seera tried to work with the clenching of her stomach, by pushing with the contractions. She lost track of time, but was beginning to feel faint. Her strength was failing her and she wasn't sure she could push him out. He was too big. There was no possible way he was going to fit.

"Fit he will," Systa replied as if Seera had spoken aloud. Seera was too exhausted to ask her how she knew what was in her thoughts.

Systa laughed lightly. "His head I see. Covered with black hair it is."

Seera managed a weak smile at her words…black like his father. Would his eyes be as well? Suddenly she could not wait to see him, to hold him, to see how like his father he was.

Finding a last reserve of strength she didn't know was still there, she pushed for all she was worth. One, two, three pushes…a scream tore from her of its own accord as she felt her opening stretch and rip.

"Cease now." Systa held up a hand to signal her to stop. Seera eased off, feeling completely depleted. "Alright, I have made sure the cord is free of his neck. Now give me one more small push."

Somehow Seera obeyed and the baby slid from her body in a final release. A euphoric sense of relief and pride washed over her as she tried to sit enough to see her son.

Systa was tying and cutting the cord, while Joka waited with a blanket. Systa cleared his mouth and the baby let out his first cry. The sound of a new life filled the space around them as Systa handed the baby to her sister. Joka wiped the baby clean of bloody tissue before transferring him to a new blanket, while Systa laid out a fresh fur and eased Seera onto it. Joka handed the baby to her once she was settled.

Tears filled Seera's eyes. She could do nothing but stare at the little miracle she held in her arms. He looked back at her out of green eyes.

He was a mixture of her and Rafn. Their love had been combined into one tiny little child.

"Thank you Lord," Seera said. Systa and Joka exchanged a look but said nothing. They had accepted their Christian guest and counted her as family.

"Your name shall be Orn," she said to him. She had decided weeks before that he should bear the name of the man who had not allowed her die in the forest. She felt him with her even then and knew he was smiling.

Systa got that strange look on her face whenever she sensed Orn's presence. Her eyes shifted around the tent as if trying to figure out where he was, but the Seer said nothing of it.

"Fine is his name," she said.

Joka knelt beside him, eyeing the new babe with curiosity. "It is befitting one of noble blood."

"A new life for one which had been taken," Seera said. Each had not been immune to loss, but for the first time they felt what it was to welcome in a new life. Even Joka, stern as she was, could not hide a smile of pleasure.

Seera saw and understood. Life was but a cycle with birth and death joining together to create the beginning and end of a continuous circle.

Baby Orn screwed up his face and let out a howl of displeasure which caused the women to laugh.

"Put him to your breast and ease his empty belly," Systa said.

With awkwardness she positioned him in the crook of her arm and tilted his face towards her. He opened his mouth in anticipation and took the nipple. Seera was alarmed at the strength of his sucking.

"Need you to keep the nipples moist with your milk so they do not crack and bleed," Systa warned. "Toughen will they in time, but first will be discomfort."

Seera nodded in understanding. She had heard other women speaking of the pain nursing caused in the beginning. If she recalled they had all claimed it eased after a few weeks.

When he was done feeding, her son fell asleep with his face buried in her chest. She eased him away so that he wouldn't be smothered and enjoyed looking into his beautiful face. She took one of his tiny hands into hers and marveled at its size.

"The mother must rest when the son does," Systa said. "It would not be good to tire yourself needlessly."

"I won't." Seera yawned with exhaustion. "I just want to look at him a moment more."

"We will watch over him while you sleep," Joka said. "He will come to no harm while I am near."

Seera looked to Joka and knew she spoke the truth. Joka would keep them safe. She had no doubts about that. "Thank you," she whispered as she succumbed to the sleep that beckoned. Systa spread a blanket over them.

Somewhere in a distant tree a raven cawed.

Systa sat outside her cottage, a metal cauldron suspended over an open fire, as she mixed its contents. It smelled awful. Though what she boiled was not to be eaten, but for something far more sinister.

As she stirred, she chanted words that made only sense to her. An old woman in her village had taught her many spells and their many uses. This one she'd been weaving ever since Joka had brought the Christian woman to their home.

The one-eyed giant was still out there, lost in a tangled web of her making. His mind had become a prison in which he wandered in confusion and madness. He would not even be aware of his slip on sanity, so cleverly had she spun her net.

It was not yet time for his final battle with the raven that searched for him, but it would be soon.

A light shone in her eyes as a clear view of the future lay before her. She could almost stretch out her hand and touch it.

The giant's foul stench corrupted the very ripple of the world around him. She continued to speak the words that bound him in the confines of the illusion she had wrapped around him.

She would not allow his escape until the Raven found him.

CHAPTER 29

Rafn and Peder arrived back in Skiringssal as the sun was setting. He allowed Fox to take his horse from him and return it to the stables so he could go immediately to the posts.

The skinny one had dozed off, but the short one watched him coming with wariness. The man he had glimpsed just days ago, who had seemed defeated, was gone. He had no doubt that the warlord was back, fiercer than ever.

Rafn held the man's eyes and stepped before him. A crowd began to filter out from the surrounding buildings. Rafn ignored them. A hushed silence kept the people mounted to their spots. Even they could see that Rafn was renewed. They could feel his power and were awed by it.

"My brother-in law has told me that he has promised you a quick death if you cooperate." His eyes narrowed as the short one straightened to face him. "I look forward to days of torture, but I will honor his pledge. What say you?"

"I say that you are a great warlord and I believe your words." He tried to answer without a hint of fear, but even he could hear it in his reply.

"Then speak," Rafn said.

"Would you allow me a warrior's death, so that I may enter the halls of Valhalla?"

"Tell me your name and I will consider your request."

"It is Abiorn, my lord." He held his head high as he spoke it.

"I would hear what you have to say." Rafn stared down at him, making him appear even more intimidating just from his sheer size. Rafn heard the man swallow before answering.

"Hwal ordered us to attack the women when they were seen at a grave on the hill above the village." As Abiorn began the skinny one came awake and widened in shock to see Rafn. Rafn ignored him, his time would come.

"Klintr, and Lene." Abiorn nodded towards the other man, who stared at him in disgust at being betrayed. "They grabbed Lady Kata, while Hwal subdued the Lady Seera."

"Continue." Rafn insisted when Abiorn paused.

"When your sister screamed, Lene silenced her while Hwal dragged your wife into the trees before your men could reach us. We ran for some time, deeper into the hills, knowing our path to our ship was not safe. We reached a cave at which time Hwal ordered me to return to Skiringssal, to watch for a chance to make our escape."

"And still you are here in my town." His voice was calm but harsh and Abiorn knew that emotions were no longer ruling him. He also knew how deadly that made him.

"Lene was sent back next, with orders that we were to remain and watch you," Abiorn said.

"This is all you know?" Rafn moved closer to him so he could stare directly into the other man's face. He saw no deceit.

"Aye, the rest is for Lene to tell."

He turned to Hachet who stood close by and ordered the man to be released from his chains. "Bring him also a tunic and sword."

"Aye, my lord." Hachet hurried off and soon Abiorn was clothed and armed. He stood facing Rafn and hoped only for a quick end.

"You may have your honorable death, for speaking truthfully with me." Rafn drew the serpent from the sheath on his back and Abiorn's eyes widened in awe at its perfection. Never had he seen a more magnificent blade. To die on such a weapon was honor in its self.

Abiorn was weak from two days of being bound naked to the post and being denied food or drink, but he held his sword steady and managed to stop the blade that rang through the air towards him.

Rafn did not release his full strength, giving the man a brief attempt at defense. His blade hacked downwards only twice, the first being stopped by Abiorn, the second finding flesh as it was brought across his throat. He made sure the cut was deep enough to end the man's life quickly but not enough to sever his head.

Blood spurted from the wound, soaking into the ground as the body fell at Rafn's feet. "Take him away." Hachet and two others came forward to get rid of the body.

Rafn turned back to the post and the man there who'd turned as white as a ghost. The look on his face told Rafn that he understood that his death would not be so easy. He had tried to kill his sister. For that he would suffer first.

"Why did Hwal send you back?" Rafn demanded of him.

Too afraid to speak anything other than the truth Lene replied. "Lady Seera escaped while Hwal slept. Klintr and I were to have kept watch, but we did not see her slip away. Hwal demanded I return here, while he and Klintr pursued her."

Rafn grew suspicious. He looked to Peder who had been watching in silence. He seemed to notice the crowd for the first time and scanned their anxious faces. He saw the hope spreading among them. A hope he was desperate to seize, but could not.

"What else do you have to say?" He met Lene's gaze and the iciness of his glare made the skinny man shiver.

"Only that we have not heard from Hwal since we were sent back here."

Rafn took the knife from the holder on his leg and held it for Lene to see. "You will not be given the honor of your friend," he promised. "You must answer for the attempt on my sister's life."

"Rafn," Kata said as she approached him. Rafn met her pleading eyes, but he would not give her what she wanted. "I did not die."

"But he will."

Kata nodded in understanding. She would not stop what was demanded of him. Her honor and his had been insulted. This man would have to pay for it.

Peder pulled Kata away from the post and kept a hand on her shoulder in comfort. If Dagstyrr were there, he would have been the one to make such a gesture, but Rafn had sent him away and it was too late to doubt his decision. He turned back to Lene, who shut his eyes in anticipation of the pain that was to come.

Rafn did not disappoint him. He sliced a deep cut underneath the one that had already begun to fester. Even as the blood began to trickle from the wound, Rafn sliced a cut on each of the man's cheeks and down the length of each of his arms. His legs received the same treatment before he turned to the man's fingers.

He severed all the fingers on the man's sword hand. A sacrifice for having held the blade that had hurt Kata.

Only then did he look into the man's eyes and see the pain that he was trying hard to contain. He was brave this man, Rafn had to admit that. He had clenched his teeth tightly, but refused to react in any other way. He was close to unconsciousness, but still he remained aware. Wanting to be done with this gruesome task, Rafn took the knife and plunged it into the man's heart.

"We must speak," Rafn said to Peder as he beckoned him to follow him to the hall, leaving his men to take care of the body. Both the prisoners would be burned before the night was through.

Rafn glimpsed the priest who was frantically praying for the dead men's souls. Rafn did not acknowledge him as he passed, but Peder said something to Father Duncun that Rafn could not hear.

Once inside the hall, Rafn ordered the servants to leave them. "We must search inland for Hwal. I will leave in the morning and would have you join me."

"I had not thought to seek permission. She is my sister and I would have demanded my right to accompany you."

Rafn nodded. They would leave with the first light and would not return until Hwal was dead. He allowed no thoughts of Seera. If she'd succeeded in her escape she would have returned to him. If Hwal had caught her, he would have killed her.

And she had not returned.

Klintr watched Hwal sitting before the hearth in the abandoned cottage. They hadn't moved from this location in weeks, and Klintr was unable to get the man to return to Ribe. Certainly the woman was long dead.

Klintr had left for a few days when Hwal had ordered him to find out information. His Jarl had been more lucid on that day. He found a small village and learned what he needed, but had not lingered because too many of Rafn's men were about, and there had been no way passed them. Since returning to inform his lord of the destruction Rafn had brought upon Ribe and the rest of Hwal's holdings, the giant had been locked within his mind.

Klintr had considered many times leaving Hwal to his madness and returning home, but thousands of Rafn's warriors stood between him and his goal.

Of Lene and Abiorn's fate he knew nothing, but if they'd been discovered, the Raven would not have let them live.

Hwal stared into the flames muttering incoherently. The man had not bathed in days and the stench coming off his stained clothing was ripe to the nose. Klintr tried to breathe through his mouth as he brought Hwal a bowl of rabbit stew.

Hwal's only acknowledgment was to squint up at him. His head, that had always been meticulously scrapped bald, had grown into an unruly mass. His beard had come in thick and was crawling with lice. For people who believed in cleanliness, he was hard to be close to.

What was there for Klintr? He could try and make a new home for himself in one of the villages in Vestfold or try and make it to one of the other territories, perhaps Smaland.

It was suicide to stay there with the Jarl. His mind worsened each day. When Lord Rafn found them...

He couldn't finish the thought. He needed to start making arrangements to flee, but even as he considered such a thing, Hwal turned and looked at him with absolute clarity, as if he'd heard his thoughts. His eyes were hard as stone and Klintr took a step back. If Hwal's mind cleared, he would not accept disloyalty.

Hwal stared at him long enough for Klintr to doubt his decision and in the end he chose to do nothing but stand by his lord and hope that it would all turn out. A raven landed on the window sill to peer inside the dwelling.

Klintr could have sworn the bird looked directly at him and knew that the omen was bad.

She was close, he knew she was. Hwal's gaze shifted around the unfamiliar room, wondering where he was, before the confusion of his mind once again claimed him.

He needed to find that woman, whose name was momentarily lost to him. Her green eyes haunted him. She was just within his grasp and he could almost touch her, almost possess her as he once had on a hard cold floor and feel the stone that cut into his knees as he took her.

A wave of erotic pleasure swept through him and he grinned in anticipation of his penetration into her warm flesh.

Blood smeared his chest. It was not his own, but came from her and it irritated him. He lost her. She was beyond his grasp. He growled in frustration as he tried to find her through the fog. Tree after tree hindered his search and he could not see what was right in front of him.

She was gone, swallowed by a world of white. Gone…gone…gone.

He reached into the empty space in front of him and clamped his fist shut. He barred his teeth as if he were a rabid dog ready to attack.

He wandered the blankness of his mind, trying to find an end to the maze. Each time he glimpsed a path to light, it was snatched from him.

He heard a quiet voice chanting unknown words. Even as they reached his ears the walls around him became thicker, higher, harder to transverse.

His heart beat louder and echoed like a drum in his head. He tore at the sharp walls until his fingers bled. He tried to climb their vertical heights, but he slipped and fell with each attempt.

Madness reached ugly talons towards him and he heard a raven's shrill call.

The large black raven flew high above the run down cottage. He circled it as he climbed higher until he was above the trees. He found a perch on the top of a dead tree, its leaves long gone. The large skeleton reached its bony fingers to the sky.

The bird settled on the highest branch and looked to the clouds above as thunder rumbled through them. He tilted his head as if listening to something.

The rumbling continued louder, but the raven remained unafraid, even as a flash of lightning shot out from the darkening sky. He simply turned his head and cawed loudly as if in answer.

CHAPTER 30

Seera woke to the rain pattering on the roof of the cottage. The sisters both slept soundly, but baby Orn stirred as soon as his mother shifted in the bed beside him. She waited for him to cry out and wake the other women, but he only cooed with contentment.

Before he changed his mind she stuck a breast in his mouth. He accepted it greedily and started making gulping noises as if the milk was coming faster than he could swallow. He let go so quickly to draw a breath that a stream of milk sprayed his face. He blinked in confusion before finding her nipple once again.

A warm happy feeling flooded her as she watched her baby feed. His body had gone from scrawny and wrinkled to smooth and round in a few short days. His appetite was a healthy one, and she did not doubt he would grow fast.

Now that her son had arrived, her mind turned more rapidly to the desire to go home, though she was still healing from the birth. When her strength returned she vowed she would not be kept any longer from her husband.

The sisters would argue of the danger, but surely Hwal had given up his search by now and returned to Ribe. Even he would not wander for months looking for a mere woman. He must think her long dead.

Did Rafn also?

Her husband had not come for her as she'd prayed each night for. Had he believed her lost to him? Had he moved on without her?

She did not want to believe he could forget her so easily, but if he didn't believe her still alive, then he would not search. Therefore it was up to her to make it home. The sisters would not stop her.

She looked down to find that her son had fallen back to sleep, one hand curled up against his face. She eased her nipple from his mouth and covered him with his blanket.

"Soon my son, you will meet your father."

On horseback Rafn and Peder went in search of trail long cold. They found a path that led from Orn's grave site, heading northwest. Believing it the most likely route, they followed it for hours until it led them to a large cave.

Rafn reined in his horse and stared at the dark opening that seemed to stare at him. Anxiety filtered through him and he had to take a deep breath to calm his nerves. This could be the first real clue to what had happened to his wife. He was torn between the urge to race into the dark interior and see what secrets it hid, and reluctant to take that step, to find the inevitable answer that his wife was dead.

Peder eased off his horse and threw the reins over a nearby bush so the horse wouldn't wander. Rafn watch his brother-in laws actions as if they were happening in slow motion. Only once Peder took a step towards the cave did Rafn jump from his stallion and follow.

It was dark within, causing them to rely on one of the torches they had thought to bring with them. Peder held it while they entered the dark damp interior. The ground was solid and scattered with rocks of various sizes.

Rafn ran a finger along the east wall feeling its cold roughness beneath his hand. It felt so impersonal. Would it yield to him the answers that he needed? He walked forward slowly making sure he missed no detail of the rocky ground. His caution proved true when his gaze landed on something that seemed out of place. "Hold the light over here."

Peder held up the torch, casting a shadowy light on the space before him. Rafn knelt down and picked up a whip made of horse hide. He clenched his teeth against the sudden punch of anger as his hand closed tight around the whip. He had to shut his eyes and take in a deep breath before he could face Peder. His control came by the time he stood.

He handed the whip to Peder, who was not so good at hiding his fury. He could almost hear the man's thoughts, but Rafn had a clearer image to draw on. He remembered all too well, Seera being whipped by Hwal in Ribe. Drenger had stayed his hand before he'd quenched his taste for her flesh. Rafn's fist clenched at his side.

Though his face remained hard, Peder was all too aware of Rafn's fight for control, and understood his brother-in law's need not to lose the fight. He would have a clear head when he met Hwal. He could afford no mistakes.

They searched further and almost turned to leave when Peder spotted a cloak forgotten behind one of the larger rocks. The softness of the material seemed alien to the cold solid surroundings. He held it up and Rafn recognized his wife's blue cloak.

"It is hers." Rafn confirmed what Peder had already guessed. At his feet his eyes fell on the bronze pin she used to hold it closed, broken and forgotten in the dirt. Rafn bent to pick it up and rub it between his fingers. He had given her the pin just after they had returned from Dun'O'Tir.

"They were here." Peder watched Rafn's silent contemplation of the metal pin.

"It must be the cave that Abiorn spoke of." Rafn slipped the brooch into to a small pouch he carried on his belt.

"If the other was to be believed," Peder said, "then this is also where Seera escaped from Hwal."

"If Lene is to be trusted." Rafn tried to picture in his mind, the desperation his wife must have felt when she crept from this cave in hopes of finding safety. He dared not hope she found it. It was too soon for that.

"It is light still." Peder stepped from the cave. "Let us continue on."

"But which way?" He made a quick survey of the surrounding land, even as Peder searched the tree line closest to the cave's entrance.

"I have found a clear path. It is close to the cave opening, and under the cover of darkness Seera could have made it here without the guards noticing," Peder said.

Rafn came over and inspected the deer trail. She would only have needed to take a few steps to reach it and therefore the most likely route she took. He peered down the path into the dim closeness of the trees. It headed north, deeper into the mountains.

"It is a place to start." The two men collected their horses and followed what they believe to be in Seera's footsteps.

They had traveled for about an hour before night descended and the path narrowed. Trying not to feel frustrated, Rafn agreed to stop and get some sleep. It did no good to rush headlong into the dark. If they took their time and chose the most logical course, they would have better luck in finding something.

Peder got a fire going, while Rafn managed to spear a hare. They roasted it over the fire and ate in silence.

"We will find more answers tomorrow," Peder said.

"Tomorrow," he replied.

Rafn slept fitfully as he pictured Seera injured and scared, racing through this very forest. Why had he looked in the wrong direction? Why hadn't he seen the path from his brother's grave? Why had he not realized when Hwal failed to return to Ribe, that he was still in Rafn's own land?

Such foolish and costly mistakes he made. Seera and his child had need of him, and he had failed them. He remembered the fog that night. It would have been a storm in the mountains.

And she did not have her cloak. Did they both die somewhere in these trees, close to where he now lay? If he listened would he hear her ghost calling his name?

Rafn woke with sweat beading on his forehead. Peder leaned against a tree, his sword across his lap. His head was tilted sideways in sleep, yet Rafn had no doubt he would be fully awake at the sound of anything out of place.

He was not disappointed when his wife's brother was alerted to his movements and opened his eyes.

Light was beginning to filter through the trees. The horses neighed as if they too were restless and ready to get started. They ate a meal of dried venison from their packs and started down the path.

It soon became too narrow to ride, forcing them to lead the horses in on foot, until the path began to branch off in too many directions to follow, bringing them to a halt.

"Thor, give me some luck," Rafn pleaded.

In answer to his plea a raven landed on a low hanging branch in front of him. He stared directly at Rafn and cawed as if in greeting. Rafn felt a strange power surge through him as he stepped towards the large bird.

"Lead me." Rafn commanded the raven. Peder watched in amazement as the bird tilted his head as if in answer before taking flight.

The bird led them through the thickest part of the trees, before they made it to a well worn path which allowed them once again to mount their horses. The trees thinned away and the raven took to the sky.

Rafn and Peder followed until once again night came. The bird had disappeared and the men were forced to spend another night. They slept beneath the stars instead of a canopy of leaves.

This time Rafn slept deeply and had strange dreams of his brother Orn. He felt comforted by his brother's memory. He woke rested and ready to face another day.

He was not surprised to see the raven waiting on a nearby rock.

Systa approached Joka who was outside sharpening her sword. She said nothing for a time as she watched her sister. Joka stopped and turned to Systa, a question on her face.

"The giant waits with terrible images in mind," Systa said. "He slumbers in a valley southeast of here. His mind will soon release and then bring with it a terrible storm."

"He will come for Seera?"

"It is what he most desires, to reclaim the lady." Systa looked around, but Seera was not in sight. "You sister, need to go to the old cottage that hides him."

"Will you tell Seera of where I go?" Joka picked up a worn leather cloth and began to polish the hard steel of her blade.

"Nay, she must not. For where the one-eyed giant waits to return, so will you find the raven."

"Her husband." Joka sensed the future that Systa had seen would be on them soon. "She would insist on coming with me."

"And must she not. Danger to be that close to the giant. The child we must protect. Here she shall wait. Soon the family will be as one."

"We will lose her to the warrior." Joka sighed for she had become fond of Seera and was losing her heart to her son.

"Never shall we lose her sister." Systa laid a hand on Joka's arm. "Twined has she become in the tendrils of our lives."

"Our home is really too small for the four of us," Joka said. She folded her cleaning cloth and slipped it back into her pouch. She stood before sliding the sword into the scabbard on her back.

"Home is but the feeling in one's heart, not the place in which one dwells." Systa reached for her hand and held it in her own. "Your weapons you will need, for the giant will not be alone." Their eyes met.

"My sword is freshly sharpened and will be deadly to any prey." Joka smiled in anticipation of a fight.

"Quickly must you go before the lady returns from the pool." Systa rushed her back to their small cottage to collect a pack of supplies and the rest of her weapons.

By the time Joka was ready to go a thick covering of clouds had rolled across the sky and the air had become cool. She donned a cloak and secured it with a serpent pin that Systa had once stolen from a man she'd been forced to spend a night with.

Having no horse, Joka would have to walk, but by doing so she would also be able to conceal herself more easily. She hugged Systa before she left and gave her a promise that she would not take any unnecessary risks.

She had practiced...now it was time to prove that she was a warrior.

Dark were the halls of his vision as he searched for the one that led from the horror of his mind. Images of death had begun to weave themselves into the corridors he wandered, strange creatures born in a nightmare that had no escape.

Light teased the corners of his vision, taunting him to seek but never allowing him to find the one that led him beyond the high walls that kept him trapped.

Hwal was only vaguely aware of Klintr's movements someplace close to him. He saw but did not comprehend the other man's actions, as if they were the dream and the illusion of his mind was the reality. He knew instinctively that he was wrong, but he couldn't escape it.

To his right appeared a path that seemed a bit less dark than the others. He ran down it, regardless of what he might find. He ran and he fell, scraping his knees on the rocks that littered the trail beneath him.

He felt the blood on his knees where his pants had been ripped. The red stood out bright even in the dark. He continued for he could not stop.

Appearing before him was a cave. A fire burned in the entrance and he approached it with caution. He heard a voice chanting from within its darkness. It was the same one that had followed him into his nightmares, as if it was responsible for the grotesque images that chased him.

It was as if every man and woman he'd ever killed had sprung to life to haunt him. They looked to him like mutilated corpses, but they reached for him as if to pull him down into the oblivion from whence they sprung.

Horror held him prisoner, until the gruesome bodies dissolved away.

Again he focused on the cave and stared into entrance. It opened before him like a gaping maw, keeping him frozen to the spot, his feet too heavy to move.

The unfamiliar words drifted to him and he felt as if a cloak was being tightened around him until he could not breathe.

Through the haze of his vision, he saw the silver eyes of a woman.

CHAPTER 31

The large bird led them for many days deeper into the mountains until they came to a valley with a river running through it. An old run down cottage was built close to an offshoot of the river. It would have looked abandoned but for the ribbon of smoke that trailed from the chimney.

Rafn and Peder secured the horses within the trees and crouched low to watch for any signs of life. The raven landed on the ground next to Rafn and he looked to the bird. They locked gazes as if in a silent communication before the bird spread its wings and returned to the sky. He sailed towards the dwelling and cawed loudly before disappearing into the mountains beyond the valley.

"It is your call brother," Peder said, still in a bit of shock that a bird had led them. He had no answer for how such a thing could happen. He knew many believed that nature could speak to you if you listened, but he had never tried, assuming it was a false testament made by pagans.

"We wait until we are sure that this is where Hwal has hidden." Rafn motioned them deeper into the shadows of the trees.

They did not have long to wait before the door creaked opened and a young man stepped out. He was tall and broad of chest, with hair the color of wheat. He frowned as if he was displeased. He carried a spear in his hand and headed off along a trail that led west beyond the river.

Rafn and Peder exchanged a look. "Perhaps he has gone hunting," Peder suggested.

"It would appear so, but is he alone." They both looked back towards the cabin.

"Kata said there had been four of them. Abiorn and Lene were sent back, but he would have kept one of his men with him."

"He would have."

"That would leave him alone in the cabin." Peder nodded to the building that was still standing by luck alone. A good strong wind would blow walls over.

Rafn studied to the cottage. "As long as he was not joined by more of his men."

"They would not have gotten through your warriors."

Rafn nodded. He had kept a tight hold on the passage from Jutland, as well as anyone trying to get into Vestfold. Thousands of warriors had joined his forces to see that Hwal was found. They kept a keen eye still.

"Then let us see while his warrior is gone." Rafn started across the open space that separated them from the dwelling.

Hwal's mind so cloaked in shadows of late, cleared suddenly. His eyes focused on the room around him and he was confused. Where was he? Where was Klintr? His gaze shifted to the warrior's pack where it rested against one of the walls.

He was not far then.

The invisible hands that had held Hwal prisoner eased their hold, freeing the giant. He remembered the dreams, the feeling of being lost. How slowly his grasp on sanity had slipped from him, until he was locked in darkness.

He'd been witched. He had an acid taste in his mouth that told him of the spell that had been wrapped so tightly around him. His first thought was that it had been Seera, but what would that Christian woman know of witching.

It had been someone else.

He didn't question why the spell had been severed. Did not wonder why it had suddenly released him from its clutches? Instead he let his fury swell in the cavity of his chest, while the only thing in his mind was vengeance.

He picked up his sword from where it lay on the ground beside him and bolted out the door, shouting as he pushed outside.

"Klintr, where are you? I demand you return at once."

He turned in search of the man, but who he found behind him was not his warrior. He snarled in contempt as he met the Raven's eyes.

Rafn stood still and calm. His sharp gaze locked on the one-eyed man he'd searched for all these months. He forced his rage to remain close to his chest, and kept the thunder simmering. He had no intentions of dying.

He stared hard at the man he'd hunted and was quick to see the man Hwal had become. He was filthy and his hair a tangled mess on the top of a head that had once been shaven bald. The growth on his face still held bits of food and Rafn sneered in disgust. It was when he met the giant's eyes did he understand that the man had gone mad.

Rafn reached over his shoulder and drew his sword. He brought the serpent in front of him and felt a tingling of power travel up his arm. His left hand clutched his shield in front of him. He had not bothered with armor. He wanted nothing to impede his deadly dance.

He warned Peder to stay back. "He is mine."

Hwal brought his sword up. "The time has come for you and I then." The giant took a step towards him.

"It has been a long time in coming," Rafn replied. "Today you will die, but first you will tell me where my wife is."

Hwal's laughter shook the ground beneath his feet, but he kept motionless.

"Her bones must be picked clean by the scavengers by now." He sneered in amusement, even as he wondered why Rafn remained so calm. His intent had been to provoke the warlord into fighting rashly. He had not expected that the Raven would be so controlled.

Peder stepped forward as his hand tightened on his sword so hard that veins bulged.

"No," Rafn said, stopping him.

While Hwal's attention was on Peder, the Raven struck. His sword sliced the air as thunder rumbled through the black clouds overhead. Hwal noticed the action in time to stop it with his own blade.

The serpent glowed with life even as Rafn shoved the giant back and circled him. He watched and waited until the man struck back. His arm was clumsy and his strike misplaced. Rafn deflected it without effort.

Hwal cursed and fought to steady his arm, forcing his concentration as the clouds opened up and the rain began. His mind, so recently lost in darkness was having a hard time readjusting. As he met the famous warlord's blade, a surreal feeling overwhelmed him. He had to keep trying to clear his thoughts, to keep connected to the fight or he would indeed lose his life.

The ground turned to mud beneath their feet, making it more slippery, but Rafn was not deterred. He'd seen this moment in his dreams too often to turn from it now. Lighting flashed over Hwal's shoulders and Rafn smiled to know his god was with him.

Rafn continued to circle the giant, bringing him back to where he'd begun. His eyes never wavered from the man's. Power surged through his muscles, centering on the serpent in his hand.

Hwal screamed in rage as he raised his sword and brought it down so hard that Rafn's shield cracked when it took the full force of the impact. Rafn threw the shield from him. Free now of its weight, he could dance with more ease through the mud.

Peder stayed back, watching through the thick rain. It took all his will not to join the fight. It would end fast, two against one, but Rafn would not forgive him. The kill was not Peder's to make.

Almost as if a silent signal had been given the two men threw themselves at each other and metal against metal rang out to join its music to the thunder that was rolling closer.

Peder caught a glimpse of Rafn's eyes and the dark hatred that speared from them was enough to make him glad they were not enemies. His feet moved as if they barely touched the ground and his blade moved quick and accurate.

As for Hwal he fought with desperation, his feet slipping on the slick ground. He had strength to rival most men…but Rafn fought with artful strokes. Hwal's size would not help him. Rafn was fearless. Peder had seen Rafn fight many times, but until that moment he had not truly understood how the Raven had won his reputation.

Rafn pushed Hwal back in the direction of the river and Peder followed to keep them in view. He stayed behind Rafn, ready to take up the man's fight were he to fall, but he knew it would not be needed.

Even Hwal must have sensed that he would not win. He fought sloppily and without thought to his next move. It was instinctual at best, but against an opponent who could almost see the next swing of his sword before he made it, he would not last long.

With Thor's encouragement ringing through the sky, Rafn saw only the man in front of him and felt the serpent's strength in his hand. He had never been as sure of anything in his life.

The battle was his.

Joka crept on silent feet after the warrior who she'd been trailing since the rain had started. He had a deer slung over his shoulder and a spear in his hand. She could see that he also had a sword across his back, but no other weapon.

The trees thinned into a valley and the man stopped. His attention was on something ahead. Night had come and it was hard to make out much in front of her, especially through the rain, but the man threw the deer on the ground and positioned his spear in his right hand.

With careful steps he began to creep across the valley. Joka hurried to the edge of the tree line to find out what had drawn his interest. Not far from them was an old cottage, but it was what went on a little ways from it that drew the man.

Two men fought with viciousness…sword against sword. A man, as handsome as the night and with an arm that must have been blessed by the gods, danced and twirled through the mud as if he did not fear misplacing his step and slipping. He was a vision straight out the stories told by the scalds when she was a child.

That he was the father of the boy she was learning to love was no doubt. He was Seera's husband, Warlord of Skiringssal, respected by those who loved him and feared by those who faced him. He was the Raven she'd heard so much about, chosen of the god Thor.

The man Seera would return to.

The other was the one-eyed giant of Systa's visions. The same man who'd beaten and raped Seera, bringing her close to death. Joka felt nothing but contempt when she looked at him.

She turned from the fight to focus on the young warrior who was moving into position behind the Raven.

She took note that another man stood not far from the fight, watching the warlord's back. He remained yet unaware of the threat that crept up on them both and would not stop it in time.

The warrior threw his spear as Joka sprang forward, her sword ready to strike. The man turned at the last second to see her bearing down on him and managed to grab his sword in time to stop her blade. It vibrated down her arm, but she held it tight and kept her eyes on her opponent.

A warrior she would prove herself to be.

Peder jumped as a spear sailed over his head and landed without harm in the ground beside Rafn. His fight continued without pause, unaware of the weapon that almost found him.

Peder turned to search out the threat. The man he had seen earlier was there, but as Peder was about to react, another charged forward and attacked. The man barely managed to get his sword in his hand to prevent being killed.

Peder watched in stunned amazement as he realized the attacker was a woman. Her wet hair was braided and held back by a leather head band. On her belt he saw an axe as well as a knife. On her back was a quiver of arrows that she shrugged off and let fall beside a bow she'd already dropped.

She could have easily brought the man down from a distance with one of her arrows, but instead she chose to engage the man in hand to hand combat. He saw how her muscles bunched for she was wearing a sleeveless tunic with no cloak. He had never seen a woman possess such strength.

He looked back over his shoulder at Rafn and knew the man did not need him. He stepped instead towards the other fight, but decided not to interfere. The woman seemed to be holding her own and he was not disappointed when she screamed like one of the Skelkies, female gods that claimed warriors from the battlefield.

Lightning flashed in the sky above and rain fell in sheets to wrap around her, clinging to her smooth flesh. Her feet seemed to float over the muddy puddles, while the man's balance was altered each time he slipped on the slick ground.

Briefly her eyes flicked over Peder as he approached, but soon turned her attention back to the man she fought.

The man frowned in frustration at not being able to finish off the woman, and this made Peder smile. He found the woman most appealing.

Klintr swung out with all his strength and knocked the woman's sword from her hand. Peder stepped forward to stop him, but the woman already had a dagger in her hand. The man seemed confused by how it got there and it broke his concentration as she crouched and rolled away from him.

He turned to find her as her arm lunged upward and drove the dagger deep into his chest. Klintr's eyes widened in disbelief and he stumbled back with the knife still imbedded below his heart. The woman was on her feet again before the man fell.

The man was not yet dead, his eyes wide with shock. Peder moved to stand over him and the warrior looked up at him.

"You fought well," Peder said. His head cocked in the woman's direction. "But she was better."

Peder brought his sword down through the man's heart to end his pain. He looked up to find the woman glaring at him with displeasure. Water streamed down her face, already washing the blood from her hands, and the mud from her body.

She snarled. "I could have finished him."

"You already did," Peder said. "I just ended his suffering."

"Why?"

"I was feeling pretty useless watching two fights I was not needed for." Peder shrugged. "I just needed to wet my sword a little, so I could continue to call myself a man."

"Of course you are a man." She shook her head at the strangeness of his comment.

"You are hurt." He indicated a cut down her left arm. He stepped towards her but the look in her eyes stopped him.

"It is nothing...what of them?" She gestured in the direction of Rafn and Hwal.

"It will be over soon enough."

Hwal wasn't willing to give up so easily. He recalled who he was. He was a man who brought terror to others. He was a monster who brought pain and death simply because he could. More important, none had ever stood before his strength and lived.

With a howl of rage he let the beast out. He screamed as he charged Rafn. He took the warlord off guard and Rafn's foot slipped in the mud knocking him off his momentum. Hwal's face contorted in madness at having interrupted the Raven's perfect dance.

Hwal aimed for the man's chest but at the last second Rafn stepped back and his blade cut across the warrior's leg instead. A cocky laugh escaped him as the blood escaped the wound. He would put the Raven in his place.

Set off balance Rafn stumbled backwards as he clenched his teeth against the sudden pain that speared his leg. He allowed only a second for the agony to flare before he pushed the weakness aside. He met Peder's gaze and saw concern reflected in his eyes.

Peder's worry was misplaced. His jaw hardened as he faced his enemy. Rafn readied to finish off the giant once and for all. His leg did not hinder him as he sprang forward to lock hilts with Hwal's sword. Their faces were but inches from each other, each determined to fight to the death.

"For my wife and child, and for my brother, you will now die." Rafn screamed as he let lose the fury he'd held in check burst from him. The thunder exploded from within to match the echoing force in the sky.

A searing fire surged forth from him, carrying with it all the power of his god. His eyes reflected the storm that was inside and the air around him became filled with an electric charge as if a lightning bolt just hit him.

Hwal sucked in a breath of shock as he looked into Rafn's possessed eyes. What he saw was not the warlord, but the god. The giant understood too late that the stories told of the man were true. He'd been claimed by Thor.

For the first time in his life, Hwal felt fear as he saw death descending down upon him.

Rafn pushed Hwal from him and swung his body full round and sent his sword sailing through the air with such strength and speed that the one-eyed man couldn't stop the blade from cutting across his chest.

While the giant was still stunned, Rafn pulled back his sword again and plunged it through the man's throat. The full force of the storm seized him, the power surging through him as he fought to maintain some sense of control.

With his sword stuck in the giant's throat, he felt the earth beneath his feet tremble as he vented his anger. Blood spurt everywhere as he pulled the blade back out. The giant teetered back and forth, before Rafn's foot kicked him back with such force that he landed hard on the soaked ground.

Clutched by an utter sense of hopelessness, Rafn sank to his knees in the mud. While the rain washed over him, he raised his face to the sky and bellowed to the gods in rage.

Seera was dead—gone, their child with her. He opened his arms wide as the thunder boomed over his head and was followed by a bolt of lightning so close it hit a nearby tree.

The branches burst into flames even as Rafn cried out to Thor. "She was my life."

The rain thickened and the fire sputtered as it choked in its final moments of life. Rafn dropped his sword and buried his face in his bloodied hands.

CHAPTER 32

Peder felt the man's pain as he screamed out his rage, and his own anger swelled at her loss. But, he'd come to understand Rafn's connection to her was so much more than Peder could comprehend. His grief was beyond anything Peder imagined anyone could feel.

Peder made the sign of Christ across his chest. "Dear Lord he has such need of your mercy now."

From the corner of his vision he saw the woman's eyes turn to him and when he looked down at her she was staring at him in bewilderment.

"You are Christian?"

"I am."

He went to Rafn then and dropped to his knees beside him. Rafn faced him and Peder saw the redness in his eyes. Somehow he knew that the wetness on his face was not from the rain alone.

"Let us get dry."

Rafn allowed Peder to lead him to the shelter, not noticing the woman that followed them in.

"She…" Rafn tried to speak but could not get the words out.

Peder was about to say words of comfort when the woman came to stand before Rafn. The Viking looked at her in confusion, wondering where she'd come from.

"She is not dead," the woman said.

"What?" Peder asked for Rafn stood like stone staring at her as if she were not real.

Her gaze shifted to Peder. "The Lady Seera, she is alive."

"Where is she?" Peder demanded. The woman only raised an eyebrow at the sharpness of his tone.

"Safe."

Rafn watched the strange woman as she spoke words that seemed unreal. He wanted to accept them as truth, but part of him believed she was nothing more than an apparition there to taunt him with false words.

But then Peder spoke to her, demanding the answer Rafn needed to hear. She was alive, his wife was alive. He grabbed for the woman before she could move from his sight.

She flinched as his hands closed on her arms, but she did not resist him. "You will bring me to her."

"It is why I have come, my lord," she replied.

Rafn released her and looked to Peder before he saw the scowl that came to her face. Peder did not miss it.

"What is your name," Peder asked and her frown deepened further before she answered.

"It is Joka."

"I am Peder." He offered his name even though she had not asked. She nodded in acknowledgement before returning her attention to Rafn. Peder felt somehow dismissed and he did not like it.

"Lord Rafn. It will take two days to reach my home by foot."

"We have horses," Rafn said.

She nodded. "That is good. Then it will not take so long."

"I will get them." Rafn headed for the door but Peder stopped him.

"It is dark and still storming, we should wait until morning. Besides, your leg should be tended to first."

Rafn looked down at his leg as if he'd forgotten he'd been injured. He considered Peder's words before agreeing. "You are right. I will bring the horses into the shelter of the cottage only. As for my leg, the cut is not so deep. I will clean it and bind it once I am done."

Rafn wanted to disagree with his brother-in law, but knew he was correct. She was safe. He would be with her soon enough.

He shut the door behind him and headed towards the trees where they'd left the horses. He ignored Hwal's body as he passed it.

The wolves and ravens could have it, he thought, even as he heard the howling of wolves as they spoke to each other somewhere in the thick trees.

Joka looked to Peder and felt a bit nervous in his presence. He was a good looking man, with blue eyes and sandy hair, but certainly that was not such a consideration for her. She had vowed long ago that she would never take a man as husband. They had never been anything other than savage, greedy beasts who took what they wanted despite the protests of the women who bore the brunt of their insults. Had it not been so for her mother?

Yet she had seen the Raven kneeling in the mud crying out in sorrow for the woman he loved. She had looked into his eyes and seen life return to them as he accepted that she was still alive. She'd seen how they had softened, seen how powerful his love was.

Seera had talked of her Viking husband with nothing but tenderness and longing. Joka had not understood. Perhaps she didn't know as much about men as she'd believed. Could there be more?

She felt Peder's eyes on her and glanced up to see him studying her with curiosity. He had not interfered when she'd fought the warrior. He had acknowledged that she was capable and kept from her fight.

He'd also waited rather close to rescue her if needed, she realized. But he had not stopped her.

"What does Seera mean to you?" she asked, for she had not missed how relieved he'd been to hear that she was safe.

"She is my sister," he replied.

"That would explain why you are a Christian, here in the wild country of the Norse."

"My father is of Norse blood," Peder said. "I only follow a different religion than you."

"Seera has tried to tell me of your God."

"You did not care to listen?" He smirked as she glared up at him.

"I choose my own path, my own beliefs." She tried not to notice the flitting in her stomach when he looked at her. She looked away and refused to meet his eyes again, for she was afraid he would see the turmoil he had caused in her.

"We should get some sleep," Joka said. "Lord Rafn will want to ride hard tomorrow."

"Aye, he will." His mouth turned up into a smile and she swore she would not let it affect her.

The rain stopped by morning and the sky cleared to all but a spattering of clouds. Rafn woke early and the others knew he would not wait patiently while they lingered, so they rose also as the sun was reddening the sky.

Joka stared at the horses, and though she admired their beauty, she frowned. Two horses! She hadn't thought what that would mean. She would be made to ride with one of the men.

She looked to where they were attaching their packs and weapons to the saddles and instinctively knew which one would bear her. She was proven correct when Peder approached her.

"You can pack your things on my horse." A teasing smile lit his face and she fought not to knock it from his him.

She secured her pack and weapons on the horse. Peder leapt onto the stallion's back then looked down at her as he extended his hand. Reluctantly she took it and he swung her up in front of him.

"This should be cozy." He whispered in her ear and she hoped he didn't see her blush.

"Are you ready brother?" Peder called back to Rafn.

"Ready," Rafn replied and looked to Joka. "I will follow."

She took the offered reins from Peder.

Many emotions waged a battle inside Rafn as they rode as fast as the mountain trail would allow; which was to say not very fast at all, along a windy path that at times was so thick with overhead branches that they were forced to get down from the horses.

He would reach the end of this trail. Not even the gods could stop him making it to his wife.

The clouds returned my mid-day but the rain stayed away for which Rafn was grateful. Not that it would have stopped him, but it would have slowed their progress and he was becoming impatient as it was.

They stopped in the afternoon to allow the animals to drink from the stream that twined in and out around the trail. Rafn sat on the stump of a fallen tree and cleaned his sword. Peder and the woman took charge of the horses, for which he was grateful.

"How long has she been with you?" Rafn asked the woman when she chose a spot to sit not far from him. He watched her glance enviously at his sword.

"Since her escape from Hwal."

"Then why did you not see her back to Skiringssal?" He tried to keep the suspicion from his words, but his anger seeped out.

"My sister warned her not to leave," Joka said. "Warned her that the one-eyed giant would find her if she left the protection of the meadow."

"Why would your sister believe this?" He noticed that Joka was not intimidated by the narrowing of his eyes.

"She is a great Seer. One with the knowledge of seid magic." A hint of pride was in her voice. "She foresaw your wife's coming. That is how I was able to find her before she died from exposure and her injuries."

"This is true?" Peder who'd been listening questioned disbelieving. She turned to him with a hard look on her face.

She hissed. "I do not lie. My sister is also a great healer and she has cared for Seera."

Rafn did not respond. She was alright, what else mattered than that. "We have rested long enough."

They were forced to walk their horses again for the trail was becoming steeper and the sun had already dipped behind the mountains, pushing them into darkness. Rafn would not stop.

Joka must have understood, for she led the men through the night.

The night was dark. The trees so large and thick that the moon's light could not penetrate its canopy. Even the wind was blocked from reaching them. The path had become steep and they were making their way up slowly. They had to place each foot carefully for they couldn't see hidden dangers.

The forest around them was not silent. Wolves, owls and insects echoed out from the darkness. Rafn felt a bit claustrophobic not being able to see much past his nose. He longed to be able to look out to sea and see to the horizon, where he could once again imagine that something great lay out beyond the limits of his sight.

Rafn and Peder led the horses, while Joka walked on up ahead clearing their trail where it was needed. Rafn had to keep a close watch on her back through the darkness. He soon found she walked so quietly that he could not tell where she was unless he could see her.

The horses had to be led slow as well, for the path was not only steep, but narrow and littered with rocks. It was hard for them to find their footing in the darkness. Why one would choose to travel such a path was beyond him, but he would climb it a hundred times to get to Seera.

Rafn studied the woman who dressed like a warrior and carried the weapons of a man. It brought to mind many questions about who she was. She was strong, of that there was no doubt. They had been walking for a day and a half and she had not tired. She was used to a physical life he assessed. The solidness of her muscles was the only proof he needed. She was not a pretty woman, but she had beauty. There was an untamed wildness about her.

But why did she prefer the life of a man?

Rafn looked back at Peder and was glad that he was keeping up. His horse had given him trouble when they'd first come to the trail. The stallion had balked at its steepness, but Peder had a way with the animal. He'd had only to talk soothingly to him and offer him an apple from his pack and the horse did what he wanted. He imagined that his brother-in law used the same soft voice when dealing with the fairer sex, and undoubtedly had much success.

Impossibly the trail grew even steeper. It narrowed up so sharply it appeared to Rafn that it was almost vertical. Determined that he would not fail he coaxed the horse up the dark and windy path. The stallion brayed and tried to pull his head away from Rafn but he kept a strong grip on the reins until the horse found its footing and followed.

Rafn felt with his foot each step before he took the next to make sure that he had found solid ground. He had given up trying to watch Joka and looked to the ground instead. With patience they proceeded forward.

As it turned out the path was not vertical. It had only been an optical illusion and they were able to make it up safely if slowly. Finally they crested the top of the cliff and the path leveled out before them. Through a break in the trees Rafn could see that the sky had turned from black to gray and knew dawn was not far off.

Rafn felt anxious as he sensed they were getting close to their destination. For so many months he had been searching and hoping, filled with fear and despair. It would all end soon. It was almost done.

A sense of calm washed over Rafn, as he saw a bright light appear before him. He squinted and saw Orn standing within its glow. His brother had a radiant smile streaked across his face and his eyes glowed from within. He blinked and the light and Orn were gone.

He looked to the others but neither appeared to have seen anything, but he felt that it was not an illusion of his mind. He knew it had been Orn. And it was not the first time. He had seen him once before when he'd been brought down in battle. Then as now it had been only a moment's glimpse.

He remembered a time that he had sat with Seera at his brother's grave. They had just buried him and Seera had yet to heal. She had told him a tale of how Orn had come to her and given her strength and hope. That he'd not left her when she had need of him.

Sudden understanding came to him. Orn had come to Seera once again. He felt this truth deep inside. His brother's spirit had stayed with her, watched over her. He had been with her this whole time.

A smile of gratitude and wonder touched Rafn's face.

CHAPTER 33

Seera woke early in the morning to find that Systa was already up. She'd taken the baby, who was gone from his blankets. Seera smiled. Systa thought that Seera should get her rest, so she often watched baby Orn in the mornings so she could sleep. But that morning she could not linger in bed.

A shaft of sunlight was streaming past the shutters to tease Seera with its promise of a good day. She cleaned with cold water from the basin, not wanting to fuss with heating any. She pulled on her smock and the yellow colored apron-dress that Systa had just finished making her, now that she was free of a large stomach.

The sisters had done so much for Seera that she didn't know how she would ever repay them for their kindness. Rafn was rich and would gladly give them wealth, but she knew they didn't care for such things. She would have to think hard on how she would show them how much she appreciated them.

Seera brushed the tangles from her hair before tying it back with a ribbon. She stepped outside to find it was already warm. The sun felt so good on her face. It was going to be a good day.

Systa was close by sitting on a blanket with the baby who'd fallen asleep. The Seer smiled at her as joined her. "I could take him now," she said. "I was too awake to sleep."

"I would watch him for a time yet, while still I have the chance," Systa replied in her usual unique way of saying things. "Practice you should, with your bow. Not have you since this wee one came."

"You are right. I shouldn't allow my arm to grow clumsy."

Seera ducked back inside to eat a quick breakfast of dried venison and bread, before reaching for her bow and quiver of arrows. It would be good to practice. She found such joy in her accomplishment.

Seera straightened the wooden target that Joka had made and stepped back to the line on the other side of the practice field. Her arms felt a bit stiff when she placed her first arrow into the bow and took aim. It hit the outer ring of the target.

She could do better.

She tried again and again, each arrow coming closer to the center. She went once to collect them from the wood when it had started to resemble a porcupine. Returning to the line she went to fit an arrow when she felt a sudden disconnection.

The land around her lost focus and a glowing white light grew before her. Orn appeared as she had seen him before. His beauty never failed to awe her. What was wrong now? What danger threatened?

A slight touch of fear teased her before his smile eased it away. He reached a hand to touch her face and she felt a power rush through her.

"You have no need of me any longer," Orn said.

"You would leave?" She was shocked. She had grown accustomed to feeling his presence, even when she could not see him.

"I promised I would stay until you were safe." His voice rang in a musical tone that could only belong to an angel.

"And am I safe?" She wanted his words to be true.

"You will know soon enough." He smiled and she could have sworn there was a twinkle in his eye. "Ranka has waited patiently. It is time for me to join her."

"Of course," Seera said. He would want to be with his love as surely as she wanted to be with hers. "I will miss you."

She blinked and he was gone. She felt momentarily lost, until she felt a final touch on her shoulder and she knew she would be alright. Had Orn ever lied to her?

"Goodbye my husband's brother," she whispered as she felt her connection to him disappear. "Be at peace."

Feeling that the world was once again falling back into balance, she raised her bow with the confidence that Joka had taught her. For the first time she became one with it. She felt the power of the bow, the strength of the arrow as she looked to the center. She pictured in her mind the flight it must take and released it, understanding finally what Joka had tried to explain.

She heard the parting of the air as the arrow sailed and the thud as it hit the center. Pride took hold of her and she welcomed it.

She was charged with excitement and ready to take a rest. Her breasts were becoming full and she needed the baby to ease their pain. She went across to collect the arrows and remembered that one of them had sailed off course and landed in the trees to the right of the target.

She ducked into the bush and began searching the ground for the missing arrow when she heard a movement coming from behind a large boulder in front of her. Instantly on guard she slipped one of her arrows in her bow and stood very still.

From behind the rock a shadow moved across the ground, growing larger until a huge rabid wolf was standing beside it. His nose sniffed the air as he was drawn to her presence, while he foamed at the mouth in his madness. He picked her out across from him and bared his teeth in a warning.

She began to step backwards until she was out of the bush and once again in the practice clearing, but even as she did this the wolf began to growl, foam dripping from his open maw. Were she to run, he would be on her before she could get very far.

Her only hope was to stand her ground and not give into her fear. She raised her arms, held the bow ready and hoped her arms did not shake. She pulled back on the arrow, never taking her eyes from the snarling animal.

The wolf sprang straight for her even as she heard someone scream her name. A part of her registered that the voice belonged to Peder, but she could not let it distract her. She let the arrow fly and to her it seemed that it arched slowly through the air, but her aim was good and it hit the wolf in his throat just as he leapt in the air towards her.

A spear bearing black raven feathers followed hers, but it had been unnecessary. Her arrow had stopped the animal and she sighed with relief as she allowed the memory of Peder's frightened scream to penetrate.

She spun around, but it was not her brother who she sought, but the one who owned the spear with its familiar feathers.

Rafn was there two steps from where she stood. His black eyes bore into her and she almost staggered at the impact of his gaze.

She had but to reach for him.

They had left the horses to graze and walked across the field. Rafn spotted her at once standing in front of a wooden target with a bow in her hand, looking not at the target but off to its right. He seemed confused by the bow in her hands, but not for long. For born on the moment of relief came surprise, than fear as a large rabid wolf sprang from the trees in front of her.

"Seera," Peder had screamed a warning beside them, even as all three of them ran towards her in an instant reaction to the threat.

His heart stopped beating as the wolf leapt into the air in front of her, even as he became aware that she had been ready for him and had let loose an arrow. Somehow his spear had found its way into his hand and he threw it as he ran.

But the wolf was down even before his spear found its mark. He stopped a few steps from her and stared at her in shock and disbelief. How she'd learned to do it he did not care. What mattered was that she had turned and looked at him.

His eyes scanned her quickly to satisfy himself that she was alright. Their eyes met and he saw the tears.

"Seera," he said and she gasped at the sound of her name. That was all it took for him to take her into his arms and draw her to him.

"You found me." She sobbed into his shoulder. "I feared you would not."

"I wouldn't have, if it weren't for your friend," Rafn said into her hair. His heart had started beating again, but he struggled to slow it. He held her hard against him and let the fear slide away.

She was real and safe, and in his arms. She smelled like fresh flowers and the mountain air. The feel of her warmth against his made him come alive in a way he had not been in a long time. She was safe.

Seera pulled back from him so she could look up into his face. "What did you say?" she asked, remembering that he had said something.

"Joka led me here." He nodded to the woman standing beside a dazed looking Peder.

"It was all Systa's doing. She sent me to him."

Seera smiled. Systa had been acting stranger than usual since Joka's supposed hunting trip. She should have suspected something was up.

Peder glanced at the dead wolf. "That was impressive sister. I thought you were dead and I was helpless to stop it."

Rafn let her go, with reluctance, so that she could give her brother a hug. "I have missed you brother. I'm glad you are here."

Seera stepped away from him and as soon she was out of Peder's embrace, Rafn had her back in his arms. He would never let her go again. Did not ever want to feel what her absence had done to him again. He pulled back from her so that he could look at her and study her face. Her eyes had become more serious he decided.

A dark shadow filled his eyes as he looked at her. He had remembered something very important. Something that Joka had made no mention of.

"Our child?" He was almost too afraid to ask.

As if waiting for the perfect time to make an entrance, Systa appeared with the baby in her arms. Rafn noticed her first and caught the gleam that reflected on her face as she stood before him.

"Strong your son is," Systa said as she held the baby out for him to take.

Rafn took the small bundle into his arms. Seera smiled to see her husband holding their son with such tenderness. "A boy," he said as a smile of amazement softened his face. A son to teach and guide, to watch grow into a man. A son that was as dark in coloring as he.

"I have named him Orn."

Rafn looked to his wife with wide eyes. "For my brother?"

"Aye." It was not the time to tell him how Orn had found her near death and kept her hope alive. Of how he watched over her until Rafn could come. It was enough to see the joy on his face as he peered down at their son.

But she did not have to explain, for Rafn already knew. He didn't have to question why she had chosen the name, because it was obvious. His brother had not failed her. To honor this she had given his name to their son.

The baby squirmed in his arms as he woke and then stilled as he looked up into the unknown face. He did not cry as if he knew that this man was important, that he was not to be feared. Little Orn opened his eyes wide as if to examine his father closer, and they shone with the emerald green that had always belonged to Seera alone.

"He's got your eyes," Rafn said in wonder. He couldn't seem to look away from the tiny perfection of his son.

She laughed. "But, the rest of him is all you."

Rafn pulled Seera closer and kissed her. He had never thought to feel such contentment again. Thought he'd lost that peace forever.

"Alone we must leave them," Systa said as she turned and walked away.

Peder smiled to see the family reunited. To know that his sister was safe and that the storm in Rafn had quieted. He was glad to have been there to witness it.

"Come." He offered Joka his arm. She looked at him with contempt at him making such a gesture. Peder chuckled when she turned away, ignoring the gentleman's offer.

She walked ahead of him and he had to lengthen his stride to catch up with her. She was heading to a cottage across the clearing and he managed to fall in step with her before she reached it. He could tell she was displeased, but she did not send him away.

"You taught her to shoot like that." Peder realized it must have been her that had taken the time to teach Seera a skill that had saved her life.

Joka turned abruptly and looked up at him. He saw anger pass across her face. "If you had wanted to be a good brother, You should have taught her!"

"What?" He was stunned by the accusation. "I have always cared for my sister. Thought only of what was best for her." What right did this woman have to speak to him so? She did not know him.

She glared at him. "If that had been true, you would have shown her how to defend herself when you could not be there to protect her."

Peder opened his mouth to argue, but the truth of her words rung true, even to his ears. He hadn't been there to stop Drenger from taking her. Rafn hadn't been there to stop Hwal. Twice now she could have used the knowledge that Joka spoke of. Seera had been through the worst sort of hell, more than once. If she'd been prepared, it could have been prevented. It was a truth that was hard for him to admit, but admit he was forced to do.

"You are right," he said. He had cosseted his sister all her life, especially after their mother's passing. He loved her more than he'd loved any other. She had been his best friend through many years. The purity he had long coveted was stolen by men who did not treasure such things.

She had lost that youthful virtuousness. She had given up her innocence harshly to the world that sought to take it. From it she had grown from a girl into a strong woman that had faced the savage world and survived it.

Joka lost her anger at the look in the man's eyes. She had not thought he would agree with her so readily. Men always wanted to be superior. To know they held power from a woman. To give a woman such knowledge was to give her an advantage. What man would accept that?

Peder's gaze held hers and she realized that perhaps he was such a man. This lord from Dun'O'Tir was different from those she'd grown up around. He was so unlike the father who beat her mother. From the man who turned his abuse on his own daughters. Deep inside her memory she could still feel the pain of the bruises on her skin.

If at first she had cried in terror when he was angry, she soon hardened against it. She and Systa had survived him, even after their mother's death. It had become worse then, but Joka had bided her time, had watched and learned. When she was ready and poised to strike, she had killed him.

The smell of his blood on her hands still came to her in the dark dreams of her sleep. The years of pain and humiliation had been enough to fuel her strength and she'd caught him unprepared. He had not expected a daughter to fight like a son. That had been his mistake.

The sudden pain of her memories must have reflected on her face for Peder had turned to stare at her in concern. She saw a question in his eyes but she was unprepared to answer it.

She dropped the veil of concealment over her eyes before he saw too much. He reached out a hand to her, but she stepped away from it. Composing herself she turned from him and quickened her pace.

She wanted no concern from this man. She had lived without such compassion her whole life and she did not need it now.

She felt him still behind her, but he kept back as if sensing that she needed her space. She peered over her shoulder and he watched her still. His eyes were like the sky on a clear day. She felt them pull her in as if to ensnare her.

Joka turned at Systa's laughter. Her sister was staring at her with an odd gleam in her eyes.

Joka did not like it.

In the night Systa crept off to sit in her small cave. She sat very silent as she shook the runes between her hands. The runes were made of animal bones on which she had carefully sketched the symbols used by her people. She breathed her life into the runes so they might help her find the answers she sought.

Haunted had been her dreams lately and she needed to find some answers. She stopped the movement of her hands and brought them, while still closed over the runes, to her mouth and pressed them against her lips.

With a soft prayer she tossed them across the cave floor in front of her. She closed her eyes and willed calmness to travel through her before she dared to open them to see what the runes would tell her. She leaned over the scattered bones to study them.

She read them carefully...and knew what the next step must be.

It was time for Joka to know the path that must be taken.